Cathi Unsworth began her journalistic career at nineteen on the music paper *Sounds*. Later headhunted by *Melody Maker*, she worked there as a freelance feature writer and reviewer for several years before joining *Bizarre* magazine. She now works as a sub-editor and lives in West London. *The Not Knowing*, her first novel, was published by Serpent's Tail as well as her edited collection, *London Noir*.

Praise for *The Not Knowing*

'*The Not Knowing* is gutters full of blood and moon, bodies and dreams, streets full of cries and whispers, secrets and lies – fiction every bit as fraught as the nightmares from whence it came' David Peace

'Those of us who mourn the loss of Derek Raymond and believe we will never see his like again have huge reason to celebrate…He is reincarnated in Cathi Unsworth…all the noir, the Black Novels we delighted in are restored to us in the guise of C. Unsworth…she has not only taken on his mantle but reinforced it with a freshness and vitality that makes you gasp in sheer amazement… I haven't been as excited by a new writer since I first read Ellroy or stumbled across the very first James Sallis' Ken Bruen

'Brilliantly executed with haunting religious imagery, interesting minor characters, great rock 'n' roll references and a spectacular ending. *The Not Knowing* is a cool and clever debut. Sleep on it at your peril' *Diva*

'Hugely entertaining debut from a future star of gritty urban crime literature' *Mirror*

'Unsworth's debut ushers the reader into an early '90s twilight world of Ladbroke Grove bedsits, dingy magazine offices and seedy Camden pubs – a louche, lovingly evoked milieu… Unsworth has concocted a powerful story' *Time Out*

'Cathi Unsworth is the new cool…Unsworth ups the tempo by way of a dark, pacey plot and perceptively witty metaphors, making this near perfect debut very hip indeed' *Buzz*

'Consider it full immersion in a downright good crack about rubbishy gossip with your best mate' *The Crack*

'Cathi Unsworth has long been an accomplished writer. With *The Not Knowing* she weaves together all her passions: music, cultural journalism, hip London, crime novels and edgy films – to give us, in the tradition of Derek Raymond and Ken Bruen, angiographies of contemporary London and of lives gone all edge' James Sallis

The Singer

Cathi Unsworth

A complete catalogue record for this book can
be obtained from the British Library on request

First published in 2007 by Serpent's Tail,
an imprint of Profile Books Ltd
3A Exmouth House
Pine Street
London EC1R 0JH
website: www.serpentstail.com

Designed and typeset at Neuadd Bwll, Llanwrtyd Wells

Printed in Great Britain by Clays, Bungay, Suffolk
10 9 8 7 6 5 4 3 2

The paper this book is printed on is certified by the © 1996 Forest
Stewardship Council A.C. (FSC). It is ancient-forest friendly.
The printer holds FSC chain of custody SGS-COC-2061

Acknowledgements

Thanks and love to Brenda and Phil Unsworth, Yvette and Matthew Unsworth, Cath Meekin, Danny Meekin, Frances Meekin, Eva Snee, Ann Scanlon, Joe McNally, Pete Woodhead, Ken Bruen, Martyn Waites, Lydia Lunch and Marc Viaplana, Caroline Montgomery, John Williams, Pete Ayrton and all at Serpent's Tail, Raphael Abraham, Damon Wise, Damjana and Predrag Finci, Johnny Volcano, Max Décharné, David Peace, Ben Newbery, Lynn Taylor, Emma and Paul Murphy, Florence Halfon, Mari Mansfield, Helen and Richard Cox, Ken and Rachel Hollings, James Hollands, Roger Burton and everyone at The Horse Hospital, Michael Dillon and the company of Gerry's, Suzy Prince, Joolz Denby, Tommy Udo, Rod Stanley, Terry Edwards, David Knight, Ruth Bayer, Karl Blake, Margaret Nichols, Claudia Woodward and Tony Stewart and the Sounds massif for getting me backstage in the first place.

Special thanks for the punk memories of Richard Newson, The Shend and Billy Chainsaw. And the music of John Lydon and Johnny Cash.

For Michael Meekin

Did you forget The Folksinger so soon?
And did you forget my song?

—Johnny Cash

Prologue

You can tell it's love by the expression on their faces.

Four, maybe five hundred of them, packed together so tightly they've formed a kind of human sea, rolling and lapping in waves around the rim of the stage. A couple of girls sway on the shoulders of their boyfriends, loudly beseeching the white spotlight that rests on the microphone in the centre of the stage. Like most of the rest of the assembled worshippers, these girls have long black hair, crimped into corrugated ribbons then teased upwards with the help of Boots' Ultra-Strong Hairspray. Thick black liner magnifies their eyes against china-white foundation and slashes of red lips. The negative image of the crest of a wave, their clothes as the colour of their hair, their faces full of yearning, waiting:

For the man.

A big punk rocker with arms thick as tree trunks pushes his way to the front, elbowing and swearing, pumped up with expectation and adrenalin, the forthcoming catharsis of violence in song. His head is a black crown of soaped-up spikes, four inches long, liable to have someone's eye out – or so he would hope. Round his neck a dog collar of spikes, ditto on his wrists, a visual dare for anyone to start on him. He's ripped the sleeves off his GBH T-shirt, exposing flabby white flesh smudged with home-made blue tattoos, right down to his waistband, where a pyramid stud belt coils around the top of his tight black stretch jeans. No doubt he's got steel toe-capped Doc Martens on his feet but you can't see that from here. You just see the flash of his eyes as he wades through the waves to the front, hauls his upper body up onto the stage and starts pointing, shouting abuse to the wings, where he knows they'll make their entrance.

Waiting for the band.

Then the house lights go down and a huge roar erupts.

A vein stands out on the punk rocker's neck as he screams his lungs out into the white noise around him, punching the air with a hammy fist.

Slowly, they coil out onto the stage.

The bass player first, a tall, willowy black man, cigarette dangling from his bottom lip, black suit and white shirt and shades, the image of Don Cherry in the Ornette Coleman free jazz days. His bass guitar is slung low around his hips, and without looking up at the crowd he stands sideways and begins to pluck the strings, a low, loping, insistent sound.

Cigarette smoke swirls across the stage from the bassist's lips.

The drummer has by now climbed behind his kit and begins to join in the tattoo, the undulating refrain quickly becoming hypnotic, the goth girls swaying on their boyfriends' shoulders, waving their arms like seaweed underwater. Their mouths form the words of a name.

Of the singer.

For five long minutes the men on stage continue to make their rumble. Then from stage left, the guitarist emerges. Compared to the bassist he is wide and solid. His round, slightly battered face peers out from under a black Homburg hat. He looks like Gene Hackman as Popeye Doyle, and he knows it, cultivates it. Broadshoudered, bandy-legged, he wears a second-hand sixties suit like it was handmade for his personal use from Savile Row.

The guitarist faces the crowd, rocking slightly on his heels, a flicker of amusement across his broad features, and slashes into his guitar like he's taking a razor to soft skin. The jarring sound resonates through the crowd in a synaptic rush, wiring their collective conscious for action, and none more so than the punk rocker, who is by now attempting to get his feet onto the stage. A bouncer rushes from the darkness of the wings to push the spiky head back down, back into the sea of arms and backcombed hair. You can see his fists rising above the heads of the others and with them his feet, and yes, he is wearing Doc Martens, eighteen holes with steel toe-caps.

Meanwhile, the guitarist, grinning now, stalks the front of the stage, shaking a violent heehaw from his strings, making a mangled blues turn red.

Punk rocker's head comes back up. He screams the name of the singer.

Who comes tripping out of the darkness, as if somebody's pushed him or he's reeling drunk. If the other guys looked the epitome of louche cool, he actually looks frightening – long long legs in black leather, a shock of black hair greased into a glistening pompadour, a T-shirt printed with a picture of a gun bearing the legend: SMITH & WESSON: THE GREAT EQUALIZER.

His arms are snaked with elaborate tattoos – skulls, dominos, women, dice and crosses. His eyes are wide and bulging, his lips a thin line across a taut jaw.

He lurches towards the mic stand, pulls it towards him, leans into the face of punk rocker and screams: 'Your funeral is about to begin!'

The crowd lets rip a mutual roar and a thousand hands shoot skywards.

Clearly delighted, punk rocker grabs hold of the singer's T-shirt, pulling him down into the throng. Long insect arms and legs flail above the hands of the faithful, pieces of T-shirt ripped off his back and delivered up, consecrated in hair grease and sweat. The mic has gone with the singer into the pit; at first it must have been grabbed out of his hands by the punk rocker, who shouts into it: 'You're a fucking arsehole,' in a South London accent.

By now two bouncers are wading in from the stage, trying to separate the writhing form of the singer from the mass of arms that want to keep him. He has wrestled the mic away now, words are discernible, cutting in and out of earshot, more guttural howl than singing – '*I am the king of this wasteland*'.

It sounds like, '*Blackened, empty, fill my eyes…*'

The bouncers now forcing him out seemingly against his will, long legs lashing, T-shirt long gone, traces of blood trickling down pasty white skin.

Belt buckle of a Colt .45.

All the while, that voodoo beat pounding, that guitar shrieking.

The singer thrashes his way out of the bouncers' grasp, teeters on the edge of the stage. He pushes his hair, now standing up like porcupine quills, out of his pale saucer eyes, stares into the writhing throng of his flock as if stupefied. Their hungry hands try to catch him again, but this time he is too quick for them, leaping sideways, almost colliding with the guitarist, who leans backwards against him, his white Custom Les Paul at crotch level, pumping away at those mangled notes as if he's fucking some girl against an alley wall.

Punk rocker making the wanker sign, shit-eating grin on his face.

The singer raises the mic to his lips: '*I am the fucking king/The wretched king/Of all this shit/Of all nothing*!' he screams. The congregation scream back their approval.

He glances over at the guitarist for a second. An almost imperceptible nod. Then he runs to the front of the stage, leaps back into the crowd, who open up and swallow him in a grateful frenzy.

The scene dissolves into a studio shot, one of those chirpy tosser presenters that were everywhere in the early eighties, paisley shirt with the top button done up, waistband of his jeans practically under his armpits, mullet hairdo with blond tips.

He opens his mouth to say something and dissolves into static.

Gavin gets up laughing, turns the video recorder off.

'That was all they did!' he whoops, still in disbelief, twenty years later. 'That one song. That was the whole gig. It was a riot. They had a record number of complaints for putting that on the TV too.'

'That,' I tell him, still staring at the blank screen in astonishment, 'was fucking amazing. Why the fuck wasn't I around then?' I add to myself.

'Ahh, you young 'uns,' Gavin sits back in his armchair, cracks open another can of lager. 'You missed out. Those days were the shit.'

Gavin Granger is fifteen years older than me but he's still whippet-thin, still wears a crumpled lounge suit with bonhomie, knows he's still good-looking enough not to care about the salt-and-pepper streaks in his shaggy hair. Maybe it's because he's Australian. Brought up on sunshine and cold beer and shrimps on the barbie – not roast dinners and cold winters and Surrey motherly love.

Whereas I, Eddie Bracknell, am twenty-nine and already running to flab, already starting to lose my hair, already in a permanent state of anxiety. As a result of all those things and probably more.

But at this moment I don't give a shit. At this moment, my

palms are sticky with elation, sliding down the side of my tin of Red Stripe, which has crumpled and turned warm in my grasp.

There are so many questions I want to ask him.

'What happened, then?' I start with the obvious one.

'To him – to the singer?'

Gavin lifts his eyes and then his can to the ceiling.

'A chick happened, mate,' he finally says. 'Isn't it always the fucking way…'

Part One

1

Potential H-Bomb

May 1977

Stevie Mullin was already halfway through his second jam doughnut, on top of the new school sports centre, when he realised what all the shouting was about.

He liked it up there, on top of the world. Ever since he'd found a way how – a tree, a rope, the top of the boys' changing rooms – he'd been spending the best part of his lunchtimes high above the playground. As Stevie spent more time twagging than actually in lessons, no one missed him much. To be frank, most of his peers were actually relieved by his absence. It made him laugh that no one had ever so much as looked up and noticed him.

It was a good place for a smoke and a raid on the day's takings from the school canteen, or cornershop, whichever was most vulnerable to his wandering hands that day. But the thing he liked about it most was that you could see the big cranes of the docks from up here.

Stevie's Grandad Cooper worked on Hull docks, and he was Stevie's favourite relative. A rubble-faced Yorkshireman, as short as he was broad, with fair hair that stood up like Stan Laurel's, a permanent roll-up hanging from the corner of his mouth and a permanent 'bastard' on his lips. He'd taken Stevie up one of those cranes once, when he was seven.

'Don't worry, son, I'm right behind you,' he'd said, as the wind whipped through Stevie's hair and his little hands gripped the freezing iron rail tightly. 'Steady as a goat.'

But Stevie hadn't been frightened, he'd been exhilarated. He could see everything from here – the mouth of the Humber curving grey out to the North Sea, the city stretched out beneath him like it was nothing but a toy town, and away to the north, the outline of the distant moors. It instilled in him an urgent desire to be places he wasn't supposed to be, to see things other people didn't see.

Eight years later he could still feel that weird yearning in his stomach that he'd felt on that day, still kept it close. But Stevie wasn't dreaming about the dockyards as he crammed the sticky stolen bounty into his mouth that day. Instead his head was playing over and over The Sex Pistols' 'God Save the Queen', a single that had been on his turntable incessantly since he'd liberated it from Sidney Scarborough's record shop at the weekend.

He just loved the way Johnny Rotten said: '*We mean it, maaaaaannnn*,' like one drawn-out sneer.

He also loved the way Steve Jones played guitar, was glad that his name was Steve too, because Mullin also harboured a dream of playing in a band. He knew the guitar he had to have – a white Custom Les Paul. At the moment all he had was a thing called a Holner which cost £40 from Band Box second-hand music shop and was supposed to kid you into thinking it was a Hofner. It sounded crap and it hurt his fingers trying to keep the notes down, but he had begun to riddle out how to get those chords, if not the monster sound that Jones achieved.

He was lost in his reverie for some time, picturing the fretboard and how his fingers had to fit there, until gradually his subconscious drifted and harsh noises filtered through the veil.

'Fuckin' nignog,' rang out clearly from below.

'It's Chalkie,' came another, a bad impersonation of Jim Davidson's bad impersonation of a West Indian accent, 'Chalkie White!'

'How you doin' den, Chalkie?' Another comedian. 'You want some ban-an-na?'

Stevie was on his feet and over to the side of the sports hall.

A group of his classmates had cornered the new boy by the side of the boys' changing rooms where any patrolling teachers would be hard-pressed to see.

There were five of them – the hard men of the fifth year. Gary Dunton, stocky, red-haired, trying hard to grow his first sidies and bumfluff moustache was the ringleader and chief Davidson impersonator. Then there were Malc and Martin Carver, twin bruisers with Kevin Keegan perms and thick eyebrows that formed single lines across their Neanderthal foreheads. Hull Kingston Rovers scarves and donkey jackets buttoned up despite the warmness of the day, going 'Hur hur hur,' like two cast-offs from *Planet of the Apes*. Skinhead Barney Lee, Dunton's second-in-command, Rovers scarf as well and a Leeds Utd thumbs-up patch sewn on his demin jacket, waving a banana and pretending to scratch under his armpits. Lagging back from the others, shortarse speccy Kevin Holme, their lackey, keeping a lookout for teacher.

Their prey was pressed up against the bricks of the changing room wall, breathing heavily. From his head burst a fuzzy mass of black candyfloss, a thug beacon that would stand out a mile anywhere in Hull, especially in the place he'd been consigned to for his education. His black skin gleamed like crude oil in the sun, shockingly dark and exotic against the acne-riddled, raspberry-and-cream complexions of his tormentors. Beads of sweat broken out on his forehead, eyes a mixture of fear and rage.

Lynton Powell was too tall for his school uniform, but not yet broad enough to fill it out. He was taller than any of the others, in fact, but so skinny and slight they wouldn't look upon that as an advantage.

Dunton took a swipe at him, trying to grab his bag from off his shoulder. Lynton jumped sideways like a cat, bag falling onto the concrete, his other arm coiling round into a fist, every inch of him shaking.

'Get off me,' he hissed, barely audibly.

'Ooo! Ooo! Ooo!' Lee and the Brothers Grim started making their monkey noises, bouncing up and down like they were baboons. Speccy Kev giggled nervously behind his hand.

'All right, you bastards!' shouted Stevie.

The hard men stopped their ape japing and looked around, bewildered, in every direction but up.

He actually heard Dunton go: 'Durrr?'

'Up here, you fuckin' divs.'

Five lumpy porridge faces cracked round in his direction, wet red mouths going slack when they realised from where and to whom they were speaking. Signs of astonishment betrayed.

Dunton was the first to regain his composure. 'Paddy,' he sneered. 'The fuck you doin' up there, you spaz?'

You had to hand it to him. Only the most vicious ginger cunt in the playground could rise to the top by being the first and most aggressive to racially slur everyone else.

Stevie – whose accent was every bit as East Yorkshire as Dunton's – broke into a broad grin.

'You're a funny bastard, aren't you, Dunton? Real comedian. That were a good show you were puttin' on there.'

They couldn't tell if he was joking or not, and in the seconds it took for them to eye each other, then him, then each other, Lynton took the opportunity to scoop up his schoolbag and race back towards the safety of the school.

'Somethin' wrong with you, Spudhead?' Dunton had decided he was being mocked, although he still wasn't quite sure how or why. Lynton forgotten, he squinted his piggy eyes, affected what he thought was a Brian Jacks judo stance in Stevie's direction. The others moved in closer, formed a circle around their leader.

Stevie belched loudly, taste of jam and sugar in his mouth. 'Nowt much,' he continued to smile. 'Part from this.'

Dunton, the brothers and Barney watched transfixed as Stevie Mullin casually unzipped his trousers and pulled out the most enormous cock any of them had ever seen.

Stevie winked and affected his Dad's Belfast accent. 'It's the luck of the Irish.'

Their mouths were still wide open as the first splashes of hot piss hit Dunton's lips. Only then did they all recoil screaming: 'Ugghhh, Jesus! You dirty fuckin' paddy bastid! You fuckin' homo queer! What the fuck are you doin'?'

Stevie's whole body shook with laughter as he rolled his weapon round in an arc, catching all five of them with his deadly fire. He was still literally pissing himself when a sharp teacher's voice demanded: 'You boys! What's going on out here!'

And he couldn't get it back in his pants quick enough to avoid the accusing fingers that shot up in his direction, the hard man voices now turned to whining, spragging victims: 'It's Mullin, sir, he's on the roof and he's pissing on us!'

'Language!' stormed Mr Smith, aka Herr Schmitler, the German master and worst of all possible teachers to be caught by.

'Boy Mullin, what are you doing on that roof? Get down here immediately!'

In his rush to hide his modesty, Stevie almost fell over backwards.

'And you boys,' he turned his attentions back to the others, 'what do you think you're doing here? You know this area is out of bounds at break-time. What are you playing at, eh? Eh?'

Stevie almost got expelled that time.

The cane, detention, his parents up the school to talk about his future; all that shit. It was all worth it for the expression on Dunton's thick face, which would continue to keep Stevie happy for years to come. It gave him further pleasure that while his own reputation as a mad fucker not to be messed with was increased, Dunton's became tainted by Chinese whispers that suggested he was some kind of sex pervert who liked drinking men's piss.

Stevie didn't waste a moment of his month of detentions. While his right hand robotically wrote out I WILL SHOW RESPECT FOR SCHOOL PROPERTY AND SCHOOL RULES 1,000 times, his head neared completion on the notes for the Steve Jones riff. The left hand holding the paper down was at the same time forming chord structures with its fingers.

From the classroom where he spent his penury he was able to make a further interesting discovery.

A music group met after school every Thursday. He watched them going in and out of the school hall.

One of them was speccy Kevin Holme. He was always carting the most kit into the hall, which meant he had to be a drummer. Away from his gang, he had a secret life.

And finally, one Friday, as Stevie strolled out of the gates of the now deserted school at five o'clock, someone was waiting for him.

Hanging nervously around the gates, left hand absently rubbing right bicep, eyes darting up and down the street, peg-leg trousers halfway up his shins, blazer sleeves halfway to his elbows.

'Ey up, Lynton,' Stevie was surprised. 'Waiting for summat?'

Lynton glared up at him then back down at the ground. He took in bandy legs and drainpipe trousers, yellow socks and brothel creepers, white shirt and bootlace black tie, blazer slung over one shoulder. School uniform like no one else wore it.

Lynton's eyes both fierce and fearful. 'I wanted to say thank you.' His voice came out as barely a whisper, a southern accent with a bass rumble. Then his head came up again, eyes more fierce, volume turned up. 'What you do it for, man? Why d'you help me out?'

Stevie shrugged. 'Dunton's a cunt,' he said simply, liking the way the two words almost rhymed.

Lynton liked it too. Couldn't suppress a surprisingly high-pitched giggle.

'Dunton, Cunton, the fuck's the difference? Reckon us paddies and nignogs should stick together against the likes of him.'

Lynton stopped laughing for a minute, frown forming across his brow at the word 'nignog'. He did look quite frightening when he scowled. Then he smiled again, a wide, brilliant smile that lit his whole face up.

'You're right, man.' He held out his hand. His fingers were long and elegant, his palms light pink, which further surprised Stevie, who had never been this close to a black person before.

Stevie's own hands seemed big and clumsy in comparison, despite all the training he'd been putting his fingers through.

But they shook, and then Stevie clapped his new friend round the back, a gesture that almost winded the slighter boy, though he did his best not to show it.

'So, Lynton,' Stevie said. 'What d'you think of the Sex Pistols?'

'The what what?'

They started to walk down the street together.

It was nearly the end of term, long summer holidays beckoning, and already the weather showed signs of repeating last year's scorcher. Like every other town, city and village in the land, Hull was in the grip of Jubilee fever.

Red, white, and blue Silver Jubilee bunting fluttered from every lamp-post, every windowsill and drainpipe. Some folk had even gone so far as to paint their houses with the Union Flag, from roots to rafters.

'You never heard of the Sex Pistols? Don't you watch TV?'

Lynton scowelled again. 'You're havin' a laugh, ain't you? There ain't no TV programme called that.'

Stevie laughed. 'S'right, mate, there's not. Sex Pistols is a band.

They've been on the news an' all sorts, swearin' at TV presenters and gettin' their tour banned all across country. Loads of old women up in arms against them, forming prayer groups outside their gigs.'

Lynton's eyes sparkled with wonder. 'A band? What kind of music?'

Stevie's smile broadened still further. 'Punk rock is what it is. Music you don't have to learn an instrument for. You just get up and do it, make all the noise you like, and say what you like an' all. That's what they did. I read it in *Sounds*.'

'Sex Pistols?' Lynton tried the unfamiliar words out. 'What kinda name is that? What does it mean?'

'It's a weapon. Same kind as I used on Bary Cunton.'

Lynton dissolved into another fit of giggles. 'That's funny, man,' he finally said. 'That is some good shit. Where do you get it from?'

'Me? I stole my copy from Sidney Scarborough's,' Stevie shrugged. 'You can come round and hear it if you want.'

Lynton stopped his laughing and made a careful study of Stevie's face.

It was a wide face with a thick nose and a generous mouth. Eyes that crinkled round the edges when he smiled. Thick blonde hair sprouting in all directions, haphazardly rising up off his crown and all over his forehead. Lynton couldn't detect any traces of mockery in that face, didn't feel like he was being set up for an ambush this time.

'I would like to,' he said warily. 'But tonight my mum is expecting me home. In fact, I'm late all ready.'

'No bother,' Steve shrugged magnanimously, 'we can always do it another time.'

Lynton looked both relieved and grateful. 'That would be good. Wh-why not tomorrow?'

'All right, you're on.' They had reached the crossroads at the end of the street. 'Which way you headed?' Stevie asked.

Lynton lugged a thumb left. It wasn't the way Stevie was going, but he was curious to see where his new friend hung out.

They crossed the road together. There wasn't much traffic about. A few kids on Chopper bikes practising wheelies. Dogs lying down in driveways, panting in the heat. One of those golden summer evenings that can gild even the back streets of North Hull.

'D'you know how to play any instruments?' Stevie asked as they continued on their way.

'I've been trying to learn the trumpet for the last five years,' Lynton sighed. 'I wanna be like Miles.'

'Miles?'

'Miles Davis.'

It was Stevie's turn to frown and Lynton's to laugh. 'You never heard of Miles Davis? You're kiddin' me! Miles is the king of jazz. He was the original bad boy.'

'I'm just a pig-shit ignorant paddy,' Stevie shrugged, putting on his Da's voice again. 'We only have the ceilidh in our house, the fiddles and the whistles and the bodhrans…'

'Tell you what,' Lynton was really pleased now. 'Tomorrow, I'll bring Miles and you bring your…Sex Pistols. Then we see what it's really about.'

'You got yourself a deal,' Stevie clapped his hand round Lynton's back again, making the other boy buckle at the knees. 'You show me yours, then I'll show you mine.'

2

Unknown Pleasures

November 2001

By the time Gavin had been through his stash of old videos and we'd emptied all the cans in his fridge it was 5am on Sunday morning. Much too late for going home.

'D'you wanna crash here tonight, mate?' Granger read my thoughts, let his eyes travel from mine to the sofa. 'I'll get you a duvet.'

I was fast becoming a regular on that black leather couch, getting used to the fact that, despite being a three-seater, it still wasn't quite long enough for my legs. But, mildly uncomfortable though that was, it was preferable to going back to Camden Road.

'Yeah, cheers,' I gave him the thumbs up, lit the last of my packet of Camels and screwed up the empty box. My throat was already raw with the amount of cancer sticks I'd got through that evening, but I still had half a tin of Red Stripe left and a drink was too wet without one.

Gavin left me like old man Steptoe, rolled up in a duvet, draining the dregs of my can and tipping the ash into its empty predecessor.

'See you in the morning,' he winked, shutting the door.

I'd first met Granger on a job two months ago. We were on a junket to New York to meet Sony records' latest 'alternative' signings, who ironically enough were actually from Oxford. But to convince us of their faith in whining psuedo-U2 miserablists, the men's magazine I worked for and a bunch of other titles were being flown out *en masse* to the city that never sleeps.

Actually listening to them, at private showcase gig at CBGBs, was the only pain I felt, but even that was tempered by the new friendship I'd just struck up with the photographer from a Sunday magazine.

I knew him by reputation first, of course, but who didn't? Well, anyone who knew their past would know. Granger had been the *NME* photographer in the 1980s, his iconic black-and-white images of Ian Curtis, John Lydon, Siouxsie Sioux glaring dissent from every best-selling cover. He always managed to capture the pure essence of his subjects, the source of their very difference: Curtis drawing on a fag, lost inside a greatcoat, already a ghost's shadow imprinted on the grey Manchester streets. Lydon smiling through crooked teeth and manic eyes, the host of Death Disco. Siouxsie in bondage gear and cigarette holder, harsh, glossy ice queen.

I'd discovered all these while avoiding work at my former employer's, a second-hand magazine and photo stills shop in the dirty raincoat end of Soho. It was the Lydon cover I first noticed, Johnny's first since the Pistols' bust-up and the introduction of his new band, Public Image Ltd. Granger's portraits were as edgy and fractious as his studies, like he really had managed to capture a bit of someone's soul with the flick of his shutter.

When I had enough freelance work to finally stop working with used linens, I took with me a stack of *NMEs* bearing the Granger hallmark. For some reason they made me feel nostalgic for a time I was too young to actually remember. A time when music really meant something, really said something about the times and people's lives. When bands got together because they were mates, they could write their own songs and tie their own shoelaces. People like Lydon and Curtis were men you could look up to, heroes, self-made, self-taught. Forged in the Winter of Discontent from the grimmest inner cities.

No more heroes in 2001, just endlessly manufactured, mix-and-match outfits, aggressively marketed at eight-year-olds. Boy bands to your right, girl bands to your left, comedy metal for the rebels and, worst of all, bands like the cunts I was watching on this night – the thirtysomething angst bands.

Coldharbour, they were called, a name they probably picked at random off a map of South London and thought it gave them cred. The singer played a piano and wailed about the alienation he felt from his peer group of rugby-playing inbred Sloany tossers. Probably. He had one of those haircuts that screamed the name Jeremy, and much as he dressed himself down in frayed cuffs and distressed denim it was blatantly obvious that neither he, nor his equally bland and innocuous band, had ever really been anywhere near a place like Coldharbour Lane.

'Christ, what an arsehole,' came a voice in my ear as the singer's wailing reached crescendo.

Gavin Granger lounged against the sweaty CBGB's wall. There was a camera around his neck that he was paying no attention to, a bottle of Rolling Rock in his hand. He had a black shirt unbuttoned almost to the waist, and black pinstripe trousers. Big silver braclet on his wrist. Shaggy hair down to the shoulders, curling up at the ends with the humidity.

He looked a fuck's sight cooler than anyone up on stage.

'You read my thoughts,' I laughed and he raised his bottle to clink it with mine.

'Don't know what the fuck we're doin' here,' he drew me into a conspiratorial whisper, gesturing at our surroundings, the fabled birthplace of American punk rock. A narrow little cave of a place with graffiti all over the walls, walls that leaked sweat and stank of a million spilled pints, a million fag ends ground into the floor.

Only tourists came here now, to drink at the little tables that ran down the side of the bar, buy the T-shirt, try and catch the memories that were fading as fast as the carpet.

'Is this supposed to mean we're witnessing the birth of a legend? Why don't they be more honest and set up a showcase in a shopping mall.'

'Are you supposed to be taking pictures of them?' I asked him.

'Yeeeaah,' he slouched back against the wall, took another pull on his bottle. 'But fuck 'em. I've got all I need for the feature we're doin'. Don't really need to waste any more film on no marks like these.'

'Who are you working for now?' I couldn't help but ask, aware that my voice reeked with deference and fan-worship.

'*Sunday Times Magazine*,' Granger sneered. 'You know the sort of pictures they'll want. Although how you can make this look at all glamorous is beyond me.' He started laughing, pointing a long bony finger with a vicious-looking nail towards the postage stamp-sized stage.

'This tosser here,' he was singling out the plump bass player with the lights shining through his receding hairline, 'already looks like my accountant. But…' he stopped laughing abruptly, waved his empty bottle like a baton. 'Guess that's why they get into music these days. It's a career choice.'

'Join the manufacturing industry,' I agreed. 'Maximum exposure for minimum effort.'

'You got that,' Gavin nodded vigorously and I felt childishly pleased.

'Can I get you a drink?'

Apart from the half-hour set aside for me to probe the deep recesses of Coldharbour's collective mind, I spent the rest of the two days we had left in New York hanging on Granger's every word. Starting the moment the gig finished and we'd said our fake congratulations to the PR and got the hell out of CBGBs. He knew a bar down the road in Tompkins Square Park that was like an English pub and had a punk rock jukebox. Over margaritas and beers and the good taste of Lucky Strikes he told me his rock'n'roll stories while the very people he was talking about blasted out of the speakers.

John Lydon, Ian Curtis, Elvis Costello, Ian Dury – the whole post-punk spectrum caught in his lens. But he had one favourite, a bloke I had to admit I'd never heard of, who fronted a band equally unknown to me.

'Vincent Smith,' he said, eyes misting over. 'D'you ever hear of him?'

'Mark E. Smith,' I misheard him. 'The Fall?'

'Nah, mate, although Smithy's another one of the champions. Vincent Smith. He was in a band called Blood Truth. They were the best bloody band I ever saw. Fuckin' riots happened when they played.'

'Yeah?' I leaned closer to my source, hanging on every utterance. 'How come?'

'They used to do things like turn up, play one number, have a fight with the audience and leave.'

'Wow,' my jaw dropped open.

'And you gotta remember, the audience in those days really wanted a fight. It was all factions, and they'd all turn up at the same gig. Punks hated pyschobillies, psychobillies hated rockers, rockers hated everyone and goths were just in there for a punch bag.' He chortled at the memory.

'But Vince Smith, he was a big bastard, about six foot three. And the guitarist, Steve Mullin, he was a big bastard too. Very stylish with it. It was like Smith was Lee Marvin and Mullin was Robert Mitchum, but they came from Hull which made them even harder. Yeeeesss,' his eyes were far away, savouring the memories.

It pushed all the right buttons with me. Lee Marvin. Robert Mitchum. Blood Truth.

'So they were, in fact, the Wild Bunch?' I joked.

'Fuckin' right,' Granger nodded. 'About as far away as you can imagine from the bunch of wankers onstage tonight.'

'I don't know,' I drained my bottle and stabbed a straw at the remains of the ice in my margarita, aware it was my round next and wondering if the dollars in my pocket would hold up to it. 'I can't help thinking I was born in the wrong time…'

Granger's eyebrows shot up quizzically.

'Why d'you say that?'

'Well, you've just spent the whole evening pointing out why it was better twenty years ago than it is now. I'm twenty-nine and the wildest thing I've ever seen is my grandmother loose at the January sales. If wankers like Coldharbour are the alternative choice then I don't think there's gonna be another John Lydon… or another Vincent Smith.'

'*Touché*!' Gavin laughed.

As if in agreement, someone put 'Cretin Hop' by The Ramones onto the jukebox.

I staggered towards the bar in search of more margaritas, the germ of an idea already forming in my brain.

Back across the ocean, through another sea of time in old videotape and second-hand memory.

That idea more certain now I had seen the video.

I was picturing a big hardback book jacket. Black and white frontispiece; one of Gavin's classic shots from the eighties. Maybe the one he had shown me earlier of Smith with his head flung back, veins bulging on his neck, hair a mane of jagged black points. Big black letters spelling out:

VINCENT SMITH – THE LOST BOY

BY ED BRACKNELL

WITH PHOTOGRAPHS BY GAVIN GRANGER

I was even beginning to anticipate some coverline quotes as I drifted towards alcoholic slumber.

'Where rock biography meets investigative journalism and blows the lid off popular culture' – *Time Out*

'Bracknell goes back to where history got off and brings back to life a forgotten icon of the twentieth century' – *The Times*

'A riot all of his own' – *The Face*

That kind of thing.

Before long, I was snoring, an insistent bassline throbbing in my head.

3

Dance to a Different Song

May 1977

'Where are you from, Lynton? An' how did you end up in a shithole like Hull?'

Lynton sat on the end of Stevie's bed, trying to take everything in. Stevie's house was unlike anything he'd ever encountered before.

For a start, he lived on Hessle Road, *Hezzle* Road as the locals said it. Near the wasteland where the gypsies camped and a pub patrolled by surly Teddy Boys, who smoked roll-ups and gobbed onto the pavement like it marked their territory.

Which in effect, it did.

As they had walked down the streets towards Hessle Road earlier this evening, Lynton had become aware that the word 'fishwife' did actually describe a proper Hull sub-species. Pinning out their endless washing in their front yards, they continually screeched to their offspring and each other, fags clamped in the side of pink lipsticked mouths, hair in rollers under nylon hairnets, sleeves rolled up on arms the size of hams. They looked like miners in drag. Some of them even had tattoos, ships anchors, love hearts, etched in blue ink on corned-beef flesh.

The youngest of their offspring – those not yet capable of passing themselves off in the pub – combined football and kicking the shit out of each other into a kind of game to be played in the middle of the road. Monkey boots and bright orange balls scuffling over the tarmac, screams and insults flung into the air to the encouragement of the constantly baying mongrels running amongst them.

Only when they noticed Lynton, they seemed to freeze. One bain stood with his finger stuck mid-nostril, jaw swinging open like it was on a hinge. He carried on staring with dead eyes, drool flowing unconcernedly from the corner of a mouth crusted with orange baked bean stains.

He made Lynton want to throw up. He tried to look away, down at the pavement, painfully aware of their prods and whispers. The Hessle Road juniors weighing up whether to make a comment. They had never seen a black person before and were, for the moment, more curious than aggressive. What kept their gobs shut was the fact the stranger was accompanied by one of the Mad Mullin family.

Five brothers, three of them big and a dad who was a legend for skippering ships on ramming raids against the Icelanders during the Cod Wars of '75 and '76. A local hero, the hardest of the hard.

Stevie clocked their stares too and stared them back like his Da would.

Yet: 'Gollywog!' squeaked a high-pitched voice.

Stevie stopped in his tracks, slowly began to crack his knuckles. 'Did I hear a skate gob?' he asked.

That was enough for now. Monkey boots running away up the Hezzle Road, trailing mumbles and stifled laughter behind them.

Lynton looked at the ground, his cheeks burning, feeling real fear and not wanting to show it. Wishing, not for the first time, that he had a formula for turning invisible.

Stevie's house was an end-of-terrace. Like all the others,

washing hung in the front yard, kids' trikes, scooters and a Space Hopper lay strewn haphazardly across the path. But unlike the fishwives' houses, the front gate had been recently painted, and flowers did grow in what little earth there was.

To Lynton's relief, Steve's mum didn't look like a miner in drag.

She still had five of her children living with her, Stevie being the oldest, little Gracie at four the youngest. Not to mention the dogs, the cats and whatever other creatures her children could coax or steal home with them. Her husband was out on trawlers most of the time, down the pub the rest of it, only stopping home to drop off the spoils of another catch, try for another addition to the family.

Despite all this, she still managed to look slim and blonde and about twenty-five, still managed to always be smiling as she grappled with the endless stream of traffic through her kitchen. She had welcomed Lynton with the same beatific smile she used on her whole family, offered him a supper of cabbage, bacon and mash. Only the broad delivery of her Hull accent clashed with the delicacy of her features.

'It's all right, Ma, we had us chips on the way home,' Stevie was eager to get upstairs and away from the mess and madness that unravelled around his younger siblings at mealtime.

But Lynton felt embarrassed that he'd had those chips when she had been cooking. He wouldn't have treated his own mum that way. And she wasn't even his real mum.

He smiled and said lamely: 'Sorry, Mrs Mullin.'

'Don't you worry, love,' she smiled back at him, 'I've plenty more mouths need feeding. It never stops round here.'

Stevie's bedroom was small and cramped, smelt of stale biscuits and ripe socks. A heavy old wardrobe and chest of drawers took up most of the space, narrow single bed shunted into a corner. Stevie had only got a room of his own when his brother Connor had moved out to get married last spring. He was inordinately proud of the improvements he'd made since then. A small Dansette record player leaned against the wall beneath the window, beside it, a stack of albums and singles. The curtains were permanently closed and Stevie had pinned a Jolly Roger flag over the top of them. Small glimpses of luridly patterned carpet were just visible between the piles of discarded clothes and music papers.

But what really struck Lynton were the walls. Every inch of them covered in pictures of four very strange young men, all ripped out of newspapers and the music press. A big banner tacked to the ceiling, a gigantic A surrounded by an even bigger O, looked to be home-made, Airfix paint on bedsheet. Lynton's eyes traversed the newsprint gallery.

The same figure leapt out at him each time. He had orange hair and staring eyes, was wrapped in what looked like a straitjacket with DESTROY and a swastika on the front of it.

He looked like he came from another planet.

'S-sorry,' he realised he'd been spoken to. 'What did you say?'

'I said,' Stevie pulled off his school tie and hurled it into a dark corner, started scrunching up his hair in the wardrobe mirror, 'where do you come from? Originally, like. 'Cos it ain't from anywhere round here.'

'Ain't that the truth,' Lynton weighed up what to say next. His fingers worked at a thread on Stevie's tartan bedspread. 'My parents lived in London,' he said eventually.

'How d'you end up here then?'

Lynton's eyes in Stevie's mirror looked like burning coals. ''Cos they didn't want me,' he said bluntly. 'She was one of them "gymslip mothers" you read about. Irish, I think. And he was some Rude Boy from Jamaica. Paddies and nignogs stick together, yeah? Well, not back then they didn't. I don't remember either of them. Soon as I was born, I got given to someone else, a white family with a nice house in Essex. We just moved here 'cos my dad's got his self a job at Hull University in September what pays more than the one he had before. I don't think they realised I would be the only black kid in the whole of the city, otherwise we might have stayed were we was. In Essex, it ain't such a big thing. But that's how I come to live in this shithole.'

'Oh,' Stevie staring back through the mirror. 'I'm sorry, mate,' his voice was gentle. 'I didn't mean to stir up bad memories.'

Lynton looking fierce again, not wanting Stevie to see him looking sad.

'I just knew it must be weird for you here,' Stevie went on. 'Surrounded by white, lardy Yorkshire cunts. Must be like some kind of bastard nightmare.'

Again, just the way Stevie phrased things made his companion laugh out loud.

'What do you think?' Lynton chuckled his agreement. Then, seriously: 'But to tell you the truth, I think I would feel weird anywhere.'

Stevie met his eye, held the gaze for a heartbeat. 'That's right how I feel. I know our family's got that reputation that we're all mad bastards and it's good, like, 'cos they leave you alone. But I'm not mad like they are. I don't want to end up on some bastard trawler, freezing my bastard knackers off in middle of North Sea, for fuck all.'

Both boys blinked at each other a moment longer. Then Lynton realised what Stevie had been rubbing into his hair the whole time they had been speaking.

'Man!' he exclaimed, clapping a hand over his mouth to try and stop from laughing. 'Are you putting toothpaste in your hair?'

Stevie's face cracked open into a wide grin.

'Yeah, I am an' all. It's how you get it into spikes.'

Lynton couldn't control his giggles any longer. Within seconds both of them were in hysterics, Lynton lying on the bed, Stevie leaning against the wardrobe, clutching his stomach. Only when they had exhausted themselves did Lynton weakly gesture towards the pictures on the wall. 'Are these the Sex Pistols then?'

'Aye,' Stevie wiped tears out of his eyes, hauled himself onto the side of the bed.

'Which one's that?' Lynton pointed at the alien.

'That's Johnny Rotten.'

'This singer?'

'Aye. He's fuckin' brilliant, he is. He don't go on about girls or love or any of that shit stuff pop stars sing about. He sings about the IRA and the Queen and council estates, stuff like that. He don't really sing, either...' Stevie started delving into his pile of singles, pulled one out of a red and beige paper sleeve. 'But don't tek my word for it. You see what you think.'

Stevie dropped the needle onto the vinyl and pulled his white guitar from on top of the wardrobe. The room filled with a roar like jet engines taking off. It almost knocked Lynton backwards. It took him a while to realise what he was actually listening to was guitar and drums and by the time he did an eerie voice was snaking over the top of it all: '*Riiiiight. Naaaaaaaawwwwwww*!' it went and then dissolved into a maniacal cackle.

Stevie, affecting an axe-slinger's pose, was playing his amp-less guitar along for all he was worth.

'*I am an anti-Christ!*' went the alien's voice, '*I am an anarcheist!*'

The music got louder and louder. Lynton felt like it was about to blow him out of the room. Stevie's fingers flew up and down the neck of his cheap guitar, and he mouthed along to the words with his eyes locked shut.

''*Cos I wanna beee-ah, Anarcheeeeeeeee*!'

It was like nothing else on earth, Stevie was right about that. And in amongst the sheet metal guitars and power-driving drums and the acidic voice of the alien, Lynton sensed something very powerful, taking shape and rising like a phoenix.

He sensed freedom.

The single clattered to its end with the sound of lacerated

fretboards, crashing cymbols and the alien's last, drawn-out command: '*Deeestrroyyyyy*!'

Lyton got the shivers all down his spine. 'Put it on again,' he whispered.

'You like it?' Stevie was clearly proud as punch, standing legs apart with his guitar resting on his crotch, his hair stuck up with globules of Signal.

'You want to start a band, don't you?' Lynton realised.

'Yeah,' Stevie nodded. 'Yeah I fucking do. You want to join me?'

Lynton's eyes travelled from Stevie to the newsprint alien and his mad-looking eyes.

We're all aliens, he thought. *We're all in it together*.

'Yeah, man!' he said defiantly. 'Yeah, I fucking do too!'

It was the first time he had ever said the word 'fuck'. It sounded as liberating on his lips as the Pistols did to his ears.

'You won't need no trumpet for this though,' he considered the situation quickly, 'so I will play bass.'

'Oh! D'you know how to do that an' all?'

'No – but I'm going to find out.'

'What about Miles Davis though?'

Lynton thought. Miles in his bag. So sure he would blow Stevie away with it. Now it felt old and out of place, another time, another man's battle.

This was the sound of the future.

'What about him?'

Stevie let out a whoop of delight, leapt up punching the air.

'*Anarcheeeee!*'

4

Pump it Up

November 2001

It was after 4pm when I finally staggered up that wind tunnel of Camden Town tube, stomach keeping a tenuous hold on the fry-up Granger had cheerily provided, the couple of hairs of the dog at the Market Bar, the first cigarettes of the day.

After four, and the sky already darkening. Bags of old men slouched around the Camden Road exit, holding up greasy palms for alms that were never going to come. Not even bothering to speak any more, just staring up with red, accusing eyes. Crumpled cans of Special Brew at their feet; the thirst that could never be slaked. More of them these days than ever, and there always was a wino army around here.

Once you got past them, there were the drug dealers, skinny, rangy black kids slumped into oversized jeans, jabbering with each other and anyone that passed, as wired and aggressive as the winos were pathetic and old. More of them these days too; in fact, Camden now resembled King's Cross with novelty yoof shop knobs on. The party days were long gone. It seemed more like a million years ago since we first moved here than ten. Days when the sun shone all summer, when the pubs were run by Irishmen with rock'n'roll 45s on the jukeboxes and musicians, not dealers, were hanging on every corner.

It was after four and the lights blinking on up Camden Road, the last dribbles of pink fading into the grey sky. It was freezing too, the kind of cold that seeps into your bones, embalms you from the inside.

I knew it would be cold in the flat too. I trudged past Sainsbury's, past the queues for the bus overflowing onto the pavement. The other side of the road all second-hand and cut-price shops, the one last Irish bar that had been left given a Hoxton makeover six months ago and now standing empty. Someone had been shot there the night it opened and it had remained closed for business ever since.

Past Camden Road station, idling the last few steps to my front door. The churning in my stomach combined with a feeling of dread. I looked up to our flat, first floor, above the fruit and veg shop. Blinds down. Dark panes reflected back nothing but the street lights.

I breathed a sigh of relief, fumbled in my jacket pocket for the key. Even waved a cheery 'Hello!' to Ali in the shop as I opened the door, ever the urban gentleman, never the dirty stop out.

Pressed the hall light on, ignored the pile of junk mail on the spindly table at the bottom of the stairs, creaked up to the flat. Inside it was colder than out. Spotlessly clean and ordered and empty.

My eyes swept round the room anyway. It was minimalist, the way we both liked it. Well, Louise especially. Black Ikea furniture, stripped floorboards, aluminium blinds. Her concession to ostentation a bookcase full of thick titles, philosophy, sociology, fine art and old movies – still not sure which part of her studies I made up. My concession, the widescreen TV and DVD player. The reason the flat was so cold, I'd rather spend my money on toys like these than central heating.

In the kitchen, a Duellit 1950s style toaster, a Smeg fridge, all the other things that looked good and so were more important than feeling comfortable.

A Polaroid of me and her tacked to the side of the fridge. Smiling, laughing.

Ten years ago. When the librarian and the libertarian still made a winning combination.

She didn't even bother to leave notes any more. The kitchen table was empty, but for a fruit bowl containing a shriveled-looking lemon.

Me and Louise today.

I stooped to turn on the fan heater, pointed it towards my desk, fired up the G3. Filled up the kettle and put it on to boil.

The answerphone was blinking in the corner.

But it was just the routine Sunday night call from Mother, sounding, as usual, like a battle address from Margaret Thatcher. I didn't have the will to return it.

By the time the kettle had boiled, the G3 had powered itself up. It wasn't a bad machine, considering I got it off the IT department at work with a shitload of software installed all for nothing. But the new iMacs looked so much better. So small and neat and Futurist.

It was still too cold to take my coat off, so I sat down with my instant coffee, clicked on the Internet Explorer icon.

She wouldn't be able to phone here now, even if she wanted to. Her or Mother.

I went straight to Google. Typed in four words: *Vincent Smith Blood Truth* and watched the pages come up.

The first hit was called **Careless Love: Doomed Rock Relationships**. Underneath it listed Kurt and Courtney, Sid and Nancy, Paula Yates and Michael Hutchence, **Vincent Smith and Sylvana…**

A chick happened, mate.

'You and me both,' I said aloud as I clicked onto the link. The site was done up like a pulp magazine, with lurid headlines in *LA Confidential*-style typefaces. I scrolled down pages and pages about Sid and Nancy and Kurt and Courtney, the authors deliberately comparing and contrasting the women, their blonde hair and bombed eyes, clear implication: *deadlier than the male*. Skipped past Paula and Hutch, a story far too depressing for Sunday afternoon turning into Sunday night. I'd always secretly fancied Paula, couldn't fault Hutchence for that, not like hapless Sid and Kurt.

Finally, under the headline: **Kiss of Death: A Gothic Love Story**, a big picture of the couple sprawled across the back seat of an old Cadillac. Vince with a pompadour oiled and gleaming, black Tuxedo and a blood-red shirt, cigarette dangling from one hand, the other arm around the shoulders of the most beautiful girl I had ever seen.

She almost looked like a doll. Little porcelain face and red bow lips, huge green eyes peering up from thick lashes, framed by a Ronnie Spector-style bouffant of bright red hair. Red velvet dress with a white lace collar, the sort they put on those antique Victorian figurines, looking tiny and surreal in Vincent Smith's embrace.

Vincent and Sylvana Smith, just married, Paris, January 1981 read the caption. Only six months later, Sylvana would be dead…

The hook was too good to resist. I read on:

Largely forgotten now, in the post-punk era, Vincent Smith was the self-styled King of Nothing and his band Blood Truth made the most searing and unholy racket of anyone around. Their live shows were legendary for starting riots: Smith did his best to incite the volatile mix of punks, goths and skins that made up the ranks of his following, with seemingly half his audience turning up more for the prospect of a fight than the music. Just as well, legend has it that the longest show they ever played lasted thirty minutes.

Blood Truth were formed in Hull in 1977, by Sex Pistols-mad guitarist Steve Mullin (who always emulated the playing style of his hero, Steve Jones), bassist Lynton Powell and drummer Kevin Holme. They met Smith, from Doncaster, at a Sex Pistols gig in that town in August of that year. He was two years older than the then sixteen-year-old upstarts and able to relocate to Hull, where he immediately took charge of the fledgling band, picking out a name and writing the lyrics for their songs in earnest.

Smith was obsessed with Americana, in particular Elvis and the writer Flannery O'Connor, from whose classic novel *Wise Blood* he was inspired to take band's name. The Memphis King had been dead for only a week when he met up with Mullin and co., and Smith saw this as his sign to resurrect the fallen Presley in his own performance as the anti-establishment Elvis. Coupled with Mullin's natural flair as a guitarist, this gave them a different edge on the post-Pistols sound than any of their rivals from the industrial North. Blood Truth's other secret weapon was Powell, a brilliant musician who had studied jazz trumpet for years before meeting Mullin and reputedly learned the bass overnight in order to play in the band. Even by the time they had scraped together their first single 'Blind Preach/Dockyard' in January 1978, they had the beginnings of a distinctive sound that was all the stronger for their disparate influences. They also looked brilliant – along with Siouxsie Sioux, Vince Smith can genuinely be traced back as the first gothic role model.

Initially managed by local entrepreneur Don Dawson, who put out their first records on his own Dawsongs label, Blood Truth set about conquering the North in '78 with a succession of gigs that saw them rise from supporting the likes of The Damned and The Stranglers to their own headline tour before the year was out. A string of further singles accompanied their gradual rise, and the mini-LP that spawned their legendary track, 'King of Nothing', fell into the hands of new London-based label Exile. Ever the champion of all things batwinged, they signed Blood Truth early in 1979 and quickly recorded their first full-length LP *Down in the World*, which rapidly made them the darlings of the music weeklies. Their propensity for outrageous behaviour claimed yet more column inches and a front cover for NME in which Mullin persuaded a young woman to be tied to the front of their tour van half naked as their figurehead, a photograph that nearly landed the paper in serious legal trouble.

More albums followed. *Ruined* (1979), *The Crooked Mile* and *From the Bottom of the Glass* in 1980, when the band hit a creative and commercial high, denting the bottom of the official chart and staying at Number One in the Indie charts for six weeks solid.

It looked as though 1981 would be the year of their commercial breakthrough, but fate had another idea: Sylvana Goldberg.

Sylvana, an American Jewish princess from a rich New Jersey family, had come to London to follow the Pistols in '77 and never left. She'd met a young Scottish musician, Robin Leith, at a Damned gig, fallen in love and formed the band Mood Violet with him and guitarist Aliester McTavish, a schoolmate of Leith's.

Thanks to the fact that Sylvana (who generally dispensed with her surname) sounded as exotic and eerily childlike as she looked, Mood Violet soon attracted a cult following. Leith's inventiveness with synths and atmospheric guitar style lent them an assured accessibility beyond the grasp of most of their goth peers. By the time Sylvana met Vince, at a New Year's Eve party hosted by Exile records' founder Tony Stevens, Mood Violet were a breakthrough act who'd had three singles in the Top 20.

According to legend, the attraction was so instant that Vincent and Sylvana slipped away from the party within half an hour of meeting – leaving her hapless then fiancé Robin Leith stranded over the canapés…

The sudden vibration of my mobile in my jacket pocket startled me out of my reverie. I checked the number and sighed, giving in to the inevitable.

'Hello Mother,' I tried to sound cheerful. 'Yes, just walked through the door five minutes ago…'

'You're on that Internet again, aren't you?' she said. 'How much money is that costing you? And this mobile phone – you know I hate calling you on it. It's twice the price of British Telecom...'

'I'll ring you back on the landline, shall I?' I tried not to grind my teeth as I made a bookmark of the Careless Love website, turned the remote access off.

'If you don't mind, dear.'

She always got her way.

Live and loud from Guildford, thirty minutes of further interrogation followed. How was work? Fine, Mum. I'm lining up another trip to the States. Why do I like it so much there? Just, well, it's different, isn't it? I know they have strange values, Mother, and what that President Clinton got up to and how he got away with it. Terrible, yes, quite so.

And on and on, until she got to the really excruciating bit, the sore spots she always stuck her voodoo pins into with unfailing accuracy.

'Louise not with you then, tonight?' A thoughtful pause as I tried to mumble out an answer, followed by a swift: 'That why you're wasting all that time on the Internet?'

'Actually I'm doing research, Mother,' the annoyance resounding down the line, giving her the reassurance of my discomfort she so dearly needed. 'I'm thinking about writing a book.'

'Really?' her tone poised between scepticism and sudden interest. 'What kind of book would that be? A novel?'

'No,' I should never have started this. 'A biography...'

'Has someone asked you to ghostwrite their memoirs?' her tone getting fruitier, more expectant.

'No, it's not authorised. It's just an idea at the moment. Probably nothing will come of it.'

'Who did you say, dear?' Not letting me back down again now. 'Anyone we know?'

I pictured Dad in the background, hovering like a little grey ghost, nodding earnestly at her every exclamation.

'No, no one you would have heard of.'

'One of your musician friends, then?'

'Yes, Mother. Vincent Smith. Ever heard of him? He was very big with skinheads and punks in the eighties...'

'Really?" she said again, this time it sounded more like a sigh. 'Well, that's lovely for you, dear. And have you a publisher?'

'I'm seeing someone tomorrow,' I lied. 'I'll tell you all about it when there's actually something to tell. Now, I'm going to have to get off now and get myself some dinner...'

Shouldn't have said that either.

'She isn't there, then, Louise?' Mother scenting blood. 'I didn't think she was. Is there something you're not telling me, Edward?'

'She just went to Sainsbury's to pick up a few things,' I blurted the first thing that came into my head. 'She'll be back any minute to get the dinner on, that's what I was trying to tell you.'

'There's no need to shout, dear.'

'Sorry Mother.' No, there's every need.

Teeth grinding spontaneously. 'Ta ta for now then?'

'Well, enjoy your dinner,' she concluded, her voice saying she knew it was actually going to be a bowl of Crunchy Nut cornflakes, eaten alone. 'Give my love to Louise. *When* she gets there.'

'I will. And give mine to Dad. Bye now...'

I put the phone down feeling fat, useless and one hundred years old.

Still freezing inside this room.

My breath hung on the air.

Still empty.

Interminable Sunday night blues coming down.

After Mother's interrogation, it was nearly five o'clock, but there was no way of telling how long Louise had actually been out. Seeing as I hadn't bothered to either come home last night or phone her to tell her I wasn't, there was no way she was going to extend me any such courtesy. This was designed to make me suffer.

A gremlin in my head said: What if she didn't come home last night cither?

I pushed it away, banged my hand down on the mouse and brought the G3 back to life. Hit remote access status to reconnect and put the kettle back on as it loaded up. I actually could have done with Louise's fictitious trip to Sainsbury's. That was the last of the milk, which meant not even cornflakes on the menu, unless I could be bothered to go downstairs to Ali's.

Which I couldn't. Just have to eat them dry, I supposed, taking the packet back to my desk. Back to the eighties.

'What followed sounds like an unholy amalgam of *Spinal Tap*, *Fatal Attraction* and *Panic in Needle Park*,' I read on:

Leith was none too pleased about the sudden exit of his girlfriend and quickly mounted an escalating campaign of stalking, threats and attempted violence against Sylvana and Smith. Their immediate reaction was to get married in Paris, announcing they were to relocate to the City of Lovers to get away from the 'drag' of the London scene. This in turn didn't go down too well with Vincent's band, but Blood Truth were contractually obligated to a month-long tour of America before anyone could actually settle down anywhere.

Sylvana's presence on the tour bus added to the tensions, as did Uncle Sam's lacklustre enthusiasm for Blood Truth, especially in the Southern states where Smith's Elvis apparel was viewed as an insult. The band struggled through their commitments before flying back to London to record their new album, nursing grudges and burgeoning substance problems.

Initially, Smith left his new missus in Paris, either to protect her from the attentions of Leith or to shield himself from an increasingly irate Steve Mullin. The on-edge band began recording at Nomis studios in March 1981. Within a week, Sylvana was back at Vincent's side and maintained a Yoko-like presence there during the rest of the torturous month-and-a-half long session. In that time, Mullin was arrested for drunken disorder, Kevin Holme was hospitalised for injuries apparently caused by the rest of the band, and Lynton Powell began quietly following in Sylvana and Smith's trackmarks.

Even so, the resultant 'Butchers' Brew' (Powell's idea, now that he was seeing more clearly where Miles had been coming from) remains a post-punk masterpiece, up there with Joy Division's 'Unknown Pleasures' and PiL's 'Metal Box'. Whatever conflicts they endured only seemed to galvanise Blood Truth into even greater musical feats. On the week of its release, late in May 1981, it entered the UK national charts at 25 and the band headlined the Lyceum Ballroom, their biggest London date and a total sell-out. Smith and Mullin managed to keep it together for what aficionados generally regard as the greatest gig of the band's career.

Sadly, this triumph was to be short-lived. Three weeks later, after a violent argument with her husband, Sylvana Smith took a fatal overdose in Paris.

Blood Truth never played together again. The split was so acrimonious that Mullin vowed he would never so much as step into the same room as Smith again, blaming the singer not only for putting a woman before his friends to the cost of his band, but also (and with some justification) for turning Powell into a junkie. Smith remained in Paris for six months after Sylvana's death, depressed and alone. Finally, he packed up his belongings from their shared apartment in Montmartre and disappeared into the night on New Year's Eve 1981, never to be heard of again.

In this post-Richie Manic world, Vincent Smith's exit from the music business would have been spectacular, ensuring for him enduring notoriety and endless front cover features on every anniversary of his moonlight flit. But in 1981, a nearly-popular goth/punk band were never going to be the stuff of such legend. Smith remained a curio for the next couple of years, like his hero Elvis he popped up in supermarkets and bars on three continents, but it didn't take long for everyone to move on to something else. The Birthday Party, Southern Death Cult, The Sisters of Mercy – skinny young men with black hair and mysterious personas were a booming genre.

Today it is likely that Alien Sex Fiend have left a more lasting impression than Blood Truth, which, like the rest of this tale, is a tragedy. Anyone moved by this Gothic Love Story is urged to seek out the compilation *Shots*, released by Exile on CD to an indifferent world in 1997, and listen to the future as it could have been.

My heart was pounding by the time I reached the end of all this.

Fuck.

Who was the author of this piece? It was signed MG.

I scrolled back up to the top of the web page, looking for elaboration on these credits. There was a little editorial box on the side of the page, listing contributors: David Burbeck, Andrew Hain, Sara Spedding, Kenneth Cox, Annie Hanson, Mick Greer…

Mick Greer. The name rang a vague bell somewhere in the memory vault.

Sweating now, I pulled off my overcoat and scarf and threw them onto the sofa.

Fuck. Mick Greer. I knew that name. About to punch Granger's number into the mobile when it came to me.

Greer was Granger's old partner in the *NME* days. The one that provided most of the ink that went with his images – the John Lydon piece, the Ian Curtis, the Siouxsie Sioux. Of course. They must have done their Blood Truth pieces together, the two Gs.

Fuck. What if this Greer cunt had already had the same idea that I did? What if he had it ages ago? If he already had a book deal? He knew the fucking band, for Christ's sake…

Back over to the sofa, rummaging for my fags in my coat pocket. Only a book of matches swiped from the Market Bar to light them with, fumbling to rip one off with sweaty palms, practically ripping the book to pieces before I had the fag alight, sucking down the nicotine, telling myself: Calm down. You haven't heard the name in years. Means he's not working for anyone big. If he's writing for a web fanzine that proves it.

I moved back to the desk, nodding to myself, thinking: Print that one out and look for some more. Start compiling a dossier.

I turned the printer on, fed through the first few sheets by hand until it got the idea. Mick Greer's feature dropping out onto the tray while I went to the next site, Exile records.

It was a plug for the *Shots* album Greer mentioned, complete with biography penned by…Mick Greer.

I was starting to hate the guy already. What he'd written for Exile was a less flowery version of the *Careless Love* feature, concentrating more on the music and how highly Vince Smith rated on Greer's personal genius scale. It did provide more of an insight into what the rest of the band got up to in the years after, however, with a handful of quotes from Lynton Powell (reformed junkie, now respected jazzer), Kevin Holme (now backing up Lou Feane, the former singer with a weedy early eighties pop band who reinvented himself as a loungecore act) and finally, the thoughts of Steven Mullin, successful record producer and occasional collaborator with Powell.

'Sixteen years later, it's easier to look back on the actual music we made, rather than the madness that went on around it. Tell you the truth, there were a time when I never wanted to hear a fuckin' note of it ever again. But now that I have, sat down with Lynton and gone over the whole of the back catalogue, I have to admit it…I'm fuckin' proud of us.'

More Mick Greer humming through the printer, still more of him to come. All the fan sites I could find – and most of them were appalling goth rubbish – had posted up old *NME* articles written by the cunt, with Granger's photos to go with them. Oh dear. Granger went ballistic when he found out people had been stealing his images. As soon as I let him know what www.thedarkside.org, www.childrenofthenight.com and www.thebatcave.co.uk had been up to behind his back it would be a darker night in Gotham City than any of them could possibly have imagined.

Then I could just casually mention the infringement of Greer's copyright too, get him into the conversation, find out what the bastard was up to these days.

It was getting on for ten o'clock when the key in the front door brought me back from Vincent Smith's world.

Louise stood framed in the hall light. Black wool coat with Astrakhan collar, black gloves, black wool trousers and black high-heeled boots. Thick black hair cut into the style of her namesake, her lookalike, Lulu Brookes. Her lips were red. Her eyes were narrow. She looked like one of the evil queens from the Disney movies, the ones with poisoned apples in their handbags.

'H-hello, darling,' I tried to sound cheerful. 'Been anywhere nice?'

Louise's glittering green eyes took in the scene.

Her fat bastard boyfriend in a dishevelled suit he'd obviously slept in, sitting red-eyed among a paper mountain that spilled from the desk to the floor, a similarly towering ashtray, a coffee cup with rings around it and cornflakes all over the toffee shop.

Her red nails tapped on the doorframe. The shutters came down in her eyes. 'Anywhere,' she finally said, 'would be nice compared to here.'

'Darling,' I stood up and went to walk towards her, catching my foot in the flex from the fan heater and diving headfirst into the carpet, spilling cornflakes and print-outs like dandruff as I went down.

Louise shut her eyes like it was a monumental effort of will for her not to start screaming.

I stared up at her from the carpet, prostrate at her feet. Started to laugh, laugh hysterically at the stupidity of it all, trying to stagger back upright as I did so, clutching at the side of my chair. Hoping my stupid laughter would somehow reach out to her, explain to her that I was sorry, so sorry, for everything that I'd done wrong, for all the late nights and trips away and showbiz parties while she stayed in alone, with her books. Sorry for all the times I'd staggered in drunk and broken things, for the time I tried to take my cowboy boots off and fell through the window, for the time she found my friend Christophe asleep in the bath when she tried to get ready for work in the morning. Sorry for all the money I spent on drinking and trying to impress other people who were not her, for the fact that ten years after I so grandly announced I was going to be a writer I had got only so far as leaving a shitty second-hand paper shop for a regular gig on a low-selling gentleman's monthly. Sorry for the fact I once had the most glamorous, mysterious woman at our school and now I ignored her and dreaded seeing her and preferred the company of ageing photographers and vanished goths. Sorry for all the things I couldn't say and all the lies I told instead.

Sorry that I existed.

The ice maiden's eyelids slowly rose on her hard, cold, emerald eyes.

'You're fucking pathetic, Eddie,' she pronounced, letting each word drop like dead leaves on dirty flagstones. She didn't say anything more. Just turned on her heel towards the bedroom, slamming the door behind her so loudly my coffee cup jumped off the desk to join me in splinters on the floor.

Another night on another sofa, dreaming of a vanished rock star, and how he could save me.

5

Oh You Silly Thing

June 1977

'What you got there then, Kevin?'

Kevin Holme nearly dropped the bass drum he had been carrying into the school hall.

Lounging against the side of the wall by all the massive food bins storing leftovers to be taken away for pigswill, was Stevie Mullin. Stevie Mullin looking like he'd come in from a different planet. Wearing a leather jacket and a T-shirt all ripped up and then pulled back together with safety pins. Drainpipe jeans with luminous yellow socks and black, thick-soled brothel creepers. A padlock holding a bike chain around his neck. His hair all up in spikes. Stevie Mullin looking harder than even he had looked before. Smoking a fag on school grounds.

Kevin's eyes darted around, looking for teacher.

'What you doing with that, Kevin?' Stevie nodded at the kit, almost bigger than the awkward boy holding it.

Old Tucker already in the school hall, helping all the other kids to set up their gear. Not even looking round and noticing.

Kevin could feel his heart beating as Stevie slouched off the wall and started towards him, with a slow, menacing, bow-legged swagger.

'You play that, do you?' Stevie was still smiling as he got near enough to blow his fag smoke into Speccy Kevin's face, watch him go red and start stammering: 'Wh-wh-what's it to you, Mullin?' Kevin's voice was only just breaking and veered from high-pitched to low to comedic effect.

'I'm interested in music, me,' Stevie told him. 'Especially in drummers.' He circled around his prey like a panther. 'So that's what you get up to behind Dunton's back, eh? Playing drums in school band? You any good at it, Kevin?'

Kevin looked like he was going to shit himself. 'Look, Mullin, I've got to go in,' he sounded like a girl, pleading. 'They'll notice.'

'All right, Kevin,' Stevie said amiably. 'I've got a detention to go to myself.' He blew another line of smoke into Kevin's face, dropped the butt of his cigarette and ground it out slowly, like he didn't care if anyone saw.

Walked off just as casually. Speccy Kevin blinked, took off his glasses and rubbed them on his pullover. By the time he'd put them back on, Mullin had disappeared. As if he'd never been there in the first place.

Kevin couldn't concentrate on band practice that night. He got shouted at three times for not coming in at the right moment, and then, most mortifyingly, playing the wrong part entirely.

'Something wrong with you, lad?' enquired Old Tucker, the music teacher, normally a genial duffer but not one to tolerate any sort of mucking about. 'Been getting enough sleep, have you? Eh? Well, will you do us the pleasure of joining the rest of us then?'

The hall resounded with laughter, all eyes fixed on Kevin.

His face burned bright red and his palms were sweaty. His sticks felt big and clumsy in his hands. What he was thinking was: 'Is Mullin going to get me when Gary's not around?'

He'd never wanted to join Dunton's gang in the first place, but he didn't have much choice. As their next-door neighbour he'd grown up playing with Gary, his brothers Darren and Keith and their little sister Mandy. Their mums went to bingo and Beverley races together. Their dads to the Working Men's Club and to see Rovers, sometimes taking the boys along if they'd kept enough cash back that week. Kevin didn't have any brothers or sisters of his own, so he'd been unofficially adopted by that lot.

All the Duntons had called Kevin 'Brains' ever since he got his first glasses when he was seven. He didn't just look like the *Thunderbirds* puppet, he was the cleverest out of all of them. By the time they reached North Hull High, it was a given that Kevin would do all Gary and his mates' homework in return for the honour of being protected by them. Knowing he was too soft to be of any use in a fight, they used him instead as their lookout and scapegoat. More than once Kevin had taken the blame for something one of the others had done, especially if it meant them avoiding the cane or suspension. It did his reputation with the other kids no harm.

Kevin would rather have just been left alone but at least, the way things were, he was safe. At school and at home. Playing his drums was the only thing Kevin ever got to do that he really enjoyed. Gary had called him a puff for it, mind, but in an affectionate way. He let him get on with it. Gary weren't all that bad, really.

Stevie Mullin, on the other hand, was a mad bugger in a league all of his own. Darren and Keith Dunton could handle theirselves all right, but the Mullin boys were mental, had a reputation for it. And as for their dad…Their dad drove boats into Finnish trawlers in the middle of the North Sea.

It didn't bear thinking about. If Stevie was after him, Gary or no Gary, Kevin was really in trouble.

Like the rest of the school orchestra, Kevin was supposed to be polishing up on his repertoire for the end of term concert in three weeks' time. Tucker, who'd fought in Normandy in the war, still had a thing about the Big Band classics of his youth. He'd had them all learning Glenn Miller – 'In The Mood', 'Chatanooga Choo-Choo', 'Moonlight Serenade' – all that old-style stuff. Though it were right different to the stuff Gary and his mates listened to, all that Pink Floyd and Deep Purple, Kevin liked it, liked the way it really did swing. He'd learned to use brushes for the first time to get that shuffling sound, had really impressed Old Tucker both by his dedication and his natural ability.

But tonight, he was all over the place, staring into space, not concentrating and in turn, putting the others off. The rehearsal was a shambles.

'You sure there's nowt wrong, lad?' Tucker asked him gently as Kevin packed up his kit. Because there were so many bits to it, he was always the last to leave. Tonight he seemed to be taking even longer than usual over unscrewing everything and putting it all into its cases.

Kevin Holme had reached puberty later than most boys in his year, looked younger, with his specs and his puppy fat and his still smooth face. Tucker knew the crowd he hung about with, but he knew at heart that Kevin wasn't the same as them. He hoped that this one's talent for music might see him go a bit further than the trawlers or the docks, the likely careers of most he taught.

'No, sir, honest,' Kevin's voice came out high and shrill.

'Shall I give you a hand with that?' Tucker took the cymbal stand that Kevin was wavering over and began unscrewing the cymbal for him, lest the lad eviscerate himself with all his dithering.

Kevin stood hopelessly as Tucker effortlessly dismantled the rest of the kit and stowed it in its cases. His eyes kept flicking up to the big clock that hung above the stage, the hands creeping around to a quarter-to-six. He had already deliberately made himself as late as possible, but would it be late enough? The question came out of his mouth before he could stop himself: 'Sir, what time does detention end?'

'Detention?' One of Tucker's bushy white eyebrows shot upwards. 'Detention ends at five o'clock sharp, son. You waiting for someone? You're a bit late if you are.'

'No, sir,' Kevin avoided the teacher's eyes, but the way his shoulders slumped indicated his relief.

Tucker didn't press it any further. 'Right, let's put this lot away.' He lifted up a case and was pleased to see the little lad smile back at him.

After they'd lugged the kit back to the music room and locked it all up, Kevin had reassured himself. They'd walked across the playground twice and there had been no sign of Stevie Mullin hanging by the swill bins, or anywhere else. Mindful of the sports hall incident, Kevin had glanced up there too, but couldn't see anyone crouched on top of the building, nothing but seagulls up there, wheeling across the sky.

The caretaker was waiting to lock the gates as Kevin left for home. Only, out of the shadow of the kindly music teacher, without Gary and the others around, he suddenly felt vulnerable again. Kevin looked left and then right before he started down the road.

All he could see was an old boy out walking his dog, a gaggle of biddies in nylon overalls gossiping outside the corner shop and a couple of bains doing wheelies in the road.

Kevin walked quickly, looking around him every time he took a corner. It was a humid night and overcast, the sky a dreary grey, but the closeness of the atmosphere making him sweat. He tugged at his school tie, trying to loosen it, but only managing to tighten the knot. His bag of books felt heavy on his shoulder, the monkey boots he'd got his mum to buy 'cos Gary's lot all had them chafed at his ankles, making his stride uncomfortably slow.

Kevin navigated the little sidestreets that took him onto the Beverley Road as if caught in a bad dream, spooking at every gang of little kids running out of an alleyway, every dog barking up at a gate. All the time he was humming to himself, almost without realising, humming to keep his spirits up the song they had just been practising: 'In The Mood'.

Once he got to top of Road, he felt safer again. The constant, heavy traffic reassured him, as did the amount of people walking back from work in the city centre and mums pushing prams, the chip shops that had just opened for the evening and their comforting smells of fresh hot batter and frying fish. It were too busy here, Kevin rationalised, for Mullin to jump him. And only a little bit further down Road was his turn off for home, his road, effectively the Duntons' road, Davis Close. Stevie wouldn't do owt there either.

The chippy smells made his stomach rumble. Normally, Kevin would have eaten by now, even on a normal night's band practice. He was half an hour later than usual and hoped his dinner wasn't too burned in the oven where his mum would have left it for him. Thursday night were a good one, usually his favourite week night – band practice followed by sausage and mash and Mum's thick onion gravy. Just thinking about it, he could almost taste it.

He was tasting it as he turned left onto West Street, tasting it as he swung around the corner for Davis Close, the corner where two tall fir trees stood and from behind them out jumped: Stevie Mullin.

'All right, Kevin?'

'Whaaa!' Kevin recoiled backwards, his face white with shock. Stevie Mullin here, on the end of his road.

'Eh up, lad,' the spiky-haired, grinning mug moving in on him fast, amusement glittering in the staring eyes. 'Just wanted to finish our talk. You know, about you bein' a drummer?'

'Whaaa!' shaking Kevin repeated, his hungry stomach lurching into sick fear.

As Stevie continued to walk towards him, he found himself backed up against a garage wall. The fir trees gave cover from the Davis Close side of the road. Nobody could see them.

'Well, what it is like,' smiling Stevie looming over him now, 'is we need a drummer. For band we're startin'. And I thought about you, straight off. Only thing is,' he turned his head and smiled in the direction of the firs, 'young Lynton here's going to take a bit of convincing.'

Kevin followed the direction of Stevie's stare, and to his horror, saw another shape emerge from the deadly shade of the trees.

A long, dark, sinuous shape. Only somehow different to the last time Kevin saw him. Lynton Powell with his hair shaved into a flat top, wearing a long drape jacket and a white shirt and skinny black tie. Lynton Powell no longer cowering scared in the playground but looking as hard and weird as Stevie did.

Staring at him with jet-black eyes that bored right through his skull.

Kevin felt his bowels loosen, strained to keep his sphincter tight.

'Lynton feels you owe him an apology,' Stevie continued. 'For what you and your mate Cunton were saying to him.'

'I-I-weren't saying it!' Kevin stared with pleading eyes from one to the other of his captors. 'Honest, I said nowt. It were all Gary and Lee. I were just lookout for 'em. I didn't like what they were saying, honest I didn't…'

Which was actually true. Kevin had cringed inside at their monkey jokes. It were like when people called him 'four-eyes' and 'speccy swot', but worse. It were just bloody cruel.

Stevie tutted. 'I can't hear an apology there, can you, Lynton?'

They moved in closer on him, so close that he could smell the mixture of sweet cider and tobacco on Stevie's breath.

'I'm sorry they said it, they shouldn't have.'

Lynton saw the smaller boy's eyes fill up with tears, knew it would only be seconds before he dissolved completely. 'I'm sorry I helped them,' his voice cracked and snot blew out of his nose.

Lynton put his hand on Stevie's shoulder, muttered, 'S' enough, bro,' and stepped back a pace. Stevie did likewise, cocked his head to one side as he watched Kevin wipe his nose on his sleeve.

'All right, Kevin, so Cunton makes you do his bidding. We know you're not really from same side of trough as he is. And you won't have to worry about his lot any more. From now on, you'll be with us.'

'Worry?' Tears were streaming down Kevin's round face now. 'Worry? Gary lives next door to us. What d'you expect us to do? I can't…'

But Kevin couldn't go on with the sentence. Overwhelmed by tears, he crumpled up into a heap, crouching on the pavement, torn between the fear of Dunton and the fear of these two figures of nightmare.

Lynton crouched down beside him, put a hand on his shoulder.

He looked up at Stevie, who was trying his best to suppress a grin as he rocked on his heels, surveying the damage he'd done. Said: 'Be cool, Stevie. He won't be no use to us if he's gonna be like this.'

Kevin had clamped his arms around his bowed head.

'Listen,' Lynton said to him softly, 'you won't have to tell Gary nothing. And we won't tell him neither. You like playin' the drums, don't you, Kevin? You like being in the school band?'

Kevin continued to bury his head somewhere between his knees. But Lynton thought he saw a nodding movement.

'OK, so come in with us, you can be in a band the whole time. It's the holidays soon, we can start then. Don't worry about nothing until school is over.'

'That's right,' Stevie added boastfully. 'Me and Lynton are still at songwriting stage ourselves right now. Once we've writ 'em, we can learn 'em together. We can start first day of holidays.'

'Now, Kevin,' Lynton ignored him, continued talking in the same soothing way. 'Is that kit you play yours or the school's?'

'School's,' a small voice whimpered up from the depths.

'Right then,' Lynton looked challengingly at Stevie. 'To prove to you that we're serious about what we say, me and Stevie're gonna get you your own kit. We can keep it at my place. That way, we can all rehearse together and Dunton will never know.'

At this, Kevin's head came up. Through smudged glasses and bleary eyes, he stared up at Lynton incredulously.

'H-how you gonna do that?' the smaller boy whispered. 'You've not got that kind of money?'

'We don't need money,' Stevie gloated. 'We've got…contacts. Contacts in all the right places. No sweat, Kevin. We can take care of it.'

Kevin's gaze travelled from Lynton to Steve and then back to Lynton again. Those deep, dark eyes that had so scared him only moments before were now warm and kindly. Even Mullin was looking at him earnestly, palms outstretched in a 'trust me' gesture.

He couldn't quite work out what they were up to. He thought they were going to kick shit out of him, but here they were promising him his own drum kit.

'I don't believe it,' he finally said.

'Don't have to,' Stevie smiled. 'We'll prove it to you. You mark my words, Kevin. First day of holidays and it'll all be ready for you.'

Kevin stumbled to his feet, began self-consciously brushing the dust off his trousers and sleeves.

'You all right now?' Lynton asked him.

Kevin nodded his head, not looking him in the eye.

'All right then, we'll be off,' announced Stevie. 'We'll be in touch, Kevin.'

'Have faith,' added Lynton, raising his palm in farewell.

Kevin watched them drift back in the direction of Road. Both of them over six feet tall, wearing their weirdo's clothes proudly, laughing easily with each other as if this nerve-wracking exchange had never even taken place.

Kevin did a final check to make sure he wouldn't look to his mum like he'd been rolling in the mud. Got his glasses case out

of his schoolbag to give them a polish with
Maybe if he could see clearly then the events of th
hours would start making sense.

Kevin's stomach reminded him of sausage and mash.
walked towards the sanctuary of his own front door, he coul
help but think: This is the strangest day of my life.

6

I Wanna Riot All of My Own

Winter 2001

'What do you think then? Think anyone will give us a go?' With Granger again already and it was only Monday night.

At a bar called Lounge on the Portobello Road, his manor infinitely preferable to mine. Christ, it was posh around here now. While Camden had remodelled itself into an open-air lunatic asylum/young offenders institute, Ladbroke Grove had taken a decidedly upmarket turn.

This bar, for instance. Moroccan, Bedouin tent theme, with lavish drapes hanging from the ceiling, heavy wooden tables complete with hookahs, chaise longues and huge scatter cushions everywhere. Brian Eno and David Byrne's *My Life in the Bush of Ghosts* the soundtrack. Jocasta and James and their friends sipping Pinot Grigio and showing off their lizard foot tattoos, while a couple of Heroes of Britpop – the ones whose daddies were millionaires to begin with – slouch at the bar, pretending not to surreptitiously eyeball everyone who's surreptitiously eyeballing them.

This bar used to be a dirty, dingy old man's pub called The

Black Fort, with a brass-topped bar and a carpet that stuck to your feet. London Pride was the brew of choice, real Rastafarians dealt ganja openly and emphysema was the soundtrack of the day. Every eccentric weirdo in the vicinity congregated here at the altar of greasy optics: the old git with the motorised wheelchair, banging on its horn and poking at you with his stick, yapping Jack Russell cavorting at his side; the black lady with the big blonde wig and the even bigger Russian fur hat, selling voodoo candles from a bag that trailed human hair; Jangling Jack, a twitching, angular heroin addict, doing the withdrawal shuffle across the floor. And the cast of old timers who considered this their front room, dozing in the dark corners, studying the racing pages or just staring into their pints in search of visions.

Not for the first time, I beseeched myself: Why didn't we move here instead of Camden?

Granger had done so well. He'd bought his pad in the eighties when this was still considered an undesirable district. Now he could look out onto the park behind his garden flat on Elgin Crescent every morning knowing he lived on the very road that signalled Martin Amis's definition of success.

The photographer took another swig on his Hoegaarden, wiped the foam off his lips and gave a wry grin. 'I dunno, mate,' he sounded uncharacteristically pessimistic. 'I tried to do one before, with me old mate Mick Greer, but no one was bitin'.' He gazed into his glass sanguinely, swilling the last of his beer into foam.

'When was that?' I tried to keep my tone light, but already I could feel beads of sweat pricking my forehead.

Granger swivelled round so that his back was against the bar now, leaned back and gazed into space as if trying to see back through time. His arms cut graceful arcs through the air to illustrate his points as he spoke.

'Lemme see now, about four years ago? Yeah, 1997 it was. Year that Exile did the CD remasters. We thought there might be some renewed interest off the back of that, but we were way off the mark. All everyone wanted to know about then was bloody Britpop.'

This last sentence said loudly for the benefit of those responsible for that atrocity here present.

'Mick Greer?' I feigned interest. 'Isn't that the guy you used to work with on *NME*? What's he up to these days?'

'Moved back to Oz,' Gavin finished his dregs with a final swig. 'Work was gettin' too thin on the ground for him here. It's not just that good bands get forgotten. Great writers do too. Yeah, Mick got tired of the weather and tired of living like a student. He's doin' much better now back home.'

I nodded earnestly. 'I can imagine.'

A wave of relief swept over me. Poor old Mick Greer, back on the other side of the world. As far away from me as possible.

'It's a bloody shame 'cos it would have been good to do that book,' Gavin continued, pricking a new vein of paranoia. 'Mick had all the great interviews from the early days, plus he still keeps in touch with all the guys.'

He leaned back round to catch the barman's eye. 'Same again please, mate,' he called over, then to me: 'What about you?'

'Yeah, uh, same again here.' Another thing I liked about Gavin, he never seemed to notice it was always his round.

As he handed the folding stuff over, he asked: 'What makes you think we'd have any luck with it now?'

I could see the flicker of hope in his eyes and the sly curve of his mouth, and inspiration hit me like a sudden boner.

'Well, Britpop might have got in the way of your plans four years ago,' I said, 'but in case you hadn't noticed – and I'm forced to notice, living in Camden – we're in the middle of a goth revival. There's hundreds of little Marilyn Manson clones sprouting up all over the place, there's that Slipknot band walking around like the cast of the *Evil Dead* and *Kerrang!* is selling more than *NME*. It's taken a fuck of a long time, but it's actually happened. The children of the night are back and singing. You should do a search on the Net. Actually, last night I did, and I found three goth websites straight off that had all posted up those very features from *NME* that you were just talking about.'

Gavin's eyes narrowed. 'Oh yeah?' he said, darkly.

'Yeah,' I smiled earnestly, 'I bookmarked them when I found them, 'cos I thought you might like to pay them a visit.'

'Too right,' he nodded, then brushed the minor annoyance aside for later. 'So you reckon people are starting to get into this stuff again? I mean, the good stuff, not just this modern shit?'

'I think it's just waiting to happen,' I looked him straight in the eye. 'These people are into their Lord Byrons and Bram Stokers and all that Decadents shit. Now Vincent Smith is a genuine lost boy, a proper decadent, a real rock'n'roll legend. You know that better than anyone. He invented the way they all look, for Christ's sake. And from a selling context – and I'm not comparing him to the twat, only the effect he seemed to have on an entire generation – he's like the Richie Manic of goth, isn't he? And then there's the love interest, Sylvana, the goth Ophelia...'

'Yeah,' fresh light came into Granger's eyes, 'and actually...' he paused and clicked his fingers. 'If you're lookin' at it that way, then the love interest kinda makes him Kurt Cobain, stroke, Richie Manic.'

Our pupils locked.

'Genius,' said Granger. 'Precisely the sort of shit they're eatin' up these days. You're right, mate, the timing's there now...'

I could see the gears shifting in his head.

'Are *you* still in touch with the rest of the band?' I asked him.

'We-eell,' he considered, 'not really, but I've never fallen out with any of 'em. They still used my pictures for *Shots* and if I see them about they're always friendly. We go back a long way. I don't reckon it would be difficult to get 'em to talk...'

''Cos what I was thinking,' I leaned in closer, painfully aware of every James and Jocasta in the place as a potential, better-connected rival, 'is that we could present this not only as a music biography, but also like a true crime book, an investigation. You know, try and pitch it to them like we're actually really looking for him.'

Gavin's eyes slid from mine as I made this comment and darted around the room, as if he was mentally snapping an image of everyone in it.

He was obviously thinking what I was thinking.

Room-sweep finished, his eyes came back to mine. 'Don't say any more, mate. We've got to keep this to ourselves,' he said. 'Walls have ears.' He tapped the side of his nose. 'Let's leave these drinks and get outta here. Go back to mine.'

By the end of the week, we had our dossier. A pile of clippings from Gavin's files, the Internet, and various zines and anthologies. Plus his favourite black-and-white prints redone, mindful of a slew of recent punk picture compendiums that had all made a mint out of the Spirit of '77.

Plus – and this was the really good bit – Gavin got on the phone. Made some inquiries. Because of their past history, Lynton Powell and Kevin Holme agreed on principle that they would speak to us if we had a deal. As did Tony Stevens, their record company guy, who still remained somewhat of an indie legend even after his label had busted through to the mainstream. That only left Steve Mullin, who was in LA recording some trendy metal band, but Powell promised to put in a word and didn't think it would be a problem.

All of them seemed to think it would be a bit of a miracle if we did get a deal, though.

Gavin and I didn't. We were men on a mission. I wrote up our synopsis over fevered nights in Camden Road, where the flurry of activity seemed to raise the temperature not just of the flat, but of the two women in my life as well.

Mother, for a start, couldn't resist poking her nose in.

Regardless of the fact she had no idea who Bono was, let alone Vincent Smith, she had heard the magic words 'writing a book' and started to dwell on what this could mean. After only a few days, she could start to hear the distant chiming of cash registers, smell a faint, tantalising aroma of success. I could feel her, itching for a bit of fame by association, something to boast about to the other mothers at the Con Club, the ones whose sons had gone on to be surgeons and barristers and were rolling round in cash. Something to make her feel justified at last.

And seeing me at it, night after night, with my reams of notes and cuttings at least backed up my story to Louise that all my late nights with Granger had been for a reason. For the Furtherance of my Career, that noble pursuit that was of as much importance to her as it was to Mother. Louise had probably never seen me work this hard since those far-off days of cramming for A-Levels. I noticed a change in her attitude before she started to speak. She was actually taking note of what I was doing, studying me from behind her books at the other end of the room.

'So you're actually serious about this?' were the first words she spoke to me after Sunday night's debacle. It was Thursday by now, and I had been at home every night since Monday, diligently tapping away and not drinking either. I'd kept to my place on the sofa at night, kept the kitchen stocked with supplies and hadn't left a single thing out of place for her to moan about.

The surprising side effect of this new, responsible sobriety was not just that I'd been putting this synopsis together but that I'd managed to rack up a whole heap of work and freebies from the magazine too. Including tickets for the premiere of the new Coen Brothers film, something I was keeping under my hat, something Louise would be hard-pressed to be able to resist.

I looked up from my keyboard to see her holding up a newsprint copy of the Vince'n'Sylv wedding picture. She appeared to be examining this artefact with the expression of someone watching a slug emerge from their plate of salad, but that countenance, coupled with the disdainful voice, was actually pretty much Louise's full range.

'Yes,' I said as neutrally as possible. 'Yes, I really am.'

Her green eyes flickered from the newsprint to me and then back again.

'Do you want to know why?' I asked, pitching it halfway between amiable and pleading.

Louise did her Roger Moore eyebrow trick and said: 'Go on then. Amaze me.'

She sank down into the armchair facing me, crossed her legs and tapped a red fingernail against her temple.

'I realise,' I began humbly, 'that my career is not exactly progressing at the speed it was supposed to. I think journalism is tougher to get into now than it was when I first had my teenage dreams about writing for the *NME*, and I've realised that in order to carve a future for myself, I'm gonna have to do a bit more than write articles for a low-circulation men's lifestyle mag.'

A half smirk played across her lips.

I took a deep breath and continued. 'So, I'm gonna try and take it to the next level and become a proper author. And it's not just some silly, adolescent book about dead pop stars, Louise,' I added imploring Lady Di eyes to this statement. 'I think I have a story here that's real dynamite. It could get me up there and it would sell shitloads and if that happened,' I leaned as forward in my seat as I dared without toppling over at her feet again. 'If that happened, I could get us out of this shithole and into somewhere better. I know this isn't ideal any more, this whole place is depressing and dangerous and I want us to have more than that. I know you think I've just been wasting my time hanging round with Gavin, and I admit, I have been using some of that time to get more wasted than I should have done. But he's given me this, this story, and I really believe that this can be our way out. Our future.'

The smirk disappeared and she regarded me in silent solemnity.

The seconds on the clock ticked by, louder in the small room than Big Ben.

'You're actually thinking about *our future* now?' she said eventually.

'Yes, I am. I've been doing a lot of thinking since Sunday, Lou-Lou,' I dared to use the pet name she once, a long, long time ago, used to find so amusing. 'And I know I've been letting you down for a long time. So I'm trying to do something to make it up to you...' I was so convinced by what I was saying and the way I was saying it that my voice started to break without me wanting it to. 'I don't want to lose you, Lou,' I stuttered, feeling hot tears suddenly jerk into my eyeballs.

'Dear, dear!' she exclaimed, looking more puzzled than anything else. It was like she didn't want to believe me, but despite herself she did.

'Look,' I waved a hand in front of my face, reached in my jacket pocket for a handkerchief. 'I'm sorry, I didn't mean to be embarrassing.'

'Edward Bracknell,' she rose to her feet as languidly as a cat taking a stretch, stood over me with her feet apart. 'I almost think you mean all this.' She cocked her head to one side. 'I almost believe you.'

She smiled. 'But don't think that means you can come back to bed yet.' She cuffed me round the head with the newspaper clipping, then dropped it back on the pile. 'I want to see a bit more evidence first. Actions speak louder than words.'

And with that she stalked back to her frosty boudoir.

But something had melted in her, if only a droplet. I saw it in her eyes.

And as luck would have it, she didn't have to wait too long for her evidence either. Once the synopsis was finished, Granger took it straight round to an agent friend of his with a long history of music biz association, Madeline Fuller, a Marianne Faithful lookalike with the same nicotine-ravaged but posh baritone.

Granger said she'd reacted exactly as he had done in the Lounge bar. Wanted to place the synopsis in a Swiss bank vault or something. Whatever her fears, her powers of persuasion were most impressive.

Before Christmas, we saw three publishers who were interested and naturally went with the highest bidder, a well-established and pretty well-heeled house who gave us a reasonable advance for it and a year to deliver the manuscript.

That Christmas was the warmest one in recent memory, not least because I finally blew a wedge of my advance on some heating for the flat. Following the film premiere, the flow of work I'd pulled in for the magazine and the speediness of mine and Granger's contract, I was allowed back into the Ice Queen's newly cosy lair.

I was careful to keep the drinking down, and the attention to Louise up, keeping the friends she found so undesirable away from the flat and myself away from the pub. The interesting by-product of this was that I found myself happier than I had been since I couldn't remember, with a purpose to my life, a clear head set to achieve it, and the grudging admiration of the woman who I'd realised almost too late I didn't want to live without.

Mother was all over me at Christmas, parading me to the ceaseless round of old biddies that dropped by for mince pies and sherry as if I'd already won the Booker Prize. Louise stayed on the sofa, exchanging knowing glances with my father, but both she and Mother seemed to be making more of an effort to be cordial than I'd ever seen before. And when we got the hell out of Guildford for new year, Lou was even happy for me to invite over Granger, along with some of her workmates, to see in the New Year with good food and wine and all the promise of the work we were about to embark on.

We stood watching fireworks explode above the gothic towers of St Pancras Station from our window over Camden Road, all of us linking arms and attempting 'Auld Lang Syne' while cracking up with laughter, toasting each other with champagne.

'Here comes the biggie,' Gavin winked as he knocked his glass against mine. '2002. Somethin' tells me, this is gonna be our year!'

Louise was leaning against me, smiling her cat smile, almost purring. 'That's right, Gavin,' she nodded. 'The year Eddie is going to take me on to better things.' She said it semi-sarcastically, but there was humour underneath her tone and almost a touch of pride, I thought.

'I'll drink to that,' Granger raised his glass again.

'To better things,' he said.

'To better things,' we chorused as our glasses clashed and the bubbles rose up their stems and the sky was full of stardust and coloured lights.

Just like my dreams.

7

Heart Attack Machine

August 1977

It was one sticky hot evening in August when Stevie heard the news. He was due at practice, in Lynton's dad's garage by six-thirty. But now it was pressing seven and his brother Connor still wouldn't let him out of the pub.

'Just 'old your 'osses, our kid. You're gonna like this, believe me,' Connor plonked another half of Tetleys down on the already sodden beer mat in front of his brother, while Stevie fidgeted with his hair, his cigarettes, and his hang-nails impatiently.

Inside the King's Head on Hessle, you could see the dust swirling in the shaft of sunlight from the open pub door, just the way the cloudy beer swum down from the tap. It was over 70 degrees outside, and still Connor insisted on skulking down in the snug, where he had command of the jukebox, the dartboard and a view of the entire room.

Stevie's brain was churning. Five weeks they'd been getting the band together, scraping and shaping the frameworks for songs. Lynton's dad had let them have the garage, he was so grateful to see his son finally settling in with local folk. They lived in a big house on the Avenues, far enough away for Kevin to be safe from Dunton's prying eyes. And with the kit that Stevie had promised him, the speccy twat was finally coming into his own.

Lynton, who was after all the expert, said Kevin could play. Stevie realised it straight away. It weren't just a question of technique, it were more like, he could swing. And Lynton, with the bass his parents had got him second-hand, twanged along with him, mastering the notes with seemingly apparent ease, scratching the beginnings of a deep, menacing rumble.

Stevie could keep up with them, just. The more he practised, the bigger the noise he could get out of the Holner, which he'd painted with a Union Flag to match the 'God Save The Queen' cover. It wasn't quite the Jones sound he was after, though. The way it came out was more fractured, nervy. It suited the sound they were making.

In fact, the tentatively titled Dead City even startled themselves at the way they intuitively worked together. It was almost like the music they were hatching had already been lurking there, somewhere in the atmosphere, waiting for them to grab hold of it.

Only trouble was, none of them could sing. The other two had naturally assumed Stevie would take that role, but two things went against him. One, he still found it too hard to remember his chord sequences and sing at the same time. Two, he sounded like a foghorn.

Kevin claimed he couldn't sing either, and Stevie didn't make him prove it. Only cunts like Genesis had singing drummers anyway. And Lynton...Well, Stevie suspected that he could, but he didn't want to. Lynton wanted to be in the background. He was too thoughtful and shy to stand up front.

What were they gonna do about it was what Stevie was wondering, as the reason for his imprisonment in the King's Head came bowling through the bar.

Terry Gough and Barry Hill were two lads in thick with Connor. Like Stevie's brother, they dressed like Teddy Boys, with thick, greased-back hair that they were always running combs through, lurid coloured drape suits and thick-soled brothel creepers.

Terry and Barry were the source of Kevin's drumkit, and the black drape suit that Lynton wore in homage to Rotten. They worked as roadies-cum-bouncers for local entrepreneur Don Dawson, who ran a handful of pubs and clubs in Hull and Doncaster.

Stevie had been helping them out on and off a lot that summer and it really had opened his eyes. Barry and Terry had a lot of scams going with the man who employed them and acquiring brand new bits of kit was one of the bonuses they could collect for a job well done. Poncy bands from down south and the long-haired record company men that came with them never had much of a mind to complain about missing items to folk like Don Dawson.

All Stevie had to do to get Kevin's drumkit was do a couple of nights' humping for Terry and Barry. He did all the loading in and out, the gaffa-taping of equipment to the stage and that, while they sat around reading *Knave* and *Fiesta* and combing their hair. Fair play, thought Stevie, being backstage at any gig was a newfound thrill for him any road. Despite their constant piss-taking of his hairstyle, Terry and Barry liked Stevie too. Even said they'd keep an eye out for a white custom Les Paul.

''Ere 'e is!' bellowed Terry, who obviously modelled himself on Rory Storme, with bleached blond hair and metal tips on his Western shirt collar. 'The lad 'imself.' He clasped hands with Connor, then looked down at Stevie. ''Ow dy'er fancy doin' a spot of work for us tomorrow? Special, like?'

'How so?' Stevie only had to look at the glances exchanged by the roadies and his brother to know they were up to something.

'Oh, it's something you'll like all right,' Barry, darker and smaller with a bumbfluff moustache he was trying to cultivate into something more stylish, lit up from his Zippo and his eyes twinkled in the flame. 'Up in Donny.'

'Yeah,' Stevie was getting impatient. 'What is it?'

'SPOTS,' said Terry, as if he were stupid.

'Whaddaya mean, spots?' Stevie looked from leering face to face.

Terry took his time saying it, enjoying the impact of every word. 'Not spots like on yer face, Stevie, though you should know. SPOTS. Sex. Pistols. On. Tour. Secretly.'

Stevie's gob fell open. 'You what?'

'Callin' theirselves The Tax Exiles for this one,' Barry, the fount of all knowledge, nodded. 'At Exile Club, Donny. Tomorrow night. We've gotta be more like bouncers for this one, so we thought you might want to help hump gear. But, you know, if you've got owt else to do…'

'Can I bring a mate?' Stevie was on his feet, head already sprinting away down Hessle Road.

'What d'yer reckon, Barry?'

'Go on, you might need extra hands.'

'Well there won't be owt extra cash,' Terry's eyebrows raised.

'Don't matter. Go on, let us bring us mate.'

The two Teds looked at his imploring face and burst out laughing.

'All right Stevie. Just meet us outside here tomorrow. Five o'clock sharp.'

'Yes!' Stevie's punch hit the air.

So here they were in Donny, pulling up in a pub car park in the back of Terry and Barry's Transit. Stevie and Lynton sat on an old mattress covered in dog-eared porn mags and copies of the *Sun*. The whole way down they'd been listening to Elvis, eight days after the King had left the building for the last time, dropping off his throne in Jubilee year.

To say they were nervous would be an understatement. Nerves crackled with excitement and something else churned in Lynton's guts. Something connected to the way those Teds had looked at him when they first saw him. The whispered comments and laughter. Then they'd referred to him as Chuck Berry for the rest of the journey.

Now they were sliding out of the van, towards the back of the pub, where an extension had been built to house a small stage and dressing room. Usually, it served small-time pub bands, local comedians, talent contests. Tonight would be something different.

Don Dawson met them at the back door. A big bloke, like you had to be in his line of business, hard as granite, but softened up to the untrained eye with all the trappings of Northern *nouveau riche*. The oiled hair swept back off his low forehead with some fancy pomade. The sharp Italian-style suit. The cloud of aftershave. The gold rings on every finger.

Dawson had seen something different from most blokes his age in the coming of punk. He'd seen young people turning up to see these snotty-nosed, foul-mouthed yobs like they'd never turn up for local comedians and talent nights. He'd been around the clubs investigating, keeping abreast of the local trends, across the Pennines to Manchester, on up to Newcastle and back again and he'd read all the signs. He'd smelled the cash from chaos.

Now Dawson was extending his businesses into the punk arena. He had a mind to start up a record company too. Tonight he intended to learn all he could from a money-spinning master – Malcolm McLaren.

Dawson clocked the Teds and their mate Stevie, the latter of whom he was most interested in, representing as he did Dawson's whole new demographic. Clocked the darkie too, but said nowt.

Darkies didn't irk Dawson the way they did most blokes his age either. Say what you like about them, their money was still green.

'Right Terry, right Barry,' he greeted the older men with handshakes, then turned his attention to the schoolboys. 'Stevie,' he recognised, 'and this is?'

'Lynton Powell,' Lynton said huskily, meeting Dawson's eyes for the briefest of moments.

'We've told them they're workin' two for price of one,' Terry said hastily, trying to explain Lynton away. 'But that's how eager these young folk are for their punk rock.'

'Pleased to hear it,' Dawson smiled beneficently. 'Now then, let's get started.'

It wasn't as glamorous as Stevie had hoped. The first job Dawson gave them was making sandwiches. Endless sandwiches from sliced white loaves, industrial-sized tubs of margarine, ham and pickle, cheese and coleslaw. They had to slice them into little triangles and pile them onto salvers, do the whole lot up with clingfilm, put them in the backstage room with a keg of ale and a load of cheap tins of lager.

'Is this what Johnny Rotten really eats?' Lynton frowned in wonder.

The Pistols' bus must have arrived by then, but there was no sign of their heroes. Just some roadies from London who had them doing the dirty work, humping the speakers and building the stack of amps, setting up the drumkit and gaffa-taping mic stands to the stage floor. All the shit stuff, the hard graft. Maybe the equipment came separate from the band.

Then they saw a shock of red hair bobbing across the floor, a man in a garish tweed suit swooping into Dawson's office.

Stevie nudged Lynton in the ribs. 'Malcolm,' he hissed.

Soon after that, one of the London roadies asked Stevie: 'Do us a favour and take them sarnies out to the bus. They don't want to come out 'til it's showtime. We'll take care of the beer.'

'I bet you will,' muttered Stevie, but a sudden pang of sheer joy hit him as he carried the salver across the car park to the big coach that was parked there. The blinds were down on all the windows, but it was them in there all right.

The door whooshed open and Stevie walked up the steps.

There stood Steve Jones, in a pair of white underpants and yellow socks.

'Cheers, mate,' said Stevie's hero, relieving him of his burden.

Then the vision turned and shouted: 'Grub's up!' before hurling a handful of Stevie and Lynton's specially made bread triangles down the other end of the bus.

Stevie walked backwards off the bus, awestruck.

Now they were letting them in through the front door. Terry and Barry were front-of-stage security, the London roadies took care of equipment. All that remained for Stevie and Lynton to do now was watch the show.

It seemed like the whole of the North was piling into the room, a constant stream of home-made punks with food-colouring in their hair and artfully ripped T-shirts. Some still looked more glam, with feather cuts and Ziggy make-up. Others still wore their Bay City Rollers tartan. Some of them – quite a lot of them – were even girls.

'Lynton,' noted Stevie seriously, 'there must be every freak in Yorkshire in this room.'

'Mmmm,' Lynton nodded, 'who would have thought there was so many?'

Lynton was getting that feeling again. As the bodies in the room caused the temperature to rise and the condensation to start running down the walls, he could smell it in the hot, smoky air. Like the night in Stevie's room when he first heard 'Anarchy', only magnified.

Every freak in Yorkshire who could had got their hands on a ticket, inspired by the Pistols-led soap opera that had flashed across their screens all summer. The boat trip down the Thames on Jubilee Day and subsequent arrests had made the band Public Enemy Number One. Men wearing brown suits and handlebar moustaches queued up to spill their outrage from the studios of *Nationwide*, proclaiming that it would be better if Johnny Rotten was dead.

Every freak in Yorkshire wanted a part of that.

The jukebox was playing The Stranglers, guttural grunts twirled around a fairground organ, a big, black, boot-crunching bass riff.

The freaks were already pogoing to it, throwing themselves around at the front of stage. Boys and girls, bug-eyed, robotic, narcotic.

Stevie and Lynton headed in the direction of the bar, more by the will of the crowd than by design. It seemed there were only seconds between the blur of hands passing across the tiny, sticky counter and the chance to gulp back a mouthful of the warm, watery fizz before there was another surge, back in the direction of the stage.

'Fuckin' hell,' breathed Lynton.

Johnny Rotten stood smiling at the centre of the stage.

There was a sudden roar of feedback as Steve Jones plugged in.

'Evening all,' said Johnny.

The first chiming chords of 'Anarchy in the UK' roared out from beneath Jones's fingers. The room moved as one. Like everything had been struck with an electrical charge and the separate entities that had formerly made up band, audience and bouncers had fused to make one giant Godzilla of a beast, a spiky-haired, pogoing punk-rock machine. A hundred fists punching the air, Johnny leaning into his mic and saying: *'Riight! Naaaaaaa aaaoooooowwwwwww!'*

Stevie and Lynton were near the back of the beast, the wildly vibrating heads and arms in front of them obscuring their view. It didn't matter. It didn't matter either that hands pressed on their shoulders, that elbows jammed into their sides, that all they got were fleeting glances of Johnny and Steve, of Sid Vicious, the new bassist, looking cool and wasted in his black leather trousers and permanent sneer. It didn't matter that they had beer splashed all over them and their carefully elevated hair had wilted in the heat.

What mattered was that they were here, in the eye of the hurricane.

'Anarchy' segued into 'I Wanna Be Me', segued into 'Seventeen'. Stevie and Lynton slowly manoeuvered themselves forwards, as exhausted revellers fell away from the front and the rest pushed steadily forwards from behind.

'New York' was followed by 'EMI', Johnny's taunt to the company that had just so spectacularly dropped them. Then Stevie's new favourite, 'Holidays in the Sun'. From where he was now he could stare directly at Jones. The guitarist was standing, legs apart, arms windmilling, playing the fattest, juiciest, most searing riff he had ever heard. Stevie felt as if his head might blow clean off his shoulders.

Then somebody broke away from the throng, staggered straight towards him.

Tall and skinny with luminous white skin.

Leather trousers and a head of thick, shining black hair.

For a second Stevie thought Sid Vicious had jumped off the stage to come and inspect the audience. Then the figure barrelled into him with eyes out on stalks. Stevie instinctively caught hold of his shoulders, pulled him back upright.

'You all right, mate?' he asked, staring into bugged-out, red-rimmed, pale blue eyes. He thought maybe the other fella was gonna faint. 'Have some of this.'

An eager hand grabbed for his pint, necked the dregs of it down in one long gulp. He had a ring on his middle finger, a big thick silver thing, with a fat blue eyeball set in the middle of it. Stevie watched it in fascination as the stranger knocked back his pint, threw the empty plastic glass to the floor, and swayed, catching his breath.

'Ta, mate,' he eventually drawled, wiping a hand across his mouth. 'Thought I were a gonner there.'

'Aye, it's bastard hot in here.'

'I'll get you another,' the stranger's face suddenly cracked into a smile, as blotches of red colour flushed back into his cheeks. 'After, like.' He nodded towards the stage, where the emaciated figure of Rotten now stood up on the monitors, steadying himself with a hand on the ceiling, ranting: *'Now I've got a reason/Now I've got a reason/Now I've got a reason/The Berlin Wall…'*

And pushed his way back into the bodies. Stevie could see his slick black head making steady progress to the front.

'Who was that?' Lynton shouted.

'Some nutcase,' Stevie mused.

'No Feelings' was next, then 'Problems'. His eyes fixed on his alien mentor, Lynton felt that he was having some kind of epiphany, that his life was changing for ever, from being in this room, with these people, right now. He felt like he was growing wings, that any minute they'd burst right out of his back and he'd be up and soaring.

We have to do this band, he realised with fevered intensity. It has to work. It has to get us out of Hull…

As if in agreement, Jones struck up the first chords of 'Pretty Vacant'. The room erupted in a second wave of flailing limbs and plastic glasses hurtled towards the ceiling.

Five seconds later, Barry pushed past, propelling the Sid lookalike through the throng on the end of his arm. Blood was running down the kid's face, but his expression was rapturous.

Stevie's head swivelled round to follow their progress. Barry pushed the kid up against the bar, waved a warning finger in his face. The kid just smiled back at him, slouched against the bar like he owned it, despite the trail of gore sliding down from a cut above his right eyebrow. Barry stomped back past them, heaving his way to the front of the stage.

'No fun/My friend/No fuuuun,' Johnny was sneering, while Steve Jones powered the Stooges' original industrial guitar. Sid with his foot on the monitor, blood running off his chest too.

Steve wondered if the two things were connected.

'Mate,' he suddenly heard in his right ear, and a minute later there was someone with his arm around his neck, pushing a pint of lager in his face.

'The drink I owe you. Sorry it's late.' The kid's face was covered in blood but his eyes were bright and round, the pupils like pissholes in the snow.

'Er, ta,' Stevie's big fingers gripped the plastic pint jug, his new-found friend still hanging round his neck.

'What you do to your face?' he couldn't help but ask.

'I kissed Sid Vicious's bass,' the eyes now rapturous. 'Trouble was, fucker kissed me back!'

Stevie looked at him, incredulous, then started to laugh and started to pogo, the gig nearing its end, the crowd moving in one final surge towards the dirty godheads on the tiny stage.

'No fuuuuunnnnnn/No fuuuuuunnnnnn...'

Lynton knew it was about to be over, never wanted it to end. His eyes still stared at the spot where Rotten had hunched over his mic even after the band had left the stage, the crowd had finally accepted they'd gone and Terry and Barry tried to push everyone back out of the doors.

No one had called him a nigger tonight, Lynton realised. He hadn't even heard 'nignog', 'chocolate drop', 'wog' or 'Chalkie'. Not a one.

Stevie brought him back to reality. 'Eh up, Lynt.' He felt

a tugging on his sleeve. 'I think duty calls.' One of the London bouncers was motioning them towards the stage.

'Tek care of things a minute,' Stevie urged. 'I've just got to nip out back a sec. Tell 'em I won't be long.'

Lynton nodded, moved towards the stage, then looked back to see what Stevie was up to. His friend was headed towards the load-in door. He seemed to have a large, bloody, Sid Vicious lookalike attached to his neck.

'Get started on that,' the London roadie ordered Lynton in the direction of the drumkit. It wasn't long before Stevie was at his side, unscrewing the kit and stashing it into boxes. Dismantling seemed to take even longer than setting up, and both were tired now the euphoria of seeing the band had diminished into the slog of tidying up after them.

The floor was a carnage of crushed plastic and spilt beer, discarded scarves and pools of vomit by the time they had finished. A pissed-off looking middle-aged woman with a fag clamped to her bottom lip was out with a mop and bucket.

Don Dawson smiling from the bar, a thick roll of money in his hand. 'Well done, lads,' he clapped Stevie across the back as they assembled for their wages. 'I like to see you young 'uns having fun.'

Barry didn't look like he echoed his boss's feelings. 'Bunch of fuckin' yobs,' he muttered, flexing his fist. 'We had some right bastards in here tonight.'

'Bastards they might be, but their money's still good for me,' leered Dawson gleefully, licking his fingers and peeling some notes off. 'Here, lad, tek some extra.'

'Cheers, Don,' Barry's eyebrows raised.

'And you lads, tek this between you,' he proffered a fiver at Stevie, nodded towards Lynton. 'I'd like to know more about this punk-rock lark from you what know it best,' he told them. 'You'll have to come up and see us some day.'

Stevie and Lynton exchanged glances.

'Terry tells me you have your own band,' Dawson furthered. 'I'd like to know more about it. I'll let you know when's convenient.' The big man stashed his roll back safely in the pockets of his faux Italian suit, nodded to one and all. 'Right then, lads, we'll call that a night.'

As they got back into the van, Stevie whispered a strange thing to Lynton. 'Sit over here. Don't go near that.' Something long and large had been bundled in the back of the mattress and covered over with sheets.

'Have you nicked something?' Lynton hissed back in alarm.

Stevie shook his head furiously. 'Just don't touch it. I'll explain it to you later.'

They were halfway back down the A63 when the sheets suddenly shook into furious life.

'What the…?' Lynton began.

A hand emerged, then another, then a shock of black, shiny hair.

'Where the fuck am I?' moaned the Sid Vicious lookalike, rubbing his head that was caked with dried blood.

'What bloody hell is that?' Barry's head spun round from the front of the van. 'Not that bastard!' He recognised him instantly. 'What's he doing in our van?'

'Calm down,' Stevie moved forwards, palms oustretched. 'That's just me mate Vince. He said he needed somewhere to stay the night and I said me Ma'd put him up. He's completely harmless, honest.'

'No he's bloody not,' Barry fumed. 'He nearly had us eye out earlier.'

Vince started chuckling.

'Shurrup!' Stevie warned him.

'What you playin' at, Stevie?' Terry's eyes in the driver's mirror were stern.

'Nowt, honest,' Stevie started, then relented. 'I think he had a bit of concussion like, from Sid's bass. I thought he needed a lie-down so I just put him in here while we loaded out…and then I kind of forgot. I'm sorry, Terry, But we can't just chuck 'im out on motorway.'

'Can't we?' Barry was fuming.

Vince had by now struggled upright and was staring in awe at the Elvis pennant that hung between Terry and Barry's seats.

'You're true believers,' he said, glassy-eyed, pointing at the object of his awe. "True believers in the one King.'

Then he slumped backwards. Seconds later he was snoring.

'I've heard it all now,' said Terry. 'Heard it bloody all.'

8

A Brand New Switch

January 2002

We did the first interview in the first week of the New Year, with Tony Stevens of Exile. His company was still run from an end-of-terrace house on Shepherd's Bush Green, the place it had all started from in 1978. From Granger's pad on Elgin it was a short stroll through the languid luxury of Holland Park and then a sharp descent into the badlands of the Bush.

The night before, my all-seeing smudger had given me his personal lowdown on Stevens, along with some freshly reprinted black and whites of the signing itself, which had taken place on the green, with the Exile office in the background.

I stared long and hard at the young faces in the frame. Stevens could have been no more than thirty, but he had that slightly older, Nick Lowe air about him with the suit and the skinny tie, tousled but not spiky hair, and a strong, determined jaw. He was beaming avuncularly as he shook hands with a clearly delighted Steve Mullin, still wearing his Popeye Doyle hat and a battered leather jacket. Next to him, Lynton Powell stood with his hands in the back pockets of his skinny black jeans, wearing a hipster's turtle neck sweater and shades and laughing. To the other side of Stevens, spiky-topped Kevin Holme wore a Damned T-shirt and looked about fifteen. Next to him and leaning into the camera, Vincent Smith, in a white T-shirt under an unbuttoned black shirt, yawned openly.

We approached the very spot across the litter-strewn green the next day. A couple of skinheads sauntered past us, sucking nonchalantly on bags of glue and reassuring me that not much had changed in this part of West London. Least of all the Exile building itself, which looked just like an ordinary house and had nothing by way of sign, plaque or awning to tell you what its function actually was. The receptionist, with her ironic eighties wedge cut and black eyeliner only added to the eerie feeling that time was standing still on this corner of W12.

That was, until Stevens himself appeared from upstairs and it became clear that more than just his tie had filled out in the past twenty-four years. He was a big, robust, Germanic-looking man with a florid complexion and an enviable thatch of thick, unruly blond hair. He still had that firm jaw and eyes that sparkled with pleasure as he recognised Gavin and reached out his hand in greeting. With his camel-hair coat and hand-tooled shoes, Stevens really was the money.

When he took us round the corner and into the vastly more upmarket Brook Green for lunch in a chic little bistro, the impression cemented in my brain. Stevens had come from money in the first place; he didn't have that chip on his shoulder that so many self-made men do. As Granger had already told me, he'd made his company's fortune from a couple of astute signings in the early eighties that still continued to pack stadiums in America. This had allowed him the money to develop less conventional acts at his leisure, some of them taking nearly ten years to make back their advances before success had finally come. It was like a creative kindergarten and many were the comfortably-off, middle-aged rock stars who claimed they owed it all to Stevens.

Yet, despite his magnanimous nature – which extended over three hours, four courses and vintage wines to match – I could sense there was something granite at the core of Tony Stevens.

The first time I got a flash of it was when he mentioned Don Dawson. Listening back to the tape, I could hear how his voice hardened, even though he'd kept the smile on his face.

We were still on the starters, general pleasantries having extended through the bread rolls. I'd asked him about the first time he ever saw Blood Truth, and why it was he wanted to sign them. Stevens was a natural raconteur; he enjoyed looking back on the whole story and bringing it back to life, and he'd leaned over to fill our glasses before settling comfortably into his tale.

A friend of his, Paul King, who now ran Exile's publishing arm, Outlaw Songs, had tipped him off. King was working for Chiswick at the time, and Blood Truth had got the support slot on The Damned's pre-Christmas tour. As soon as he saw them, King knew Stevens would want them, and sure enough he was so blown away by a twenty-minute set they played at the Electric Ballroom that he was backstage wanting to make an offer before the band had even wiped the sweat off their brows.

'The only thing I couldn't work out,' Stevens had said, twisting his glass between his fingers, 'was why no one else had got in there first. There was a lot of competition coming straight after punk, anything with spiky hair and legs normally had a scrum of A&R men all waving their chequebooks around it. There were plenty in the audience that night, as I recall, most of them majors, so I made sure Paul got me into that dressing room even before the set had ended. I thought I was gonna be smacking them off, and I knew they all had more money than me.

'But as it happens, no. Apart from their girlfriends, I'm the only one in there. Paul makes the introduction and I'm chatting up Vincent straight away, with Steve and the others looking more interested by the second. Then suddenly, boom, the door bangs open and there he is…the cock of the North, Mr Don Dawson.'

Stevens's eyes had narrowed slightly and on the tape, his comments sounded more weighted than they had at the time, when it had all seemed a bit jovial.

'He had the full get up, just so you understood. The suit, the rings, the football manager's sheepskin and the great smell of Brut coming on after him. Aha, I thought – so that's why everyone else pissed themselves and ran away.

'As soon as he clocked what I was doing, he was ready to start throwing his weight about, but—' Stevens paused, sighed and examined his cuticles '—that's not the way I do business. I made sure Vincent had my number and we took it from there...'

'Did Dawson threaten you then?' I had asked at this point, and my voice came back highly overexcited.

'He tried it on,' Stevens said. 'The problem was, he was their manager, their agent and their record company. That's a clear conflict of interests and should it ever have got as far as a courtroom he wouldn't have had a leg to stand on. No. Dawson used those old dog's tricks that had worked for him before when he was building his ropey empire on slots and comedy clubs up North. Well, they might have worked for him there...' a shit-eating grin lit up Stevens's face, 'but it don't wash down here.'

Then the subject of Dawson was closed, except in my head, where I wondered if the old bastard was still actually alive, and if so, how I could get hold of him.

Stevens spent the rest of the main course fondly discussing the band and their achievements. They certainly came alive as characters, the way he told it. Stevie as a combination joker and grafter, the one who put it all together and kept it all together. Lynton as a modest musical chameleon. Kevin Holme as the drummer.

But it was soon evident that Stevens loved Vincent the most. He saw him as a total genius, not just as a songwriter, singer or performer but almost as a visionary, a punk-rock William Blake who was too far ahead of his time. Following this analogy, he even offered the surprising revelation that Vincent was a secret church-goer. Stevens didn't say if Smith ever saw any angels floating around in trees, but he did say the singer got a lot of inspiration from visiting the houses of the holy.

'That's why he was so pleased when he first got a place near the Sacré Coeur in Paris,' Stevens revealed. 'You wouldn't think so from his lyrics, but there you go. Maybe it was an extension of his faith in Elvis…'

Despite his comic flourishes, there was a level of respect in Stevens's voice when he talked about Smith that he didn't apply to the others. He regarded them with a more fatherly affection.

'I've seen Stevie Mullin punch a bloke from one end of the bar and out the door,' he reflected, 'but then I've seen him more protective and sensitive than Mother Teresa, especially when Lynton got himself into bother…'

Naturally, the record company boss didn't want to talk too much about the darker sides of the story. 'If he wants to tell you, then that's fair enough, but I ain't telling any tales out of school about personal problems. It's already on the record that Lynton got strung out, I can't exactly deny it. Poor bloke was always too sensitive for his own skin, not surprising, really, considering where he grew up. Came across in his playing, though. He's the best natural musician I've ever met, Lynton. You ask him how he learned the bass,' Stevens raised an eyebrow.

'I will,' I nodded, remembering with slight distaste know-it-all Mick Greer's testimony on Powell. 'But if you don't mind me asking, all the articles I've read seem to blame Vincent for Lynton's drug problems. Was that what you saw?'

Stevens pursed his lips and shrugged. 'The trouble was with Vincent,' he considered, 'all along, he could do stuff that nobody else could. It just didn't affect him in the same way. Spliff, speed, smack…it was the same to him as a few jars is to us. A way of winding down, something amusing to pass the time. He could take loads of everything, drink like a mule at the same time, stay up all night writing songs, or laying down tracks, or just talking in the bar, and there never seemed to be any payback. So what Lynton saw was pretty different from how it affected him. I don't think Vincent had a normal constitution, therefore I don't think he did that old junky's trick of turning on everyone around him. I know this sounds strange, but there didn't seem to be any form of chemical or booze that he *could* get addicted to.'

'Apart from love, mate,' Gavin had said then.

Which was when I saw Stevens harden for the second time. 'If you want to call it that,' he muttered, then smiled, shaking his head as if casting off a bad feeling.

The waitress came then to take our dinner plates and offer us the dessert menu. Stevens continued his commentary as his eyes scanned down the list.

'Little Sylvana,' he sighed. 'Don't make me speak ill of the dead, Gavin.' He looked up and straight at me.

'You want to be careful what you write about her. Seriously. Her family are loaded, they could shut you down like that,' he snapped his fingers.

'Well he's gotta write something about the bitch,' Granger noted. 'Otherwise, it's not gonna be the whole story. You can't libel the dead, whether the Schmoldberg family like it or not.'

Stevens continued to eyeball me in a way that was almost uncomfortable. 'She was nothing but trouble,' he told me, and on tape it sounded nonchalant, nothing like the moment it actually happened. 'Other people will probably tell you, continue to proliferate that tall story about them falling in love with each other over the sausage rolls at my Christmas party…'

Granger winced a bit at that and I suppressed a smile. So Mick Greer wasn't so all-knowing, then.

'Don't you believe it. She had him in her sights a long way off. She was working up to it, and she seized her chance that night. You want my opinion? You can write her down as Nancy Spungen – came over here to try and bag a Sex Pistol, wound up with some poor little effeminate Scotsman who she quickly turned into a cripple. She got her own band out of it, and yeah, they were pretty good for a while, but that wasn't really what she was all about. Little Sylvana wanted to write herself into some rock'n'roll legend and she did so at the expense of everyone around her. Vincent, the band, that poor bastard Leith – all the ones with the talent.' Then he turned on that smile again. 'Fancy some dessert?'

'Just deserts?' quipped Granger drily, and everyone laughed.

'Seriously,' Stevens looked at both of us with a twinkle in his eye. 'Get someone else to dish the dirt on that one. I don't really want to talk about her. I might have the most successful band in the world on my roster – but she lost me the best one.'

'Fair play,' Granger shrugged and the subject was dropped. I didn't mind one bit. Stevens's reaction to her after all this time was fascinating enough; I couldn't wait to fill in the gaps elsewhere.

I waited till after dessert and cheeses, for the haze of brandies and cigars, before asking probably the trickiest question of all: 'What do you reckon happened to Vincent?'

Stevens's eyes followed the smoke upwards and he smiled sadly. 'I change my mind about that on a frequent basis,' he admitted. 'Sometimes I think he must have took a vow of silence with some dodgy monks somewhere and they're still keeping him prisoner. That's the only way of explaining how someone as noticeable as he was has stayed AWOL so long. 'Cos, I don't know about you,' he nodded at Gavin, 'but the Vincent Smith I knew wouldn't just walk away from everything and go and be some old goat herder in Tibet or something.'

Gavin agreed. 'Can't see that myself either. He wasn't exactly cut out for manual work.'

'Or mucking in with the locals, fading into the background,' Stevens nodded. 'Nah, but that's a fantasy really, a distraction from thinking about the fact he's almost certainly dead.'

Gavin looked down at the tablecloth, as if those words were a bit too strong for him to take, and muttered: 'Yeah. I came to the same conclusion myself.'

Stevens puffed on his cigar. 'You can't trust the police to find out anything,' he said evenly, still looking at Gavin. 'And foreign ones, forget it. So I did hire a sort of a private eye myself to try and find out what happened in Paris.'

'You did?' Gavin looked amazed.

'Yeah,' Stevens blew a long plume of smoke up to the ceiling. 'After about three months, when it became obvious he wasn't suddenly going to turn up on the doorstep again. Course, the trail was long cold by then. Found out fuck all. Vincent and the lovely Sylvana were surrounded by dealers and junkies while they lived in Montmartre, and you know how they all melt away when the cock crows. You can't find out anything of substance from people like that.'

'Is he still around, this private eye?' I blurted, and Stevens blinked at me, totally amused.

I thought I'd said a stupid thing and he was going to laugh in my face, but instead he said kindly: 'I might be able to dig him out for you if you're really interested. If he's still alive and even remembers it. But I could show you his report and you'd be none the wiser.'

'I just want to get a feel,' I explained, 'of what it was like there in Paris, just of what it felt like at the time, before he...went up in smoke.'

Stevens nodded. 'I understand that. Give me your number and I'll get back to you.'

He still sounded genuine when I played back the tape. I was soon to realise that that lunch had been something of an initiation ceremony for me. Stevens already knew and trusted Gavin, but if he hadn't liked me, I don't think that anyone would have talked. After we'd gone our separate ways that day, with Stevens footing the entire bill, Gavin started to get the calls.

Lynton Powell was first. He rang Gavin to say he could meet

us in a month, after he had finished the production on his latest album, which he needed to do in Los Angeles. Which was lucky, because that was where Steve Mullin was still hanging out with the metal boys, and he would put in a word for us while he was out there.

A few days after that, Kevin Holme agreed to meet. Of all of Blood Truth, he was the one who had always said the least. Some of the articles I had in my archive scarcely even mentioned him, and Mick Greer's only seemed to point out the amount of abuse he'd got off his fellow band members. So I was determined to let him have the say that no one else had ever allowed him. Hoped that would get him to open up, get me the inside line.

As it happened, on the day we were due to meet Kevin, Gavin got a commission from the *Sunday Times* and had to jet off somewhere, so I ended up going it alone. At first, I was a bit wary of how it would pan out without Gavin making the introductions, whether it would be so easy to get the instant rapport we had with Tony Stevens.

But going it alone, it seemed afterwards, was a stroke of luck.

Kevin had asked us to meet him in his local, the Red Lion, off Stoke Newington Church Street. It was a cavernous old ginhouse that slumped across the corner of the road, decked with garish banners offering various lager promotions, big screen football fixtures and dubious claims about being the 'home of live music'. The list of upcoming attractions was a veritable *Who's You?* of pub-rock dinosaurs and tribute bands, mirroring a clientele of aged hippies, wizened roadies and threadbare one-hit wonders, who basked around the fruit machines in the lounge bar and looked up sullenly as I walked in for my one o'clock meeting.

They all looked as dull and hungover as the day was outside, and for a moment I felt an overwhelming anxiety that I wouldn't recognise Kevin Holme amid the lined faces and faded tattoos that sat there with their roll-ups hanging from their thin lips, yellowed fingers clawed around their flat pints of bitter.

But Kevin had chosen this venue because, he said, he was friends with the landlord and could get us a private room upstairs. I remembered I was supposed to ask at the bar for him and did so with relief.

The only bar staff around was a slight teenager with long, dyed black hair and a bolt piercing through his eyebrow. He looked like most of his flock probably had the last time they were famous, in around 1984. Again, I had that weird sense that time was going backwards and made a mental note that this had to come through in the writing. The London of the rock community like some kind of Swiss cheese, riddled with wormholes in time.

Bar goth perked up when I asked him if I could find Kevin Holme anywhere. 'Ah yih,' he said in the Kiwi accent that was now *de rigueur* of London barmen. 'Go upstairs, mate, and turn to your lift,' he pointed round the corner of the bar. 'He's in the function room. You can't muss ut.'

'Great,' I smiled. 'Can I get a pint of Four X to take with me? And d'you know what Kevin likes drinking?'

'Don't worry about that, he's swit,' the pasty youth told me. 'Kivin only drunks muneral water, eh.'

I clocked his Sisters of Mercy badge as he poured my pint and thought to ask him: 'Do you like his band, Blood Truth?'

He frowned. 'Nuver heard of 'um, mate. I jist thought he was a sussion guy.'

'Ah,' I handed over a fiver. 'You should check them out. I think you might like them somehow.'

I left him scratching his head and wondering.

The function room was obviously where they had the bands. Thickly carpeted and smelling vaguely of stale biscuits, it was a drab little hole, where I imagined the not-even-hopefuls of the bar downstairs went through the motions, dreaming of days gone by.

Kevin Holme was perched on a barstool, leaning against the deserted counter, reading a paper and sipping his fizzy water thoughtfully. He was shorter than I'd imagined, and still wearing the sort of thing he always had on in his press shots – black leather jacket, black jeans, pointy boots and a white shirt with purple stripes. A small pair of wire glasses rested on the top of his nose, and he still sported a bit of a mullet, though the face, when he looked up, was thankfully less battle-scarred than the undead downstairs.

He looked like a middle-aged pixie.

'Hello,' I put my pint down and extended my hand to him. 'Eddie Bracknell.'

'All right, Eddie,' Kevin said. He sounded like a pixie too, or Willie Carson. He looked over my shoulder as he spoke, and his hand felt small, dry and delicate, not what you'd expect from a drummer.

'Gavin not with you then?'

'No, I'm afraid he had to go on a shoot at the last minute. In New York. I hope you don't mind him not being here.'

'Not at all,' Kevin looked almost relieved and ushered me onto the nearest barstool. As I rummaged my dictaphone out of my bag, he carefully folded up his paper and said: 'Gavin was Vince's friend, really. He took some good pictures of us, but we didn't talk much.'

He sounded quite sad and suddenly I felt sorry for him. He looked so easy to pick on.

'Is it all right to turn this on?' I asked, placing the dictaphone between us.

'Yeah, sure,' Kevin looked like he hadn't seen one of those in a long time, if ever. 'It's a bit strange, somebody wanting to talk to me about Blood Truth. After all this time. It feels a bit like a different world.'

'I've read a lot about the band,' I told him, 'but there never seems to be very much about you.'

'Well, there wouldn't be, would there?' he laughed to himself softly. 'Do you mind if I ask you, why are you doing this book?'

'It's Gavin's fault,' I shrugged. 'He played me a video of one of your gigs. That was enough to get me hooked. Then, the more I found out about the band, the more I thought, God, here's a story that needs to be told. It's amazing that people have forgotten about you.'

Kevin nodded thoughtfully, then looked me straight in the eye. 'You're not going to try and find Vince, are you?'

I barked out an unconvincing laugh. 'Well, I'd obviously like to try and find out what happened to him…'

Kevin was shaking his head.

'I don't think you could,' he said. 'Or, maybe I don't think you should. He's better off lost…' he blinked and almost whispered, 'and forgotten.'

Then he seemed to shake himself out of it. 'Look, sorry, Eddie, this isn't a very good beginning. I don't mind answering your questions, but I think I should be honest with you about one thing, 'cos no one else will. They'll all idolise him and lionise him, the way your friend Gavin does. But take it from one who was actually there and actually sober – Vince Smith was a very bad bastard. Right from the start…'

Then Kevin Holme started to tell me his sad, bad tale.

9

The Last Gang in Town

August 1977

Stevie was having a nightmare about cheese. He was in a desert of melting cheddar, surrounded by big holey mountains of edam, all of it going rank and sweaty in the relentless heat. He was trying to move but his feet were stuck in bubbling gunge and the smell of it all was unbearable. 'Uughhh!' He shook himself awake, but the hideous smell still lingered.

And no wonder. A long pair of feet, encased in filthy, sweaty socks was propped right under his nose. They protruded from the end of his bedcovers, from where they joined a long, angular ridge under the sheets that led right along to a shock of black, greasy hair spilling out of the bedstead. Bleary from sleep as he struggled up to his elbows, Stevie tried to remember how he'd ended up in bed with Sid Vicious.

The events of the night before came back in a rush as he stumbled out of the twisted sheets, his T-shirt, Y-fronts and socks clinging to his clammy skin. Oh aye, he thought, my new friend Vince. Stevie went over to inspect him.

'Uughhh,' he repeated, examining the congealed gash on

sleeping beauty's forehead, the great clumps of blood stuck in his already matted black hair.

The room smelled worse than a docker's drawers, so Steve staggered to the window, pulled back his blackout curtains and, wincing in the bright light of 10 a.m., pushed the sash window up and open.

He leaned out to breathe in the fresh air, take in the panorama of the rooftops stretching towards the big refineries on the docks. The bains were already at their football in the street below, racing up and down the street with their big orange ball.

Another beautiful day, he noted with some poignancy. Summer holidays were almost over now. No more days spent practising in Lynton's garage. No more nights humping gear.

He had a flashback to Steve Jones in his underpants and his face cracked into a wild grin. Now, that – that had been a moment in a lifetime.

'Nurrrghhhhh,' came a sound from the bed. Underneath the black hair, something stirred.

'Nurrrghhhh, am I?' it seemed to say.

'You're in Hull, mate,' replied Stevie.

'In Hell?' Vince Smith emerged from the covers, eyes screwed up against the sunlight. 'How did I get here?'

'You stowed a lift in our van, remember?' Stevie watched with some amusement as his companion tried to focus.

'Can we have a bit less daylight?' frowning Vince asked. He sounded much posher than he had the night before.

'Why, does it turn you to dust?' quipped Stevie, thinking, aye, and he doesn't half look like a vampire and all.

Vince put his hand to his forehead and instantly recoiled. 'Ow! Jesus, what have you done to me?'

'I've not done owt,' Stevie shrugged. 'Sid Vicious did that to you. You were right pleased with it at the time.'

A sudden grin lit up Vince's face. 'Sid! Oh yeah, I remember – I communed with him!'

'He cut your head open with his bass,' Stevie nodded. 'Do you feel all right? S'pose I should have took you to the hospital. But it were hard enough stopping Terry and Barry from throwing you out of van.'

'Ah, it's all coming back,' Vince began shakily to stumble to his feet, one hand clutching the bedpost, the other gingerly examining his skull. 'Shit, you saved my life last night. And I don't even remember your name.'

'It's Stevie. Stevie Mullin. And I didn't really save your life – unless you count stopping Barry from givin' you a batterin'.'

'Stevie,' Vince extended his hand, the one with the eyeball ring, took Stevie's and shook it with a strength that belied his skinny frame. 'Believe me, you did save my life. You got me away from Rachel for the night. If she'd seen state of this...' He eyeballed himself in the mirror on Stevie's wardrobe.

'I won't ask,' mumbled Stevie. 'D'you want to get cleaned up? Then we'd best get out of here. The old man's due back off boats today and if he finds you in here, he'll think I've gone queer. Believe me, no one will be able to save your life then.'

Vince started to laugh, sending stars shooting through his eyeballs. He clutched his wounded skull, muttering: 'Maybe I'm dead already.'

Stevie hung round the top of the stairs nervously while Vince was in the bathroom. Downstairs the telly was on full blast and he could hear little Gracie and his youngest brother Milo laughing to *The Banana Splits*. His mum was hoovering and the smell of breakfast bacon still lingered on the air. Stevie was starving but he couldn't risk it. Getting Vince in in the middle of the night was one thing. Smuggling him back out unnoticed would be a whole lot harder and the thought of his dad barging in on them sharing a bed was already causing his stomach to turn somersaults.

'Hurry up, hurry up,' he muttered nervously to the locked bathroom door, his fingers drumming on the banisters. Vince was taking ages. Stevie himself had pulled on new underwear, last night's peg leg trousers and a white T-shirt, fluorescent yellow socks and his brothel creepers. He'd rubbed some of the toothpaste he kept to do his hair with around his teeth, sprayed on some deodorant and figured he could save a bath for later. But obviously, when sober, Vince was a little more fussy about his appearance.

The bains outside smashed their football against the front door, causing the dog to erupt. Stevie thought he was going to have a heart attack.

'Will you shut up!' his mother yelled, turning off the hoover.

For one second there was silence in the Mullin home, and that was the moment Vince pushed open the bathroom door, and stood framed in the doorway in all his splendour. His hair stood up on end again and the skin all red and shiny around the two-inch scab that was forming on the centre of his forehead. His T-shirt was ripped and covered in dried blood. On his left shoulder, Stevie hadn't noticed the night before, was a tattoo of a naked lady sitting in a cocktail glass. On his right shoulder was the Virgin Mary.

If Stevie's dad saw that…

'Is that you up, son?' Mrs Mullin's voice came.

'Uh-oh, yeah, Ma,' Stevie winced. 'Top of the morning.'

'D'you want something cooking?'

Stevie and Vince stared wide-eyed at each other across the top of the stairs.

'You're all right, Ma, I'm late as it is. I'll get summat out.'

'Late for what?' Stevie's mum appeared in the hallway, looking up at him in puzzlement, one hand around the dog's collar, the other still trailing the Hoover lead. 'I thought you were working last night?'

Vince shrank back into the bathroom. Stevie dropped his gaze just in time.

'For band practice, Ma. We've not got many days left now.'

'Well, it's not like you not to want your breakfast.'

She eyeballed him suspiciously.

'I know, but it's 'cos I had a late night,' Stevie said the first thing that came into his head. 'I've slept in and now I'm gonna be late. Don't worry, Ma, I'll be all right.'

She shook her head. 'Well I don't know.' She shrugged, and made to turn away. 'All right, son, I've got enough on my plate as it is. Your dad'll be home any minute and I'm not halfway through the cleaning. You carry on. Go on and have a good time.'

Her voice resounded with sarcasm, but Stevie didn't rise to it. Instead he smiled sweetly. 'All right then, Ma, see you later.'

She scowled at him and disappeared from view, turned the Hoover back on. It was now or never.

Stevie threw Vince's leather jacket at him. 'Come on!' he hissed. 'Let's get out of here!'

They ran down the stairs, shot out of the front door before Stevie's mum could finish asking: 'Stevie? Have you got someone with…' and were halfway down Hessle Road before they stopped running and started laughing.

'Did you just say—' ventured Vince, clutching his sides and trying to get his breath back '—you've got a band?'

'Aye,' nodded Stevie. 'We're not bad neither. We've been practising all summer. Only trouble is, we've not got a singer.'

'Well,' smiled Vince, 'you have now.'

Lynton and Kevin reviewed this new prospect with a mixture of horror and awe. Lynton couldn't quite believe the mad bastard was still with Stevie. He agreed with Terry and Barry – Vince should have been deposited in a lay-by somewhere far from here. That bloody face and all his gibbering about Elvis Presley had made Lynton shudder. The last thing he expected was to see this vision of mad badness swaggering into their rehearsal room, laughing and joking with Stevie with an ease that suggested the two of them had been friends for years.

With his finely tuned instinct for personal danger, Kevin regarded Vince with mute terror. Vince said he was eighteen and had left school already, but he looked much older than they did, much more knowing. And the way he had passed his eyes over the little drummer reminded Kevin too much of the expression on Dunton's face when a new boy turned up at school. Like he couldn't wait to get on with the torture.

From the moment they'd assembled in the garage, on Stevie's orders later that afternoon, it was as if Vince had taken over, assumed the gig was his before he'd even sung a note. Worse still, Stevie didn't even seem to have noticed.

Instead he was boasting to his new friend about how they'd taught themselves a few cover versions over the summer – 'Anarchy', 'New Rose' by The Damned and Link Wray's instrumental 'Rumble'. Vince decided instantly that demolishing Dave Vanian would be the best way of demonstrating his skill.

Doesn't want to measure himself up against Johnny, thought Lynton, tuning up his bass. Kevin was so nervous it had taken him forever to set up his kit, crashing around all fingers and thumbs, dropping cymbals left, right and centre. Lynton had helped him in the end, then sullenly wired up their only vocal mic, while Vince and Stevie jawed on about the gig last night, oblivious to their discomfort.

'All right, you ready?' Stevie slung his guitar around his neck.

'Yeah,' Kevin's voice came out high and shrill, making Vince snigger.

Lynton just nodded. I'll show that freak, he thought. Bet he knows nothing about music.

'New Rose' had an explosive intro anyhow, drums, bass and guitar all crashing in together, and the moment the three of them got going it was like a shower of sparks went up. Stevie nailed that subverted rockabilly riff the way a surfer catches a wave. Kevin drummed faster than he'd ever managed before, drummed like his life depended on it. Lynton felt hairs standing up on the back of his neck as his fingers flew up the fretboard, finding the notes as if of their own volition.

Then Vince grabbed hold of the mic, swung it backwards and let rip a deep, almost yowling voice. That it wasn't entirely pleasant on the ear wasn't the point. From the moment his fingers touched the mic, Vince Smith looked like a star. He moved that microphone back and forth with a louche magnificence, like a hellbound punk Gene Vincent, already caught in the spotlight's glare. It didn't seem like he knew most of the words, or maybe he was just making up couplets that amused him more. But there was an aura about him that was electrifying. You couldn't stop staring at him.

Jesus, thought Lynton, that freak is showing me. And then he had to smile as his heart filled up with the rush – the four corners had touched and magic had come forth. They actually sounded like a band.

That three minutes was the best noise they had yet to make together. When it was over, they stared at each other, almost shocked by what they'd done.

'Oooh 'eck.' A flushed Stevie looked round at his bright-eyed companions. 'Was that really us? Shall we do that one again and prove it?'

They spent another two hours messing around in Lynton's garage that day. They went through what they knew, what they'd been working on and tried to put a few of their own tunes together with Vince's own lyrics.

Vince already had a lot of these to spare. He kept them on him at all times, scribbled down on a tiny girl's notepad he kept in the arm pocket of his leather jacket. As he explained to the others, he'd been looking for a band for quite some time. He'd enrolled for an art foundation course at Doncaster College, thinking he'd meet some like-minded people there. But, oh no, they were all pretentious middle-class wankers playing at being punks. Not like this. This was off the streets, real working-class rage. This was the real thing.

Without even Stevie realising, Vince's voice had gone back to a thick Yorkshire brogue now. 'What d'they call you?' he asked.

'We thought about Dead City, 'cos that's what Hull is, d'you know what I mean?' Stevie shrugged. 'But that's the nearest we've got to a name we all liked.'

Vince frowned. 'Yeah. Sounds a bit depressing, mind. Reckon we should have a name with a bit more mystery to it.'

Lynton and Kevin exchanged rolled-eye glances. 'Yeah?' Lynton growled. 'Like what?'

'I was reading this book,' Vince smiled at him, 'that gave me an idea. It's called *Wise Blood*. It's about a preacher who doesn't believe in worshipping Jesus so he forms the Church Without Christ. You might like to borrow it some time,' he raised one eyebrow slowly, laughter lines deepening at the corner of his mouth. 'I think you might like it, Lynton.'

Vince seemed to enjoy the look of confusion that passed across the bass player's face, but he didn't push it. 'Anyway,' he continued. 'This preacher, he meets this country hick who he thinks has got wise blood. I like the idea of wise blood. Like, the music's in our blood, we bring it out of us when we play together. Blood brothers, you know what I mean? We should call ourselves after it. Call ourselves…Blood Truth.'

'Blood Truth?' Stevie swilled it around his mouth like he was testing wine. 'Sounds fuckin' weird all right. What d'you reckon, Lynton?'

Lynton had at first thought that Vince was taking the piss out of him with all this Church Without Christ bollocks, like he'd figured out something about him that the others didn't know. But the Blood Truth thing he could really understand. That's what it felt like when they played together.

Still, he remained suspicious. He'd recognised that look in Vince's eye as well as Kevin had.

'It's good,' he nodded. 'What about you, Kevin?'

'I don't mind,' squeaked the drummer, dropping his eyes to the floor. 'Whatever you think.'

'Right,' said Vince, pleased with his first victory. 'That's that then. Blood Truth we are. Anyone fancy drinking to that?'

'Just one thing,' Lynton cut in. 'How can you be in our band if you live in Donny? I mean, this is our rehearsal space, we're all set up here, so we ain't coming to you.'

'Don't worry about it. My girlfriend's got a car,' Vince said airily. 'You tell me when you want me,' he looked pointedly at Stevie, 'and I'll be there. Now then, about this drink…'

Stevie went willingly off to the pub with him, leaving Lynton and Kevin to clear everything away.

'He were a bit mad, weren't he?' understated Kevin when they were alone, not sure if Lynton would agree with him or not.

'You are not wrong there,' Lynton nodded. 'Not wrong at all.'

'What did he do to his head?'

Lynton grimaced. 'Apparently, he run into Sid Vicious's bass. I'm not sure if it did enough damage, though.'

Kevin giggled.

'Thing is, though,' Lynton had to admit, 'he is good. It's like…' he spread his arms, tried to explain how he felt to Kevin. 'You never wanted to be in a band with us, did you? We had to force you. Then, soon as you was, you was brilliant. We all played together and it was like…something special, you know what I mean?'

Kevin nodded. He did know.

'And now, this mad Vince comes along, and I don't want to play with him neither. I'm gettin' bad vibes from him. But Stevie forces me. And then the same thing happens again. He is good, seriously good. It felt good playing with him. He was right about it being in our blood.'

Lynton's eyes beseeched Kevin to agree. He smiled sadly in reply. 'Guess we're stuck with him then, aren't we?'

Lynton smiled. 'Guess we are.'

Kevin walked home across the city, lost in thought. Lynton had been right, he hadn't wanted to be in a band at first, especially not with those two. But now that he was, now that he did know Lynton and Stevie and what they could achieve together, he didn't want to give it up. Despite their obvious differences, the three of them had grown strangely close over the past five weeks. For the first time in his life, and because of his talents, Kevin had actually been treated like an equal. His opinion had counted; he was a vital part of something good.

The four weeks Dunton and his family had spent in their caravan in Brid had helped a lot too. Kevin hadn't seen Gary for so long now that he had almost dared to imagine a life without him.

But now, he had a horrible feeling that with the arrival of Vince, his fleeting happiness, like the summer holidays themselves, was coming to an end. A feeling that only intensified when he rounded the corner of Davis Close. It was almost dark and people were starting to switch their lights on. The Duntons' car was back in their drive. Every light in their house was ablaze. Even as he walked towards his own front door, Kevin caught sight of Gary through the living-room window.

Dunton appeared to have grown another foot over the past month. His bumfluff moustache was now fully formed into a thick, bristling band and his hair had been fuzzed into a Kevin Keegan perm. He appeared to be demonstrating newfound strength to go with his height by holding Barney Lee in a headlock. Wearing a Leeds United football shirt, he looked like a genuine hooligan.

Kevin shrank away up his own garden path. But at that moment, Dunton saw him, dropped Barney and looked at him with a puzzled expression. Then he smiled – top lip curling, more like a sneer – and beckoned him to come round the side of the house.

Heart sinking, Kevin turned and tramped towards the Duntons' front door just as Gary pulled it open.

Dunton looked down at him, feigning amusement, while something deadlier played in his eyes.

'What's all this then, Kevin?' He reached forward and rubbed a big sweaty hand through Kevin's first feeble attempts to make his hair stand up a bit. 'You look like one of those punk-rocker dickheads. That's not like you, is it? Anyone would think you'd been hanging out with Paddies—' Dunton's eyes narrowed, into evil little slits '—or even worse, nignogs. Get a load of this, Barney,' he shouted over his shoulder. 'Come and look what's happened to Kevin.'

Then he turned back to Kevin and hissed: 'I don't know what you think you've been up to while we was away. But it looks to me like you need sorting out…'

Lynton kept the fear away until all the lights were turned out. Then, alone in his bed, Vince's words pushed their way unwelcomely back into his head. 'The Church Without Christ…you'd like that, Lynton.'

'No,' Lynton turned, pulling his bedsheets over his head, 'get out of my head.'

But it was hot and sweaty in Lynton's bedroom, even with the window open. He had never been the easiest of sleepers and tonight presented the perfect conditions for rampant insomnia. 'Church Without Christ, Lynton. Church Without Christ.'

His hand burrowed under his pillow, finding the little leather Bible he kept there. The only thing his real mother had left for him when she'd gave him away. Because of this, he had always happily accompanied his foster parents to church, thinking that it was what she had wanted for him. Because of this, he feared evil. Feared Vince's casual blasphemy had more behind it than just punk posing. In daylight hours the thought would have been stupid, could have been brushed aside. But alone in his room at midnight, that taunting took on a new dimension, the words twisted into accusations. 'Church Without Christ, Lynton. That's what you want.'

'No!' he gripped the book tightly to his chest, started mouthing the words to The Lord's Prayer at the same time thinking: I am not going to be evil, I am not going to be turned, I do love you, Jesus.

Repeating it over and over, every time the mocking voice made a comeback, threatened to drown him out. Over and over, sweating and afraid in the oppressive darkness. I love you, Jesus, love you, Jesus, love you.

It wasn't until he heard the first birds singing just before dawn that Lynton fell into an exhausted sleep.

Stevie turned his key in the door as quietly as he could and stole into the hallway. It was ten o'clock and he'd left Vince heading in the direction of the station to catch the last train home. Dawdled his way back through the streets, avoiding going past any of the pubs where the old man was likely to be, the exhilaration of the past two days fading into a knot of dread, tight in his stomach.

The old man was home. Stevie had slammed the door in his Ma's face. Now he was going to get it.

He took his shoes off on the corner of his street, wanting nothing to give him away. The place was eerily deserted, like every house knew and was silently watching him, catching their breath, waiting for the storm to break.

The TV was on loud, as usual, covering his tentative steps in the darkness. Stevie had made all of two silent steps up the stairs when the living-room door flung open and the great hulk of his father appeared in the harsh electric light.

'What d'you think you're doing there, Steven, sneakin' off like a thief in the night?' His voice was soft but his eyes were hard, the overture to a rage.

Stevie froze, said nothing. His father snapped the hall light on.

'Will you take a look at that!' he exclaimed, eyes sweeping up and down his son's artfully distressed appearance. 'What in the name of God have you been doin' while I've been out breaking my back for you? You turning queer, son, is that what it is? Is that what makes you think you can treat your own mother like dirt?' His voice was rising now, prodding at Stevie like a jabbing finger and he walked towards his errant son, balling his right hand into a fist. 'Have you got a tongue in your head, Steven? I asked you a question.'

'No, Da…' Stevie started.

His mother slunk silently through the living-room door, placed an arm on his father's shoulder, her eyes round with worry.

'Leave it, love,' she whispered. 'We can talk about it in morning.'

'I'm not leaving anything,' he stated. He shook the hand off, continued to stare at Stevie, his face flushed, a vein pumping hard on his temple.

'D'you know what I think? I think you're taking the piss, son. What kind of people have you been bringing into my house, Steven? What kind of heathens have you been entertaining behind my back?'

'I've not, Da…' Stevie heard himself croak, knowing that was precisely the wrong thing to say.

'You what, son? What are you saying to me? You didn't have anyone here? That's not what your mother's told me, Steven. She distinctly heard two of yous running out of here this morning, slamming the door in her face. So you're calling your mother a liar now, are you?'

'N-no…' Stevie stared for a second more into those mad, bulging eyes, then tried to make a run for it. He got to the top of the stairs before his father's fist connected to the side of his head and a shower of stars exploded before his eyes.

'Are you calling your mother a liar?' Screamed into his ear. 'Are you, son?'

His sister Gracie waking up, crying.

'Are you?'

His mother pulling at his father's legs, trying to get him off him, sobbing: 'Please don't hurt him, please…'

Sparks in his eyes and red pain hammering down across his head, his shoulders, his arms where he tried to protect himself. Crying 'No, no, no, no, no, no, no.'

The end of the summer holidays.

The start of Blood Truth.

10

Steps Through the Unmarked Door

January 2002

I was halfway through Kevin's transcript when Louise got home from work, dropping her black leather handbag and a Sainsbury's carrier of food down on the kitchen table with a concentration-shattering bang.

'Eddie,' she turned round and stared at me. 'We've been getting weird phone calls.'

'What?' I pulled my mini-earphones out of my lugholes.

'Weird phone calls,' she repeated, lips pursed. 'While you were out yesterday someone left a constant stream of drivel on the answerphone. I don't know if you've bothered to listen but I can't understand a word of it.'

'I'm sorry, I didn't realise...' With her usual accuracy, Louise had pinpointed the first time in months I hadn't instantly played back my messages once I'd got in. Probably because I had been so full of triumph after my encounter with Kevin Holme, my feet had somehow taken me from Camden tube up to the top of Inverness Street, to where Christophe worked in Joe's Jump-Jive Shack. We'd got talking and ended up celebrating my book deal over a few jars in the Spread Eagle. It was the first time we'd seen each other properly all year, after all. So I'd got back late when Louise was already asleep. Then today I'd just got up wanting to get back to it, and after a leisurely 2pm breakfast I had. With Granger still out of the country, I guess I hadn't expected anything important to come in.

Trust some loony to catch out my first act of transgression in 2002.

Louise's red fingernail hovered over the playback button. 'Do you understand a word of this?'

The voice was slurred, with a thick Scottish accent. But having had more experience listening to incoherent drunks than Lou, I could just about make out what he was saying.

'Ah'm lookin' for an, ahm, Eddie? Uh, Eddie B-brack…nell? Eddie Brack-nell. Ah've go' somethin' furr youze…'

The phone was cut off with a shrill BEEEEEEEP.

Next message: 'Ach, shite, fuckin' heel.Wha' I was sayin' was – Eddie, are youze there? Wha—' BEEEEEEP.

'Jesus,' I shook my head, thinking, has someone given my phone number to an old wino from Arlington House for a joke? 'Sorry,' I said to Lou. 'I've no idea who this…'

The next message cut through my sentence with a clarity missing from the others. 'Eddie, eh, this is Robin Leith. You've heard of us, eh?'

'Holy shit!' I exclaimed.

Louise put her finger down on the stop button. 'You mean you do know this moron?'

'Yes, er no, I mean I know who he is. He's someone I need to speak to for the book. Shit, let it play back!'

'Why should I even be surprised? I'll leave you to it then.' She gave a sigh of disgust, pressed play and stalked back to the kitchen to noisily unpack the shopping.

But I was transfixed by the voice on the tape. It was poised somewhere between intoxication and menace. 'If youze ah thinkin' ah talkin' about Sylvana, youze come tur me first. Ah wanna meet with you, eh…' There was a moment of crackling silence before the voice resumed. 'Wha's today? Thursday, aye. Reet, Eddie, ah want you to meet us…' BEEEEEEP.

'Fuck!' I exploded. 'Fuck, fuck fuck—'

'Sunday, Eddie, ah want yous to meet us ahn Sunday. One o'clock in the Devonshire Arms. Thash Camdun Town. Yuh know it, eh? See youze then, Eddie.'

END OF MESSAGES.

I was stunned. Robin Leith. The man Tony Stevens had described as a 'cripple' – alternately, a 'stalker' in Mick Greer's testimony. Who had told him? How had he tracked me down? And when?

'Lou-Lou?' I moved tentatively towards the kitchen. 'Did you say you were in when he called?'

Louise was sorting stuff into the fridge. She didn't turn round. 'Not when he left those messages, but he must have tried calling back in the evening. I thought it was a dirty phone call.'

She slammed the door shut and turned round. 'Just heavy breathing on the line so I put the phone down on them. Then it rang again almost immediately and I was about to switch it over to the fax and burn their ears out when it spoke. Or should I say it mumbled. It was that voice all right, but I couldn't make head nor tail of it, so I hung up and then put the fax on. He didn't try it a fourth time.'

'God, I'm sorry, darling, you should have said.'

She sniffed. 'I just assumed it was some random loony.'

'Well, believe it or not, he's someone I need to talk to,' I told her. 'For the book. His story's really important.'

Which was what I kept repeating to myself as I slouched down to the Devonshire to meet him.

Granger was due back that night, but that was too late, and he didn't have the kind of mobile you could call in America. I knew he hadn't given Robin Leith my home phone number, but I desperately wanted to ask him who he thought could have done it. As far as I knew, only a handful of people knew we were doing the book, and none of them were friends of his. Still, there was one thing for certain – gossip travels fast in a small world. And the faces of the early eighties new-wave scene were a pretty exclusive club these days.

I'd spent most of the past two days finding out everything I could about Leith, Sylvana and Mood Violet, which included a couple of battered old albums salvaged from the bargain bins in the second-hand record shops along Inverness Street. They both had artfully blurred covers, blue and pink dreamscapes with little arcs of fairy lights and the shadowy silhouettes of a band in motion. The inside sleeves, replete with incomprehensible lyrics, had small band portraits in them.

On both, Sylvana was gorgeous – huge green eyes, deep red hair and matching Clara Bow lips. It was hard to reconcile those angelic features with the acid comments Gavin and Stevens had made about her. The music itself was like some dreamy electronic lullaby and she sung her Edward Lear lyrics in a voice as pure and ethereal as her face. Not only could I see where Vincent Smith was coming from, but I really had to commend him. You couldn't not want to give that one. Maybe Granger and Stevens were both secretly gay.

Still, they both said she had sent Leith round the bend, and those phone messages did nothing to disprove the fact. I'd played them back again so I could tape them on my dictaphone, and shuddered at how belligerently wasted he sounded. You'd imagine some hulking great Rangers fan waving a broken bottle on the other end of that voice. But from his picture at least, Leith looked like a frail, skinny bloke, with a carrotty crimped wedge haircut that didn't do much to enchance his pasty face. You could still see the acne on his temples.

Don't think I could blame her for running off with Vincent either.

The Devonshire Arms as well, that was a funny one. And not as in amusing.

It was a Goth Heritage Site of Olde Camden Towne, with a bloody great plaque on the outside of it proclaiming: Goth/ Alternative Venue and a jaw-dropping painting of a vampire woman's face on a spider's body to illustrate the point.

Was Leith taking the piss? Did he realise I lived in Camden and wanted to put me through the exquisite torture of being seen going into this shithole? Or was he, like those sad old gits at the Red Lion, trying to keep his past in limbo by drinking in the same pub as the children of his original fans?

Whatever it was, I was taking certain precautions with Leith. Because I wasn't sure whether he was going to talk to me or try and do me over for besmirching the memory of his precious Sylvana, I had arranged back-up. Christophe was going to be in the pub from half twelve, so that when he saw me come in he could keep an eye on proceedings from across the room. Leith might know who I was, but he sure as hell didn't know Christophe, and Christophe – half Romany, six foot two and dressed like Henry Hill – was not the sort of person you'd want to find out about the hard way. In the ten years I'd known him, he'd only lost one fight, and that was to some ju-jitsu master who'd kicked out one of his front teeth. To reproach himself for his lack of attention to detail, Christophe had never had that tooth replaced. With him at my back I had no reason to feel nervous.

I walked through Sainsbury's car park, which came out practically at the Devonshire's door. That way, I hoped, no one would see me go in there.

I looked at my imitation Tag Heuer watch before I went in. It was five to one. I had no fucking idea what Robin Leith was going to look like now, but it was safe to assume he was probably going to be the oldest person in the room.

Sunday lunch in the house of heathens was a sight to behold. The place was heaving with Euro goths, wobbling on top of twelve-inch wedge boots with bloody great armour-plating all up the front of them. Every spare inch of their faces had been pierced, bolted and chained, and crowning glories of red, black, fuchsia or canary-yellow mohawks and spikes burst out over deathly faces of uniform blank gormlessness. Marilyn Manson was grinding out of the jukebox, moaning on about the beautiful people in a way that, in that moment, transcended irony.

Above the spiky heads, I could just make out Christophe standing at the bar, looking like he should have changed his name to Pissed Off. He was reading *The News of the Screws* and drinking a pint. Wearing a camel-hair coat and a fedora, his neat little goatee trimmed to a strip between his lower lip and his chin. When he saw me, he raised one eyebrow and subtly nodded to the dimmest corner of the room.

With porridge face and staring eyes, Leith looked like some golem who had sat in these shadows for twenty years, purposefully avoiding all daylight. Time had not filled him out at all, instead he was skinnier still, and as I neared his table, the acne scars and hollow cheeks became more visible. His hair had been cropped back to a number three, and great patches of white had spread amongst the carrots.

He was wrapped in a black crombie and he rocked slightly back and forth as he stared out of the window with hooded, watery blue eyes. An untouched pint of Guinness sat before him on the table, a packet of rolling tobacco, skins and a box of matches beside it.

I cleared my throat and his head snapped round, his eyes seeming to take a few seconds to focus.

'Excuse me,' I said to him, 'are you Robin?'

His eyes were so pale they were almost translucent.

He looked me up and down, raised a roll-up to his lips, sparked it up slowly and inhaled. 'Eddie,' he said softly, indicating the chair opposite with the merest tilt of his head. 'Ah see you got the message.'

There was a curious stillness, like dead air around him. He was a man who had waited so long already he could sit here for another eternity before telling me what he really wanted. So I resisted the urge to ask how the hell he got my number, and smiled encouragingly instead.

'Can I get you a drink?' I asked.

Leith looked at me as if I was some kind of fool and did another one of his almost imperceptible nods towards his brimming glass. 'Ah've got one.'

'Right. Ah…I'll just get myself one then. Won't be a minute.'

I dived into the space by Christophe's elbow, my back towards the decomposing goth spectre. Looking ahead, I muttered: 'I'm glad you're here.'

Christophe concurred. 'Looks like a right fucking nightmare.'

'Thanks for this,' I told him, leaving another pint on the bar in front of him and taking my own back to Leith's table.

He was looking out of the window again, but the gaze was seeing far beyond the remit of Sainsbury's car park.

I fumbled into my seat, pulling my fags and lighter out of the pocket as I did so. Leith continued to stare into space. So I took a long gulp of lager and lit up myself, wondering how to begin this conversation.

'S'pose yer wonderin' how ah came by yer number, eh?' my companion growled, not moving.

'Er, well, yes I did wonder,' I admitted, trying not to sound too perturbed about it. 'Do we have a mutual friend?'

He swivelled his head round to look at me.

'Well, ah have plenty to wonder about mahself,' he told me, and nodded to himself. 'Like, wha' are youze up teh? Young guy like you. Wha' de youze know about anything, eh?'

Anger flared in those watery eyes. I held my hands up, palms open.

'Look, I don't understand…'

'Nah.' Leith shook his head vigorously. 'That's obvious. Youz dunnae understand shite. Take a look around youze,' he swung his arm around wildly. 'Look at all these wee gobshites fuckin' twenty years outta date. Ahsh just a funny wee fashion to all of youze, eh? And youze,' he jabbed a grimy fingernail right under my nose. 'Youze wannin' to make some money outta all this, eh? Thash why youz writin' this book? Youze wanna make some money outta my girul?'

He practically screamed this last sentence, flecks of spittle flying from his rubbery, toothless mouth. Not that anyone noticed above the industrial jackhammer noise thumping out of the jukebox.

Jesus Christ, I thought, he is a fucking Grade A berserker. But he'd sussed me out in a second – that's why he'd brought me to this bloody awful goth pub. The thought sent a small tremor of fear up my spine.

'You've got it all wrong,' I said, surprising even myself with the calmness of my voice. 'I'm not trying to exploit anyone at all. I'm actually trying to find out the truth...'

This made him laugh and it was not a pleasant sound. 'The truth, aye, that's a good one. Wha' truth would that be then, eh?'

'Your side of the story,' I tried to encourage him. 'You know what effect Vincent had on Sylvana. Everyone I've spoken to so far has painted her as the villain, but they're all people who had their own investments in him succeeding. You could be a vital counterpoint to those accusations. You could tell them what she was really like.'

A good point well made, I thought, but Leith just carried on laughing, as if he couldn't believe what I was saying.

'Well, don't you even want to put the record straight?' I battled on. 'I presumed that's why you got in touch with me?'

'Och, dear, that's wha' youze *presumed*, is it?' he cackled, stressing the word in a mockery of my accent and virtually clutching his sides with glee.

I looked at his smug, sneering face and the fear started to transmute into anger.

'OK, you tell me,' I snapped. 'How did you get my number and why did you ask me to meet you when you obviously only want to sit here and insult me? Just a way of getting your jollies, is it?'

'Nae, is no.' Leith's countenance suddenly turned to stone. He leaned forward, clutching his coat around him like the wings of a big, greasy crow and hissed. 'Ah'm deadly serious, pal. Youze goes proddin' around amongst the deed like this an' don' be surprised a what springs up outta the coffin.'

I slowly wiped off the saliva he'd just sprayed across my face.

'Are you threatening me?' I asked.

This made him smile again. 'Ach Eddie,' he tilted his head to one side, 'are youze gonna start throwin' yer toys outta yer pram now?'

I groaned aloud. I should have known better than to respond to this weirdo. It steadily dawned on me that no matter how he got my number, if I hadn't have shown up today, he wouldn't have even known it was the right one.

Fools rush in and all that.

'Do you actually have anything of interest to say to me?' I asked wearily.

'Yeah,' he smiled. 'I knew Sylvana and youze didnae. That means youze have nae right wha'soever to write abou' her. Ah've asked youze here so's ah could suss out wha' type of guy you really are – no' that there's much hope with any of youze journalist types, youze all the same. And frankly, Eddie, ah don' really like wha' ah see. But ah'm gonnae ask youze once nicely. Stop writin' this book. The worruld doesnae need to know any more about the stupid mistake mah lass made with tha' big prick Smith. Storp glorifyin' that bastid an' let her rest in peace. Otherwise I won't let you, d'yuh ken, pal?'

I was starting to get the picture.

'Now I know that is youze number,' he continued, 'an' I know what youze look like. Soon enough I'll know where you live.

Ah'm pretty sure you wouldnae want me to be makin' regular visits, eh?'

I stood up, heart hammering, red fog coming down. I wanted to pound this prick into the pavement right then and there, but that was probably exactly what he wanted. He did look like he thrived on pain.

'You know, Robin,' I said to him instead, 'everyone told me you were a fuck-up and a nutter but I thought no, I'm not going to take their word for it, I'm sure he has his own story and it's a story worth hearing. Well, how wrong I was. You are a nutter. God, what a fucking nightmare it must be, living in your head.' I grimaced sarcastically. 'Tatty bye then, Robin. Let me know if you ever make it back to the real world.'

Before I slammed out of the door, I looked over at Christophe who had moved closer to our table, obviously noting things weren't turning out well. He caught my eye and nodded.

Outside I walked up Kentish Town Road as fast as my legs would carry me. My hands were clenching and unclenching and I was grinding my teeth, hissing a stream of expletives under my breath. Fear and rage combined – rage that I had been duped so easily by such a lowlife; fear that he would carry out his home invasion threat and Louise would get caught in the crossfire.

I wondered if this was part of the prick's plan too, get me to leave in a huff and lead him straight back to my door. A C2 bus was pulling into the stop in front of me. Without looking back to check, I made a dash for it and swung myself on board.

As I moved down the aisle I looked out of the window just in time to clock us passing Robin Leith, halfway between the pub and the bus stop. For a second our eyes met and I feverishly hoped he'd noted I was going in the direction of Hampstead Heath.

A few paces back, Christophe was walking behind him.

Jesus Christ, I thought, falling into a seat. This was supposed to be easy. A few lunches with some middle-aged musicians, how much trouble can that get you into?

I rode the C2 all the way up to the Heath, where I got off and headed up into the wilds, stomping against the wind through the thick grass until I was on top of the hill from where you can see the whole of London spread out before you. Horrible day though it was, there were still people up there, jolly Hampstead types flying kites with their kids and walking their Weimaraners, so I didn't bother to take in the panorama, just kept on walking, getting as far away from them as possible. The weather matched my mood: a dismal symphony of thundering grey storm clouds whipped across the sky by a spiteful north-easterly wind.

I must have spent a couple of hours up there, trying to work out what the fuck I was going to tell Louise if that nutter ever did turn up on our doorstep, when my mobile started vibrating in my pocket, pulling me back to reality.

I took care of that thing for you the text read and I smiled. Christophe was using our *Goodfellas* code. *I'm in the Stanley now if you fancy a decent drink.*

This was more heartening still. I made my way back to civilisation and grabbed the first cab I could find.

11

The Flesh is Willing

October 1977

'I hear you've got yourself a band, Stevie. A punk band, am I right?' Don Dawson smiled across his desk, revealing a row of pointed teeth that reminded Stevie of a shark. A shark with a lot of gold fillings.

'Well, aye, I have,' Stevie shrugged. 'But we've only been goin' a few months. We've only just got ourselves a singer...'

Dawson chuckled, relaxing back into his leather chair. 'Thought that was what it were all about, Stevie lad, just pick up some instruments and gerron a stage. You don't need to practise owt, do you? I didn't think you young 'uns cared if it sounded shite? I thought—' he blew three smoke rings out of his cigar and firmly eyeballed his youthful charge '—it were all about the attitude.'

This room was all about the attitude all right. This was Dawson's inner sanctum, the room at the top of Hull's biggest nightclub, the Ocean Rooms, and everything about it spoke of the man's progress in the world.

Dawson sat behind a heavy mahogany desk, on which were

placed a giant table lighter, a cigar humidifier and some kind of sculpture-cum-ashtray that was supposed to give off a whiff of high culture. His throne was a big, black leather upholstered armchair that swivelled around, facing another set of black leather chairs that had no such facility, so that his associates could feel comfortable but know their place at the same time. To Old King Hull's right was a teak cocktail cabinet on which crystal decanters full of Scotch and brandy stood on a little turntable that spun gently around and played a dinky tune when you took out the stoppers.

To his left was a rack of pool cues. Seeing as there was no actual pool table in the office, it didn't take much imagination to work out what they were there for. On the wall above the desk hung a portrait of Mrs Pauline Dawson as the youthful beauty queen she had been when they'd first met in the sixties, a tiara resting on her black, bouffanted hair, a blue sash around an elegant white cocktail dress. The frame was ornate, dull gold rococo and likely as not the safe was hidden behind it.

There were other framed photographs around the walls, Don meeting various celebrities at his clubs – Bernard Manning, Joe Bugner, Harvey Smith, Brian Jacks, Julie Goodyear, Hurricane Higgins. These were more discreetly done, as if to say, I know them, aye, but I don't have to boast about it.

Stevie had been summoned here this Saturday morning by a message relayed to his brother Connor by Terry and Barry. Don wanted to pick Stevie's brains, they'd said, which had made them all laugh. As if he had any.

But Don had counted the takings for that night at The Outlook and confirmed his suspicions about where the future lay. Lately he'd been filling his clubs with concerts by more of these punk types. Gen X. The Damned. The Buzzcocks over from Manchester. It were starting to look like a licence to print money.

Stevie mulled over this last question before answering.

Since Vince had joined the band, Blood Truth's progress hadn't simply been about getting a useable live set together. They'd had other, personal stuff to sort out first.

Going back to school had put a bit of strain on things. Gary Dunton had caused havoc with Kevin, accusing him of all sorts and threatening him with a kicking for getting out of line. Actually, Stevie suspected Kev had taken one hiding already, although he hadn't said owt. He were all for settling the cunt once and for all, but Kevin had to live next to Dunton and pleaded with Stevie to leave it. At the moment, they were getting away with using Kevin's 'orchestra' night as an excuse, but sooner or later it were obvious that would fall apart.

Most nights, Lynton and Stevie rehearsed together, working out songs and trying out new ideas. Just as he'd picked up the bass so quickly, Lynton was getting pretty handy on drums too, so they could shift instruments around when they wanted. If they weren't playing their own music they'd be listening to John Peel or playing Stevie's latest pickings from Sidney Scarborough's. Lynton's folks didn't seem to mind Stevie being round their house the whole time, which were a bonus, considering he didn't want to be anywhere near his own.

Then, at weekends, Vince's girlfriend Rachel would bring him down in her horrible orange and white Citroen Diane and he'd have more lyrics to put to their budding creations.

That Rachel were a weird one, Stevie thought. She obviously came from a rich family, had that look about her that she'd never wanted for owt. She looked too clean, her clothes too well cut, however skinny and arty she was. With clear, almost translucent skin and dyed black hair, she was willowy and remote, always hiding behind sunglasses and never speaking. Not that she hung around much any road, just dropped Vince off and then picked him up later, fuck knows what she got up to in between. Maybe she joined Pauline Dawson in the beauty parlour, getting her hair done by experts.

Now that it had been a few weeks, even Stevie had noticed

an air of tension afflict Lynton whenever Vince walked through the door. He'd go all stiff-legged and prickly, like a cat with its hackles up, which were funny really, 'cos Vince always seemed to go out of his way to be nice to him, asking him loads of questions about them old jazzers Lynton liked so much. And Lynton always answered him politely but he never let things roll into an actual conversation. Stevie couldn't quite work out why, but something told him not to bring it up when they were on their own. Everyone had things they didn't want to talk about.

Still, once they got playing they didn't need words. They were just brilliant. They'd all loved 'New Rose' so much they'd decided it needed to be in the set, although they'd ditched 'Anarchy' 'cos Vince didn't want to sing it. What he did love, though, was Link Wray's 'Rumble', a tune Stevie had picked up from Terry and Barry's tapes. They'd told him it were the original punk rock, the first record to get banned for starting knife fights in the States – and there weren't even any words. Not only had Link invented distortion, he was also a Red Indian and looked like Crazy Horse with a quiff. That made him a fucking hero in Stevie's book.

Vince had never heard of Link but he loved the slow menace of his signature tune so much that he'd suggested it be the first number in their set, priming the audience before Vince made an entrance. They were gonna try and segue it into another tune they'd been working on, which Vince had the words for but no title and the two had started to fuse into one seething mass which Stevie dubbed 'Grumble'.

So they had a start and they had an end, but in-between it were all a bit sketchy. Though Dawson had a point, that weren't supposed to matter.

'Why?' he cocked his head to one side and smiled back at the club manager. 'What you after?'

'That's my boy,' Dawson grinned. 'My lad on the inside. I've seen the future, Stevie, as well as you have. The money that these bands make…' He watched another smoke ring drift up towards the ceiling, then looked Stevie straight in the eye. 'I'm looking to expand my business interests, lad. I've done right nice putting these punk bands on at my clubs, right nice indeed. Made a lot of interesting contacts and all. Makes sense to build on that. Tck a leaf out of that McLaren's book, eh? So, what I need is some raw, home-grown talent…'

'What you saying?' Stevie wanted to get this clear. 'You want to be our manager or summat?'

'That's right,' Dawson nodded. 'I knew you weren't daft.'

'But you've not heard owt.'

'I don't need to,' Dawson leaned forward across his desk. 'I know it's not Frank Sinatra, son, and that's as far as my musical appreciation extends. Punk rock, funk rock, heavy metal – it's all the same racket to me. But I saw you and that coloured lad at Sex Pistols show. You know what it's all about, what kids want,' he nodded meaningfully and continued.

'Stevie lad, I couldn't give two shakes of a pygmy's ballbag what you sound like, but I do trust your judgement. You be the ears of this operation and I'll be the brains.'

He let that one sink in for a minute, enjoying the huge, shit-eating grin that slowly stole across Stevie's face.

'So when you've had enough time to get your little act together, come back and see us, all of you.' Dawson made a bit of a show about fishing his business card out of the inside pocket of his jacket and handing it over. It was gold with black writing and a little DD emblem with a pair of dice underneath it.

'Only don't take too long, eh?'

Dawson had them sign the contract the night they played the gig. It was 31 October, Halloween, and two days after the Pistols had released *Never Mind the Bollocks* to another firestorm of media outrage. Dawson had watched that record shop being closed down for stocking 'obscene material' on the news and chuckled to himself at fate's providence. The tickets for Blood Truth's debut gig at the Ocean Rooms had already sold out. They had a lot of friends, them Mullinses.

Just so that Stevie felt a true measure of his power, he'd had the lad help with the fly-postering campaign, running round the city centre after dark with a roll of the posters that Rachel had designed, a bucket of paste and a ladder. Copper had caught him halfway up his steps outside Sidney Scarborough's.

'What's that there, lad?' he'd said.

'Fuck,' Stevie had replied.

The copper had made a long show of studying the poster, making sarcastic comments as he did so, like: 'One of those punk rockers are you? Flamin' puff rock if you ask me.' Finally, he'd squinted at the bit that mentioned the Ocean Rooms.

'One of Don's, is it?' He leered up at Stevie, still wobbling on his perch.

Not trusting his own mouth, Stevie just nodded.

'All right then, son,' copper said. 'I'll pretend this never happened. But don't let me catch you again, like.'

Stevie had fled into the night. The copper and Dawson had a right laugh about that later, over a whisky in Don's office.

'Let the lad know who's in charge here,' Dawson had said. 'Just in case he gets any big ideas when money starts rolling in.'

He looked at them now, eagerly scrawling their names across the papers he'd had his lawyer draw up in the name of his latest company, Dawsongs. Papers that gave Dawson fifty per cent of anything the band were likely to ever earn. They could have said anything, mind. But they were too keen to even read the large print, the lot of 'em. Well, who else was gonna take this lot seriously? Who else was gonna nurture their teenage dreams?

He looked at Stevie, big and hard and Irish, with that rogue's smile and wandering eyes. He had brains enough but wore his longings so transparently on his sleeve it wouldn't be hard to keep him happy. Lynton, long thin and nervous, rolling his huge eyes up and down, too shy to hold a gaze for a second. Would be no trouble from that one either – long as they kept him away from British Legion, like. Little drummer, what were his name, might have a problem convincing people he was legally old enough. The only one of them who caused a slight flicker of doubt to momentarily cross Don's cash register of a mind was Vince Smith.

Terry and Barry despised him, but that were their lookout. He was just a thug who fancied himself as far as Dawson could see, sprawled out on his chair with his great clodhopping zebra skin brothel creepers hovering annoyingly close to the corner of his desk.

Vince Smith wore dark shades so you couldn't look him in the eye. His hair was thick with what looked like boot polish and he had a dog chain padlocked around his neck. He smoked endless cigarettes and dropped ash on the floor; he were a lout with no manners but that didn't worry Don. What actually made him uncomfortable was the girl he brought with him and made stand at the back of the room while they all did the business.

Tall, skinny wraith in a stripy black and white top, she looked more like a beatnik than a punk. Dawson caught the unmistakable undernote of money in the way that her hair had been cut – his Pauline often lectured him on how you could tell the difference between a good cut and Choppy Chops on the High Street, and this one looked like she'd been sheared by Vidal Sasoon himself. She were wearing shades an' all, but Don had caught a glimpse of something underneath as she'd meekly bowed her head down and tried to turn away rather than shake his hand and greet him. A purple streak, under her left eye. Could have just been her make-up like, but Don's instinct told him it was what he thought it was. His impression was backed up by the way lass stood meekly up against the wall, head bowed, obviously not wanting to be there but taking her orders nonetheless. He watched Vince slash his name across the paper in a big, spidery scrawl and thought: I've got a live one here.

Not that he let any of it filter through his smile, mind.

'Right, lads, that's that sorted out,' he said, standing to shake each one of the weird-looking tykes by the hand. 'Now, I believe it's showtime.'

Lynton stared out between the gap in the curtain at the side of the stage, across their assembled equipment: the drumkit, the mic stands, the wall of amps and the monitors on the front of the stage to the audience beyond. It gave him a rush, halfway between ecstasy and sphincter-clenching fear to see how many there were of them. He'd no idea there were this many weirdos in Hull.

The ones near the bar at the back looked older, the seasoned gig-goers nonchalantly swilling their pints, friends of Stevie's brother in their leathers and greased-back hair. There were still some hippy types in there too, but assembled around the front looked to be the entire audience from the Sex Pistols gig transplanted into the Ocean Rooms. They brought with them the hum of expectation and chatter, those ripples of excitement he had felt so keenly in Donny. Only this time, it wasn't going to be Johnny Rotten up there on stage. This time it was gonna be him.

They'd worked it all out so many times now, and closing his eyes for a moment, Lynton recalled the exact chord sequences he needed to play to. His bass was slung over his shoulder, its thick neck a comfort to his nervous fingers, as he silently plucked out the trusted notes. Lynton was going on stage first.

He felt a hand on his shoulder.

'All right, Lynt?' Stevie sounded calmer than he felt, but his eyes were wired, sparkling pinpricks as he surveyed their impatient audience. 'What a fucking turn out.'

'I know,' Lynton nodded. 'It's unreal.'

'You ready to do this?'

They locked eyes. 'I'm ready, thank you for this, man.'

And with that he stepped beyond the curtain, out onto the stage, the only black man in the room. He daren't even look at them, but he heard a cheer go up and his blood rushed to his ears. Nimbly, he plugged his bass into the monitor, hit the strings and felt the roar of noise amplified louder than anything they'd ever gone near in rehearsal. Felt that surge of power again as his fingers formed the chord and he started to play the undulating rhythm. At first he kept his eyes shut as he swayed on the spot, letting the music take him. Then, when he heard Kevin come in behind him and touch the drums with his brushes he opened them.

The whole crowd was swaying along with him.

It was a blur of colour and heat, their eyes all turned towards him not in mockery or hatred, but in what looked like awe. The great slabs of noise he was generating were holding them there, in the palm of his hand.

Miles, he thought, this is what you knew. This is what you were trying to tell me.

Then suddenly Stevie was beside him and another cheer came up from the throng as his fingers skidded across the guitar sending great screes of sound shrieking through the atmosphere. Stevie looked like he had swelled to twice his size, buoyed up on adrenalin and excitement. The punks down the front started pogoing, someone shouting: 'Go on, Stevie!'

Stevie's Link Ray bastardisation sounded brilliant – cacophonous, discordant, wild as its original author had intended. If 'Grumble' had sounded good in rehearsal with their tinny amps and the reverb from the garage walls, it sounded completely awesome to the band's ears now.

Then, like a thin black streak, Vince slunk out of the sidelines, his hands raised above his head, palms outwards, fingers splayed. Reaching the centre of the stage, he lurched at his mic, pulled it off the stand and coiled the lead around his fist. Putting his right foot up onto the monitor, he leaned out over the crowd like the deranged preacher of his vivid imagination. His lips touched the mic and he began to whoop and holler: '*Whoooo! Whooooo! Do you believe?*'

The effect was electrifying.

Hands reached out from the audience, punching the air, some trying to grab at his T-shirt. The girls in the crowd looked as if they were witnessing the arrival of the Messiah; Lynton could see their eyes widen as they took in this spectacle, this raggedy, raven-haired king.

'Do you believe?' demanded Vince.

'We believe!' one punk shouted back.

'Do you believe?' Vince pointed his skinny finger out accusatorily around the room.

'Fuck yeah!' someone screamed. Then the rest joined in. Fists flew towards the ceiling. The throng around the front of the stage took one form, became one amorphous being, swaying under Vince's imaginary pulpit.

It was as if an aura of power formed around his long, skinny frame. He stepped down from the monitor, began intoning the lyrics he'd had scrawled down in his little girl's notebook, pacing the stage in circles like a panther in captivity, coiled and ready for attack. Lynton and Stevie shot each other a glance that said: Is this really happening?

Then, from out of the corner of his eye, Lynton saw something coming from the side of the bar. A flash of red hair, frizzed up into a ludicrous ball around a wide, ugly, all-too familiar face.

Oh no, he thought. Not him.

But it was.

A face contorted in anger, a mouth forming vile words, a sausage finger jabbing the air, pointing towards him.

Gary Dunton, surrounded by Barney Lee and the Brothers Grim, Malc and Martin Carver. All standing at the bar, wearing their hooligan uniform of flared jeans, denim jackets and Leeds United shirts. It didn't look like they'd stopped in to buy a drink either. They were here for one reason and one reason only:

Trouble.

Lynton's eyes flicked over to Kevin. Absorbed in his playing, he was looking down his sticks; he hadn't noticed yet.

Stevie was grinding away next to him; he hadn't noticed either. Lynton felt the cold chills running down his spine. He couldn't drag his eyes away. Dunton appeared to have worked his way into a thermonuclear rage. Everything about him was red – his hair, his face, the whites of his eyes. He looked like a slab of raw steak sizzling on a spit. For a moment or two, he and his cronies argued amongst themselves. Maybe they weren't too sure of themselves in present company, maybe even they realised that here it was them who were out of place.

Whatever their beef was, Dunton wasn't standing for it long. He turned away from them, gesticulating with his arm that they should follow, and began pushing his way through the crowd.

Kevin looked up. Kevin noticed. Kevin heard Dunton scream: 'Nigger lover! You're fucking dead, Kevin Holme.'

'Keep playing,' shouted Lynton. 'Don't listen to him.'

Kevin dragged his gaze away over to the bass player and nodded almost imperceptibly. He kept moving his arms up and down even as his stomach hit the floor, kept beating away at the skins as he watched with horror his next-door neighbour burrowing through the punks and freaks, his eyes wild with hatred and rage.

By now, Stevie had clocked it too, had moved right to the front of the stage, yelling: 'Fuck off out of it!'

'Ooo! Ooo! Oooo!' Dunton and his apes chanted back, drinks flying up in the air as they bulldozed their way through the crowd.

'Dead, Kevin!' Dunton repeated. 'Dead, d'you hear me, you traitor!'

'Fuck off!' screamed Stevie. Lynton and Kevin exchanged nervous glances, but kept on playing like their lives depended on it. Perhaps at that moment they actually did.

Dunton got right up to the lip of the stage, Barney and the brothers pushing people off him left and right. Terry and Barry were winnowing their way towards the knot of trouble, but by now they were also having to deal with outraged members of the audience thinking that they, too, were trying to start a fight. The whole area in front of the stage had become a teeming pit. From three minutes of sheer rapture, it looked like everything was about to go to hell.

Then Vince leaned down from the stage and pushed his hand right in Dunton's face. Long fingers crunched into his cheekbones, a palm pushed his noise back so sharply a bright pain brought tears into his eyes.

'And ah see we have one here who does not believe!' Vince roared into his mic.

Dunton's hands flailed in front of his face, trying to bat his assailant away. But Vince was much taller, his reach much longer, his grasp as rigid as iron. As the singer leapt down from the stage, Dunton felt a sickening crunch and blood spurted out of his newly broken conk. His legs threatened to buckle under him but already, Vince was propelling Dunton backwards and the crowd parted involuntarily to let them pass.

Slow on the uptake, Barney Lee at last tried to swing for Vince but Stevie was right behind him, thwacking him round the back of his bony shaved head with the stock of his guitar.

'Get them!' he yelled across to Terry and Barry, motioning with his head to Malc and Martin Carver, who were having problems of their own with a couple of hefty punks. 'I'll deal with this shite.'

But it was Vince who was really dealing with things. The crowd started to cheer as he continued to march Dunton backwards at the end of his arm, pouring scorn non-stop through his still-wired microphone while globs of blood and snot ran over his hand and his prey choked for breath.

'We have a sinner in our midst! This snivelling worm at the

end of my arm thinks that he is a man! We will show him his folly! The error of his ways!'

Barney Lee weaved unsteadily around in front of Stevie, as if trying to focus. Stevie headbutted him and he dropped to the floor.

Lynton and Kevin continued to play; luckily they knew their parts off by heart as what was unravelling before them was enough to break anyone's concentration. Giving them the thumbs up, Stevie hauled himself back on stage for a better look.

Vince's mic lead was on a long cable, but it was about to run out as he neared the back of the hall. He thrust it into the hands of one of the Teds standing by the bar. But he didn't let go of Dunton.

Everything Dunton had imagined would happen this evening had been totally turned on its head. The little thug had not forgotten what Stevie Mullin had done to him at school and how he had then had the cheek to go on and take Kevin away from him. He had brooded all summer long on how stupid Kevin was to think that he, the all-seeing Dunton, wouldn't realise what was going on. But all the same, he had bided his time, while building himself up with his dad's Bullworker and extra judo classes. Much as he hated him, he didn't underestimate Mullin. Tonight, however, he'd felt ready. Ready to rub Kevin's nose in it for defying him. Ready to knock Stevie's block off.

He hadn't reckoned on this. On this wild-eyed maniac with superhuman strength; where the fuck had he come from? Dunton couldn't see where he was being pushed, could hardly stay upright, his only blessing was that he was too wired with adrenalin to actually feel the pain that would soon come crashing down around him.

Vince pushed the flailing, flapping creature right out of the room and out of the door, right past the bouncer at the entrance and didn't stop until they were standing by the top of the stairs.

Then the singer dropped his preacher's voice and said in a voice as cold as steel: 'Don't ever try to fuck with my band again. Or next time, I'll really hurt you.'

Then he let go of his hand and Dunton fell backwards down the stairs.

Terry and Barry appeared in the doorway, the Brothers Grim in armlocks in front of them. They looked at Vince now with new eyes. Maybe the daft bugger had his uses after all.

'Ta, mate,' said Barry.

'Yeah, you can go back to work now,' added Terry.

Vince smiled a twisted smile and watched Malc and Martin go toppling after their leader. Then he turned back into the room where the Ted still had hold of his mic and an incredulous expression all of his own.

Vince snatched it back.

'Brothers and sisters!' he roared. 'Ah have expelled the sinner from our midst!' He opened his arms wide as if he had just witnessed a miracle. His right hand was smeared in Dunton's blood.

From the stage, Stevie cheered, cranked up the 'Rumble' riff in double speed as a salute to his conquering comrade. Lynton and Kevin both thought about Vince too. He had really stood up for them. He had fucked off Dunton without having to be told, and what's more, he had taken the audience's loyalty with him, when everything could so easily have gone the other way.

From the wings, Don Dawson chuckled softly to himself, lighting another cigar with his gold Ronson lighter. He'd had his heart in his mouth for a moment when it looked like it were going to turn into a proper ruck, but the neat way that Smith had turned it round had impressed him. A live one all right, he ruminated. It reminded him of the Teddy Boy tours he'd witnessed in his youth, the Jerry Lee Lewis, Gene Vincent, Little Richard package put on by Don Arden – one of his business role models, who he hadn't forgotten when he put his faith in punk. Gene Vincent, that were who lad reminded him of: all black hair and leather. Danger on two legs.

His eyes travelled across the room and he drank in the admiration shining back at the singer from every face. He might be a nasty bastard, have that streak in him that went beyond the exuberance of youth, but what came with it was that rarest of commodities: star quality. The one thing that money couldn't buy.

Vince tried to make his way back through the crowd, but it was not to be. They hoisted him into the air and carried him back to the stage on their shoulders. He wiped their hair with the gore from Dunton's broken nose, kneaded the rest of it into his own raven crown.

First blood.

Part Two

12

Head Over Heels

April 1978

'That's it,' said Donna, pursing her lips at her reflection in the mirror. 'Before the night is out, Dave Vanian will be mine!'

The results of two hours plastering and preening gazed back at her. Donna's thick black hair had been crimped, sprayed, backcombed and bouffanted upwards into an enormous beehive shape so that she resembled the Bride of Frankenstein. Although Bride of Dracula was more what she was aiming for, Dracula himself being the equally raven-haired singer of The Damned. Tonight might be her last chance – it was the band's farewell gig at the Rainbow and Donna had been loudly proclaiming how she was going to ensnare him all day long.

As usual, Helen had been roped in, in the role of her dresser. She had to admit, she'd done a good job.

Underneath the virtually vertical mane, Donna's face was as white as death, thanks to the powder and foundation she had half inched when Helen showed her the theatrical shop on South Molton Street that they used for college supplies. Along with the black liquid eyeliner and false eyelashes that batted back to her from the mirror. The purple and white Reflections eyeshadow, Rouge Noir blush and Black Cherry lipstick were all by Miners, swiped from Woolies on Portobello Road.

They had first bumped into each other about a year and a half ago, down the 100 Club. Literally bumped into each other. Donna had emptied a pint of beer over Sylvana's head, for absolutely no reason at all, then stood there smirking while her victim's eyes filled up with tears. Helen, who had been more or less taking care of her very unworldly-wise American friend since the first day they'd met at the London College of Fashion, took charge of the situation. Using the technique that had so often subdued her brother, she'd grabbed Donna's arm and twisted it up around her back till she was in agony. Then she'd asked: 'What do you think you're doing?'

Donna had then apologised profusely, helped Helen mop Sylvana down in the bogs. That should have been that, but Sylvana, who genuinely believed it had all been an accident, had had to go and mention that they were fashion students. And that clever Helen was doing theatrical costuming. Donna had stuck fast to them for the rest of the evening. When she'd seen where they lived, there had been no getting rid of her.

Admittedly, Donna's sense of style was strong and her instinct uncanny. She often boasted about her rubberwear from Sex and the Seditionaries T-shirts that she'd taken while still in her school uniform, but as soon as she saw too many other people wearing the same, she would ditch them and move on. When she saw Helen's pattern-cutting blocks, the corsets she had been required to make for coursework and her first experiments in millinery – a black velvet top hat – she had been entranced. Helen loved the Victorians, and Victoriana was where Donna saw herself headed next – thanks to the influence of Dave. She had begged, wheedled and cajoled Helen into helping her fashion her own outfits, and tonight's really was some kind of triumph.

It was constructed from half a lace Victorian dress and a

Fifties net petticoat – that was Donna's way of saying up yours to the rival Teds. Helen had shown Donna how to dye the two things black by dissolving big, inky tablets into in a huge iron pot over the stove, a process that took about two days. Which, of course, had to be done in the students' flat, Donna's mum 'would have killed' her if she'd tried it at home. Then Helen had tailored the two garments together with a corset acting as the waistband. Winched inside, Donna looked breathtaking. Fishnet tights and a pair of black stilettos completed this vision of glamour *gothique*.

Yet even as she posed in front of the mirror, Helen could see the sideways glances Donna cast at Sylvana, who sat at her feet, painting her own eyeshadow on with painstaking slowness. Donna looked at Sylvana the way a cat looks at a mouse.

Donna had Sylvana totally hooked on her every word and style dictum. Gone was the thick thatch of brown hair she had come to London with; in its place a razor cut, dyed ruby red with the colours Donna decanted from her day job, hairdressing on the King's Road.

Good with her hands, was Donna.

It made Sylvana look ethereally pretty, that haircut. She would never have got away with it at home, in New Jersey, where her textile magnate parents kept her as cosseted as they possibly could. She had only been allowed to come to London as part of her training, so she would know more about the business of fashion when it was her time to take the helm. And only then because one of her uncles had this mansion flat in South Kensington, just round the corner from all the museums. Her parents had spent time there before, they knew the place was respectable. The uncle himself was hardly ever around; he was always flying off around the world, making even more money, something the family were obviously extremely good at. They had only seen him twice in all the time they'd been here.

Helen had watched Donna taking all these details in. Once the full magnitude of Sylvana's richness had sunk in, Donna had made every effort to be her best friend, showing her all the hippest hangouts, taking her to all the best gigs. And at the same time, gradually moving in to the spare room. Helen had tried to subtly hint that perhaps she might be trying to take advantage, but as Sylvana kept saying, poor Donna was from a deprived background. Her parents lived in that dreadful new tower block near Portobello Road, the Tower of Terror the tabloids called it. Everyone knew it was a dump, used by anyone who fancied it as a public toilet and shooting gallery, glue-sniffers and skagheads roaming the stairwells at all hours. Sylvana said she shuddered to think of poor Donna going back there late at night. Or even in the daytime.

'You look incredible, doll,' Sylvana said to Donna's reflection. 'How could he ever resist?'

'He couldn't,' agreed Helen, who had been ready for about an hour already. 'Although, if you do want him to notice you, we'd better get our arses down there before the gig finishes…'

They travelled down to Finsbury Park on the Piccadilly line. Most people looked away from them as they got on the carriage, as if they'd just stepped out of 1666 with a big sign saying: 'Unclean' around their necks and someone ringing a bell in front of them. Donna liked it when they looked away. It showed a healthy fear. But then there would always be one who would want to start something, and sure enough when they got to the stop for Holborn, some starched suit with his briefcase thought it was about time he passed comment. 'Disgraceful,' he pronounced, running his eyes up and down the three of them.

'Beg your pardon?' Donna shouted back. Lounging in her seat, her fishnet legs crossed in front of her with one ankle idly twitching from left to right, she was the picture of sullen disdain.

The man cleared his throat. He had a salt-and-pepper moustache and sticking out ears, pale, watery eyes, and an ordered neatness to him that suggested he had once been in the military. With his pinstripe suit and black Macintosh, shining shoes and briefcase, bowler hat and brolly, he couldn't have been more the proper city gent than Donna could have been the epitome of degeneracy.

'I said you are disgraceful!' snapped the man, his face colouring vividly. 'You look like nothing but whores!'

Donna merely raised one painted eyebrow. 'Looks like you would know,' she said.

'Well, I...' the man blustered for a second, looked round the carriage for support. Everyone else was busy minding their own business, deep in a book, the *Evening Standard*, fast asleep or catching flies. Everyone was looking anywhere but at the three punk girls and him.

And the punk girl with black hair was looking at him bold as brass, bold as *a* brass indeed with her lurid lipstick and insolent eyes.

'I won't lower myself,' he said aloud and pinged open his own briefcase, from which to extract the *Financial Times* he had already given a thorough going over once today. Ruffling the pages loudly and clearing his throat, he emulated the other passengers' studied indifference all too late.

Donna laughed herself into hysterics, Sylvana giggling along nervously. Helen wondered when this kind of behaviour would start getting really dangerous. Helen had had enough of Donna. But Sylvana was still totally in awe of her. Sylvana still had an awful lot to learn.

At the door of the Rainbow Theatre converged a scene out of the city gent's worst nightmare, a *Night of the Living Dead* on Seven Sisters Road, all come to dance on The Damned's premature grave. It wasn't just Donna who had been captivated by Dave's vampire chic, but, as her rolling eyes struggled to take in the line of potential love rivals, there didn't appear to be anyone here who looked a patch on her. Swaggering in her stilettos, a trail of glances like glittering daggers followed in her wake. It gave even more of a swing to her step.

It was a cold night for the time of year, but none of the trio felt it. A legacy of the minus zero New Jersey winters, Sylvana had brought an array of fur coats over from the States. While lesser punks made do with the fake leopardskin they could find from the second-hand shops and markets, Sylvana, Donna and Helen were warmly wrapped up in real mink and silver fox.

Inside the venue, these were quickly dispensed to the cloakroom as the temperature shot up in the humid throng of bodies, all waiting to light punk's funeral pyre. Brian James had announced in February that he wanted to leave the band, who had already lost their founding drummer Rat Scabies, and it seemed better to burn the thing to the ground in one last act of defiance than let things meander on with stick-on members plastering over their legacy.

The girls had already missed most of the support, not that this particularly bothered them. They'd already seen Johnny Moped too many times at other people's gigs and Prof and the Profettes were just The Damned's roadie and their new drummer, Jon Moss.

The final entertainment before the main event came in the underwhelming form of The Soft Boys, a bunch of Cambridge fops who sounded a bit too much to Helen's ears like her brother's hideous Pink Floyd records than anything genuinely punk. She was about to offer to go to the bar when Donna cut in, as if reading her mind.

'Ugh, I can't stand these lot. I met that singer once, down the Roxy or the 100 Club or somewhere – Jesus, he was fucking boring. I'll get the beers in, so I don't have to look at him.'

Helen and Sylvana idled their way down the side of the seats, closer to the front of the stage, to an angle where they thought they would be able to see The Damned better. Whether it was the dullness of the Soft Boys, or just the fact that things seemed to be running late, time passed awfully slowly, and every time they thought they had a good spot, they seemed to get pushed out of it by a crowd that was getting restless.

'What is she doing now?' wondered Helen crossly. The Soft Boys had been droning on for about ten minutes and there was still no sign of Donna or their drinks. It was getting really late now – approaching ten o'clock – and at the rate she was going the bar would soon be shut too.

Sylvana shrugged. 'Probably working an angle. Finding someone with an in to Dave.'

The two had found a fairly decent position by now, about halfway down the auditorium to the left of the stage, where they could get a view over the heads of the biggest guys who'd be rucking down the front the moment The Damned came on without getting dragged into their mêlée. It would be a pity to lose this spot, but those Soft Boys weren't getting any better.

Still, for the moment, most people remained seated.

'I knew I should have gone,' Helen sighed. 'I'm not going to get through any more of this bollocks without a beer and that's for sure.'

She cricked her neck and surveyed the room. Packed as it was, Donna wouldn't have been too hard to find under any circumstances. But it looked from here as if they were going to be left drinkless, and Helen fancied their chances of resolving that even less after this lot came offstage.

'Look, will you be all right here if I go?' Helen couldn't help feeling protective over her little Sylvana.

'Sure,' her companion nodded enthusiastically, wide eyes shining. 'You'll find me again OK, won't you?'

'Course.'

'But here, Helen, let me give you the money.'

Helen rolled her eyes.

'You already paid for us to be here…'

'Take it anyway!' Sylvana pressed a roll of notes into Helen's lace-gloved hand. 'And don't give me any of that "charity" crap, OK?'

'If your mother could hear you now,' said Helen, then winked and turned towards the bar.

It was a sea of spiky hair and leather that she had to wade through, and her eyesight was not the best. But by the time she'd managed to elbow her way through to being served she still hadn't seen where bloody Donna had got to. Best not buy her a drink then, she reasoned, especially as two pints are much easier to carry than three.

The Soft Boys were coming offstage. It was all Helen could do to keep the contents in the two plastic glasses she'd been given while she dodged her way back through what seemed like an army of thirsty ghouls heading straight for her. It obviously wasn't just she and Sylvana who'd been unimpressed with the support. Coins, bottles and bog rolls were being lobbed at the now empty stage. Cries of 'Come on then!', 'Why are we waiting?' and 'Where's the Captain?' filled the air. As she edged her way nervously down the left-hand side of the stage, Helen saw a huge punk rocker trying to pull up one of the seats.

She couldn't see if Sylvana was where she'd left her, because by now everyone was stood up, shouting for the band to come on. Moving out of their seats, into the aisles, pushing towards the stage. A line of red-faced bouncers was trying to keep everybody back, but Helen could feel that momentum building. Wishing she had worn her specs, she whirled around on the spot, trying to catch a glimpse of Sylvana's red hair, getting pushed and jostled on both sides. Bloody hell, this was impossible!

The seat, ripped free of its moorings, flew in a graceful arc over her head.

'Come on, you wankers!' someone screamed down her earhole.

'Hey, Helen.' A hand suddenly gripped her elbow. 'Over here!'

Sylvana had taken cover in a Fire Escape door in a recess of the aisle. And she wasn't alone. She had two men with her.

A tall, skinny guy with a thick fringe of red hair and his stockier, shorter companion who had black spiky hair and a round, smiling face.

'This is Robin,' Sylvana was making the introductions, indicating the fringe, 'and this is, er…'

'Allie,' said the smiley-faced punker, nodding vigorously.

'Pleased to meet you,' said Helen, and actually she was. There was something about his face she liked.

'The guys thought we might be a bit safer over here,' Sylvana added, shouting to be heard over the noise. 'I think things might get a little out of hand tonight.'

Helen nodded, took a sip of beer, noted that Allie's eyes were still flickering back and forth between the stage and herself.

'Don't suppose you saw Donna anywhere?' Sylvana continued.

'Don't suppose I did. She must have found her backstage pass all right. Anyway, who are these two?'

'Oh,' Sylvana smiled demurely. 'Just some guys in the protection racket. Came to look after little ole me while I was on my own in this dreadful place.'

They cackled together into their beers. 'I can't understand their accents but they are kinda cute though, hey?' Sylvana winked. 'I thought you would dig that Italian-looking one.'

Helen nodded, a wry smile forming. 'Not, bad, not bad at all…'

They turned back to their new friends.

'Did you say you were in a band, Robin?' Sylvana asked the fringe.

'I'm trying to get somethin' together,' he said. 'But I really need a singer. Me and Allie here, we're good enough at makin' the tunes but singin', no way. We sound like two asthmatic auld bastids who've been too long at the sauce.'

'I love your accent,' said Sylvana, though she couldn't quite understand what he'd actually said.

'Can you sing?' he asked her.

Just then a little fellow in a flat cap slipped by the side of them towards the front of the stage.

'Robin,' Allie dug him in the ribs, 'Rat Scabies just walked past.'

Four heads turned towards the stage, and as they did the lights went down and a huge cheer erupted, along with another couple of seats flying skywards.

Sensible, wearing a white dress and a dog collar, walked up to his mic and made the announcement: 'This is the end of punk!'

The bouncers were overpowered as a huge surge of people rushed towards the stage, and almost as a reflex, Robin and Allie found themselves pulling the girls behind them, covering the doorway with their bodies. It might have been punk rock and all, but they were good Catholic boys.

'Guys,' Sylvie suggested, 'when the coast is clear, I don't mind moving back a bit.'

'Me neither,' Helen agreed. As she peered out from under Allie's armpit, her eyes travelled around the stage and came to a halt at the right-hand side. She may not have had her glasses on, but she could take this sight in well enough. Lounging by the side of the curtain, draped all over a punk rocker in a leather jacket, white spiky hair and shades was Donna.

The punk rocker had his hand on her leg. Donna had her eyes on Dave Vanian.

She'd found her backstage pass all right.

The end of punk was a riot worthy of the original Peasants' Revolt. Virtually every seat in the Rainbow's auditorium was wrenched from its moorings and hurled towards the stage. Their blood up, the hardcore down the front wouldn't even listen to Vanian's admonishments to calm down. Gradually, Helen, Sylvana and their new-found friends edged their way backwards to the bar where they were out of the range of flying furniture. All the same, it was a pretty awesome spectacle to behold.

Rat Scabies climbed up onto the stage and the set continued with two drummers and then Lol Coxhill added to the frenzy with his honking sax, nicely choreographing the carnage below. They played The Beatles' 'Help' like they really meant it. Sensible walked off. He came back on naked and they played an encore, 'Feel Alright'.

But all the way through, Helen was watching Donna as much as the band. Her pass provider seemed to have fallen under a spell; he could hardly take his eyes off her to concentrate on the gig. What would become of him once Donna was where she wanted to be? One thing she could feel sure of – they wouldn't be seeing her again tonight.

Which was a major relief. Everyone was getting on really well here, and Helen just knew that if Donna was to turn up now, that would be the end of that. No cosy foursomes if she could help it. Only Donna could possibly be the centre of attention.

Helen said a silent prayer of thanks for whoever the bloke with the white spiky hair was. And he did seem familiar from somewhere, she just couldn't quite think where.

Suddenly it was over. The house lights came up and the bouncers pushed the peasants out of the venue as quickly and as forcefully as they could. Blue lights spilled onto the pavement outside from waiting panda cars. As they piled out onto the streets, Helen saw the massive punk rocker who'd launched the first chair getting bundled into the back of one, loudly protesting both his innocence and opinion of the great British police force.

It was so cold outside compared to in, steam was coming off people's backs. Helen shrugged her way back into her fur coat.

'Which way you headed?' Allie asked her, as the human tide eddied around them, between the tube across the way and the line of bus stops on Seven Sisters Road.

'South Ken,' Helen shouted. She wondered if she should ask

him to come back. He'd looked after her really well all night, acted like a real gent, without slobbering all over her or even acting like he had a right to. Helen hadn't met anyone she liked so much since she'd moved to London.

Allie looked impressed. 'They got a chippy there then?' he asked.

Helen laughed and put on a posh voice. 'Whatever do you mean, *a chippy*?' She pretended to stick her nose up at the very suggestion.

Allie's smile broadened and his eyes twinkled in the streetlight. Helen felt a sudden strange feeling that she had found her way home. 'You haven't tried my famous fried egg sandwiches yet,' she told him. 'You'll never want chips again.'

It was pretty bloody late, but they made the last tube back west, rammed into a carriage with the rest of the punk hordes, laughing and singing along with the rest of the carriage. Good job the city gents were long in their beds.

Helen and Allie swung from the hand rails, laughing and accidentally-on-purpose falling into each other's arms each time the train stopped in a station. Standing to the side of the doors, Sylvana fitted snugly into the crook of Robin's arm, looking as if she'd never really been anywhere else. They looked good together, Helen thought. Robin was one of those guys who wasn't so much handsome as really cool, like he was happy inside his own skin. He had a really tender expression when he looked at Sylvana too. God, things went so much smoother without bloody Donna around.

'What yer thinking?' Allie broke into Helen's reverie.

She quickly thought of something different. 'Do you think that really was the end of punk?' she asked him. That was a bit of a depressing thought too. She'd had such a good time in London since she got here, caught up in a wave of excitement, new bands forming every week, new styles of clothes to wear, new clubs, everything happening in a giddy rush, everyone joining in. She didn't like the sudden idea that this train full of happy extroverts was heading nowhere.

Allie smiled. 'Maybe. Maybe it's about time, eh? It wasn't supposed to last for ever you know, that's the beauty of it.'

'What do you mean?'

'It's like a forest fire. Unless the dead wood burns, the new shoots won't come through, dy'ken? Punk burned down everything that was old and shite and reactionary. Cleared the wood. Now somethin' new can grow out of it. Somethin' even better.'

Helen liked this idea. 'You reckon?' she asked cockily.

'Aye, I do,' he replied with a wide grin. 'You stick with me, kid. I'll show you.'

13

Shadowplay

January 2002

Christophe was smiling as I walked into the Lord Stanley. He'd managed to commandeer the leather armchairs by the fire and in front of him, on the table, a tumbler of crushed ice and whisky glowed by the light of the flames. He was staring into the grate as he pulled on a cigarette, hat tipped back on his head, expression almost beatific. With the smoke swirling around him, he looked as if he should have a pair of horns poking out from under his hat brim.

I, on the other had, felt like screaming.

'What happened?' I asked, falling into the chair opposite.

Christophe turned his head slowly, exhaling blue smoke. 'Like I said, I took care of that thing for you.' The sparks from the fire were mirrored in his hazel eyes.

'You look like you could do with a drink, mate. Where d'you get to anyway?'

'Hampstead Heath,' I spluttered. 'Look, what exactly do you mean—'

'Whisky do you?' Christophe stood up and reached for his

wallet. 'Or brandy? Must have been fucking freezing up on the Heath.'

He moved towards the bar and I tried to calm down, pulling my cigarettes out of my pocket and lighting up with shaking fingers.

'Get that down yer,' Christophe plonked a glass that must have contained at least a double down in front of me. 'And don't worry, Eddie. You know your problem? You worry too much.'

I necked the amber liquid, enjoying its burn as it raced down the back of my throat.

'But you saw the guy,' I said, as I set the glass down half empty. 'He was a fucking nutter. And he threatened to come round my house. What's Louise going to say if he turns up on the fucking doorstep? What if he goes after her…'

Christophe smiled and waved his hand as if swatting away an annoying barfly. 'And like I said, don't worry. I sussed it out for you. He ain't hard. He's nothing. He won't be bothering you again, believe me.'

'So you had a word with him then?' My hands closed back round the glass, desperate for another swig.

'Yeah, Eddie,' he nodded. 'I put him straight.'

I guzzled the rest of the whisky down, almost slamming the empty tumbler back on the table.

'Feel better now?' Christophe sounded as if he were asking a four-year-old who had just fallen over in the playground.

'Y-yeah, thanks,' I wiped a hand across my mouth, decided I had to pull myself together. 'Like you said, it was cold on the Heath. Think I'll have another one. You?'

'Ring-a-ding.' Christophe held up his own glass. 'That's more like it.'

After another couple of those, and a few pints to steady things down, Robin Leith began to recede into memory, as if he had only been a bad dream. Christophe suggested that I should go home at about seven, so Louise wouldn't be worried about where I had got to and I wouldn't be too drunk to get my story straight. It was bloody thoughtful of him, as if he hadn't done enough for me already. We walked back down the lengthy slope of Camden Road together, and he said goodbye on the corner of Royal College Street, which was his turning home and virtually my doorstep.

'Honestly,' he said, clapping his arm round my shoulder. 'You still worrying, ain't you? That chancy bastard's not coming anywhere near you. I promise you.'

'Thanks, Christophe. I really do appreciate it.'

'I know you do, mate. But it's nothing. Laters.'

'Laters.'

All the same, I thought, as I turned my key in the door, this is pretty bad. Here I am, only two weeks after I had been so full of New Year's resolutions, getting ready to lie to Louise again – and not only that, it feels vastly more natural than telling her the truth.

But, I reasoned with myself as I climbed the stairs, it was for her own good, really. She'd only get upset if she knew Leith really was a mental stalker.

Louise was sitting on the sofa with a bowl of carrot sticks and a bottle of really expensive looking red wine in front of her, watching *À bout de souffle*. If she was upset about something, she didn't look it.

'How was the freak?' she asked, without turning her head.

'Just that,' I said heartily, sliding out of my coat and hanging it up on the door. 'A freak. Totally wasted and a total waste of time.'

Hopefully, I went into the kitchen for a wine glass and then sat down next to her. 'That looks good...' I reached for the bottle.

'You smell like you've had enough cheap stuff already,' Louise sniffed, and then finally looked my way.

'So how did it get our number?'

'Ah, um, Tony Stevens gave it to him.' I almost forgot what I was supposed to say then. The wine glugged noisily into my glass.

'He probably thought he was doing me a favour, but the guy was fucking useless. I'm surprised he still remembered his own name.'

'So what were you doing all this time?'

'Well,' I shrugged. 'I had to let him talk. Let him get it all out of his system. Not that I'm going to use any of it.'

'I see. Eddie the Good Samaritan. Always there for the poor and needy,' she sighed and reached for a carrot stick. Poised it in front of her mouth and then said: 'Don't suppose you've eaten, have you?'

'Er, no, I didn't give it much thought.'

'There's a pizza in the fridge. You can get on with it while I watch what's left of this movie.'

So that appeared to be that. Full of pepperoni and delicious wine, it should have been easy to drift off to sleep that night. But I couldn't.

Instead I lay there, watching the arc of car headlights travel across the ceiling, listening to the usual midnight ravings echoing up from the street. Louise seemed happy enough with my explanation. But what was I going to tell Gavin?

Should I tell him anything? It would be pretty embarrassing to admit the way things turned out and now that Christophe had got involved maybe it was better not to say anything at all. But then, how would I ever find out how Leith got our number? What if Louise brought it up and I hadn't told him? How would he feel about that? And what if Christophe was wrong – the way Leith had acted in that pub, it didn't seem like he was going to give up easily. What had Christophe actually said to him that made him so sure?

The thoughts churned over in my mind like the red contents of my stomach. I don't think I drifted off until right before Louise's alarm announced that it was seven o'clock. Funnily enough though, once she had to get up and I didn't, I slept through to midday like a baby.

It was another grim, grey day in the hood when I finally got out of bed. I took a quick shower, wrapped myself up in my dressing gown and surveyed Camden Road from my window as I nibbled on my toast.

Across the road, a group of teenage boys were cycling down the pavement on bikes designed for their younger brothers, six abreast, pedalling as slowly as they possibly could without falling over. They all wore the same uniform – sweatshirts with hoods pulled down low, baseball caps rammed down over the top so it was impossible to see their faces. Children brought up in front of the CCTV.

It was the middle of the day, but just like the dealers across the way on the High Street, they knew that no one was going to turn up to stop them. I watched as one of them idly flicked the strap of a handbag off a woman's shoulder. He wasn't making much of an effort to nick it, this was more like a game of casual intimidation to amuse his mates.

Too scared to even look backwards, the woman grabbed it back tightly and increased her pace. Her tormentor kept dawdling behind, like an oversized, bandy-legged monkey teetering on top of his wheels, whooping and laughing at her discomfort. The woman ducked into the minimart, her face tight and white. The gang continued on their way, cutting a casually menacing swathe through the pedestrians. Pushed a staggering old drunk out of their path and into a collection of bargain mops and buckets outside the pound shop. Gave each other high fives as the poor old bastard fell, his face a picture of utter bewilderment.

Still, at least there was no Robin Leith out there, staring up at me from a doorway. I shivered.

I had to get out of this shithole.

Back to Kevin Holme.

I had gone through one tape, but another remained, and I slotted it into my dictaphone as the G3 powered up. Kevin had been pretty forthcoming in his own quiet way and the picture of

Vince that he'd painted so far was definitely the one that had been kept in the attic. I had to remind myself that maybe I wouldn't have got so far if Gavin, Vince's pucker mucker, had been with me. So maybe it was for the best that I didn't share all the details of the past few days with him.

'The best year for me was that first year, when we were on the road,' Kevin was saying as I pressed play. '1978. Don didn't mess about. He got our singles out every couple of months and then we were off to promote them…'

'Do you think Dawson took advantage of how young you were when he made that deal?' I asked.

'Not at all,' Kevin almost sounded shocked by this suggestion. 'You've got to look at it for the time that it was. The whole world was changing and Don had seen it before anyone else round our way. Not only that, but he was the biggest promoter in the North; he had all the contacts, all the clout. He paid for our records and got us on tour with The Stranglers and The Damned, who were our heroes. Who else would have done that for a bunch of sixteen-year-old schoolboys? Who else could have done it? No one. No. Ethically unsound he may well have been, but Don was like our fairy godfather.' Kevin chuckled softly at the thought. 'Ooh heck, if he could hear me say that. He were a proper man's man was Don.'

So off the band went, round and round the north of England, Scotland and Wales. Getting their motorway miles in the back of a white Transit van driven by a couple of comedy Teds called Terry and Barry.

'Course, things changed pretty quickly between the four of us. Stevie and Vince were off with the girls every night, but me and Lynton were still like the wallflowers at the school dance in them days. Suited us, mind. We got the van to ourselves at night, which were a blessing, believe me. Worked out a lot of new songs that way…'

At this point Kevin wandered off into a musical odyssey while my mind started to stray. I glanced out of the window again, still half expecting to see Leith glaring out of the doorway opposite. Started to wonder exactly what Christophe had said to him.

'So did you and Lynton write most of the first album then?' I heard myself say.

'No, not really. We worked out a lot of the stuff and I think, because it did come from the rhythm section first, that made it different, gave us our edge. But Stevie could always come up with a good riff soon as he'd heard it. He were always playing his guitar in the van, you know what I mean? He didn't really put it down until after we'd played a gig. Then Vince would come up with the lyrics…' Kevin paused. 'Well eventually he would. 'Cos he couldn't write them on his own.'

'Did Stevie help him there?' I prompted

But Kevin had gone quiet and I could recall his pained expression.

'No. Look, probably no one else will tell you this, or maybe they'll all tell you different, but it was actually a girl who wrote half our lyrics. See, as well as all his groupies, Vince used to have a girlfriend, Rachel. He lived with her in Donny when they were at art college. I think she probably supported him there, because she came from a rich family.

'Rachel was dead talented. See, that's what you have to understand about Vince. He chose his company well. He were always surrounded by talented people, people he could leech off…' Kevin started to sound angry and reined himself in.

'Any road, Rachel used to help us design our record sleeves and our T-shirts and that. And she used to write the lyrics with him. In bed, he used to say. He used to carry around a little notebook of hers and scribble things into it. Then she used to turn whatever it was he'd done into the words.'

Kevin's voice sounded faint on the tape. 'She were the first person I saw Vince destroy, Rachel. It was horrible what he did to her. Worse than Lynton and all the drugs.'

'What did he do?' No one had told me any of this.

There was a pause. 'If you don't mind, I'd rather not go into that right now. Rachel's still alive, you see, and I don't want to say anything that would hurt her any more than she already has been. Ask me something else and I'll think on it.'

Kevin was much happier talking about music than people so I had to spend the rest of that side of the tape going over what studios they made records in and how great the people they toured with were. The kindness of Stranglers and other such bollocks – all good for background, I supposed, but not really what I wanted to know. Luckily, the conversation turned dark again the moment Tony Stevens stepped into their dressing room.

'That were when it all started going wrong, really,' Kevin surmised.

'Really?' I said. 'I thought those were the glory years, with Exile.'

Kevin chose his words carefully. 'Don't get me wrong, I've nothing against Tony personally, he was very good to me, very good to all of us, in fact. But he treated Vince different to the way Don did, different to everyone else. It was like he was in awe of him, like Vince were some kind of god or something. That's what did it, really. Gave Vince *carte blanche* to do whatever he liked.

'Tony moved us all up to London, which of course we were dead excited about at time. He put us all in this house, up the top end of Ladbroke Grove. It were a bit of a wasteland, that, at the time. A lot of bands were squatting round there, so I don't think he paid for it or owt, just knew the right people to break in and turn the water and gas back on.

'We ended up living there nearly two year and in that time, this house became like Vince's court. Like I said, he always had to have a circle of people around him, but this time it weren't just talented people, it were the druggies too. That were how it started to come in.'

'But you made all your best records around this time…' I began.

'Yeah, and that were why. Getting away from the madness in that house made us right creative. Tony's studios were a lot cleaner an' all…'

Kevin was heading back to the music again. I tried to ask him about Lynton's problems, which I knew had begun around that time, but he brushed me off, saying that was for Lynton to answer. He didn't have much to say about Sylvana either, except that she made Stevie really angry.

'So was that when you had the big fight?' I asked.

'What do you mean?' Kevin sounded puzzled.

I read him Mick Greer's testimony on the making of *Butcher's Brew*: *'Kevin Holme was hospitalised for injuries apparently caused by the rest of the band.'*

'Oh right, Mick Greer said that, did he?' He struggled to keep his voice steady. 'Well, that's typical of what it was like being surrounded by Vince's mates. All putting the wagons in a circle around him, all the time. Yeah, all right, I did end up in hospital. But it was him who put me there, no one else.'

My own voice sounded faint now. 'Why? Why did he do it?'

Kevin's anger faded almost as soon as it had flared.

'Because he liked doing that kind of thing,' he said sadly. 'Look, Eddie, I think I might have gone far enough for one day. I did wonder what it would be like bringing up all this stuff again after so much time. To tell you the truth, I did think about not coming at all, but I'm glad that I did, you seem like a decent bloke. Why don't you give me a couple of days to think on about the rest of the stuff you've asked me? If you don't mind giving me your phone number, I'll definitely get back to you…'

I pressed the stop button with a jerk.

I'd given Kevin Holme my number. And after that, the phone calls from the nutter had begun. Was that a coincidence?

Listening back to the tape, it was obvious Kevin was still fucked up about a lot of stuff that had happened then. Had his 'thinking on' resulted in him deciding it would be better if

I stopped writing the book? And had he then decided to send Leith as his messenger?

I could feel my palms starting to sweat. I tried to reason myself out of this line of thinking. Kevin was the most mild-mannered bloke in the world. He'd even reproached himself on the tape when he started to sound angry. Why would he do a thing like that? Why wouldn't he just tell me himself? Come to think of it, why would he even mix with someone like Leith if he was trying to forget what had gone on in the past?

Maybe he didn't. Maybe it was that pub I met him in – it was crawling with eighties casualties. Exactly the sort of place a loser like Robin Leith would hang out. The only place he was likely to get an audience. Maybe Kevin hadn't said anything. Maybe Leith had just picked it up from the rest of the Undead that I was doing a book and Kevin was doing an interview. Maybe he'd even been in the room that day…

The phone's shrill ring cut through my paranoia like an electric shock. Oh shit, I thought. It's going to be him.

For a moment, I sat there, transfixed, staring at the jangling piece of plastic as if it was a cobra coiled up and ready to strike.

Two thoughts:

Robin Leith saying: 'Storp glorifyin' that bastid an' let her rest in peace. Otherwise I won't let you.'

Christophe's soothing words: 'That chancy bastard's not coming anywhere near you. I promise you.'

Then, as if propelled by some unseen hand, I found myself walking across the room, lifting the receiver and saying in what I hoped was a steady voice: 'Hello?'

'G'day mate,' Gavin's voice buzzed brightly down the line. 'What's cookin' in Camden?'

14

See Her Faces Unfurl

April 1978

'You did what?' Donna couldn't quite believe what she was hearing. She was possessed of the urge to smack that dozy smirk right off Sylvana's face and watch those Bambi eyes fill up with tears. Instead, utilising all the self-control she could muster, she felt her own smile freeze on her face like a rictus grin as her brain slowly processed this wholly unwelcome news.

That night at The Damned had not exactly turned out as she'd expected. Almost as soon as she'd got to the bar, she'd bumped into this bloke. Ray Spencer, his name was, she recognised his face from his byline in *Sounds*, where he was their top punk reporter, the very one, in fact, who'd announced the fact The Damned were going to split in the first place.

So she got talking to him and one thing led to another, the way they do. It was too good an opportunity to pass up and she hadn't thought the others would begrudge her that. Ray knew the band so well she'd got to watch them from the side of the stage, which was just as well, the riot that was going on in the auditorium. That was really brilliant. She'd got backstage all right too, but that was where things had taken a turn.

The band weren't putting it on, they were as angry as the audience. So there was no cosy chat and casual flirtation over a few beers to be had – instead the door to the dressing room was slammed in their faces as the noise of shouting and breaking glass intensified. One by one, each band member emerged to storm out into the night – Captain Sensible still without his clothes. Poor Dave had been so distracted, he hadn't even had the chance to look in her direction and Donna, standing powerless in the corridor with a *Sounds*' correspondent attached to her left hand, had had to quickly rethink her situation.

Luckily, Ray had no inkling of her real motives. The journo boy-wonder couldn't believe what had ended up on the end of his arm that night, and was determined to keep this transfixing vamp just where she was. As Donna had quickly found out, having Ray for a boyfriend opened up a world of advantages.

It had been a week since she had looked in on Sylvana and Helen and in that time she had been to a free gig nearly every night. Pere Ubu at the Marquee, X-Ray Spex at the Vortex, The Clap at the Nashville Rooms, Adam and the Ants at the Moonlight Club – it had all passed in a sulphate rush of backslapping and backstage interviews. Ray never went anywhere without his notepad and pen, scrawling his endless shorthand notes that to Donna looked like weird hieroglyphics. He'd made his name as the talent-finder general, the one who could sniff out the new bands faster than the rest. Along with John Peel, he had become the person every aspiring Sex Pistols sent their demo tape to first. Consequently there was nowhere he couldn't go and no one who didn't want to speak to him. The undoubted highlight of the week had been the night they spent in the Warwick Castle on Portobello, talking to Joe Strummer about the Anti-Nazi League rally that The Clash would be headlining at the end of the month in Victoria Park.

It was after that benediction that Donna could control the urge to see her fashion student friends no longer. She couldn't imagine what they had been up to since the gig; certainly it couldn't have been anything half so exciting as what she was doing.

But suddenly, the flat at Queen's Gate Gardens seemed to have grown two new tenants. Two dubious-looking Scotsmen, who had filled the front room with guitars, strange reel-to-reel recorders, a keyboard and a spaghetti junction of wires and cable. Were they some of Helen's extended family, come to stay? Or part of some strange college project? No, it appeared to be worse than that.

'I've joined the band,' Sylvana repeated. 'I'm gonna be the singer. How d'ya like that, hey?'

Donna tried to form a reply but found that she couldn't. Instead, Helen did it for her, but not in the words she would have used.

'It's brilliant, isn't it? Sylvie's been hiding her real talents from us all this time. And if you hadn't wanted to go to that gig so much, it might never have happened!'

'Yeah, cheers, for that, hen!' the dark-haired Jock, who appeared to be Helen's new beau, gave Donna a playful punch to the left shoulder then frowned.

'Where was you that night then?'

At last.

'With my boyfriend,' said Donna icily. 'Ray Spencer. You might have heard of him?'

The Jock's eyes widened. 'Ray Spencer from *Sounds*?'

Donna nodded. 'The same.'

'Did ye hear that, Robin?'

The other Scotsman appeared from behind an electric keyboard that he had been fiddling with ever since Donna arrived. Her eyes narrowed as she took him in. It looked like Sylvana had drawn the short straw there. At least Helen's had a kind of saturnine charm even if he was bit on the lardy side. This one was scrawny and ginger and she could see his acne scars from the other side of the room. The thought gave her a sudden rush of comfort. She couldn't see this manky scarecrow leading Sylvana into the bigtime.

'Aye, Ray Spencer, eh?' Robin said. 'Maybes we should give you a demo tape for him.'

'Yeah!' Sylvana squealed. 'What a fantastic idea!'

It took two weeks for them to cough up the goods, by which time Donna had formulated a plan.

Ray had his own flat on Matheson Road, just round the corner from the Nashville, in the vague backstreets between Olympia and West Kensington. An area cast in slate greys and dull greens that struggled to keep up appearances with neighbouring High Street Kensington, thanks to the thundering Talgarth Road that cut a rude swathe through the middle and the proliferation of high rises that loomed above the quieter, more modest Victorian streets below. The only splash of colour was the fruit, veg and knock-off goods market that snaked down the narrow North End Road, snarling up the impatient traffic and resounding with cries of barrow boys.

From the outside, it was a bit of a step down from Queen's Gate Gardens, but the top-floor flat itself was the hub of a much hipper social whirl. Donna hadn't taken long to decant her belongings from South Ken and the Tower of Terror to here, where she and Ray held court each night when the pubs and clubs had closed and everyone was still too wired to go to bed, listening to new records and demo tapes with a revolving assortment of musicians, other journalists, would-be entrepreneurs and less talented hangers-on. Donna loved the buzz of being at the centre of everything, of having people from the bands she had once admired from the sidelines now asking her advice. But at the same time, she had no desire to go down in history as just somebody's girlfriend, or worse, a King's Road hairdresser. Donna had much bigger ideas than that.

So she didn't let slip the fact that she had a demo of a new band even Ray could never have heard of until she'd given the tape a good listening to herself. It was a double-edged sword in a way. If it was no good, she'd have nothing to build foundations on. If it was good, then Sylvana might just pull off the one thing Donna had always wanted, but knew she didn't have the talent to do herself – become a proper singer. So Donna would just have to be the first to exploit that talent.

Ray was actually at the Nashville the first time she played it, feigning a headache to stay behind. Actually, she felt quite nauseous, with conflicting emotions churning her stomach and turning her brain.

It didn't matter how much they went on about the DIY spirit of punk and how anyone could take part, Donna could never commit herself to doing anything unless she knew she could do it a hundred times better than anyone else. Being laughed at was her worst nightmare. And much as she'd tried, much as she'd spent night after night praying for a miracle, she'd never been blessed with the gift of a golden voice. Or any sort of voice, for that matter. The music teacher at school had said she was tone deaf. She'd always suspected that was why she got straight into punk when all of her classmates were still down at the disco. She didn't like music that sounded *nice.* She liked music that felt like she did inside – icy, angry, full of the desire to intimidate and control.

She was almost wincing when she took the tape out of its box, with its little card inlay carefully fashioned by Sylvana, who despite all her training in fashion clearly still didn't have the first idea about what constituted good design. For a start it was in purple. With silver writing. For Christ's sake, didn't she realise those were hippy colours?

Mood Violet it read. *Thorn Necklace. Tracks: While You Were/ Heavenly Shades/Thorn Necklace/Crimson Contact: Sylvana on 01 942 3669*

Dear God. It sounded worse than her brother's prog-rock

collection. All it needed now were some Arthur Rackham flower fairies to seal its fate. Donna scrunched her eyes shut as she pressed play.

Found them opening spontaneously a couple of seconds later.

It was a whole lot better than she had dared expect. In fact, she realised, as track followed track and took her nowhere she'd ever expected, it was everything she needed.

Ray came back alone that night, as she knew he would if he thought she was ill. Before he did, she disposed of Sylvana's original inlay card, fashioning one herself from the heaps of music papers, fanzines and flyers that Ray hoarded, typing out the tracks again on his own typewriter. Then, satisfied that this one would embarrass no one, she went to work on herself. Shortly before eleven o'clock, she had arranged herself prettily under the bedcovers in a silky black nightie, a surprisingly risqué number she'd actually had out of British Home Stores on one of the rare occasions she'd been shopping with her mother in the past three years. She shut her eyes, tuning into the footfalls on the street outside, waiting to hear his key in the lock.

'How are you feeling, love?' Ray came through the door and straight over to her, kneeling down by the bed with an expression of genuine concern. He had such a sweet face. Despite his albino porcupine hair and the row of sleepers that went all the way up his left earlobe, he still could have passed for a twelve-year-old.

Donna pretended to blink awake, touching her forehead delicately as she did so.

'Hmmmm, a bit better, thank you,' she sat up, allowing Ray the full benefit of BHS' daringly cut bodice. 'I'm sorry I fell asleep, I wanted to stay up for you.'

She glanced at the clock. He hadn't even waited for last orders.

'Don't worry,' Ray had a laugh in his voice that was very endearing. It didn't seem possible that he could get angry about anything. 'I brought some chips up, if you fancy?'

He rustled the blue-and-white striped carrier bag he had put down by the bed and Donna's heart skipped a beat. Even if she had been legitimately off-colour, the smell of fried food would have brought her round.

They lay there companionably for a while, eating the chips out of yesterday's paper, hot and salty and drenched in vinegar, washed down with a can of Tizer. Tonight's gig hadn't been very inspiring, apparently, so she let him talk that out of his system before he got up to put the chip wrapper and the crumpled can in the bin. Nicely house-trained he was too.

Ray came back over and flopped down on the bed next to her. He gently traced the outline of her face with an index finger.

'You're gorgeous, Donna, what did I do without you?' He almost sounded in pain as he whispered it.

'I don't know,' Donna raised one eyebrow. 'I supposed you just had to make do with dirty old punk rockers.'

He leaned forward to kiss her and Donna tried, she really tried to kiss him back with the same amount of enthusiasm. He was so delicate with her, it was easier to fight the wave of revulsion she usually felt at being touched, easier to nail back the memories of other, harder, more forceful fingers probing into her young flesh, the taste of vinegar on his lips so different from the stale smell of whisky and ashtrays that always brought back her worst nightmares. She could control the urge to slap him off her and beat him a thousand shades of purple, to see him lying naked on the floor, defenceless against her stiletto heels and her fists full of rings.

Ray wasn't like the other hormonal oafs she'd made short shrift of in her time.

Better than that, he wasn't her dad.

All the same, she didn't want to get him too carried away just yet. She pulled away from his embrace smiling, put her finger on the end of his nose. 'I've got something special for you,' she said.

Ray looked slightly dazed.

'You *are* special, Donna—' he began.

'I'm gonna prove *how* special, though,' Donna slid off the side of the bed. She reached for the cassette that she'd left beside his tape recorder. 'And how clever I am.'

She flipped up the plastic lid, fitted her future dream between the spindles and clicked the machine shut.

'Listen to this, Ray. I bet you've never heard anything quite like it before.'

Ray, who had been hoping that Donna was about to show him something else entirely, lay back on the tousled bed, confused. She enjoyed watching that expression change, as the first notes filled the room with eerie wonder; that strange, scratchy guitar, those undulating keyboard swooshes, and then the unbelievable sounds that had come out of Sylvana's throat.

Another thing that was perfect about Ray. He could always be distracted from matters carnal by his truest love – music. She let him drink it in, stealing back across the room to lie beside him, soft and compliant in his arms. Ray looked like he was receiving a Holy Sacrament. Finally, when the four tracks had played themselves out and the tape recorder abruptly snapped off, he sat up and said: 'Where on earth did you get that?'

'They're just some friends of mine,' Donna replied, smiling up at him. 'Pretty good, hey?' she echoed Sylvana's words.

'Pretty amazing,' Ray scratched his head. 'You're right, I've never heard anything quite like that before. Do you know what she's singing about?'

Donna shook her head. 'No, I can't understand a single word she says. Except that it's enough to turn a man's knees to jelly.'

She prodded him there and he laughed.

'Shall I run it by my editor?' he said. 'I'm sure he'd be really interested.'

'You could do,' Donna toyed with the end of a strand of her hair. 'But I think I have a better idea.'

'What?' Ray frowned. 'You're not gonna give it to the *NME*? You couldn't…' His face started to colour in a way she'd never seen before.

'Shhh, shhh,' she shook her head. 'Course I'm not gonna give it to those wankers. I've just had a better idea than just writing about them. Why don't we put the record out as well?'

'You what?'

'It would be easy, Ray, you know it would. Who was that bloke you had over here the other night? Tony, was his name? He set up a label with a hundred quid loan from his old man, he earned it all back on his first release and still had enough over for the second. It looks pretty easy to me. I know we ain't got a hundred knicker, but you know plenty of people who'd give you that kind of backing, Ray. 'Cos they know they'd make it back like that,' she snapped her fingers.

'Everyone would buy a record you championed. Everyone knows you. And it wouldn't just be this band, there'd be loads of others would follow. Don't see why you should be making money for some magazine that you could be making for yourself.'

Ray winced at this. 'It ain't about the money, though, is it, love?'

Shit, thought Donna, those fucking punk principles. How tiresome.

'Course it ain't.' She shook her head furiously. 'That weren't what I meant, Ray, it just came out wrong. What I meant was, instead of just writing about them, you could actually help them get their records out. That Tony said it was the biggest rush he'd ever got in his life. Said it was dead easy, everyone's willing to help. And I know helping people is what you love doing most.'

She rolled him her most pleading eyes. Ray chewed his lip. He still didn't look happy.

'I've never thought about anything like this before,' he finally admitted. 'I thought I was lucky enough just doing what I do.'

'You are,' she agreed. 'Sorry, Ray. Maybe you weren't the right person to talk to about this. Maybe I should ask that Tony. He might be able to help me.'

'Maybe you should,' said Ray, but he didn't sound sarcastic, more like wounded and lost. 'Look, I'm sorry, Donna, I feel a bit out of my depth here. It's just that I love what I do. I've never thought about doing anything else but writing. All that stuff about business and other people's money scares me. I met Malcolm McLaren and I can honestly tell you, love, he scared the shit out of me. He was an evil man. He didn't want to help no one except himself. But I know you're right, Tony Stevens ain't like that, and there are plenty more like him.'

He sighed and hugged her closer. 'Is that what you want, then, a record label?'

Donna nodded. 'I'd be good at it, Ray, I know I would.'

'Course you would, and I will help you with it. I just don't want to be part of running it, that's all.'

'Fair enough,' Donna shrugged. As Ray continued to offer up suggestions of who he could get to help her and how he would do his bit in the paper, her head started to swim with the enormous possibility of it all. This was a better idea than she had ever anticipated. Instead of entering a partnership that could grow tiring, she could end up with her own business. She would become a famous entrepreneur – the first woman of punk. She could use that dumb rich Yank Sylvana to elevate herself into the penthouse league. Say bye bye to the Tower of Terror for ever. The very thought of it almost gave her hysterics.

To make matters even better, Ray seemed to think he was letting her down by not coming in with her, just dishing out all his hard-won contacts on a plate instead. After he'd apologised for the seventh time, she decided it was time the poor boy finally got his just rewards.

'Ray,' she said sweetly. 'There's something else I want to show you…'

15

Giving Ground

February 2002

There were no more mad phone calls and, despite my paranoia, I never did look out of my window to find Robin Leith staring back up at me with bloodshot, accusatory eyes. Nor did I get an icy tap on the shoulder as I walked down a dark Camden alley at night. After two weeks had turned into three, I started to relax. I hadn't told Gavin anything and I was relieved about that; I could have made a right arse of myself there for no reason. Christophe continued to reassure me of the wisdom of this course of action every time I saw him, and Louise asked no more questions about it.

But Kevin Holme never did call me back, and that still rankled, still caused a couple of nights of fretful churning under tangled, sweaty sheets. Come the grey light of morning, my fears would evaporate again and I gradually pushed the Leith incident to the back of my mind. Now that Gavin was back, it was all stations go again anyway.

I don't know whether Gavin had nudged him for me, but soon after, Tony Stevens sent me a photocopy of his private detective's report into Vince's disappearance, along with a copy of his own file of all Blood Truth's Exile press cuttings.

At first, I had been really excited to receive the report, a thirty-page densely worded document, on what would have been the standard manual typewriter of the time. I thought I would be able to find something encoded there that Dan had missed or overlooked. It started off promisingly enough.

It gave Vincent's address as apt 16, 112 Sacré Coeur, Paris Arrondissment 18 – the top flat in a nineteenth-century residential building in a quiet neighbourhood street underneath Vince's beloved cathedral. A bit of digging around on the net and I began to realise how appropriate this part of the French capital was for a man like Vince – the streets of the 18th district, combining Montmatre, Pigalle and la Chapelle, had long been home to anarchists and artists and the centre of the sex and drugs industry. Emile Zola wrote about its 'foul environments', Toulouse Lautrec immortalised its Chat Noir cabaret in oils and Picasso was put on police file on suspicion of being a robber when he lived there. Vince's historical neighbours would also have included Degas, André Breton and Max Jacob – Impressionists, Dadaists and Cubists all carved out their own niche on the hill, under the neon underskirts of the Moulin Rogue and the pure white domes of the Sacré Coeur.

Sanctity and Sin, one just above the other. The psycho-geography was perfect and I was itching to book my placc on the Eurostar right there and then, so I could go and wander those historic streets myself, drink in the atmosphere along with some bitter black espresso and Gitanes. The only thing that stopped me was the thought that Louise would probably want to come too, and then we would have to spend all our time looking at modern art rather than examining the underside of the red-light district. I would have to work this one out as a magazine trip, I reckoned, and not tell her I was going with Gavin.

Another lie, but still.

The detective signed himself M. J. Pascal and in the note Dan sent with the package he explained the guy had been recommended by a friend who'd also once been in need of a French connection – Joseph Pascal was from Paris but had lived and worked in London for years. He had his snouts on both sides of the Channel and had quickly ascertained that the French cops hadn't bothered too much with the disappearance of someone they considered little more than a criminal. Especially when it seemed there wasn't very much of a mystery to solve.

There was a thread of a story running through his report, but as hard as Pascal chased it, he couldn't find any reliable witnesses to back up any of it. Plenty of locals had heard rumours about 'les Anglais' and some of them were pretty lurid too – one witness statement from a prostitute, referred to only as 'Petite M', said that Vince's nickname was 'The Vampire' and that the local working girls were afraid of him. But Pascal dismissed this tale as the fevered ranting of an addict who had only given her statement to make some money.

However, it was common knowledge that Vince had managed to get himself barred from a couple of the local pubs and nightclubs by causing disturbances with his fists. Pascal had spoken to a couple of aggrieved Montmartre landlords who had told him that Vince had been keeping company with a local lowlife known as Marco, who was rumoured to run hashish up from Marseilles with the help of Algerian gangsters. Needless to say, Pascal couldn't find hide nor hair of Marco. His contact with the local cops told him they didn't figure him for a major player, just a boastful small-time crook who they'd picked up a few times for pimping, not drugs. People told stories about him, they said, because he looked like an Arab.

Vince had also been seen with a blonde woman on a few of his wild nights out, but she wasn't local and no one could tell Pascal who she could have been.

Pascal theorised that Vince could have got himself in even

more girl trouble, that the blonde could have been one of Marco's whores and they could have had a falling out over her. But of course, as Marco was long gone by the time Pascal reached Montmartre, he had no way of following this line.

With Vince being a junkie, there was also every possibility he could have finished his days OD-ed in some rat-infested flophouse and been an unidentified John Doe frozen in a local morgue. Pascal duly checked out this possibility, visiting everywhere there was to visit in Paris and the surrounding area, but no stiffs had ever come in that could possibly have been a physical match for Vince.

Maybe he could have just insulted the wrong person one night and been what Pascal tactfully referred to as 'disappeared' – in which case, no one would ever find him again.

But the strongest evidence tended to offer another alternative. Vince had paid his landlord in advance for the final three months of his tenancy in October. He had planned to leave when he did. However degenerate his final months in Paris may have been, his flat was left spotless, everything in order, no signs of a man interrupted. He didn't leave a single thing behind.

Pascal ended his report by suggesting that, in his opinion, Vince had deliberately 'disappeared' himself, had spent three months carefully arranging it and had taken care that no one would be able to follow him.

Stevens had obviously gone along with this summation, even if it had sorely disappointed him. His note said that he had paid Pascal for his services and forgotten about looking for Vince.

Pascal's number had turned into a mini-cab firm. Now the detective's trail was long cold. But Stevens had finished by saying that he would chase up the friend of a friend who had recommended him in the first place to see if he could find out if the PI was still around. Although if he was, he reminded me, he would be in his seventies by now.

I phoned Stevens to thank him and he was very genial,

although he hadn't tracked down the friend of a friend yet, let alone a number. Somehow I didn't expect that he would. Knowing my luck, if Pascal was still alive, he'd be dribbling away in an old folks home by now. So I turned my attention to the press file.

Just about every piece of press Blood Truth had accrued in their two years with Exile was positive, the only voice of dissent being a *Melody Maker* live review that finished with the words: '*Take this disgusting racket and shove it*', something that Vince and Steve happily told their next interviewer they were going to use on the top of all their press releases from then on. Mick Greer, was of course the *NME*'s biggest fan and had written the major feature for every release from *Down in the World* in March 1979 to *Butcher's Brew* in May 1981.

The band obviously loved the cunt; they had taken him on the road with them all over the place, providing lots of riotous copy involving copious drinking, bar fights and mad Americans trying to kill Vince for taking the piss out of Elvis. But happily, the one article that really interested me wasn't by him. It was in *Sounds*, from February 1979, and it was written by a guy called Ray Spencer.

It was called 'The Way of the Weird' and what immediately grabbed my attention was the big, black and white picture that had obviously been taken in the squat that Kevin had told me about. It looked like the band had dragged some old car seats off a breaker's yard and into their front room. Vince, naturally, was sitting in the centre of the disembodied back seat, his feet up on a tea chest, alongside an overflowing pub ashtray with SKOL written around the edge of it and a load of empty bottles. Vince, completely dressed in black and wearing a big pair of Robot creepers, appeared to be toasting the photographer with a chipped mug. To his left, Steve lounged sideways, playing an unplugged white guitar, his hat pulled down over his eyes; to his right Lynton followed the pose with his bass, a cigarette hanging coolly from the corner of his mouth. Standing behind them all,

Kevin raised his drumsticks as if he were about to start playing his bandmates' heads. If they were having a bad time of it in that squat, this picture certainly didn't show it.

'We're a long way from Hull now, Toto,' laughs big Steve Mullin, guitarist from the North's most sh** kicking beast of a band, Blood Truth, went the first sentence.

Newly signed to Exile, this band have already conquered the savage lands north of Watford, spending nearly two years riding their wheels of steel to the remotest, most punk-starved corners of our isles. A string of 45s on the Hull-based Dawsongs label lighted their trail, culminating with November's incendiary *King of Nothing* EP, which finally set the south aflame. A savage, nihilistic anthem delivered by a six-foot-four, raven-haired punk possessed like an old Testament preacher, who has a penchant for fighting with his own audience, backed up by a bunch of hoodlums who wouldn't look out of place in a Peckinpah movie. No wonder Tony Stevens wanted their names in blood.

He duly got those signatures in January and wasted no time shipping his charges down to Ladbroke Grove, where they have been holed up in his X World studios, feverishly working on the first album proper and marvelling at the atmosphere of their new neighbourhood.

'We're walking in the footsteps of The Clash here,' continues Mullin, enthusiasm spilling visibly from his lips. 'The Slits live round the corner. We're five minutes from Shepherd's Bush, where half of the Pistols come from. It feels like we're in some kind of movie. I can't quite believe it's real, to be honest.'

With his red-raw fusion of Steve Jones sonics to mangled mad rockabilly guitar (think Link Wray's *Bollocks*), founder-member Mullin is the heart of the band. He comes across as both joker and protector, a big bad brother to softly spoken bassist Lynton Powell and drummer Kevin Holme. In turn, the modest Blood Truth rhythm section are the reason this band sounds so very different from the rest of the post-

Pistols pack. The heavy, heady, swampy beats laid down by Powell and Holme have more in common with Captain Beefheart or Screamin' Jay Hawkins than the work of any of their immediate peers. Perhaps part of this otherness stems from the fact that Powell was, in his own words 'the only black kid in Hull', growing up with adoptive white parents and only an extensive jazz collection for company.

'Jazz was the original punk,' Powell points out, 'made in big cities by very angry young men. Be-bop in the fifties probably sounded like the Pistols did in '77 – like a call to arms, an alarm clock going off in people's heads. Jazz might just be some old Grandad thing to most people now, but it has definitely marked what we do and I certainly wouldn't call our music easy listening.'

The focus for all this seething intensity, however, is Vince Smith. The brilliant frontman is just as intimidating as you'd expect. When *Sounds* arrives on the doorstep of Blood Truth's house this morning, he opens the door in a lurid yellow skinny-rib Elvis T-shirt and still more eye-watering pink-and-yellow striped Y-fronts, seemingly oblivious to the sub-zero temperatures both outside and in. Showing us into the kitchen, he invites us to join him in a bracing breakfast cup of Thunderbird, a local delicacy he has just discovered, much to his delight. A ream of paper is scattered across the Formica-topped table, covered in spidery scrawl. Smith reveals he has been up writing lyrics for new songs since six.

'Want to hear some?' he offers and proceeds to recite in a booming baritone, waving his mug of wine around as he does so. It feels like being collared by a belligerent drunk on the night bus home, and we nod along approvingly, hoping he wouldn't be reaching for the carving knife to further his point, until we are saved by the arrival of a dishevelled but genial Steve Mullin.

Obviously, Smith's stage persona is not an invention.

'That were one of his tests,' Steve tells me later. 'Vince likes to see how people react by generally acting like a maniac when he first meets them. But he's all right really. Once you get to know him, like.'

Indeed, when Smith returns from upstairs for the photoshoot, dressed from head to foot in black, he is witty and charming and stays that way for the rest of the day. The band enjoy mucking around for the shots, proudly describing how they acquired their 'sofa' from a breaker's yard under the Westway.

'Tony Stevens wanted us to do a promo shoot up there,' says Stevie, referring to their label boss. 'Reckons we're warriors of the future apocalypse, like. Either that or he couldn't stretch to buyin' us any more furniture.'

All finished, the band lead us down to the bus stop to catch a lift to Exile's HQ in Shepherd's Bush. Fellow passengers give us a wide berth; one elderly West Indian woman actually crosses herself as Vince saunters past oblivious, muttering oaths under her breath as if she'd just encountered Old Nick himself.

Once at X World, a soundproof extension on the back of Exile's end-of-terrace office, we get to hear what will become the band's first album proper. Ten tracks have already been laid down, the lyrics Vince was working on are for the last two without a vocal and he's keen to try out the one he's most pleased with, 'The Old Man of King's Town'. *Sounds* gets an impromptu performance of the work-in-progress.

Vince tries out his lyrics in the booth, while Steve, Lynton and Kevin sit with us to watch him. The singer is as possessed in this sterile, soundproof room as he is in front of a seething crowd, and stamps his feet, rocks backwards and forwards and literally writhes as he spills the new words out in a ferocious, guttural roar. The music that had already been constructed is a slow, shivering, sweating funk, slashed with red shivers of Mullin's guitar.

It's difficult to make out the lyrics, there's a repeated line about: 'Running you down/Out of town' and the song ends on a demented flourish with Vince pretending to shoot up the booth, shouting: 'Bang! Bang! Bang! Shoot you down!'

Then the singer takes a bow and announces: 'That was for Don.' He looks me straight in the eye as he does so.

Don Dawson was the band's first manager. I take it this is who he is referring to.

I ask the other three about it. Kevin and Lynton nervously duck the question. Stevie is less evasive. 'Yeah, well, he tried to give us some hassle for signing with Exile, took it out on Vince mainly, so that's what you get.'

What kind of hassle?

The guitarist shakes his head. 'Nowt we can't handle.'

Smith joins us, clearly delighted with himself. 'Don't forget to write that in your feature,' he tells me. 'Don Dawson's the King of Nothing now.'

I put the feature down. I really was going to have to find Don Dawson and I knew I'd have to go it alone there – unless Kevin ever bloody called me back. So that was one trip to Gay Paris, another to Grimy Old Hull. Blood Truth truly were a journalist's dream.

But first, I had to meet with a surviving member of the band. With shy, softly-spoken Lynton Powell.

Lynton had been true to his word, fixing up some time for Gavin and me, a couple of days after he returned from his soundtrack job in LA. The bassist had moved a bit further around west London since his days in the squat, but not that much. To Latimer Road, where he had a studio set in a big, converted mews courtyard.

It was a strange kind of place, Latimer Road, a place where one world became another along the course of Oxford Gardens, a road which spanned Ladbroke Grove and began with the usual stucco mansions, set back from the road amid plenty of foliage. Only, after it crossed St Mark's Road, it was as if a boundary had been reached and immediately, the scenery changed. The houses shrank, becoming modest rows of terraces, and the gentle edges of gardens disappeared into lines of big, thick beech trees, which probably looked very grand in summer. But in the pale, watery light of a February morning, they rose grey and leafless like frozen abstract dancers, their naked branches cut back to stark nubs.

Big gates on our left hid Patrick Litchfield's studios.

'Amateur,' smirked Gavin as we passed. I got the feeling we were walking away from sophisticated bohemia into suburbia. From where it all happened to where nothing ever did. There was no one else on this stretch of the road, no trendy Notting Hillbillies or Yah Trustafari, no gangs of feral kids on bikes. Roads like this always made me feel uneasy; like you could walk down them for ever looking at the neat little houses with their unblinking, net-curtained eyes, row after row of them, until you lost your soul in their drabness.

I laughed too loudly at Gavin's quip, tried to shake myself out of the strange feeling of unease the road engendered. I couldn't help thinking about Pascal's report and the notion of 'disappearing' yourself. This would be exactly the sort of place to do it. No one would ever want to look here.

At the studios, the feeling dissolved. Behind the wrought iron gates that enclosed the blocks of buildings was a bustling little enclave, although the scene behind each plate-glass window was one of eerie repetition. Young men dressed to the latest *Dazed & Confused* dictates – semi-mohican hairstyles, Von Dutch shirts, low-slung jeans with big chunky chains hanging out of their arses and trainers shaped into cloven hooves. Plugged into their laptops over buckets of latté and beansprout ciabattas. No doubt some enterprising little Nigels with a sandwich cart made sure they were all supplied with the same provisions, just so no one felt left out. I was just glad I couldn't hear the minimalist glitch music they were all undoubtedly listening to.

Happily, Lynton's studio had tinted windows that offered nothing but a reflection of the rest of the courtyard. Gavin pressed the bell and a woman's voice answered warmly then buzzed us in.

The door opened into a bright, cheerful reception, and a very beautiful black woman in a neat pinstriped suit and heels, hair coloured with streaks of red and braided up into artful coils, was reaching out a perfectly manicured hand to greet us.

'Hi, I'm Shanice,' she said, shaking us both with an immaculately cool grip. She had long lashes and red lips. 'If you'd like to follow me, he's just through here…'

Through another door, into an open-plan studio, with a little lounging area to the right of it. On a bright orange sofa, Lynton Powell sat in a dark blue tonic suit, hair neatly cropped, a small goatee beard around an easy smile. He had filled out a bit from the pipecleaner skinniness of his younger years, the inevitable middle-age spread, but apart from that, Lynton had aged considerably better than anyone else I'd met so far.

His eyes were friendly as he stood up to greet us.

'Gavin, my man,' he crossed the room in a couple of strides, clapped my companion firmly round the shoulders and then gripped his right fist in his own. Then he turned to me.

'Eddie, right? Glad to meet you. Come on in, have a seat.'

'Can I get you all coffee?' asked the delightful Shanice from behind us.

'That'd be good,' nodded Gavin. 'Black, no sugar, please.'

'Yeah, same for me,' I smiled at her, trying not to let my tongue hang out too much. She was confusing me. I didn't even like my coffee black.

Lynton ushered us onto the orange sofa, sat himself down on a red leather armchair facing us. He and Gavin made catching-up talk until Shanice had come back with a tray bearing a cafetiere, big, round coffee cups, a bowl of sugar lumps and a plate of biscuits. I let them get on with it until she had disappeared back into reception, dropping a couple of lumps into my cup in the hope it would make it taste acceptable.

'So where d'you want to start?' Lynton asked me. His voice was a melodious rumble, judging by the red pack he had placed on the table, the result of years of Marlboro abuse. His eyes were friendly, with no traces of sadness or suspicion.

I glanced briefly down at my notes, took a deep breath and began.

16

My Love With a Knife

April 1979

Making that first demo had been the first time everything had started to make sense inside Sylvana's head. Everything she had tried so hard to create, through all that drawing, dressmaking and writing, suddenly took on its perfect natural form and flowed out of her in one almighty rush. She could hardly believe that a stranger she had met by chance had finally set her free from the dark place in the back of her mind. The place her own mother had whisperingly consigned her to, and that she had half-believed was true – that terminal ward labelled 'backwards'.

For as long as Sylvana could remember, she had seen words as colours. When she was little, this made words just about the most wonderful things – especially when her Grandma Ola was telling her stories. But once she was old enough to try to start explaining this to other people, things had taken a distinctly downhill turn.

Sylvana's mother Glo was one of those ramrod straight, frighteningly coiffured women who couldn't tolerate anything that was less than perfect. It was her mission in life to dress and deport herself better than any of the rivals she called her friends and she accomplished her aims with the steely precision of her role model, Wallis Simpson: 'You can never be too thin or too rich.'

Thankfully for Glo, her husband Ruben was always at the office, making the latter part of her mantra possible as avidly as she applied herself to the first. Grandma Ola used to tell Sylvana there were two miracles about her birth. The first was that Ruben found time between midnight and dawn to woo and win a wife; the second was that Glo found time to fit a baby in between her endless round of grapefruit diets, trips to the salon and shopping at Bloomingdales.

It was Grandma Ola who had more or less single-handedly brought Sylvana up and it was she who had filled her head with the magic of storybooks, art, poetry and clothes.

Just as well, because if it had been left to Glo, Sylvana's whole life would have been one of well-heeled misery. Spent either lying on a couch trying to explain herself to a shrivelled-up old shrink or making midnight raids on the fridge to assuage the pains of the perpetual diet she was put on. School was as bad as home – there she was surrounded by a legion of miniature Glos, all preparing themselves to catch a good husband. 'Dumpy' and 'Dopey' was all she ever heard: two of the Seven Dwarves in one and not a Snow White in sight. Only Ola could reassure her that it was good to be different from the rest of those little ice maidens.

Ola came from London, from the Commercial Road, where she'd worked in the rag trade for her father. Despite nearly a half century in America, she still spoke with a broad East End twang, her conversations pitted with Yiddish and Cockney colloquialisms. She'd met her American husband Maurice, or Mac as she always referred to him, by chance, schlepping up the Dilly one afternoon to eye the latest fashions on Regent Street. They'd fallen in love and sailed to the States on a Cunard liner, arriving just in time for the Wall Street Crash.

But Ola and Mac were canny operators with a flair for design and a skill at conjuring money. Ola may have begun bringing up her four children in a cold-water tenement on the Lower East Side but she finished up with a big house in an exclusive New Jersey suburb. Only poor Mac wore his heart out too soon. Ruben took over the business when he was scarcely twenty-one.

Ola's second son Manny had returned to the city of his mother's birth, but she hadn't been tempted to follow him. She didn't want to leave poor Mac all on his own and what would there be for her there now anyway? Sylvana used to gaze at the black-and-white photos of them in their youth, looking to her so much like film stars, and understood perfectly.

She might have been a disappointment to her mother, but Sylvana had Ola's blood. She had always known she would find her dream in London. Yet it wasn't until Robin had played her his music that she finally knew what her dream really was. It had come to her in a heliotropic rush: Mood Violet.

After that, all the years of confusion, all the strange jumbled-up poetry she'd been keeping in her journals and in her head suddenly transformed itself into actual songs. The colours she had always seen in those words – the vivid violet and silver, crimson and gold – shaded in exactly to the music Robin and Allie had made.

She finally realised the transformation was complete the day she saw her picture in *Sounds*, with the piece Donna's boyfriend had written about the band. This time there was no sign of Dumpy and Dopey – it was a red-haired, fine-boned young woman who stared back at her with radiant green eyes. She looked almost as good as Ola had in her day.

By then Sylvana had graduated her college course and her parents had expected her back in New Jersey pronto. But for the first time in her life, she had defied them. She never wanted to leave London now. Everything she had ever wanted was here.

Her band, her friends, her love.

Gentle Robin.

He was the first person Sylvana had ever told about the shrinks and the diets. So worried was she that Glo was right and she really was quite mad, she hadn't even told Helen, who was by far the best friend she'd ever had. Robin had listened to it all with no trace of mockery or malice in his face. It was strange, for someone who looked quite fragile – his thin, long limbs, his translucent skin which barely looked thick enough to protect the ropes of thick blue arteries that ran up his arms, his pale, red-rimmed eyes – Robin really was quite strong.

In a sense, Robin had run away to London to seek his fortune too. If he had stayed, he told her, he would have ended up working down the pit on the outskirts of Edinburgh that had already eaten up most of his family. And if he'd had to do that, he would have ended up an alcoholic like his Da. Luckily he had a talent for electronics and a good friend in Allie, who was likewise handy with a spanner. It meant they could earn a living anywhere as sparkies and plumbers, as well as build their own instruments. Inspired by the Pistols' Jubilee celebrations, they had bunked on a London-bound train in Edinburgh in the summer of '77 and never looked back.

But what really made Sylvana fall in love was when Robin asked her about the lyrics and she shyly admitted about the colours and the sounds, how she had always seen things this way, the way others apparently couldn't.

He told her he had always seen things exactly that way.

It had to be fate, Sylvana thought, that they had been brought together. Two lonely souls meeting in a foreign city to make music that was a direct result of their personal, misunderstood magic. Things she never thought possible had come as a result.

Like Donna. Sylvana still wasn't quite sure how she'd managed it, but Donna had got that first demo turned into an EP in the space of two months flat and had made all the music papers listen. She had fixed up gigs that had sold out purely by word of mouth, in all the right places – the Moonlight, the Nashville, the Acklam Hall.

Robin and Allie had read the signs right, people were ready for a change from the hard edges of punk into something more dreamy and ethereal. It was just as well, really, as the music continued to pour out of the band. They sold all the copies of 'Thorn Necklace' as soon as Ray had made it *Sounds*' Single of the Week. Donna got more backers. Her fledgling label Vada a going concern, they started work on an LP as soon as Sylvana and Helen graduated. *Twilight Singing* was finished by October, released in November. The first single to be taken from it, 'Honey Spike' got to number 12 in John Peel's Festive Fifty.

The best thing about it all, for Sylvana anyway, was that they all got to do it together. Like a punk-rock version of *The Partridge Family*, all her new friends were involved, sharing her good fortune.

Helen wasn't actually in the band – although she had shaken a tambourine on a couple of tracks and added some backing vocals to others – but she and Allie had grown as close as Sylvana and Robin. What Helen actually wanted to do was establish herself as a designer, which led to another of Donna's brainwaves. If Helen made all Sylvana's clothes, she reasoned, she would soon get herself noticed.

She helped Helen get a pitch on Portobello Road market and sent all her important friends down to buy new creations every Saturday. Wore the stuff herself when she was asked to comment on the latest youth scene on LWT, which was happening with increasing frequency these days. Donna, it seemed, had it all worked out.

Between times they had played gigs all over the country, driving around in the beat-up old van Allie had bought to help carry Helen's stock to and from the market. Allie drove it himself most of the time, Helen constantly stitching in the seat beside him, all of them laughing and living on chips, ginger ale and Thunderbird wine, the dulcet tones of their favourite DJ Peelie crackling away on the radio, lighting up the motorways late at night.

After about a year, they had a second album out to rave reviews and Helen had a permanent pitch in Kensington Market.

And then, like tiny flakes of glitter, the silver and gold started to slowly fall away from Sylvana's perfect world.

Almost as soon as *Ice-Tapped Vein* had been released, Mood Violet were out on the road.

St George's Day, April 1979, was the first day of the tour. Sylvana hadn't been particularly aware of this quaint English Saint's Day before, but she would never be able to forget it afterwards.

She knew all about Rock Against Racism, of course, it was something Donna's Ray had been avidly covering and Mood Violet had even played a benefit, supporting the reggae band Misty In Roots, at the Acklam Hall under the Westway on Ladbroke Grove. She was aware that the English version of the Nazis, the National Front, were on the rise and that the mood of the country was turning ugly.

In the coldest days of winter, power cuts had plunged the city into darkness with annoying frequency, almost always when they were trying to work on some tracks. It had become a habit for Sylvana to leave candles all round the room so she wouldn't have to go rummaging for them in the darkness under the sink each time. She had never seen such a thing in the States, but Robin told her that it was a fairly habitual British thing when the trades unions were angry, which they were at the moment with Prime Minister Callaghan for capping pay rises at five per cent.

In order to make him see how important their services were, lorry drivers, bin men and even gravediggers had been going on strike. At one point there were mountains of refuse sacks piled up in the middle of Leicester Square, stinking to high heaven and doing wonders for the tourist trade. The press coined a term for it, a quote from *Richard III*: The Winter of Discontent.

Sylvana's family had been fortunate enough to spend the majority of the twentieth century in America. But she knew enough about the history of Europe to realise that it was times like these, of economic uncertainty and civic disquiet, when people needed victims to vent their frustrations on.

While they had been getting ready to leave London for their first show in Leicester that day, they had been listening to disturbing reports on the radio. An NF rally was due to take place, in a deliberately provocative gesture, outside the town hall in the predominantly Asian borough of Southall.

The broadcast was punctuated by commentary from various police officers and politicians and all of them predicted this was going to turn ugly. Just at the moment they heard the horn of the van sound outside, the BBC were interviewing the public for their views.

'He's our patron Saint, he's our St George and we have the right to celebrate his day wherever we want to,' a man said in a Cockney accent. *'We ain't gonna let no dirty foreigners dictate to us our birthright...'*

'Right, that's enough of that wee bastid,' said Robin, switching the radio off. 'Ready, hen? Time to hit the road and leave those meatheads to it.'

Sylvana had followed him out of the door, trying to shake the ugly menace of the interviewee's tone from her head.

For the first time in the band's history, they were travelling in a proper minibus, with seats in the back as well as room for their gear. It was owned by their new driver, who also doubled up as their roadie, and went by the comforting name of Robber. Because his surname was Robinson, Donna had assured them, not for any nefarious reasons. Perish the thought.

Robber looked like Bill Sikes's dog Bullseye – thickset, with huge shoulders and a fat neck, arms bulging with muscles and little bandy legs in drainpipe jeans, and monkey boots carrying it all. His wide Roman nose, bright little eyes and neat buzzcut completed the illusion. He seemed very jovial, happily stashing away all Sylvana's bags as if they weighed little more than an ounce of cotton candy and giving her his hand to climb into the back seats with a cheery: 'All right, chuck, sit yourself down, make yourself at home,' in yet another strange lilt of the English accent she would later be told was called 'Brummie.'

Something else was different that day too; it was the first time they'd ever gone to a gig without Helen. She was too busy to leave her stall on a Saturday now, had too many orders to just ditch everything and join them on a tour that was due to take almost an entire month to complete. She and Allie had spent the last night together, in the new flat they'd just moved into on Lancaster Road, leaving Sylvana and Robin in what now seemed like a particularly big and empty Queen's Gate Gardens. They'd gone through the new songs together for about the thirtieth time, and Sylvana had tried not to feel like there was something important missing.

'Where to first, boss?' Robber settled himself behind the wheel.

'Lancaster Road,' said Robin, 'the left turn as you come off Ladbroke Grove, second building on the left. It's got a wee driveway at the front so it should be nae bother.'

'Right you are,' Robber started up the engine.

'Then it's straight to Leicester,' Robin continued. 'Load-in at three, soundcheck at four.'

'Easy,' their driver pointed the van down the road. 'We'll make it in no time.'

Allie was waiting on the pavement outside the 1930s block, all his bags and cases beside him. Helen had already left for work and Sylvana would have hazarded a guess that he'd been stood on that spot since half-past nine, staring up the road after her. Still, he tried to make his hellos as cheerful as he could, although he pointedly didn't join them in the back, preferring instead to sit beside Robber. Maybe he was just used to being up front. Or maybe he couldn't face seeing them holding hands just then, when he was on his own for the first time.

He had the air of a puppy left out in the rain.

Still, what Allie lacked in conversation, Robber was happy to make up for.

There was a tapedeck in the van and they all soon got to know what their driver's favourite music was – The Stranglers, Siouxsie and the Banshees, and then more Stranglers. He gave them his own personal commentary about each track. Perhaps his most golden moment was his recollection of the first time he'd heard 'Peaches' performed on TV.

'I just couldn't fuckin' believe they said the word "clitoris" on *Top of the Pops*!' he recalled with the enthusiasm of a thirteen-year-old who'd just discovered a stash of jazzmags under a hedge on the school field. 'Liberation for women, that's what I preach – yeah, not half, mate, count me in! What a bunch of berserkers!' And he howled along with Hugh Cornwell's original with all the prowess of a priapic bull terrier.

Robber's cheerful banter kept up the whole way round the North Circular and up the M1. He didn't seem to notice that no one was joining in very much. He was like a one-man Michael Parkinson show, asking himself questions when no one else was forthcoming, then providing thoughtful answers about his choice of jobs, his taste in music and how he had first made his way in London.

Then, just as they had come off the motorway to take the road towards Leicester, one of his tapes pinged out of the deck, defaulting the machine onto the radio and the middle of a news report:

'Amid scenes of chaos outside Southall Town Hall, where National Front demonstrators have clashed with police and Anti-Nazi League protestors, we are now receiving reports that a man has been rushed to hospital in a critical condition...'

'Christ!' said Allie, coming back to life.

'Oh God,' Sylvana clapped her hand to her mouth. A sudden cloud of dark, swirling reds and murky browns swam before her eyes.

'It is believed that the man received his injuries in the melee of a baton charge made by the hugely outnumbered police,' the report went on. 'The man who called the ambulance, twenty-four-year-old Parminder Atwal, told the BBC: "I saw a policeman hit a man on the head as he sat on the pavement. The man tried to get up, fell back and then reeled across the road to my house."'

'Awww, the fuckin' pigs, man,' Robber slammed his hand onto the steering wheel. 'What do they want to go and do that for?'

'Bastids,' agreed Robin.

Sylvana held her head in her hands.

'Hey, are ye all right?' he put a cool hand on her wrist.

Sylvana shook her head, dispersing the cloud like ink splashed into water. She couldn't help remembering what Donna had told her a couple of days before.

'Ray,' she whispered. 'Ray was going down to that march.'

'Ray Spencer?' Robin sounded puzzled for a moment, then put his arm around her shoulders. 'Och, sweetheart, don't fret yersen, it won't have been Ray.'

But she couldn't get the thought out of her head.

Robber, as good as his word, got them to the load-in in plenty of time. The venue was a pub down the road from the Uni, with a big back room, popular with students and the local punks and weirdos. The promoter, an enthusiastic toff with red plastic-framed glasses who was making a bad job out of looking hip, showed them to their dressing room, which was a good deal cleaner than many that had gone before, if only the size of a toilet cubicle. It must have been painted recently for the graffiti was strangely minimal and the toff, or one of his minions, had laid out some sandwiches, bags of crisps, a bowl of apples and a slab of beers for them.

'Thanks, pal,' said Robin, trying to wave him off.

But, excited by the proximity of such raw young talent, he lingered in the doorway. 'Is there anything else I can get you?' he asked.

'Do you have a radio?' asked Sylvana.

Again, Robin gave her the puzzled look.

'A transistor?' said the toff. 'I'm sure we can rustle you one up. Just a mo'...' and he scuttled off down the corridor.

'Cucumber sarndwitch?' Allie pulled back the clingfilm and proffered the plate in a plummy approximation of their host. He was getting back to his old self then, at last.

'Eww, tharnk you, I'm sure,' Robin joshed back, selecting a neat triangle of white bread and crab paste. Then he dropped the comedy accent. 'What d'ye want a radio for, hen?'

Sylvana didn't notice the sliver of ice that slipped into the enquiry.

'I need to know who that man was,' she said. 'I just need to know it wasn't Ray.'

'I'm sure it wasn't,' said Allie. 'But I know what you mean. It's hard no to worry, eh Robin?'

'Aye,' Robin nodded.

'Ah! Here we are,' the toff returned, a portable radio in his hand.

'Oh, thank you,' Sylvana smiled gratefully as he fussed around, plugging it in for her and fiddling around with the ariel.

'Now, what station would you like?' he asked.

'Whatever the best news channel is. I don't know, really...You probably know better than I do.'

'Aha,' nodded the toff. 'Well, let's find Radio Four then. They have the updates every half an hour...'

'Hey, we'll leave you twos to it,' said Robin from the door. 'We'll just make sure our Robber's no up to somethin' he shouldnae.'

'Thanks, honey.' Sylvana was still staring at the toff as he span the dial around, trying to concentrate on him and push away the red swirls that still danced round her peripheral vision.

'Don't mention it.'

The toff couldn't have known that much about radio stations either, as Sylvana must have sat through about forty minutes of the meaningless jabber of some play before the news finally did come back on.

'A man has died following violent scenes in West London this afternoon, when thousands of protestors clashed with participants in a National Front rally held outside Southall Town Hall. Amid scenes of total chaos, he was rushed to hospital with head wounds, but died shortly after arrival…'

'Sylvana.' Robin's voice cut across the broadcast. 'I've spoke to Donna on the phone just now and it's definitely not Ray.'

He was standing at the doorway, a microphone cable wound round his arm.

Sylvana almost fell out of her plastic chair. She saw his mouth moving, but it took a couple of seconds before the words sank in.

He came towards her, his eyes earnest, lifted up her left hand and started to rub her fingers.

'He was there all right but he managed to get out of it, nae harm done. He had to run about a mile to get away from the coppers though, apparently. They've arrested three hundred, she said.'

Sylvana stood up; tried her best to smile.

'Oh, thank you so much for finding that out. Oh God. Not that it isn't still so awful for whoever it is. He's dead, the man, you know.'

She felt tears prick behind her eyelids.

'So I just heard.' Robin pulled her into his arms and they stood a moment, wrapped around each other, rocking slowly. Then gently, he pulled away. 'Look, I'm sorry, but it's four o'clock. We've got to do this soundcheck now. Are ye gonna be OK?'

'Yes,' she nodded. When she opened her eyes, the colours had gone. She pulled herself together and followed him out of the door.

They found out later on that night that the man who had been killed was called Blair Peach; he was a teacher for special needs children in South London. They dedicated their last song to him, 'Splintered', one that had come to Sylvana in a rush of blood-red, with Allie's guitars like the savage strokes of black batons against soft skulls and Robin's keyboards wailing like sirens. Sylvana had never put so much anger into anything as she did that song, that night, and the crowd went with her, roaring and cheering and reaching out their arms to try and pull her in with them. Robber had to practically wrap her in a blanket and bundle her backstage afterwards or they might have made away with her. As it was, their dressing toilet was besieged by people wanting to shake their hands, local fanzine writers scribbling down everything they had to say, most of which simply boiled down to Robber's eloquent interjection: 'Fuck the Nazis and fuck the fucking pigs.'

It was well after midnight before they got away. As part of the deal, the toff had got a couple of his student mates to put them up, which meant Allie got the sofa, Sylvana and Robin got a zed-bed in a box room above the garage, and Robber got the back of his van. The students were very sweet, though. They'd kept a couple of plastic bottles of cider and some cocktail sausage rolls for them, and were keen to keep the party going as long as they possibly could.

Robber and Allie were well up for it, but Sylvana couldn't face any more. Now the euphoria of the gig had passed, she felt cold and exhausted, all her emotions used up, and crying out for sleep.

Luckily, Robin felt the same. He excused them both, and led the way up the stairs. Both the room and bed looked big enough for a toddler, their bedding a couple of sleeping bags and an ancient, orange and purple bedspread, the temperature a steep drop from the packed, sweaty pub.

And it dropped another couple of degrees the moment Robin shut the door.

'I'll sleep on the floor then, shall I?' he said.

Sylvana, about to flop onto the zed-bed, looked up sharply.

His eyes had gone to pinpoints. A little tic was working up and down on his left cheek, something Sylvana had never seen before.

'What do you mean?'

'I mean,' his voice was a hiss, 'you'll no want me in your bed tonight, will ye? Not when there are so many other men you'd like to be sharing it with.'

Sylvana felt her mouth open, but she was too shocked to make any sound come out of it.

'I mean,' Robin's voice rose up a notch, 'you'd probably rather have Ray Spencer up here with ye, wouldn't ye? Or maybe,' he cocked his head to one side, put on a mocking tone, 'you'd prefer that wee wanker of a promoter to come up and twiddle with yer dials. Ye certainly couldn't take yer eyes off him, now, could ye?'

'Robin,' Sylvana whispered, 'I don't know what you're talking about.'

But Robin was getting louder as his face got darker, until his whipcord body was actually shaking with rage.

'Or any of those students, those stupid wee fanzine writers, all those guys that were clamourin' for ye tonight, eh? Maybe ye could do the lot of 'em, eh, one after the other, is that what ye'd like, ye filthy bitch?'

He spat the last word right into her eye and she crumpled on the floor in front of him. Sobs wracked through her body, spontaneously, hysterically. She couldn't believe what she was hearing. Her gentle Robin, transformed into this snarling, twisted monster. The shock was as intense as falling into an ice bath.

He stood above her for a few moments, watching her reduced to a snivelling wreck, a bundle of rags on the floor.

Then suddenly, he was there beside her, his arms around her.

'Oh my God, Sylvana, I'm so sorry, forgive me, I don't know

what came over me, Jesus, I don't know what I'm saying.' Words tumbled out of him in rapid succession as he tightened his grip.

Her first instinct was to pull away, smack him in the mouth, run.

But then she realised he was crying too.

'I'm sorry,' she heard herself say, though she couldn't work out why she was saying it. 'Please don't cry, Robin, I'm sorry.'

'No, I'm sorry, hen, I'm a bastid, I've got a wicked temper and I thought I could control it, but just somethin' snapped inside me tonight, I don't know why. Oh God, please help me, you're the last person on earth I want to do this to.'

And he continued to cry, sobbing long into the night, while Sylvana lay frozen in his arms, wondering what the hell it was that she had done wrong.

17

Two Sides To Every Story

February 2002

Lynton Powell was surprisingly upfront when it came to the question of drugs. 'I was pretty young, pretty confused, and a lot of mad things had happened in my life over a very short period of time,' he said, with a wry smile. But he never lost eye contact for a second.

'It's a shockingly easy thing to get into when you've already been sliding towards it for a couple of years without realising,' he explained. 'The environment we were in then, everyone was doing drugs anyway – speed when you were on the road, before you did a gig, pot and weed to relax afterwards, or while you were in the studio, or when you wanted to come up with another profound idea for a song. It wasn't such a big thing to swap smoking reefer for something that made life seem even easier. And as no doubt you've heard every junkie in history say – when you start to dance with it, it does make life seem a whole lot easier.

'I was always shy, I never liked being under scrutiny,' he considered, 'even when journalists generally only had good things to say, 'cos I always thought I never had anything particularly interesting to say back to them. H just took away that worry. I stupidly thought that with its help, I could just concentrate on the important thing, the music. You gotta remember as well, all my heroes had been through their own personal romance with the stuff. If I'm being honest, I thought I was being like Miles, that I was gonna go places far outside normal, straight, boring people's existences and report back from the amazing new worlds I'd discovered out there.' He gave a short laugh. 'A common enough misconception.'

I nodded sympathetically, hiding the rush of relief and excitement that he hadn't taken this turn in the conversation badly, because the next question was ultimately just as awkward.

'So do you not blame Vince for getting you hooked? A lot of other people seemed to...'

Lynton lit a cigarette, took a puff then lifted it up in front of my nose.

'See this?' he said. 'This little white stick here is a hundred times harder to stop doing than H was. I can blame him for this, most probably, 'cos at some point in our murky past when we were spending our life on a tour bus, I took one of these bastards from him purely to see if it would stop me feeling bored. But anything else that I did was my fault and my responsibility. And,' he flashed that wry smile at me again, 'I'm still here and he ain't.'

This raised a chuckle from Gavin.

Lynton rested his cigarette back down in the ashtray, a beautiful black and gold chunk of glass that looked more like a modern art sculpture than something you should put a fag out in. He meshed his long fingers together in a reflective pose. 'What else?' he asked mildly. 'Don't worry, Eddie. Ain't nothing that's off limits to me.'

I sensed that maybe he was saying the opposite of what he meant here, but I carried on regardless.

'What about Sylvana?' I asked. 'Was it her who changed everything? I'm trying to get some sense of what she was like…'

Lynton unlinked his fingers in a graceful flourish and picked up the cigarette again. He closed his eyes as he inhaled, then blew the smoke out slowly.

'You ever heard of *amour fou*?' he asked.

I shook my head.

'Mad love. That's the French expression for it, which is sadly appropriate, as it goes. Well. That Sylvana, man, she wasn't what you'd call mad, but she wasn't really all there, if you know what I mean. D'you ever listen to her music?'

I didn't want to admit I'd spent more time looking at her picture than actually taking in the content of the albums I'd managed to acquire so far. But I got the general drift of it. So I said: 'Well, she doesn't make a lot of sense, lyric-wise, and the music is pretty away with the fairies.'

Lynton nodded. 'Well, there you go. That explains her really. She was pretty out there. Not in the way that Vince was, though, that's why we all thought it was kind of a strange attraction. He was crazy in an aggressive, confrontational way; he liked getting a rise out of people. She was more the type that always had these mystical "feelings" that she had to "go with", pretty much a hippy really. Which was why it did seem kind of strange to us that Vince would get so besotted with her so quickly.'

'Yeah, well, that was all a put-on if you ask me,' said Gavin. 'That little girl lost bit. She dumped her boyfriend quick enough and they'd been in that band together for years.'

'True,' Lynton nodded amiably, 'and Vince dropped his girlfriend just as quick, who he'd been with even longer. It ain't really fair to judge her on that.'

I clocked Gavin's scowl out of the corner of my eye.

'But what it was about her that really fucked things up,' Lynton carried on, oblivious, 'was the effect her ditzy behavior had on Stevie. Stevie couldn't stand her, man, he really could not stand her. The thing was, I think, that Stevie had always had Vince's full attention up to that point. I mean, I love Stevie and I always will; he's my Paddy soul brother from way back, but within that band there had always been kinda like two factions. Me and Kevin: the swotty ones, always staying up late to try out new chords and write new songs; and him and Vince, Los Banditos.

'Vince's first girlfriend, Rachel, she was always there, like, but she was always in the background, even when we was sharing that squat together up the hill,' he waved his arm in a northerly direction, then swooped it down to put his cigarette out. 'And when we was on tour, forget about it, he weren't thinking of her at all. So Stevie lost his alley-cat pulling partner, and for the first time since we'd been together, Vince's interest wasn't fully focused on the band. He'd changed. If you look at the records and the interviews we did from that point on, you'll notice that Vince became Vincent. It was probably a combination of the drugs and Sylvana, to be honest, but he was starting to take himself a lot more seriously.

'That's what fucked Stevie up, man, and that's why he always deals with it by twisting it round that because of Sylvana meeting Vince, I became a junkie. And no doubt he'll tell you that exact same thing when you meet him. I've had the argument with him a million times myself and it still don't work. We just leave it now,' he said with a chuckle, 'that we've just remembered things differently, that's all.

'And my man Gavin here,' he leaned over and gave the photographer a hearty slap on the knee, 'he remembers it differently again, right?'

'Yeah, right, mate,' Gavin laughed back. 'I remember it clearly. As seen through the bottom of a glass.'

That was just about the end of the interview, though we stayed around so that Gavin could take a few new shots afterwards of Lynton looking debonair on the sofa, with that beautiful ashtray arranged in front of him on the coffee table. He and Gavin laughed and joked throughout the clicks and poses; that little crackle of tension that had risen between them now lost on the breeze. I flicked through my notes one more time as they were composing themselves and realised I'd left out one important one. I saved it until Gavin had finished and was stashing his gear back into his camera bag.

'Lynton, do you mind me asking one last thing?'

'Sure, man, go ahead.' Lynton was standing up now, ready to see us out, picking up his cigarettes and putting them back into his pocket.

'Do you know whatever happened to Don Dawson?'

All afternoon we'd been talking about some pretty heavy things – heroin addiction, racism, Bible-bashing fundamentalist Yanks – and Lynton had answered all my questions with good grace and what seemed like genuine honesty. But for the first time then, I saw something flicker over the bass player's smooth countenance, a storm cloud, a flinching in his eyes, like somebody had just stood on his foot. A little trace of pain.

'Yeah I do, poor bastard,' he said quietly. 'He died, just over two years ago, on Christmas Day, as it goes. In a nursing home, back in Hull.'

Lynton stared past me, out of the tinted windows and beyond. 'He had Alzheimer's, they reckoned. He'd been slowly losing it for years. Big Bad Don, the Cock of the North, he was nothing but a tiny shell, in the end. It was kind of hard to believe…'

I don't think Gavin had caught any of this part of the conversation, because he came up to Lynton at that point, with his coat back on and his bag over his shoulder, right hand outstretched.

'Thanks again, mate, I'll send you the contacts for these,' he said. 'If you want any printed up, just let me know.'

Lynton came back to reality sharpish, grabbed hold of Gavin's palm and shook on it.

'That'd be great, Gavin, and I'll get you a copy of the new CD, once I've finished polishing it. You know it's gonna be—' they shared what was obviously an old joke, finishing the sentence together '—the shit!'

They fell about then, slapping each other on the back.

'Oh, and Stevie's definitely back next week,' Lynton added, like he'd only just remembered. 'I've got to put the bastard up for a week. So I'll make sure he spares a bit of time for you, make sure you get your story. Eddie,' he turned to me, 'it was a pleasure meeting you. Good luck stitching this all together, mate, and even better luck selling it.'

I realised this was officially the end of proceedings now and shook his outstretched hand vigorously. 'Thanks, Lynton, that's really great. Thanks for being so open.'

As if by magic, the lovely Shanice appeared at the exit door, beckoning us very politely to leave.

Out into the cold, dim twilight, the streetlights blinking on as we left the enclave and started back up Oxford Gardens. Lights switched on behind the net curtains of the little houses too, shadowy figures moving inside. Still no one out on the street itself, nothing to give the game away.

Gavin clapped his hands together, a great big grin all over his face. He was clearly delighted at having seen his old friend.

'Got time for a quick one, mate?'

I had promised Louise that I wouldn't be back late. But now there was a dull ache inside my stomach, the knowledge that I'd never get to meet one of the people I'd really wanted to talk to for the book. A knot that twisted with the knowledge that Gavin had inadvertently cut short something really interesting that Lynton was about to say.

Only one way to untie it.

'That sounds like a plan to me.'

It was a plan that cost me. I did get a cab home that night, even though by eleven o'clock the lure of Gavin's sofa and another rummage through his video collection was considerably stronger. I was greeted with a plate of incinerated pizza, left poignantly on top of the oven and a shut bedroom door that Louise had wedged the sideboard up against from the inside. When I tried to get in, gentle words drifted through the woodwork: 'Fuck off, Eddie.'

Back on the sofa again, so soon.

It took about a week to put that one right, a bloody expensive week. I ended up forking sixty quid for a pair of black suede stiletto boots and then another ton on a meal in some poncy Japanese restaurant in Fitzrovia after taking milady for a trip to the cinema.

As a result of which I didn't get the time to go through my Lynton tapes before Gavin was ringing up to say that we were meeting Steve Mullin.

Gavin was really excited about this next interview. I don't think the two of them had seen each other since that album of re-releases five years ago. He wanted me to come over the night before so we could go over everything I was going to say, watch the old videos again, and go through all our cuttings.

This time I told Lou I would probably be out for a couple of days.

'Why don't you just move straight into Arlington House and cut out the middle man?' was her reply.

We were meeting Steve in the Earl of Lonsdale on Portobello Road at lunchtime on a Thursday. By midnight on Wednesday we were listening to *Butcher's Brew* for about the sixth time. I had become fixated on one track in particular, probably because Lynton had mentioned it as epitomising the height of his skag experimentalism – he had been playing his bass while he was out of it and had stumbled across this rhythm that had actually made him feel seasick, as if the notes were propelling his stomach up and down on waves. It had something to do with how low the notes were as well as what order they were played in. He became obsessed with reproducing it on the album; he wanted to make a song that could possibly induce the listener to vomit, so that they could appreciate where Lynton was coming from while he had created it.

Vince, naturally, had loved this idea, and, having shared the same batch that had caused Lynton's revelation, understood exactly the comment his bassist was trying to make. They had just come off a disastrous tour of the States, where they'd nearly got lynched by Klansmen in Birmingham, Alabama, and the singer chanelled his own sick disgust at them into Lynton's nauseous rhythm.

They called the song 'Retch' in the end, though they had toyed with 'Kan the Klan'. It had just been the two of them on the finished track – Lynton had added some loose percussion that sounded like random, muffled thumping, like someone being beaten up in a room up the stairs, then fashioned an eerie motif to recall the Deep South on a Dobro guitar he had just been learning to master.

It was fucking brilliant.

I went to sleep with Vince's plaintive wail echoing round in my head: *'Spelt your name in beer on a bar in 'Bam/Sign of a Southern gentleman/Who waits until dark to come out and creep/Fat and afraid wrapped up in a sheet/Flames in the night light a slug's trail/Safety in numbers for the mentally frail/I'll show you the light of my purifying fire/Burn your pork flesh on my funeral pyre/Retch you wretch/Die, die!'*

I dreamed about men with pig's heads marching round holding flaming crosses and woke to the smell of frying bacon.

Gavin was humming away to himself in the kitchen, brewing up coffee and piling a ginormous fry-up onto two plates when I staggered in, feeling pretty wretched myself.

'Do you ever have a hangover?' I enquired, wedging myself into a chair round the table and reaching for the orange juice.

'Not in living memory.' Mine host slapped down a plate full

of bangers, bacon, fried bread, eggs and beans in front of me. 'But you know what they say – the devil looks after his own. Get that down you, you'll soon be right.'

He was correct about the restorative qualities of our breakfast, but I couldn't help but wonder as I ate, why it was that his would go straight through him as if it never touched the sides, while mine would immediately convert into another layer of flab. When I thought about it, Gavin didn't eat much that wasn't just meat and didn't drink much that wasn't alcohol-based. Maybe he just was the Atkins Diet in action.

'Fill your boots, mate,' he encouraged me. 'If I know Steve, we probably won't be getting any more solids today.'

When we stepped outside, it was one of those bright, mild February days that holds out the promise of spring just when you have given up hope that winter will ever end. Crocus and narcissi were poking themselves out of the ground in people's front gardens, reminding me of mother's carefully tended plot and how pleased she always was with the first bulbs of the year.

On Portobello Road, mobile phone shops and coffee bars were proliferating in just the same manner, pushing out the shops that had amused previous generations – the comix shop Fantastic Store, the goth boutique run by that tall, fit bird with long black hair that used to be next to the tattooists. I wondered what Steve Mullin would make of it all.

It wasn't long before I found out precisely.

We found him in the big lounge room at the back of the Lonsdale, which had recently been made over from its original wooden tables and chairs into a lounging area with numerous ill-matching sofas and what appeared to be half a dead tree festooned with fairy lights hanging from the centre of the ceiling.

Steve was standing with his back to us, pint in hand, examining a *Pulp Fiction* film poster. That was about as trendy as the Lonsdale got, thank Christ. It was about the only pub on Portobello that still was a pub, as opposed to a trendy Trustafarian bar.

'Steven,' said Gavin in a mock-grave tone.

The guitarist wheeled round.

I was quite shocked. Steve Mullin had not aged anywhere near as well has his former bass player. He always had had a battered look about him, but years of heavy drinking appeared to have taken a Mike Tyson-like toll on his face. All his features had coarsened; he had a double chin, a bulbous nose verging dangerously on the strawberry and eyes like slits with puffy lids. The unruly hair was still thick, dyed and spiked to attention, and he hadn't changed his wardrobe much either, it was just that his stomach now hung over the belt of his black drainpipe jeans almost obscenely. He was obviously one of those guys who only put on weight in one place, and what a concentration there was there – he almost looked pregnant.

'Fookin' hell, Digger, I see you've not changed!' he exclaimed. 'Just as bastard well, everything else has round here. What's happened to place? I just got chowed at by bastard Yanks for lightin' up in a no smokin' room – thought I'd got away from all that shite in LA.'

He frowned incredulously.

'You've been in La La Land too long, mate,' Gavin replied.

'Fookin' right I have.' Stevie put his pint down on a table and opened his arms. 'How are you, any road?'

Gavin stepped into a hearty embrace.

'I'm good, mate, yourself?'

'I'm fookin' confused I am, like. I went in bank this mornin' and the bloke behind the counter had a fookin' mohican – he only looked about twelve year old an' all. Is there some kind of punk revival I've missed out on?'

'Nah, that'll be the David Beckham fan club,' said Gavin.

'David Beckham?' Steve almost spat the word out. 'Fookin' 'ell. I think I need another pint. What you havin', Digger?'

'I'll join you in a pint. This is Eddie, by the way.'

Steve looked at me for the first time. It was not a particularly friendly look.

I stepped forward and reached out my hand. 'Good to meet you,' I offered, encouragingly.

He belched loudly, then took my hand back and shook it with a grip that made me wince. 'You're the one writin' book, are you?' he said.

'That's right,' I tried to keep a smile in place through gritted teeth.

'You want a drink?' His expression didn't change.

'I'll get them,' I offered.

Steve nodded. 'All right,' he said. 'Get us that one with the comedy German on the taps. Not the strong one, the other one – Knackerblitzen or Eidelweiss or summat.'

'Ayingerbrau,' said Gavin. 'I'll have the same. We'll get a table, Eddie. Looks like we've got the room to ourselves at least.'

Hmmmm, I thought, that might be the only consolation of the day. No wonder Gavin had wanted me well briefed for this encounter. He obviously anticipated there could be trouble with this one. Still, I mused, as I handed the barman a tenner, I suppose I would be wary if I was Steve. I'd want to suss me out too. Probably the hostility would wear off after a few jars, once he realised how seriously I was taking the book.

When the barman actually returned with some change I took it as a good omen.

Gavin and Steve were huddled in the far corner away from the sofas, sitting opposite each other across a table. Steve was mid-anecdote, a fag blazing in one hand, the dregs of his previous pint in the other.

'Billy kept goin' on about this haunted corner, that he couldn't play in there 'cos the vibes, man, were like really deadly for his mojo,' he was saying, switching from Yorkshire into LA-speak midway through. 'Well you know, there's quite a few legends about places in Hollywood bein' haunted – Grauman's Chinese Theatre for one, fookin' Chateau Marmot for another, anywhere these bastard actors have popped they clogs. 'Cos you know what they're like, they can't go on without an audience even when they're dead.'

I put Steve's new pint in front of him and he picked it up with a grunt that could have been 'ta' and carried straight on with his story.

'So, after about a month of this shite, I found out from drummer, it weren't a bastard ghost he were worried about at all. It was this fookin' sound booth where one of them poodle-haired glam metal wankers used to go an' shag 'is groupies. Once I found that out, I were like, respect to you, mate, I wouldn't want to touch it with a plastic one either.'

Gavin roared with laughter. I sat down beside him, wondering whether to get my tape recorder out of my bag or to let a couple of drinks go by first.

'Cheers, Eddie,' he picked up his pint and clinked it against mine.

Steve looked over resentfully.

'Yeah, cheers,' he said, then turned his eyes back to Gavin. 'How's your mate Mick, Digger? Where's he got to these days?'

It carried on like this for another two hours. He must have sunk six pints before he even needed to go to the bog, by which time I was steaming.

'Should I just go home and forget about this?' I asked Gavin, once his mate was safely out of earshot.

'No, no,' he put a hand on my arm. 'Just stay cool, mate, he's just sussing you out, he's always like this when he meets new people.'

'Well, I wish you'd warned me.'

'Well, if I had done, you might have felt even more awkward. I just made sure you knew your shit, 'cos if he tries to test you out about what songs you like, which he will in probably another pint's time, you've gotta be able to impress him. But honestly, mate, everyone goes through this, it's the initiation ceremony.'

He tipped me a wink. 'They did it to Mick as well. Him and Vince, it was fuckin' carnage. But I promise you, after you've survived a night on the piss with Steve, you'll have a mate for life.'

That made me feel a bit better, but not much. 'What's with all this Digger shit anyway?' I asked.

'Mate, that's how he thinks Australians speak. I think he got it from *The Paul Hogan Show* in the early eighties. He used to call Mick the Great White Wino.'

I couldn't help but laugh at that. Obviously there was a very funny guy lurking underneath that obnoxious exterior. I just had to be patient and wait for him to out himself.

Only Steve came out of the bogs in a bullish mood, swaggering across the room and coming to a halt beside us to stand, rearranging his bollocks in his too-tight jeans. 'I fancy a walk,' he announced. 'Let's go and see what manner of cunts have taken over the rest of this place. See if there's owt left I even recognise.'

Steve's idea of a walkabout was to mosey from one pub to another, staring at amazement as he entered each refurbished pile and spouting loudly of his disgust at the transformation. Predictably, his outrage reached its apex when we entered The Lounge and he saw the faux Warhol screenprint of Joe Strummer.

'I've seen it fookin' all now,' he said, stopping dead in front of it.

By this point, I'd just about had enough. At the start of our odyssey, he'd run into an old acquaintance, a huge Rasta, inside the Portobello Gold. In his delight to talk to the guy, he'd ignored both Gavin and me for the best part of an hour, which I had started to see as a blessing. But his reassurance that there was still human life in W11 took a turn for the worse when he saw the pub he referred to as Finches, but to the rest of the world The Duke of Wellington, was crawling with American tourists. He stormed straight out of there into the bar across the way and belched loudly in the barman's face when he asked if sir would like to try today's special Mojitos at two for the price of one. Taking gleeful delight that the Electric Cinema had been transformed into a playground for the glitterati, he'd stuck a foot to deliberately trip up a semi-famous TV actor who was mincing his way in there, sending him flying into a table full of shocked Yummy Mummies. By the time we'd reached The Lounge it was nearly six o'clock and the whole afternoon had been akin to minding a gigantic toddler with Tourette's and Attention Deficit Disorder.

'Yeah,' I said, 'you used to get a better class of cunt in here in your day.'

'You what?' he snapped, his bloodshot eyes blazing. 'You calling Joe Strummer a cunt?'

'No,' I said simply. 'I'm calling you one.'

And I stared him back full in the eye, the look I had spent hours learning from Paulie Sorvino in *Goodfellas*.

I was so full of adrenalin then that my hands had involuntarily bunched up into fists and I was fully prepared to swing for the bastard and fuck the consequences. But then Steve's snarl turned into a wide grin and the glint in his eye suddenly made about twenty years drop away from his face.

'I wondered how long it'd tek you to realise,' he said.

'You tested him sorely,' said Gavin.

'Aye,' nodded Steve, 'but he's finally passed.'

'You cunts!' I exclaimed. 'You're both fucking cunts!'

'That's right, Eddie,' Steve said proudly. 'We're all bastard cunts together, which is just as well, like, 'cos we seem to have found the centre of the cunt universe here.'

He surveyed the rest of the room disdainfully. 'Right, well, Digger, I think I've had enough of trendy Portobello Road now.

What say we go to off licence, get us selves a nice bottle of Jack and repair to your humble abode?'

'I'd say that was just about the most civilized idea I've heard all day.'

'Then fookin' lay on, McDigger, let's get out of here.'

Steve's story after that was long in the telling. From the first Sex Pistols record he ever nicked in Sidney Scarborough's record shop in Hull to the final showdown at the Lyceum Ballroom, he recalled it all with profane humour and astonishing honesty. Gavin, God bless him, kept us going, nipping out for another bottle of Jack, packets of fags and four-packs of lagers from the dirty offie on the Grove; even supplying blank tapes when I ran out. The birds were twittering the dawn chorus by the time we got to the end.

'I were just so fookin' angry,' Steve told me, referring to the band's fateful last night together. 'I felt like, he weren't just content to fookin' ditch us for some dozy bint, but he wanted to fookin' destroy us all in process. So, the whole way through that last gig we done, that triumphant Lyceum gig as you call it, I was thinkin' about how I were gonna kill him – and I seriously was, and probably would've done if old Stevens wasn't there to protect his investment.

'See, what no bastard realised about that gig was that Kevin, right, Kevin had nearly had his fookin' arms broken by the cunt, our fookin' drummer, he'd only just got enough strength back in 'im to fookin' play by then. And Lynton, fuck knows how he even stayed upright, let alone made a coherent noise, 'cos the rest of us might have been on a stage in London but his brain were on fookin' Mars.

'And Vince is there, poncing away, doin' all his fookin' "I'm a bad arse" shit and all the kids are lappin' it up, but little do they know, he's gonna get on a fookin' aeroplane to swan off with Gloria Vanderbilt straight after show, leavin' us lot a load of geriatric fookin' old wrecks headed straight for knackers' yard. After all's we'd been through, how far we'd come, that were how he thought it were goin' to end. So I thought, no, you cunt, that's not how it's goin' to end, it's goin' to end with my big, fuck-off, steel-capped boots walking right up your bastard neck. I grabbed hold of 'im just as we come off stage and if Stevens hadn't had his little Richardsons army with 'im this story probably would have come to an even more tragic ending.'

Steve paused, gazed up at the ceiling, and reached for another sip of Jack. 'Trouble was, though, at end of day, I fookin' loved the guy. Not to sound gay about it or owt, but the truth was, I couldn't handle fact he'd dumped me for a fookin' bird. Took me years to get over that, it did. By which time it was all too late, of course. Now there's no way I'm gonna make amends to him in this life.' He shook his head grimly.

'What would you say to him if he walked through this door right now?' I asked.

Steve stuck out his bottom lip and shook his head. 'I'd say, "Where the fook have you been, you cunt?" No I wouldn't. I'd say, "I'm fookin' sorry. Sorry for how it finished, how I behaved, and most of all, how I let you just walk off into sunset without raisin' a finger to help you when the woman you loved was dead."'

His voice sound strained and harsh.

'But there's no fookin' point even speculating about that, is they? 'Cos he's fookin' dead now too, lyin' in some cold earth, no cunt even knows where. All on 'is own. Just lyin' there.'

'All right, mate, all right, it's not your fault,' Gavin went to put his arm round Steve then, but Steve brushed him off, wagged a finger in his face.

'You know, Digger, I allus thought that bitch was such a fookin' liar and I know you did too. One night she said to Lynton that the reason her lyrics were so fookin' in the clouds were because she could actually see different colours when she heard different words and sounds. Well that fookin' proved to me she was a nutcase, amongst other things, that were really like, "Nurse! The screens!"

'But then, like, there was this programme on BBC World, or whatever the cable thing is that you can get in the States. A whole programme about folk what see words as colours, numbers as colours, sounds as colours – a whole fookin' load of 'em from all walks of life, none of them is makin' this up. It's a fookin' real condition called synaethesia and they reckoned that somethin' like one person in every hundred has got it. They even reckoned that was how language started in the first place, mebbe.'

'So,' Gavin shrugged, 'that's one thing she didn't lie about. So what?'

'No, you don't get it,' Steve looked really agitated now. 'The thing were, Vince was allus goin' on about what a fookin' genius she were and we was all too busy hatin' her guts to even listen to him. But what if he were right? All them people on that programme were fookin' brainy, I'm tellin' you. And it made me stop and think. What if I'd spent less time being a cunt to him and more time tryin' to get on with her? It never would have turned out the way it did, don't you see?'

'Mate, you're pissed,' said Gavin. 'That chick didn't top herself because of you. You can't blame yourself, especially not after all these years, just because you saw one documentary that maybe proves she wasn't quite as insane as you thought she was. It still doesn't change the fact she was completely unstable and would have done anything to get attention, including and especially wrecking the band. I think you need some sleep.' He glanced down at his wristwatch. 'I think we all fucking do.'

Steve's expression of anguish faded into weary resignation.

'I think you could be right, Digger. You usually are. Scratch my last comments, Boswell,' he said, waving an unsteady finger in my direction. 'I'll come back to you in mornin'.'

And with that, he keeled over onto the sofa and began snoring loudly.

Gently, Gavin removed the smouldering cigarette from between his fingers and stubbed it out.

'Looks like your bed's taken,' he said to me. 'You'd better come in with me – and you better not make the sort of noise that he does.'

'OK,' I nodded, rubbing my eyes. 'It'll make a change to sleep in a bed for once, even if it is with you.'

'Eddie, has anyone ever told you what a charmer you are?'

'Frequently,' I sighed. 'And one day someone will mean it.'

18

Join Hands

August 1980

Donna put the phone down with an expression of triumph.

'You won't believe this,' she said, crossing fingers plated with silver rings and black nail varnish. 'But "Cherry Coma" is number 15 and you're wanted for this week's *Top of the Pops*.'

Donna had a bright red telephone to go with her red-lacquered desk. Behind her, painted in bold black and white, was a geometric abstract mural designed and executed by two eager young students. It vaguely resembled the Rising Sun, for faux Japanese was her latest style obsession. Decorative orchids hung from the top of filing cabinets. The lampshade was a huge white paper moon. She had even piled her hair up and skewered it in place with chopsticks, although her kimono-style top, pencil skirt and winklepickers remained resolutely black.

Donna fancied herself as a high-powered businesswoman now, and this, finally, was her crossover moment. After two and a half years, approaching four albums and two previous Top 20 singles, Mood Violet were headed for the real big time. A big red smile curled across her face.

Not that their progress so far had been slow, she had to admit. They'd grown out of the toilet circuit by the end of the *Ice-Tapped Vein* tour in June of '79. It had been a major success. Demand for tickets on their final night in London had reached such proportions that Donna had been forced to switch venues from the proposed Fulham Greyhound to the Electric Ballroom in Camden, a venue that held twice the punters, and still it was a sell-out.

Watching the crowd go wild for one track in particular, Donna had been quick to release 'Splintered', possibly the most discordant track on the album and one that she'd previously not even thought of as a possible single. It had reached the low 30s in the actual charts and the press had not been slow to record their admiration for the one seemingly spontaneous political statement made by a band that some had seen up to that point as being fairly obtuse.

The times were changing and Mood Violet seemed to be capturing the encroaching harshness of a new era. By the time they'd returned to London, Margaret Thatcher had swept the floundering Labour government aside in the May General Election like a one-woman legion of Panzer tanks, promising to get tough on the recalcitrant unions and clean up the Labour-constructed ghetto. Once the iron bouffant was installed, it was important to show opposition to all she stood for, especially so far as the music press were concerned. Donna kept her sneaking admiration for the woman to herself and let her band get on with maiming her name in interviews.

With both cred and burgeoning popularity on their side, Mood Violet went straight back into the studio, delivering the *Shapeshifter* LP to more acclaim and even more sales in November of that year. No such thing as a 'difficult third', their sound had become more complex and deep with each new piece of equipment the boys could afford to buy to enhance it, still producing and engineering everything themselves.

Sylvana's vocals soared and stretched to meet the challenge. Hormonal boys not only drooled over her now, they sought to divine the true meaning of her continually obscure offerings and she furthered the mystery by refusing to print the actual lyrics and leaving nearly all the interview-talking to Robin and Allie. Notoriously difficult to interview, she had become an enigma, a beautiful enigma.

The 'Astra' single had cracked through the barriers at number 19 in December 1979, 'Dawnburst' had followed it up to number 15 in January 1980. They actually would have made *Top of the Pops* then, if the entire band hadn't been stricken with a particularly nasty bout of flu.

Then it all went quiet, for over half a year. By which time, Donna already had her flat in Holland Park, five more successful bands on her roster, a sideline career as a TV pundit and her own weekly column in *Time Out* where she shared the secrets of her glamorous, yet cutting-edge life.

In fact, the only thing that Donna was lacking in her life now was Ray. Their faltering relationship had finally imploded when she'd put the down-payment on her flat at the same time that one of Ray's heros, Sid Vicious, had come to his sordid end. When she had been more interested in furnishings than his grief at such a loss, it had finally dawned on Ray that Donna's great crusade to promote new bands was actually a sideshow to her greater ambition – the edification of herself.

It had been hard for Ray to digest that his beautiful other half had not been exactly what she seemed, even though he had been trying to deny her growing indifference to him for months. The end had not been pleasant and they avoided each other now as much as possible, but the truth was Donna didn't have to rely on Ray any more. Nowadays, people came to her.

Vada's roster were all her own signings. Bands that had come up from the suburbs, inspired by the possibilities offered by drum machines and synths and the dark romanticism woven so powerfully by Mood Violet. With her own distinctively vampish appearance itself a beacon for a new generation of bands, it was often said that Donna had pioneered her own genre.

Electro-erotica, some had called it. Glam-gothic others had said. Byronica was her personal favourite; but Donna liked the fact that however hard the press tried, they couldn't completely label her.

So she hadn't worried unduly that her biggest act were taking so long to cough up their much-anticipated fourth album. After all, they had built their own studios in some musician's co-op up on Kensal Road, pitching in their earnings with no doubt a little help from Sylvana's family. So it wasn't costing her anything for them to dick around for seven months trying to make effects out of the sound of waves breaking, or spiders spinning webs, or whatever the fuck else grabbed their muse from week to week.

They had fairly regular meetings and she heard the new tracks when the band were finally finished with them, none of which was disappointing. If anything, the multi-layered sonics Robin was so obsessively fussing over were the sort of thing that would have him heralded as a genius by those male journalists who couldn't bring themselves to admit their sole reason for going to see Mood Violet was actually the singer.

The finished tapes were finally handed over in July 1980. Straight afterwards, Allie and Helen got married in Chelsea Town Hall. Donna wasn't invited, but the service was for family only and the couple eschewed her offer to throw them a party afterwards, preferring instead to bugger off for a week in the Outer Hebrides, which all sounded very boring. Still, Helen's business continued to flourish, Donna continued to get her free samples and they genuinely seemed to get happier and happier, those two.

Of Sylvana and Robin, Donna wasn't quite so sure.

Which was why, as she announced her good news that morning, she wasn't so surprised to see that, of the three pairs of eyes pointing her way, only Allie's seemed to be registering any form of delight.

'You're joking?' the genial guitarist suggested.

Donna shook her head with a smile. 'Would I do such a thing to you?' she said.

But Robin didn't look anything like happy. The permanent scowl that seemed to haunt his features these days only deepened with the news. 'So, we've got to put on a show for the kiddies now, have we?' he sneered.

Sylvana's gaze didn't rise from the floor. She was getting skinnier and skinnier, her hair longer and longer, so that a rose-red cloud now obscured most of her face.

'Hey, c'mon, Robin, think off all those bastids back home who'll be watchin',' Allie chivvied his friend along, as he always did. 'Think about the expressions on their faces, eh? I think it's great.'

'Aye, perhaps we can hire a Punch 'n' Judy show to go with it, eh?' Robin responded.

Allie looked crestfallen. He muttered under his breath, something Donna couldn't quite catch.

Sylvana looked up then, peered through her curtain of hair. 'I think that's really great, thanks, Donna,' she said, not altogether coherently.

'Sylvana.' Donna studied her New Wave goddess closely. 'I think it's time you paid a trip to the salon. There's a great new one opened on Kensington Church Street. I checked it out last weekend and they said they'd always have a spot free for you. Let me take you there this afternoon, while the boys sort out what they need for the television.'

She flashed a glance at Robin, her eyes narrowing. Daring him to say anything else out of order. Black talons tapped on the hard surface of her desk. This time it was his turn to look at the floor.

'Good idea,' said Allie, a mite too enthusiastically. 'Let's go and get on wi' the bloke's stuff, Robin, let these girls do what they do best, eh?'

Robin was clearly unhappy with the idea, but he left without making any more comments. When he had finally shut the door, casting a hostile glance behind him, Donna went over to sit next to Sylvana on the sofa.

That was when the smell of brandy hit her. The eyes behind the curtain were unfocused, swimming. The beautiful engima was completely out of it.

Donna was shocked. From what she had seen, Sylvana was never a big drinker. Something must have happened to cause this. Judging by what had already gone on here this morning, something pretty bad.

Donna always felt awkward showing sympathy for anyone, but she realised she was going to have to go gently here. 'Is everything all right with you two?' she asked her, placing her hand on an arm that was stick thin.

Sylvana swayed a little bit, trying to focus on Donna's concerned gaze. 'Yeah, sure, honey, why sh-shouldn't they be?' she slurred.

Fucking hell, thought Donna, the state of her. 'Well, Robin didn't seem his usual chipper self this morning, did he?' She tried to keep her tone light. 'Do you know what's up with him? You lot should be really happy right now – the album's finished, the advance orders are amazing, you've got *Top of the Pops* this Thursday, for Christ's sake – things are going really well for you.'

Sylvana shrugged, the motion of a beached octopus taking its last breath.

'D-don't worry, Donna. He's just a bit…y'know…precious about the record. He gets kinda nervous before a new release. But I'm happy. Really I am.'

This listless act didn't cut any ice with the frost maiden herself. Donna tried another tack. She snapped her fingers in front of Sylvana's nose and watched her suddenly flinch. 'Then why, if everything's so perfect, *honey*, do you stink like a tramp?'

The fear that bloomed in those green eyes was real enough to see. Sylvana started to shake. 'I couldn't sleep so good, that's all,' she whispered. 'A bit of brandy's the only thing that knocks me out.'

'I see,' Donna tapped her patent leather toe on the black vinyl floor. 'Well, in that case, let's go and have some lunch before we hit the hairdressers. You need feeding up, girl. You don't look like you've had anything decent inside you for months.'

While Sylvana was being shorn and styled by the lovely Louis, French *friseur extraordinaire*, Donna marched down Church Street and across the main road into Kensington Market. A couple of vague imitations of herself nudged each other as she stomped her way in, but Donna had no time for their sort today. They could stick their autograph books up their arses. She was too busy chastising herself for not paying enough attention to the inner workings of her band. She could not have Sylvana swaying across the *Top of the Pops* stage like a clump of bloody seaweed.

Helen, having a quiet afternoon reading *iD*, looked surprised to see her.

'I need a word,' Donna announced, cutting straight to it with not so much as a preliminary 'how are you?' 'Could you put the curtain up for a minute?'

Helen frowned, folded up her magazine slowly and put it down on the table. 'What's wrong?' she asked.

Donna put her hands on her hips. 'Our mutual friend. The Quiet American.'

Donna didn't normally talk in code. With an inward sigh, Helen stepped out from behind her till, put the chain across the entrance to her space with the BACK IN TEN MINUTES sign on it and pulled the heavy velvet curtains across the doorway.

'Helen, I'm worried.' Donna spoke in a whisper, terrified of being overheard. 'She came in for a meeting this morning, an important meeting, out of her head and reeking of brandy. I could scarcely get a word out of her, so I took her down the greasy spoon and filled her full of coffee and chips, but she's still not altogether there.'

'Then where is she?' Helen asked.

'Over the road, in The Cruellest Cut. I'm getting Louis to do her hair.' Donna spoke impatiently. 'I've only got about twenty minutes before I'd better get back to her, I'm too scared to let her wander off by herself. But I need to ask you – what's going on with her and Robin?'

Helen inhaled slowly. She had been harbouring enough worries of her own about Sylvana over the past year, but the last person she wanted to share them with was bloody insensitive Donna.

'I'm not entirely sure,' she hedged. 'We don't see them half as much as we used to as a couple, and I can't remember the last time I saw her on her own…'

'Well, you wouldn't see that much of her, would you, there's hardly anything left to see,' Donna started, then reined herself in. 'Look, sorry, Helen, I don't mean to sound out of order, I'm pissed off with myself to tell you the truth. I haven't seen much of them while they've been making this record either, and I just assumed they'd been happily getting on with it. But this morning, there was something wrong with both of them – he was in a filthy mood and I've told you what she was like…' She stopped and looked Helen straight in the eye. 'Have they been having rows, do you think? Only she told me that the reason she was still pissed at ten o'clock in the morning was that she can't get to sleep without a bottle of brandy these days.'

Helen winced at this, raked her hand through her short, spiky hair. 'Like I said, Donna, I'm not sure, but…' Her hazel eyes were pained. 'But yeah,' she finally said. 'Yeah, I think they have been.'

So good at keeping her own secrets, Donna was an expert at divining others. She nodded thoughtfully. Obviously, whatever Helen did know, she didn't want to share. She had always been protective of Sylvana, not to mention suspicious of herself. What Donna was going to have to do now was find a more tactful way to get Helen onside without causing any unnecessary inter-band friction.

'Well, look,' she said, 'we'll keep this between you and me, but I think we should keep more of an eye out for her in future. I know you've only just had your wedding and everything…'

She saw Helen's eyes narrow then.

'And I know the hours you work and what they put in at that studio,' she hastily added. 'But why don't you suggest you have a girl's night out – or a girl's night in, whatever you think's best. Try and find out what's been going on. Because I'm afraid to say it, but I think she needs your help.'

She let that one hang in the air for a moment, gave her something to chew on. 'Now then, I'd better get back to her. But if you want to talk some more, in private of course, please just give me a ring. And I'm sorry to lay this on you and then run, but believe me, I don't want to see her getting into this kind of state.'

'Of course.' Helen looked like she was about to say something more, then thought better of it. Instead, she turned and pulled back the curtains; took down the chain, a tight frown creasing her forehead.

'Thanks for telling me this, Donna,' she said sincerely as they stood in the doorway. 'I'll be in touch as soon as I can.'

'Thanks,' Donna nodded. 'Take care of yourself. And more to the point, take care of her that needs it.'

Even after she'd got the sobered and perfectly styled Sylvana back to her flat in one piece, Donna couldn't rest. She tried to hang around a bit and get something more out of her singer, but it was futile. Sylvana now had a late afternoon hangover, which made her even more pathetic than the drink did. She asked Donna if she knew how to make chicken soup, but when the answer came that she knew how to take the lid off a tin of Campbell's, Sylvana waved her away, saying that in that case, she'd better lie down and sleep the rest of it off.

Two days before they went on show to the world, Donna's once pliable little princess was coming off the rails and she didn't like it one bit. Helen had been precious little help, so she decided what she needed now wasn't some dimwit friend but the advice of a professional.

Back in her office, she called Tony Stevens. The man who'd inspired her in the first place, that night up in Ray's bedroom, was now a virtually self-made millionaire. He had kept his parsimonious instincts intact, mind, establishing his office in the perpetually unglamorous Shepherd's Bush, not an area Donna cared to visit, even if it was only five minutes down the road.

Still, Donna admired Tony greatly, more than anyone else she'd ever met in the music business. But more than that, she understood him in a way few other people did.

Donna's dad was a small-time criminal, too addicted to the bottle to be anything but petty. He had driven vans for people occasionally, but his main line of work was holding and fencing. Since she was tiny, even in the days before the Tower, when they lived in a two-up, two-down off Goldbourne Road, Donna could remember strange men coming in and out of their home at odd hours of the day and night.

The first time it had happened, she'd been terrified. She'd woken to find a big, shaven-headed brute heaving away at something underneath her bed. She'd screamed the house down, thinking it was a monster, until her mum had come to whisk her out of the room, turning to swear at her father, cuddling her and telling her everything was OK with a fag still hanging out of her mouth.

After that, she had had to get used to the traffic of pasty-looking men calling at all hours, commandeering the kitchen to play cards and drink whisky late into the night, leaving their cardboard boxes under the bed, in the wardrobe, all over the house. Sometimes it had its benefits – she'd had a Tiny Tears, a Slinky, and pair of rollerskates before anyone else she knew. Her mother's range of kitchen gadgets were the envy of the estate and, on the rare occasions she ever got taken anywhere other than the pub, she had a wardrobe of fancy evening dresses and fur coats to wear.

The first time Donna had met Tone, there was something about him that immediately took her back to the circle of men in the kitchen. Something about the way he carried himself, the way he spoke, the way he smoked a cigarette pinched between his fingers and thumb, pointed towards his palm. Only there was nothing petty about Tone, she realised that too. He didn't come with the cheap aftershave and blue tattoos, the haunted eyes and ragged, oiled-back hair of her dad's associates. Because Tone came from criminal royalty. His dad had done business with the Richardsons.

It wasn't something he told people, of course. Tone was the white sheep of the family, determined to make a legitimate business out of something he really cared about, even if his first release had been bankrolled by the old man. It was something Donna had found out about herself, one of the few times her wally of a brother had come up with the goods on anything. She had stashed it away in the 'useful' drawer in her mind, although she'd never had to use it. Tone had liked her from the start.

At first, she had read his interest slightly wrongly. There had been one night when Ray was out of town, on the road with The Damned, of all people, who hadn't actually split up for long at all. Tone had invited her to watch one of his bands and had taken her to a club afterwards.

It wasn't the sort of club she'd ever been to before. It was a private members club, hidden up an alleyway besides St Martin in the Fields in Trafalgar Square, the sort of place you'd never find again if you didn't have someone to show you. It was on about three floors, with old panelled walls hung with sporting prints, tanks full of tropical fish, shaded lamps and heavy leather furniture. Tone had told her it was the place he came to when he wanted to truly be away from everyone in the business.

At first, she had thought the reason he was taking her there was to seduce her, away from prying eyes. But after they had got there, and they'd settled into their armchairs with huge balloons of brandy brought to them by a waiter, he'd put a business proposition to her instead.

He really liked her, he told her, really admired her guts. He hadn't seen any other woman operate with half the nous that she had, coming out of nowhere and wanting to make something of herself so fast. He especially liked the way she handled people, he'd said with a knowing wink, young people – she'd got their measure all right. He liked the band she wanted to sign as well, and he wanted to help her out, but he didn't want other people to know that.

'Why?' Donna had asked, totally confused by him.

He'd leaned forward in his chair and smiled. ''Cos you're like me, Donna. We come from the same place. I didn't have any sisters, but if I had done, I would have wanted them to be like you.'

Donna had frowned. 'I still don't get it. You don't really know me, why would I be like your sister?'

Tone had put his huge right hand over her delicate left one and looked deep into her eyes. 'I know you, Donna.'

Then he'd looked up at the waiter, the handsome young waiter, who'd been hovering close by all the time they'd been talking, made a slight motion with his head. The waiter came over immediately with two fresh balloons and Donna saw Tone palm something into his hand and wink as he placed the glasses down. She watched Tone watch him walk away and suddenly everything fell into place.

'We all have our secrets,' he said. 'Keep 'em close, Sis, trust no one and you'll do just fine.' He lifted his drink to her. 'Here endeth the first lesson. Cheers.'

Tone had been a silent partner in Vada ever since. In fact, the name had been one of his jokes, one that Donna didn't even get – she just thought it sounded cool. He'd given her the initial investment she needed and taught her a lot about business and in return, she had provided a glamorous companion when he needed to be seen with one – at events and socials where members of his family or their associates would be present.

The one thing – the only thing – Tone was scared of was his dad finding out about his 'peculiarities'. So Donna's double life as his stunt girlfriend was carried out far away from the eyes of their music biz friends. No one knew about his stake in Vada, not even Ray. They kept their working life as distant as possible, rarely attending each other's gigs, being merely polite when they did meet on the scene.

They both enjoyed the duplicity.

So Donna was quite surprised when, having told him that she needed to see him, he suggested that she came up to his offices after work. She'd rarely been there before and he knew she hated going to that part of town.

'Get a taxi, Sis, I'll pay for it,' he insisted. 'There won't be no one around, except the night watchman to let you in. I've just got a few things that are gonna keep me back tonight, but if you don't mind hanging about, I'll take you up the club later for a bite to eat.'

He meant the club off Trafalgar Square. He knew how much she loved it there, how much she thrived on exclusivity.

Donna clomped up the stairs to his office at about eight-thirty that evening.

The old boy on the door had told her to go up to the second floor and turn right. On the way up, she'd peered in at the office on the first floor. The lights had all been turned off, but the room was still partially illuminated by the streetlights shining through the bay windows from the street below. It was a cramped arrangement of desks and filing cabinets, decorated largely with flyposters of various Exile album releases and the odd spider plant, the picture of organised chaos, held in suspended animation now that the phones and typewriters were all silent for the night.

She carried on up the stairs, following a pool of light that spilled out from under an open doorway. She could hear the sound of laughter.

Funny, Donna thought. He said there wasn't going to be no one here. She reached the open door to Tone's office and stood hesitantly behind it for a moment, not sure if this was really where she was supposed to be. Then she shook herself out of it, stepped over the threshold.

Tone was sitting behind his desk, a wide smile all over his face. A cigar burned in his ashtray and a bottle of Glenfiddich whisky was open on the desk before him, a cut-glass tumbler of the pale amber liquid in his hand.

He looked up: 'Ah, there she is. Donna, you haven't met Vince, have you?'

Donna turned her head slowly to the right. Sprawled out on the two-seater sofa opposite Tone in decadent glory, was the most beautiful man she had ever seen.

He must have been six foot four, a long, spider's frame, encased in black Sta-Prest trousers, a black open-necked shirt and winklepicker boots that went on for ever. A silver cross hung round his neck, a belt with an enormous buckle snaked round his hips and his crowning glory was a shiny black quiff that was maybe four inches high and spiked in all directions. He peered over the top of his gold and black shades, a pair of violet blue eyes that really shouldn't belong on a boy, sizing her up in one long, lustful glance from head to toe.

Donna felt rooted to the spot, not a sensation she was at all used to. She had once thought Dave Vanian was the epitome of male beauty. But compared to this he was an alley cat looking at a panther.

'Hello, Donna.' The apparition stood up, put his glass of whisky down on the coffee table, and extended a hand that was as adorned with thick silver rings as her own. His voice was deep, with a trace of a northern accent.

'Hello, Vince.' Donna took the hand, feeling suddenly wildly out of control.

He smiled louchely. 'Shouldn't we have met before?'

'Donna's got her own label,' said Tone from behind them. 'She's the first businesswoman of punk.'

'Well,' said Vince, coolly raising one eyebrow, 'I'm impressed.'

He dropped her hand gently and motioned for her to sit down next to him.

'Vince here is the singer from Blood Truth, as you probably know,' said Tone, reaching into the cabinet by his desk for another glass. 'We just had a few details to sort out before these guys go back on the road.'

'You heard our new album?' Vince asked her.

To her inner fury, Donna seemed tongue-tied. 'N-no,' she heard herself gibber.

'Tut tut, Anthony,' said Vince, standing up. 'Can I give her one? If she's the first businesswoman of punk then I think she'd better hear it.'

'Go ahead,' Tone blithely waved his hand towards the shelves.

Vince picked out an album and passed it over.

The shiny, just-pressed cover had on it a picture of Vince and three other men, sat around a table in what looked like a Wild West bar, with a bottle of bourbon in front of them and four empty glasses. Dimly lit with a woozy green filter, it had been taken with one of those fish-eye lenses so that it gave you the feeling of drunkenness. Vince sat in the middle of the table, wearing a cowboy hat and a white T-shirt. To his right was another guy in a different kind of hat, who closely resembled Gene Hackman. To his left was a black guy with a hostile look in his eye and a cigarette burning between his raised fingers; and to the black guy's left was a nondescript little fella with spiky hair, a paisley shirt and round glasses.

Above them was written in a semi-circle in a typeface that was supposed to resemble a long lasso: *Blood Truth*. Below, in larger, more swirling, yellow letters that mirrored the above arc: *From the Bottom of the Glass*.

'Can you see the concept there?' said Vince, smiling. 'Or is concept a dirty word to you?'

Luckily, Tone intervened with a glass of whisky for her at that moment before her jaw dropped completely open. It was as if her brain couldn't keep up with the sudden rush of blood from her heart; some kind of blind instinct she had never felt before was rendering her not just speechless but truly dumb and she didn't know whether to slap the bloke or kiss him.

'Thanks, Tone,' she said, as coolly as possible, taking the glass in one hand while continuing to examine the record in her right, desperately trying to claw back her composure.

'I think so,' she returned to Vince's question. 'You've got the cowboy, the copper out of *The French Connection* and the black guy…I don't know what that other one is, but the rest of you, are you doing a tribute to the Village People?'

Tone laughed. 'No flies on you, hey, Sis,' he joked.

She waited for some stinging reply from Vince, but he simply took off his shades and pointed at her. 'We want you,' he bellowed, 'we want you as a new recruit!'

Then he picked up his own glass of whisky and downed it in one, put his glass down on the table and shrugged on a long leather coat that had been lying over the arm of the sofa.

'Anthony,' he put an arm around his boss's neck, 'I'm off. Thanks for the chat.'

'Any time,' Tone slapped him round the back heartily, making a show of male bravado. But Donna noticed the colour rising around the collar of his shirt where Vince's arm rested, noticed his pupils dilate the way they did around certain handsome young men.

Oh shit, she realised. This isn't just business. But they can't be…Not the way that Vince just looked at me…

As if reading her mind, Vince disentangled himself and gave a graceful bow to her. As he did, his eyes met hers again over the top of his shades, that same wolverine look that matched precisely how she was feeling inside.

'Nice to meet you, First Lady,' he said. 'I hope you find time to enjoy our disco classic.'

And with that, he was gone.

She wasn't mistaken. For a second, Tone's eyes followed Vince out of the door, for a second they looked wistful, almost sad. Only for a second though. The next he was clapping his hands together, saying: 'Right then, Sis, let's get out of here. I don't know about you, but I'm Hank Marvin. I'll just get all my bits together…' He hefted up a leather briefcase onto his desk, put some files into it and snapped it shut, chattering away while he did so.

Donna let him get on with it, her mind still reeling. All she could see was Vince and the way his vivid eyes had bored into her. She had wanted nothing so much as…

'Now then, how much was that cab you got here?' Tone pulled out a money clip from his trouser pocket, peeled off a fiver. 'Will this do it?' he flashed it under her nose.

'Uh?' Donna looked up from the carpet, startled.

Luckily, Tone misread the situation completely. 'You are worried, ain't you, girl?' He put a paternal arm around her. 'We'll get a cab down there and then you can tell me all about it…'

'Thanks, Tone,' Donna smiled up at him, thinking, tell you about what?

Suddenly Sylvana was the last thing on her mind.

19

New Dawn Fades

February 2002

I didn't stir from my half of Granger's pit until about five in the evening, another day gone by and dark again already.

Expecting carnage in the front room, I found instead Gavin and Steve sipping tea and reading the papers like a couple of old dears, *Richard and Judy* on TV in the background.

'Fookin' 'ell, Boswell,' Steve greeted me. 'You look rough as arseholes.'

'G'day, mate, do you want something to eat?' asked Gavin.

I stared at them in disbelief. Why was it only me who suffered the next day? Was I carrying the burden of their sins upon their livers and waistlines around with my own?

'Yeah, 'cos me and Digger fancy steppin' out for a bit in a while,' Steve carried on. 'See if he can show me somewhere decent to sup this time.'

The very thought of drinking any more alcohol made me want to heave. 'Er, could I just have an orange juice, please,' I pleaded feebly. 'And have you got any Nurofen?'

I eventually staggered out of there at seven, by which time I had finished off half a packet of digestive biscuits in an attempt to not feel quite so sick, and drunk about three pints of orange juice. As I left Gavin and Steve on the corner of Ladbroke Grove and Lancaster Road for the tube, the old punk rockers were still highly amused at my inability to keep up with them.

'You sure you'll not just have one?' Steve said, peering suspiciously at me. 'It's Friday night, you know.'

'Yeah, I realise, but the missus…' I began.

'Ah,' Steve rubbed the side of his nose. 'That old chestnut. Say no more, Boswell, me old son. Say no more.'

And chortling to themselves, they bade me goodnight.

I don't know what the rest of the day had been like, but the freezing cold wait for the tube put paid to yesterday's fantasies about the arrival of spring. Huddled up with only a copy of the *Guardian* for cover on a bench on the station platform I felt even more like a geriatric old git. The pain in my kidneys was all too real, while my head felt like it was stuffed with cotton wool and my mouth thick with yesterday's smoke.

When I finally arrived back in Camden it was eight o'clock and the place was crawling with jabbering freaks doing drug business outside the tube; Italian goths on their way to the Dev; and a swarm of children dressed in sportswear buzzing the wrong way up the roads and all over the pavements on their undersize bikes.

'Jesus!' I exclaimed as one veered away only inches from me on the pavement by Sainsbury's, then screamed a torrent of abuse at me to 'Watch where you're fuckin' goin', you wanker!'

And Steve thought the Portobello had taken a turn for the worse. I'd have to invite him over sometime. I'd like to see his methods in action up here.

Imagining the bike-riding hood rat sailing through a plate-glass window cheered me on and into Ali's shop, where I picked up another packet of digestives and a huge bottle of Lucozade. Mother's standbys were still the best at a time like this.

In fact, I was almost whistling as I turned the key in the lock, thinking about the enjoyable televisual tat of *Never Mind The Buzzcocks* and *Friday Night With Jonathan Ross* to come.

It's funny, those almost absurdly mundane moments you have like that, which come just before your world falls apart and linger around to taunt you long afterwards. As if to say, yeah, and that's all you cared about, wasn't it?

From the moment I walked through the door, my hopes of a recuperative Friday night in front of the box with my health food were dashed.

Louise was standing in the front room, talking to someone on her mobile. Her coat was draped over her arm like she was just about to go out. At her feet was a packed suitcase.

'I'll see you later,' I heard her say, cutting the connection as she saw me.

'What the…' I started.

'What do you think?' She cut me off, eyes glinting like slits of hard emerald. 'I've had enough, Eddie. It's started all over again with you, hasn't it? I suppose you're about to tell me you just had to have one more to get the story you needed, aren't you? That's why it's eight o'clock at night and you've only just turned up from an interview you supposedly did yesterday lunchtime. Why don't you tell me the truth for once in your life? That you'd rather hang out with a load of deadbeat old men than me. You can't, can you?'

'But I…' I was flabbergasted with the severity of this assault.

'No buts, Eddie. You said this book was an attempt to get us out of this place. No, Eddie, it's not. It's just another excuse for you to spend your whole life getting pissed and hanging out with your fellow adult babies.'

'That's not true, Louise! Listen to me…'

'No!' she snapped, her voice resounding through my aching head like a claxon. 'You listen to me for once. I am going to be thirty years old this year and all I do is work, work, work, while you just sit around on your arse. Most people have settled by my age. Most people have a place of their own and a husband they can rely on. What have I got? A rented flat smack bang in the middle of Crack Central and a boyfriend who's spent his entire life trying to avoid any form of real work. If I keep on listening to you, I'm going to end up a dried-up old maid with nothing to show for myself, while you are going to end up in the terminal ward of a hospital for alcoholics. So I've decided. I need to get away from here and do some serious thinking, because from how it looks from here, you and me don't have a future.'

As I tried to take in the scale of her ranting, a car horn sounded outside. 'That will be my cab now,' she informed me, peering out of the window to make sure.

'But where are you going?' My voice came out a pathetic whine. I could feel childish tears springing into my eyes like a just-slapped infant.

'I'll call you in a week's time,' she said. 'If you happen to be in, maybe we can talk then. If you don't, you can forget all about me and you. Now get out of my way.'

And with that, she flung on her coat, shoved her mobile in her pocket, lifted her suitcase and slammed out of the door, running down the stairs.

I was too shocked to even try and stop her. 'Louise...' I whispered to the air where she'd just been.

I moved to the window in time to see her get into a black cab. The driver did a U-turn up Camden Road and headed away southwards, while my vision blurred into his red tail lights.

I'd really fucking done it this time. The biscuits and the Lucozade dropped out of my hands as I crumpled onto the sofa. I'd really fucking done it.

I saw the dawn come up that Saturday morning, still sitting on the sofa. I'd never felt so empty or alone.

Ten years we'd been together and she was right, we did have

nothing to show for it. I couldn't even begin to think who she could be staying with, I'd never paid any real attention to her friends, dismissing them all as boring arseholes because they didn't know or care who Johnny Rotten or Ian Curtis were. I'd arrogantly turned a blind eye to about half of my girlfriend's life. And she was right: I'd never once even mentioned the dreaded 'M' word. Despite her sour expression every time we attended yet another of her friend's weddings and someone had said, 'I suppose it will be you next.' I still thought that marriage was something boring grown-ups did, not allowing myself to think that I could ever become one of them.

'Thirty years old this year.' Her words rang in my head.

In a vain attempt to distract myself, I turned the TV on. Cheery old Mark Lamarr and Jonathan Ross were long gone, replaced by plummy Sophie Raworth and a twitchy Jeremy Bowen on the *BBC Breakfast News*. Bowen looked lost on that comfy sofa when he should have been out in his safari suit, mixing pink gins and dodging bullets in the Middle East somewhere. Raworth reminded me of a junior version of Mother. I never thought I'd see the day that I was watching this shit on a Saturday morning.

I flicked over the channels; on ITV it was even worse, Eamon Holmes and some blonde android secretary making what they thought was witty banter with some washed-up seventies footballer who was now a recovering alcoholic. For a second I was so filled with rage I almost put my foot through the screen.

But I could hear Louise's voice in my head saying: 'That's just the kind of childish shit I'd expect from you, Eddie.'

And my heart hollowed out at the thought of her never being here again to insult me, complain or put me down. I broke down in tears again.

I guess I must have fallen asleep sometime after that because suddenly the phone was ringing. I woke up disorientated, for a blissful minute, not remembering the details of the night before.

Then it all came crashing back and in one second of mad optimism, I expected it to be her, saying she'd slept on it and realised she had acted in haste.

But it was only Christophe. 'All right, mate,' he said cheerily. 'I've got something for you.'

'Is it a loaded shotgun?' I replied.

'Nah,' he replied. 'Why, do you need one?'

'Something like that. Louise has left me.'

'Nah.' He sounded disbelieving. 'You're joking, ain't you?'

'I wish I was.' I rubbed my bleary eyes. 'But I got in last night and she was standing there with a suitcase. She said—' my voice wobbled '—she'd had enough of me.'

'Jesus,' Christophe sounded serious. 'You sure she ain't putting you on, testing you out or something?'

I stared out of the window. Shafts of bright sunlight mocked me. 'She said she needs time to think about whether we have a future or not.' The chasm inside threatened to open up again. I fumbled for a cigarette, finding a crumpled packet in my inside jacket pocket.

'You still there?' Christophe asked, as I tried to light the thing with shaking fingers.

'Yeah, yeah, I'm still here.' I took a hard drag. 'She said she'd call me in a week's time to see what she's decided. In the meantime, I'm not even allowed to know where she is.'

'Fucking hell. And you've got no idea?'

'No,' I shook my head. 'That's the thing. I've got no fucking idea whether she's staying with some mate of hers or…' I didn't even want to think about an alternative to that, let alone say it.

Christophe caught my drift, strove to put a stop to it. 'If you ask me, she's just testing you out, mate. She wants to pull you up by the short and curlies. It'll be one of her mates put her up to it, they'll probably spend the whole week bitching about you while they're eating ice cream on the sofa watching Julia Roberts' movies. Then she'll come back when she thinks you've learned your lesson. Believe me,' he sighed. 'I know what fuckin' birds are like.'

There was some crumb of consolation in this, which I was desperate to grab at. All the same, I wasn't so sure. 'Thing is, she's never done anything like this before,' I said. 'She's threatened it about a million times, but she's never actually got round to doing anything about it. God knows, I gave her reason enough…' I could hear my voice going up an octave again.

'Nah, that's bollocks,' Cristophe said firmly. 'You were getting your act together, for fuck's sake, writing that book. She ain't got no reason to complain about that. Was there something else? She didn't mention getting married by any chance?'

'Yeah.' I watched little flecks of ash falling from my cigarette onto the floor. 'As a matter of fact, she did.'

'Well, there you go. That's what this is all about, mush.'

'You could be right.'

'I'm always right. I told you, I know what birds are like. Thing is, what do you want to do about it? Do you want to walk up the aisle with her?'

Right at that moment, I wanted nothing else, but I couldn't admit it to him. 'I dunno,' I said instead.

'Well, you better think on about that,' Cristophe advised. 'In the meantime, you probably need some cheerin' up, don't you?'

If cheering up meant alcohol then yes, yes, I did.

'I pack up here in half an hour,' he continued. 'I've got a half day. Why don't you come over and we can go and have a pint or something?'

Well, I couldn't stay there in that empty flat. That was like fucking torture. So I ran myself a hot shower, stayed under it for ten minutes until I could feel my limbs working, then stepped out and into some clean clothes.

The suit I'd worn round Gavin's reeked like a thousand ashtrays. I threw it into the laundry bin, checked my slightly dishevelled reflection and stepped out to find what little solace Camden Town had to offer.

Christophe wanted to go to the Spread Eagle, but I made him

stop off at the Good Fayre on the other side of Parkway first. By now I was starving, and wolfed down the biggest fry-up they had on offer – eggs, beans, bacon, sausage; the works. It seemed like years since that last breakfast at Gavin's place and Christophe watched me neck the lot while sipping delicately on an espresso and chainsmoking Rothmans.

'I see you've made a recovery,' he noted.

'Fucking hell,' I protested. 'You don't know what I've been through in the past two days. This is the first time I've eaten since Thursday morning.'

'So I see. It went all right then, did it, your last interview?'

'It did eventually,' I nodded.

I put down my knife and fork and stared into the remains of tomato ketchup and congealing egg yolk like a burst spot on my plate.

'To my cost.'

'Aw, don't get all maudlin on me again, Eddie. Like I said, she'll come round. You'll see.'

'Yeah,' I wiped my mouth on a napkin. 'Yeah, all right. Come on then, let's go to the pub.'

He could get quite narky if he had too much blood in his alcohol system, could Christophe. He cheered up a bit once we had a nook in the Spread Eagle and a couple of pints in front of us.

'Now then,' he said, rustling inside one of the carrier bags he always carried around with him. 'I found you this.'

He handed over a magazine, folded in the middle. It was a glossy A4, though it looked like it had seen better days. The page it had been left on had a big black-and-white photograph on it, and a headline I couldn't understand, except for two words: *Vincent Smith*.

I saw what the picture was straight away: Vince and a girl in a bar. She had messy, spiky blonde hair falling over her eyes, was sitting on a high stool facing sideways wearing a mini-kilt, ripped fishnet stockings, a big lumpy jumper and pointy ankle boots. She held a cigarette to her pouting lips and her heavily made-up eyes were shut in an expression of disdain.

He was standing next to her, but looking towards the camera with a startled expression on his face. Dressed all in black, his hair a bird's nest, it was the least together I'd ever seen him look.

'It's a Frog style mag from the early eighties,' Christophe told me. 'I found it in Vintage. I didn't understand much of it, and I didn't think you would either, but this bird I know translated it for me.'

He handed across a page of neatly handwritten notepad paper.

One of the last-known pictures of English punk singer Vincent Smith, who went missing from his apartment in the 18th district a month ago, was taken by freelance photographer Didier DuVerniers, who was taking photographs of streetlife around Pigalle for a planned book on the subject of Paris lowlife. He was unaware whom he was capturing for posterity until he read an English music paper's report on the vanishing of Blood Truth's frontman. But his memories of that day are vivid.

'I thought this punk couple made an interesting subject, as they stood out from the normal crowd in Max's at 18th, an old jazz bar now frequented mainly by prostitutes and their pimps. So I just picked up my camera and fired off a couple of shots. The man noticed me straight away, unfortunately, and began shouting at me. I could not understand much of what he was saying, but when he started coming towards me with a very angry expression on his face, I got out of there fast. He started to run after me down the street, but the girl came after him and stopped him on the corner. I could hear them arguing, but I carried on running and she must have dragged him back inside, for which I was very thankful. He was a big, nasty-looking fellow.'

I couldn't help but laugh at this. 'A big, nasty-looking fellow!' I repeated.

'Yeah.' Christophe looked pleased with himself. 'Well spotted.'

'And that's all it says?' I turned the note over in case there was more.

'Yeah, bloody enigmatic Frogs for you.' Christophe nodded. 'But I thought that photo would be worth trying to get hold of. I don't know if you've ever seen it before, but if it is the last one ever taken of him, then you want it, don't you?'

I was touched. So touched that I had to glug down half a pint in one and then light another fag before my emotions got the better of me.

'It will be worth it,' my companion said, as if reading my thoughts. 'This book is gonna prove to her how serious you are *and* it's gonna set you up as a proper author, put you where you wanna be. So you gotta get on with it.'

He was right. And seeing that picture gave me another idea. 'You know what,' I told him, 'I was thinking of booking a trip on the Eurostar over to Paris to have a look around Pigalle for research. I was just gonna go with Gavin, but maybe I should turn it into a romantic trip for Louise. I mean, it's not as if I'd find anything else out now, I just wanted to get the atmosphere right for when I get to that part of the book. So all I'd need is an evening hanging round the Moulin Rouge or something and the rest of the time she can look at as many art galleries as she likes.'

Christophe nodded thoughtfully. 'You could give that a go,' he said. 'And if she turns you down, I'll come with you.'

I was surprised for a moment, but I shouldn't have been.

'See, that bird I got to translate this for you, she comes from Paris. I reckon she could show us about,' he gave a wry grin. 'There's a bit of a French Connection I want to make myself. So if your bird lets you down, let me know.'

Good old Cristophe. He let me moan on about Louise for most of the rest of that day, and walked me up Camden Road when it was kicking-out time. He was going to go to some rockabilly night at the Boston Arms where I guessed this French bird he was after would be, so I declined his kind offer to go with him. I had had just about enough by then.

Exhaustion and depression coming down; Sunday morning following all too soon. Ali sold me a bottle of Jack, under the counter. I reckoned I might need it to get to sleep in the uncertain week to come.

I had no trouble getting off that night, mind, it was the waking up that was the ordeal. Opening my eyes to find half the bed empty, her pillows cold, the flat all eerily silent. The only thing that I could kind of call a blessing was that I had so many tapes to transcribe it would take me the rest of the week to get through them. Maybe they could take my mind off the punishment of isolation, of waiting for that call to come.

Not to mention Mother's Sunday night broadcast.

I spent the day in the company of Mr Mullin's memoirs. So entertaining were they that I managed to forget the rest of the mess I was in. Not only that, what Steve had given me that night was enough to provide the backbone of the book. Despite the amount of booze he had got through in his life, he seemed to have total recall, describing his schooldays in the same vivid detail as the long days on the road in America with the band falling apart.

He put this down to the fact that he had never taken drugs. 'One thing my grandad Cooper told me long ago, and I've never forgotten it. "Never take any bastard drugs, son. A drink or two will see you all right. But don't mess around with owt else, or you'll turn most important thing you have to mush – your brain." I loved my grandad. Hard old docker he was, had to go out and fight for his job every bloody day when he were young, so course I listened to him. Glad I did an' all. I never got into the fookin' state some others did.'

I had six tapes full of Steve, thank God. I pushed to the back of my mind the little voice that said: 'the six tapes that cost you the girl'. Instead, I worked out in advance what I'd say to Mother when she made her inevitable enquiries at seven o'clock sharp.

'She's out at the theatre with some of her friends,' I said, glancing at a page in the *Observer* I'd prepared earlier. 'She's gone to see *Mother Clap's Molly House* at the Aldwych,' I continued authoritatively, suppressing the urge to laugh when the play's title went completely over her head. 'Wish I could have gone with her, like, but I've that many tapes to get through…'

'Edward,' Mother enquired, 'why are you speaking in that funny accent?'

'Oh, er, ha, ha!' I hadn't realised Steve's earthy qualities had rubbed off on me quite so much. I spent the rest of the next hour listening to her whittle on about the latest Con Club intrigue and Dad's lumbago without managing to get a word in edgeways. Which was just as well.

After that, I really was exhausted. I brought out the bottle of Jack, filled up a glass and went to sleep watching *Panorama*.

It took until Friday to finish Steve's stories. I worked from the moment I got up until the moment my eyes shut of their own volition, snacking on cornflakes and toast and drinking nothing but coffee. So long as I stayed with Steve, I was fine; I didn't have to think about anything else. By the end of it, there were twenty thousand words, about a quarter of the amount I'd been commissioned to write. I could tell her that, I reckoned.

You think I've been slacking, do you? Well I've got a third of it done, in two months flat. That's why I had to do that interview, you know?

I tried her mobile a couple of times, as I had done all week, but it always switched to answerphone, as soon as she saw who it was.

It made me feel a bit self-righteous. Did she think I was blowing up my liver last week for fun? No, Steve was vital, and so were the methods needed to get such an interview out of him.

I ran my cursor up and down the now gigantic file I had of his words. Avoiding hard work? This was the hardest work I had ever done in my life. But also the most rewarding. Now that I had an authoritative and compelling voice, I really felt the book was coming alive as a proper entity. Even if I didn't get to speak to half the people I wanted to, at least I had the goods from the guy who started the band in the first place.

So yeah, I was feeling ready for Louise's call by about five o'clock on Friday. I presumed she'd be as good as her word, call sometime around eight, like she had said.

She'd left some decent bottles of wine in the rack and I had made sure I didn't touch any of them. But after all that work, and with a third of a book and Paris on offer, I thought I deserved a little something to wind down with when it got to be about seven o'clock.

I chose a Burgundy with a picture of a chateau on the front of it. They were usually good, but not, I didn't think, the most expensive ones she bought. I reckoned I had seen the same thing in Sainsbury's and could get a replacement easily enough.

I even let it breathe for about half an hour, while I went through the TV listings in *Time Out* and worked out what the best plan of entertainment for the evening would be. Strangely, I didn't feel like watching Jonathan Ross or Mark Lamarr any more. I thought I'd watch a Channel 4 documentary about clown dancing in Los Angeles instead.

The Burgundy was good, so was the documentary. It almost kept my eyes from drifting away to see how the clock was doing. When it finished at half-eight and she still hadn't called, I just poured myself another glass and switched over to BBC2. *Crime and Punishment* they were showing. An adaptation of one of Louise's favourite novels.

I tried to concentrate on it, but my eyes kept wandering back to the clock, while a thousand permutations of torture spun through my mind. Louise really watching *Mother Clap's Molly*

House, laughing with her mates, forgetting she'd even said she'd call me. Louise at her favourite Japanese restaurant, spearing sushi with precise strokes of her chopsticks while making sparkling conversation to an appreciative audience and paying no attention to the clock whatsoever.

Louise doing those things not with her friends, but with another man. Someone taller than me, better looking, with more money in the bank and more hair on his head. Someone with 'prospects'. Someone a thirty-year-old woman could 'settle down' with.

Before I knew it, I had finished the first bottle. Before I knew it, I was uncorking another, similar-looking Claret, not waiting for this one to take the air and see if it liked it.

I imagined Jeremy, or Justin, or whatever his name was, ordering something similar with a knowing authority, smelling the bouquet without needing to taste it, proffering his arm to the waiter to pour for madame…

When the phone suddenly sparked to life, I nearly dropped the whole damn thing on the floor. I was halfway through the bottle by then, halfway through pouring another glass.

'Hello, Eddie,' her voice was steady, flat.

By now it was ten-thirty. I guessed this was another test for me to go through.

'Hi, Louise,' I tried to keep my voice on an even keel.

'So you can stay in on a Friday night then?'

'I've been working,' I said. 'As I have been all week.'

I should have been remorseful, but something about the coldness of her tone, coupled with the mental imagery of my successor ignited a little flame of rage in my head.

'And as you didn't give me the chance to explain a single thing to you last week,' I went on, 'I just thought you would like to know that I have now completed a quarter of the book. That interview I did last week was probably the most important thing I had to do to make the whole thing work. That was why I had to stay out longer than I promised…'

'OK, Eddie,' she cut me off. 'It might come as a shock to you, but this is what life is like for most of us. Working for a living. Anyway, we need to talk, don't we, so let's try to be civilized about it.'

That sounded ominous. The spark snuffed itself out. Fear crawled into its place.

'I've been doing a lot of thinking this week,' she said. 'I am aware that I may not have been all that fair on you last week, but the build-up to this has been going on for years, rather than months. The trouble is, we're both stuck in the habit of being together, aren't we? Sharing a flat, getting by.'

'Well, I know I haven't been the ideal boyfriend in the past, but I was trying to make amends for that, you know that,' I started, nauseously aware that my voice was starting to whine. 'And I honestly have been working my arse off on this, you know.'

'The trouble is,' she said, and even she sounded pained, 'it's all a bit too little too late.'

'What do you mean?'

'Eddie,' she said and sighed. 'Eddie, I'm sorry. I should have done this long ago, but I didn't have the courage. Now I think I've found it. I want something different from my life and I've only got one chance to go out and get it. Obviously we're going to have to get together and sort out all the details, the rent, our possessions and so on, but the bottom line is…I'm not coming back.'

Her voice caught then, like it had taken all her energy to say her piece.

'What do you mean?' I repeated, like an automaton.

'I'm not coming back to you, Eddie,' she said, and I could hear her start to cry. 'It's over…' she whispered.

'No!' I cried. 'No, Lou-Lou, you can't do this! I was going to take you to Paris and propose to you there. We could get married and put down money on our own place and have everything you wanted…'

'Please don't, Eddie,' she said.

'But that's what you said you wanted! To get married, be stable – well that's what we'll do, I promise you Lou-Lou, I'll be a new man, the best you've ever seen…'

'I can't go on,' she croaked. 'I'll call you in a couple of days, we'll sort something out. But there's nothing you can say to change my mind.'

'No! Lou-Lou no! Don't do this to me!'

But the line went dead.

And so did my heart.

20

1-2 Crush On You

August 1980

Donna didn't have to wait long before she saw her sudden object of desire again.

Six-thirty the next evening, when nearly everyone else had gone home and Tracey, the receptionist, was just about to, a call buzzed through to Donna's office. 'Some bloke's just turned up to see you, Donna.' Tracey sounded somewhat harassed. 'His name's Vince Smith. He didn't have an appointment or nothing, but he said you'd want to see him. Shall I tell him to piss off before I go? Your taxi'll be here in five minutes.'

Donna had just been about to put her own coat on in readiness to go and stand over Mood Violet's last TOTP rehearsal. She was intending to take Tone's advice and spend as much time with Sylvana as possible. Make sure nothing could get out of hand.

But all it took were those two little words and suddenly she was rooted to the spot, a strange feeling washing over her. It was as if someone had just waved a magnet over her brain and erased every important thing that was previously on her mind.

'No, it's OK, Tracey,' she heard herself say, 'you can let him through.'

Her voice sounded calm and businesslike. Nothing like she felt inside.

Through the frosted glass between her room and the next, she could see his outline. Tall. Lean. Dark. Dangerous.

'You sure? You never mentioned nothing about this before…' Tracey's voice squawked through the spell.

'I'm positive, Tracey, let him through and you can go home. I can manage to lock up behind me, you know.'

'What about your taxi, though?'

God, she could be annoying. 'I'm still getting my taxi, you don't have to worry. Now off you go.'

She watched the outline of Tracey put the phone down, shrug and gesticulate to the shadow of Vince, which formed a kind of indolent question mark as it lounged against the doorframe.

By now Donna's heart was hammering, her palms sweaty against the receiver. A decade's worth of the ice that had held her heart together was starting to melt. Her eyes flicked across to the mirror on the wall opposite. Donna prided herself that she looked perfect at all times, but suddenly she was worried. She ran a hand through her hair, smoothed down the front of her black lace blouse, her mind running away with lurid possibilities of what could happen next.

Then the door opened, and there he was, in that black leather coat but without the Elvis shades, giving her the full benefit of those iridescent violet eyes. 'So,' he said. 'Is this the hub of your punk empire then?'

His eyebrows twitched with mocking humour.

Donna rose slowly from her chair, subconsciously winding a coil of her hair around her index finger. 'How did you find me?' she asked, her head full of static, blanking out everything but the heady desire she felt in his presence.

Vince smiled, turned his head and watched as Tracey went

out of the front door, shooting him a filthy look as she closed it behind her. His own smile deepened. 'I can always track down what I really want,' he said, turning back to fix Donna with a stare that burned her down to her core.

She walked towards him, as if in a trance. For a moment, everything seemed to be happening in slow motion. Then his lips touched hers and it was like a roman candle going off inside her. The next thing she knew he was ripping open that lacy blouse she had taken such pride in keeping neat, was pulling up her tight pencil skirt and grunting like some hungry animal at what lay beneath – the tight basque, the fishnet stockings that were elemental to her uniform. His hot mouth was on hers and she was letting go for the first time in her life, swooning, delirious. Seconds later he was inside her, his long and hard in her wet and hot, pushing her up against her desk, frantic, the phone falling off and crashing onto the floor. He fucked her sideways, lengthways, widthways, all over the office, while somewhere in the distance a taxi sounded its horn. Nothing else mattered but the feel of him and the frenzy that brought them together.

Donna screamed as she came, over and over, while outside, the disgruntled cabbie put his light back on and drove away.

Then they collapsed onto the floor, a tangle of ripped clothes and high heels, red lipstick smeared up the side of her face, hair plastered to her skull with sweat.

They lay, panting, in each other's arms. Donna looked up through her tangled mane with the expression of a woman who has wandered long and far through a desert before finally being given a glass of ice-cold beer.

Vince smiled back down at her, lascivious. His left hand groped for his discarded coat and pulled it towards them. He fished out a packet of cigarettes, pulled out two, lit them and passed one over.

Donna had never smoked before. Until that moment it had disgusted her, reminded her of her dad and all his furtive, greasy, ugly friends. But that gesture of Vince's seemed so romantic to her then, that she took it gratefully in her shaking hands.

Vince watched her puff and not inhale, an amused expression on his face.

'I take it you liked our album then?' he finally said.

Donna burst out coughing and laughing at the same time. She hadn't taken it out of its wrapper. 'You were right. It's up there with The Village People,' she said.

He took the cigarette out of her hands and crushed it on the floor. Her beautiful, black floor.

'Do you know what you get for being cheeky?' he said, and with one lean but immensely strong arm flipped her over on her stomach and started slapping her bare arse.

Donna screamed and struggled, but really she was laughing, it was turning her on again. He pinned down her flailing arms with his spare hand, put his knee in the centre of her back as he leaned over her, shooting hot breath down her ear. Donna dimly realised this was all the wrong way around; that normally it was she who liked to dominate and inflict the pain. But at that moment she felt a deep, dark jolt of joy in letting go, submitting herself totally. For a second, she had the absurd thought that if she turned around she would see red horns poking out of Vince's head, like the Devil himself was doing this to her and she never wanted him to stop. This was fucking dangerous, but she was about to come again at any second and she would have licked the cigarette ash up with her tongue if he'd asked her to.

She squirmed and buckled under his grasp until she was spent and he let her go, let her roll over on her back, suddenly feeling somewhat immodest, pushing her skirt back down.

She stared at him with glazed eyes. He was everything she wanted. And she had never wanted to want any other human being that much in her life. It was as if every cell in her body had been electrified, as if she had never been properly alive.

Suddenly she couldn't look at him for a moment longer. She scrabbled to her feet and turned to see the mirror's harsh verdict, the vision of a wrecked, sated, lust-filled apparition she had never made the acquaintance of before.

'God, what a fucking mess!' she exclaimed.

Casually, Vince got to his feet, tucked himself back inside his black jeans. 'You look beautiful,' he said, standing behind her, running a finger up her neck and round her jawline.

With his fingers on her skin, Donna felt as if she was made of liquid and could melt and form new shapes around him. She wanted to attach herself to him so he could never cast her aside; actually become a part of him, breathing through his lungs, seeing through his eyes, feeling through his fingertips, tasting through his mouth…

Then, with a sudden jolt, she realised that this thinking was insane. Her stomach dropped ten storeys as the static cleared from her brain and all too late those important matters she was supposed to have been attending to pushed their way back into stark relief. She saw her face flush bright red in the mirror and something like panic took over.

'Never mind about that,' she snapped, pushing him away. 'I have to be somewhere. An hour ago.'

'Really?' He put his hand between her legs.

Donna almost let go again.

'Really!' She pushed him away harder.

He lifted his hands, palms outwards in submission, shrugged and moved away.

Donna scrambled frantically around, trying to rearrange her clothes, her hair, find her handbag from where it had been kicked behind the desk. From hitting the heights of ecstasy only moments before, she suddenly felt close to despair. 'Shit!' she exploded.

Vince was back inside his leather coat, looking as calm and

collected as if he had only just walked in off the street. He lit a cigarette, inhaled slowly, picked a bit of stray tobacco off his bottom lip. 'Where do you have to be?' he asked

'Rehearsal studio. Kensal Road. But now I'm gonna have to go home first and get changed. Shit! Shit! Shit!' Donna's voice was harsh but she was almost in tears.

'Can I give you a lift?' Vince asked calmly.

Donna swung round. 'You got a motor?' she said. The thought of him driving a car almost astonished her.

Vince winked. 'No man with a good car needs to be justified,' he said.

'You what?'

'It's right outside,' he continued. 'Come on, I'll get you there a lot quicker than some bastard cabbie. And after all,' he put an arm around her shoulder, 'I got you into this mess, so it's only right I get you out again.'

A comforting wave washed over Donna's addled brain. Of course everything was going to be all right. They could wait an hour for her in their studio, God, it was practically their home from home. She'd just tell them there was a really important last-minute meeting with their tour manager – as actually, there had been earlier in the day. Vince could get her home in five minutes, she could get changed and ready in half an hour, then it was only ten minutes more up to the studio. It would be fine. The office could wait – she'd just get up early and sort that out before anyone else got in. It wouldn't be the first time she'd got in before any of her staff, would it?

'OK,' she looked up at him, smiling. 'Take me away.'

Vince didn't seem to want to leave her when they did get to her flat. He offered to wait around and take her back up the road. While she hurriedly showered, painted on a new face and threw on another outfit, he lounged in her front room, watching the telly. Donna tried to get her story straight in her head, but all the while a little pulse of excitement beat deep inside her. He was here. In her flat. This was the start of something. Something wild and secret. It filled her with a reckless joy.

Good as his word, he dropped her off outside the studios. 'You'll be all right now?' he asked.

'I'll be fine,' she assured him. Although now, when it had come to the point of leaving him, she felt an irrational fear that she'd never see him again, and hesitated before reaching to open the door.

For a second she remembered the sad look in Tone's eyes as Vince walked away. As if sensing this, he pulled her into his arms and kissed her hungrily, as if he was never going to stop. When finally he did, he put his finger on the end of her nose and said, 'I'll be seeing you again soon, First Lady.'

'I hope so,' she smiled, then frowned. 'One thing though. Don't tell Tone about any of this. I don't think he'd like it.'

'Anthony?' Vince looked extremely amused for a moment, then assumed a grave expression that she couldn't tell was sincere or not. 'You don't have to worry about him. You got my word on that. Now, get your sexy arse out of here and go and run your empire.'

Donna tried not to, but she couldn't help turn around and watch him drive away before she pushed the bell on the studio door. One strange thing struck her – that Northern accent he had had when she first met him seemed to completely disappear tonight. Tonight he had sounded…almost posh.

She shrugged and pulled herself together. As he said – she had an empire to run.

The sight of Donna staggering in nearly two hours late with lipstick smudged across her face came as something of a shock for the four people inside the studio. 'Mein Kommendant' as they referred to her behind her back had never ever been late before, and was always unduly harsh to those that were. The band had been diligently practising the song for so long now that all they really wanted to do was go home.

Watching them, ostensibly just to offer an opinion, Helen had been sitting on an uncomfortable plastic chair, getting more anxious by the minute. She had already had a drawn-out couple of days.

After Donna had burst into her shop the day before and put into loud, demanding voice all her secret fears, she and Allie had spent the evening having a long, painful conversation.

Helen loved and trusted her husband for being an honest, decent human being and she realised that for him to tell tales on his oldest friend was going to be difficult. She had shut her stall up early that day, so that she could spend an extra hour making his favourite lasagne, getting the flat tidy, opening a bottle of Chianti and generally easing him into the conversation.

She had seen the trauma written right across his face as he slowly told her some unpalatable truths that he had been carrying around with him for years. It was a conflict of interests, a kind of betrayal for Allie all right. But also, a kind of relief.

'What you have to understand, hen,' he had begun. 'Is that Robin didnae have a very good start in life.'

He'd unravelled it to her then, starting from when they were five, and met on their first day at infants school. Robin got picked on from the start – he was ginger and scrawny and conspicuously poorer than all the other children. This wasn't because his family had less money – just about everyone there had a Da who worked down the pit, it was the major industry in the region – but because Robin's Da spent most of his at the miners' social.

Allie himself came from a big, close-knit, religious family, who always put the emphasis on doing as you would be done by. Big for his age, happy and good-natured, Allie was the opposite type of child from the scrawny misfit in their midst, the type that would never have an enemy in the world. He instinctively took it upon himself to be the Good Samaritan and look after Robin. As they got older, and the bond of trust grew between them, he realised the extent of what his friend was going through.

Robin was a clever child but he didn't get any help at home. He was brilliant at practical things, like woodwork and metal work, could get his head around maths and science better than most. But it was music that he most loved and that aptitude he had for figuring things out was effortlessly applied to learning new instruments. Allie could keep up with him, but only just. Robin had more pent-up feelings to let loose than he did. Because Robin had to watch his dad do terrible things to his mum. He didn't tell Allie what they were but Allie could fairly surmise most of it. Sometimes Robin's mum couldn't leave the house for weeks on end. Sometimes she stood at the school gate with livid colours around her eyes, or walked with a hobble. Robin had to look after her most of the time, do the washing, cooking and cleaning. He spent a lot of time at Allie's house, but a return invitation was never offered, and Allie knew better than to ask. As well as his friend's talents, he had also witnessed the black moods that crippled him, the thin, angry red lines that appeared on his arms when he'd come back from a couple of day's unexplained absence from school.

Helen hated to hear these things. She felt terrible for extracting Allie's secrets, even worse for the sort of childhood Robin had suffered. But at the same time, she felt terribly afraid at what this was all leading up to.

When they left school, Allie and Robin had both served apprenticeships to become electronic engineers. They stayed close; their spare time spent travelling to Edinburgh to see bands, reading music papers and buying singles, listening to John Peel every night for tips. When punk dawned, with it came the realisation that maybe they could try their hand at it too.

But that wasn't the real reason they left Scotland in a hurry. Allie sighed as he let this information out, looked at the floor, too ashamed to meet his wife's eye. Then he plunged on, willing her to understand why.

The real reason was because Robin had been in a spot of bother. He'd started seeing a girl, his first ever girlfriend, and he was really happy about it. Only, after a couple of months she'd wanted to break up with him. She was fed up with his mood swings, as most people got to be, after they'd known Robin a while.

Robin hadn't taken the news very well. He started stalking the wee lass, who was still only a schoolgirl, from the gates of the playground to her house every day. Hung around outside, staring up at her window, making calls from the phone box over the road at ten-minute intervals, that kind of mad stuff. Of course it wasn't long before her Da, who was also a miner and knew Robin's Da by reputation, got thoroughly pissed off with the situation. He'd come out to threaten Robin with a beating if he didn't leave his daughter alone.

Robin had just smirked at him. He disappeared that day, but sure enough, was back the next, ready to start the charade all over again. The Da, though, was cleverer than Robin. He told Robin's old man what was going on, probably reckoning that what Robin would suffer next would be worse than anything he could mete out.

He was right. Leith Senior was feared even by the hard men he worked beside because of his unpredictable, hair-trigger temper. That time he outdid himself. Robin had to have his jaw wired back together after he'd finished. He had bootmarks on him that took months to fade. It was from his hospital bed that they'd hatched their scheme to run away, because Allie was fearful of what would happen to Robin if they stayed.

Allie's boss had a brother who'd moved down south. He helped sort them out some work and digs before they jumped on that train in the summer of '77. And Robin had flourished here, away from the madness of his previous life. He'd been happy and outgoing in a way Allie had never seen before. Of course, both of them were delirious to be at the hub of punk's revolution, to see the bands they'd read about night after night, to take those ideas and start to form their own music out of it. When they'd met Helen and Sylvana it had seemed like the icing on the cake.

'So,' Helen said tentatively at that point. 'Sylvana's only his second girlfriend?'

'There were a couple of others before her,' Allie said. 'Nothin' serious though. Nae one ever lasted the course with him before. Nae one ever clicked with him like she did.'

Helen hated herself for pushing it, but she had to ask: 'Did he follow anyone else around like that in London?'

Allie shook his head. 'Not that I know of, and believe me, I wouldae known if he had. I thought he had sorted his shit out, put it all behind him. But...' his voice caught in his throat and he had to look away for a second. 'But,' he continued, scrabbling for Helen's hand. 'But...Aw, Jesus Christ, I shouldae told you when it first began. It was that first tour without you, the first night an' all. Sylvana got upset about Blair Peach. When we first heard it on the radio, she thought it was Ray who got his head kicked in.'

'I don't understand,' Helen frowned, casting her mind back, remembering only how sad she had been that she'd had to stay behind without Allie.

'You remember that guy, Blair Peach, who got killed by the cops on that anti-fascist rally? Yeah, well, apparently Ray had gone on that march too, and Sylvana was really upset about it. I could see her point well enough, but Robin couldnae. I could see it startin' right then. I could see his imagination runnin' away with hisself. I tried to talk him out of it an' all. Christ, Ray was Donna's boyfriend, and he'd done us a lotta favours hisself, the poor lass was only worried about him. I thought I had brought Robin round...But I can see now, that was the start of it. Things have been different since then.'

'How do you mean?' Helen gripped his hand tightly.

'I've tried to ignore it, I admit I have. But nae one's been the same since that tour. He's got more and more of a control freak – over the music, and over her. He won't let her out of his sight, he makes her practise over and over while he fucks around tryin' to get one tiny portion of the sound perfect. They never come out, do they? They never come round here, there's always some excuse. It's studio, home, studio, home, every fuckin' day. I've been so happy with you that I've pushed it to one side. I didnae want to worry you, didnae want nae conflict. But the cat's outae the bag now, eh? Donna's seen it right enough, and I shouldae faced up to it long ago. I shouldae told you, hen, I really shouldae. But I was just hopin' if I kept my head in the sand long enough it would all go away, eh?'

'It's not your fault.' Helen had tears in her eyes now. Poor Sylvana, was all she could think. While we've been so happy, what has he been doing to her?

Eventually, when they were both so tired they had to go to bed, Helen had decided on a course of action. She was going to spend more time with Sylvana. She was going to come on as many dates of that tour as she could afford – she had a trusted assistant who could mind the stall for her when she needed. She wasn't going to say anything, but she was going to make sure she was there and Sylvana knew she was there, if she needed her. Making money, being a happening designer or whatever she was supposed to be, was nothing compared to what her friend was going through. She should have acted on her fears before.

That night had been the first time she'd seen Sylvana in weeks. The first time she'd really seen through the weight loss, the tiredness in her friend's eyes. Through those two long hours as they waited for Donna, she became uncomfortably aware of everything Allie had said and how blindingly obvious it all was now those words had come out.

Robin did nothing but niggle and criticise Sylvana and she did nothing to defend herself, just meekly said sorry and tried to do better, while he stared on, an expression of scorn on his face.

It had been fifteen months since that tour without her, Helen realised. Fifteen months. Sylvana had been worn down completely. She had no defences left.

Donna didn't even meet Helen's eye as she came through the door. 'Sorry I'm late,' she said breezily. 'I got caught up in some tour business…'

As she continued to gabble out her excuses, Helen got to her feet. 'So I see,' she said, staring pointedly at the red lipstick smeared halfway across Donna's cheek. 'Well I hope he was worth it.'

Donna's mouth dropped open and for the first time in Helen's knowledge, she didn't have a smart word to say.

'You want us to run through this for you one more time?' said Robin through his curled upper lip. 'Only I reckon by now we could just about do this in our sleep.'

Donna nodded quickly and sat down.

But as the first swirling chords of 'Cherry Coma' rose through the room, it seemed like Sylvana was the only person left in the room oblivious to the static in the air, the only one who still could get lost inside a song.

21

Jumping Someone Else's Train

April 2002

The next four weeks of my life passed in a hideous blur of alcohol, pleading and self-recrimination, one long lost weekend so smudged around the edges I hardly know where to begin.

Louise wanted to discuss our separation 'like adults'. At first, she came back to the flat, even though I knew she didn't want to. But I told her I just couldn't face meeting 'on neutral ground' as she suggested, and pleaded and pleaded until she eventually gave in.

It didn't go very well. I had spent two days trying to keep it together without resorting to the malicious decimation of the rest of her wine collection, pacing up and down, trying to work out in my head a way to bring her round. When she got there, I just ended up begging.

'Please give me another chance, Lou, please let's just call this a trial separation and I'll finish this book and show you I really can get my shit together.' That sort of thing.

She just sat there, shaking her head, tears slowly rolling down her face without any sound coming out. She had to look so fucking perfect, even in despair.

So then I lost it and got sarcastic with her, mocking her boo hoo hoo, demanding to know who she was really leaving me for.

'Myself,' she said, getting up to go.

I grabbed hold of her, tried to force her to stay. Ripped her fucking coat as she pulled away, both of us yelling and screaming then, years worth of unsaid hurts and tenderly nursed slights let loose like a hail of poison bullets.

Words said that unmade everything and every chance I ever had of getting back what we'd once had. Words that left me howling in the doorway at her disappearing back, the sound of her heels clattering heavily on the stairs resounding through my brain for hours after.

It was over. Done. Finito. Once I knew it, I went down like a dog.

I spent a month moving from one pub to another, with Christophe, with Gavin, with anyone who'd let me try and drink those words out of my head. Actually, it was mainly Gavin. He had the kind of sympathetic ear I needed right then. Gavin had always travelled light, as he put it, never got entangled within the treacherous roots of domesticity. Like the musicians he'd spent his life alongside, he still saw himself on a perpetual open road. It was the kind of philosophy I needed to hear right then, over and over again, particularly when coupled with an outlaw soundtrack of Johnny Cash, Lee Hazlewood, Willie Nelson, Waylon Jennings or, even better, David Allen Coe, all night over at his place.

Christophe, on the other hand, was busy getting his feet under the table at la Maison Française. I think he felt a bit guilty about that, as if he was letting down a friend in need, 'cos he kept trying to compensate by bringing me more stacks of old music papers and magazines from his mate at Vintage every time we did meet. He had the good grace not to even mention Paris, though.

The worst time was when Louise arranged to come and fetch her belongings. We, or rather she, had decided that I could stay on at the Camden flat while she would sort out somewhere else to live. I had just enough money to keep going until the next payment from the publishers, though I really couldn't think ahead more than a week, let alone a couple of months. But she was adamant that she didn't want to see me again after our last encounter, and I sure as hell couldn't face seeing half of my life carted out of the flat in one afternoon.

The last conversation we had comprised a few short sentences, mainly consisting of me promising not to be there.

The night before I knew it was happening, I went out with Gavin to see some alt country singer songwriter at the 12 Bar Club in Tin Pan Alley. Some creepy guy from America who looked like a trailer-dwelling geek but sounded like the spirit of Leadbelly had somehow lodged into his soul. Just what I needed to hear.

After that, we moved along with some mates of his through the drinking clubs of Soho, ate breakfast at Balons on Old Compton Street – well, if you can call a Bloody Mary and some crisps a breakfast. I stayed for two days in the same clothes on Gavin's sofa afterwards. He knew I didn't want to go back and face it. So he came back with me, in a taxi, on a Monday morning. Said that the best way to deal with it was sober and in daylight.

It was like being taken to a prison cell. Gavin hovered by the doorway as I took it all in.

Oh, she'd left me most of the stuff we bought together, I'll give her that. Obviously cutting her losses and running at that point was all she wanted; all she'd cared about doing, getting out clean.

I still had the leather sofa, the widescreen TV, the Smeg fridge and Duellit toaster. My computer, scanner and printer gazing coldly from my office corner, my stainless-steel filing cabinet alongside.

The bookcase had gone, though, and all her books with it. The fruit bowl and the coffee maker and all the black and white pottery she'd collected over the years, that she used to laugh about and say she was a housewife on valium because it was called Homemaker. The Art Deco wardrobe and all of her clothes, her one hundred and one pairs of shoes. The paintings we'd picked up cheap off Brick Lane that looked like lost Cubist masters. Hidden memories rose back to the surface as I took in the absence of all these things and what they represented, the times we'd spent, the bargains we'd gone home laughing about, the careful way she'd arranged everything. Everything that makes a house a home.

On the kitchen table, she'd left me a cheque for another month's rent, with a short note saying that she wished me the best. The sort of thing you'd write a distant aunt to thank her for a Christmas present you didn't want.

And her keys, where the fruit bowl used to be.

And that Polaroid of us, ten years ago, still laughing down from the fridge door. Mocking me.

'You got some coffee in the house?' Gavin appeared behind me.

'I, er…' I fumbled to make sense of the request. 'I don't know.'

'Let me have a look,' he said gently, and began opening the cupboards.

'Here we go.' He brought out a jar of instant muck. 'Let's have a brew.'

I stood and watched him fish out some cups from the back of another cupboard, the prim Tory blue ones Mother had given me as a moving-in present, the ones we'd laughed about and hid until the rare occasions she deigned to visit. I guessed there weren't any other ones left.

'Black coffee,' he continued, filling the kettle and plugging it in. 'That's what we need right now.'

He didn't ask any stupid questions, didn't try to offer any platitudes. He just made us strong black coffee and carried it into the lounge where we sat down on the sofa, sipping in silence. Or what passes for silence on Camden Road.

'Ah, well,' Gavin finally said as he placed his empty cup back down on the coffee table. 'Not the best brew I've ever had. But not the worst either.'

I still couldn't think of anything to say.

'Now mate,' he said, gentle but firm. 'There's only two ways you can go on this. You can either go back down the bottle until you never come back up, or you can haul yourself out through that little bastard there.' He nodded towards my computer.

I followed his gaze. The tape recorder looked back at me from beside the keyboard. The next tapes to transcribe, with Lynton Powell's interview on them, sat in a neat pile beside it, wearing a thin layer of dust.

'See, we've still got a mission, you and me,' Gavin went on. 'We've made a bloody good start on it already, but we're still only part the way there. We've gotta get you shipshape and start you moving again. It's the only way, mate. The only way.'

I dropped my gaze to the floor. 'I know,' I finally whispered.

That disappeared singer and what was left of his band were my one hope left. Without them I was nothing but a failure. The drinks were lined up on the bar of the Last Chance Saloon all right.

'Good bloke.' Gavin put his hand briefly on my shoulder. 'Now, what I suggest is a trip to the supermarket. In order to do what's required of you, you're gonna need some decent coffee...'

Mother would have been proud of the way Gavin took charge of the provisions that day, making sure I had everything I needed in my fridge and my cupboards.

'*Bush Tucker Man*!' he said proudly as we stacked the last of it away. 'Bringing the hard world of Outback survival into your home.' He swung the door of the fridge shut in triumph.

As he did so, he dislodged the Polaroid of Louise and me, and it dropped to the floor like a stone. I swooped down to pick it up, held it for a moment in my palm.

'You want my advice?' said Gavin, looking over my shoulder. 'Put it away, mate. Hide it somewhere.'

'No,' I said, suddenly filled with a sense of resolution. 'No, I'm gonna keep it there. To prove to her what I am capable of doing.'

'That's my man!' Gavin laughed and I joined him.

I had to hand it to him. He fired me up. 'Thanks, Gavin,' I said. 'I won't forget this.'

Although after he was gone, it was hard to keep hold of that sudden moment of calm and purpose I'd had there in the kitchen. I could feel the holes opening up again inside me as the day dissolved into dusk and the streetlights blinked on outside. Hard not to look at the spaces where her things had been for so long, in these rooms.

Music. That was what I needed to keep me straight.

Only I didn't turn to any of the men-in-black for solace this time. Instead I picked up that Mood Violet record I'd found in the bargain bins of Inverness Street. I'd dismissed it as ethereal bollocks before, but something about the colours on the front cover, those twilight pinks and blues and the arc of gold light, like the edge of a lens caught by the sun, seemed to chime with the way I was feeling inside.

I flipped it over and looked at her again. Sylvana Goldberg, with her heart-shaped face and long red hair. She was even more beautiful than Louise. Or at least, she had been. Poor, dead Sylvana. At that moment, I really wanted to hear her story. Wanted to feel it was vastly more tragic than my own.

The sound washed into the room in deep, comforting waves. Moody synths and that echo-driven guitar that was such a big deal in those days. Compared to a modern production, it actually all sounded a bit weedy, but for the first time I could sort of tell what they were getting at; trying to put a mood in your mind through sound. And, despite the crackles on the worn old vinyl, the occasional jump and hiss, age could not diminish the stark sensuality of her voice.

I stood there, transfixed, staring out of the window, over the misshapen hunch of the city, the rooftops, spires and domes that sprawled far into the distance, at the Dog Star high above. Something about this music went so perfectly with the melancholy afterburn of sunset, the fading of all colours into black. Something about it kept me calm.

'Vince said she was a genius.' I heard Steve Mullin's words in my head again. When the first side was finished, before I flipped it over, I turned my computer on for the first time in a month. It was time to knock those words of Mr Mullin's into shape. With a little background help from the woman he'd so despised.

It was funny, really. For a bloke I had found so obnoxious on first meeting, Steve really did keep me sane for the next couple of days. His big, foul-mouthed Yorkshire presence filled the room as if he was really there with me, and I was quite reluctant to let him go and turn my attention to those Lynton tapes that had been gathering even more dust.

So to spin it out a bit longer, I started trawling the Net and those old magazines of Christophe's for more information on Mood Violet.

I had been somewhat spooked about doing this before, superstitious even, that calling them up would bring that wanker Leith back to my door. Now I truly didn't care. There wasn't anyone here for him to terrorise any more, was there? The fear I'd felt about him was all for Louise, not for myself. Stupid, smack-addled toerag couldn't hurt me now.

Besides, I'd started to become rather addicted to his former lover's tonsils by now. If this story was going to work, I needed to know a lot more about her than anyone else had been so far willing to tell me.

A familiar name popped up again from my web searches: Ray Spencer.

He'd been an early champion of the band, had interviewed

them several times. So here was a link between the two factions who seemingly had only had good words to say about them both.

He appeared to have been a pretty big name in his day, did Spencer. Yet unlike his more famous peers, the Burchills, Parsons and Morleys, he didn't seem to have had much of a public life after about 1984. I'd never seen his byline in any of the Sunday supplements or on the bestseller lists, never caught him lounging around in a swivel chair, pontificating at length on *The Late Review*. I wondered what had happened to him.

There was a photo of him in one of the magazines Christophe had given me. *Noise!* it was called. It had come out as a glossy sister magazine to *Sounds* in the early eighties, and had categories for Punk, Electrobop, Psychedelix and Heavy Metal. It hadn't lasted very long. Maybe because of the terrifying photo of Garry Bushell's gurning mush leering out of the Punk section.

Spencer's picture was alongside this monstrosity. By comparison, he looked very cool, very youthful, with spiked-up peroxide hair, a line of sleepers down his left ear and a black-and-white stripey mohair jumper. While Bushell waxed lecherous about Becki Bondage, he was enthusing about GBH.

I asked Gavin about him, but he was pretty dismissive. '*Sounds* were the enemy, mate,' he told me. 'Particularly him. He went after all the same stories as me and Mick. Got there first a few times too. He was a nice enough bloke, I guess, but we didn't really hang out a lot. I haven't seen his name around for years.'

I finally found an email address for someone called Ray Spencer not on any of the punk sites, but on the Fulham FC Supporters web page. This Ray Spencer was one of the organisers of the Save Our Cottage campaign – whatever that meant. It possibly wasn't the same person at all, but I didn't see the harm in dropping him a line. He could only laugh at me, after all.

After that, it was time to start on Lynton's transcription. Compared to Steve, he was a bit of a damp squib.

It was funny. I had memories of that day going so well, and

him being so open with me. That's one of those things that sometimes happens with interviews – gremlins get inside the tape recorder while it spins and turn all your fantastic quotes into banal rubbish. Plus, you get to hear yourself sitting back and letting them do it, only occasionally throwing a fatuous platitude into the mix when you could have actually asked a question.

It was because Lynton was so smooth. He had politely and graciously talked about every subject put to him – but he hadn't really answered with anything of substance. No bad things to say about anyone, nothing controversial; if shit had happened, well, that was down to his youth and inexperience. Which was essentially all he had said about heroin. I had obviously just been so pleased he didn't slap me upside the head for asking about it I'd deluded myself that I'd got a Pulitzer-winning quote from him.

By the time I'd got through all of the tapes I was staring out into another starless Camden midnight, realising just how gracefully I had been conned.

Sure, I could use bits of detail about music and tours, but for deep insight into how these people interacted with each other, I was going to have to look elsewhere. It was impossible to harbour a grudge against Lynton, mind you. If I had lived through what he had, I probably wouldn't want to give any more of myself away either.

So now it was the end of April, and I was supposed to show the book's editor at least a third, preferably half of this book in a month's time.

Who was I going to turn to?

I clicked onto the Internet to check my Hotmail, not really holding out too much hope. It was two days since I'd sent off that email to Ray Spencer and if there was a reply, I expected it to be from some meathead football fan calling me a poof.

But I was wrong. There was an email from Ray Spencer, sent the day before. It read:

Dear Eddie,
I'm quite shocked that anyone remembers, but I am the same Ray Spencer who used to write for *Sounds*. I'm intrigued that you are writing about Blood Truth and Mood Violet, of course I remember them and the sad ends that they came to. I suppose it would be quite a good time to reappraise them now that everyone seems to be living back in the early 80's again!
I would be happy to meet you and perhaps do an interview for the book. Where are you based? I'm still in London, I presume you are but I could be wrong. I work in Camden five days a week, so if that's any good maybe we could meet up one evening? It would be interesting to take a trip down memory lane…

He gave me a daytime phone number and signed off with a matey, *Cheers*!

Wow. Who would have thought it? The illustrious punk scribe was here, right under my nose. I wrote back:

Dear Ray,
Thank you for replying so quickly - and for being the same Ray Spencer I was looking for! By strange coincidence, I live in Camden, so meeting up couldn't be easier. Name a date and a place and I'll be there. So long as it isn't the Devonshire Arms.

I put both my numbers down for him, resolving to give him a call anyway the first thing tomorrow. After everything that had happened over the past couple of months, it was about time something went right.

It turned out Ray was working on a women's magazine up on Oval Road – there was a big publishing house up there I didn't even know existed. He was a sub-editor these days, having turned to a more reliable way of making money when he got married and started having children. Though he still seemed to have kept his hand in a little, reeling off a list of new bands he was keen on that I'd only vaguely ever heard of, and telling me about an anarcho-punk shop on Plender Street of which I was blissfully ignorant. All in all, he seemed a really nice guy. He liked my comment about the Dev too.

'Cor blimey,' he said. 'You want to keep away from a place like that. You get vampires going in there.'

Didn't I know it.

Seeing as most of the bars in Camden were pretty noisy and anti-social, we decided I'd meet him from his work and we'd go for a pizza on Parkway instead. Because Gavin had given me the impression he wasn't that keen on his old rival, I didn't bother to tell him about it.

It would be nice to hear this story from a different angle.

Ray's office was a hideous old sixties block that sprawled like a grey behemoth across the corner of Jamestown and Oval roads. A flurry of people was spewing out of it as I arrived at six o'clock, most of them women and none of them the trendy, youthful types you'd get in the world of men's magazines. Not an iPod nor a Hoxton Pyramid in sight. This lot looked more like they were hurrying back to the kids in suburbia, eager to be away from the squalid environs of Camden.

Ray was easy to spot. He'd shaved his hair to about a number three, and only had one sleeper left in his left ear, but apart from that, he really wasn't so different from that photograph in *Noise*! He was tall and slender, and like Steve Mullin, still was fashioned indelibly out of punk. Only Ray's choice of black StaPrest, black Harrington jacket and vintage Robot creepers looked so sharp as to be almost cutting-edge contemporary. With his high cheekbones and cool blue eyes, he could still teach the kids a thing or two about style.

He greeted me with a warm smile and a steady handshake. He had a nice voice too, full of good humour. We walked amiably up Oval Road towards Parkway with him asking most of the questions.

'Blood Truth, eh? What made you want to write a book about them? Brilliant band and all that, but not one that ever gets mentioned. It's Gang of Four the kids all seem to be going after these days.'

'That's it really,' I explained. 'The mystery of them. The fact that they did disappear at the peak of their powers and haven't been slogging it round the reunion circuit ever since.'

He nodded. 'Yeah, there is that, isn't there? It's strange how they got overlooked, but I suppose there were so many bands that came after them which sounded more or less like them that they just got lost in the ether. It wouldn't be like that nowadays. Imagine if no one remembered Kurt Cobain but there were a load of new bands banging on about the glory of Counting Crows.'

I laughed. 'Maybe there will be in ten years' time.'

'Maybe. It was a different world then, that's for sure. So many scenes coming up, one after the other, so many brilliant new bands. I suppose it's not surprising that some of them got lost. So how did you find out about them?'

'Gavin Granger got me into them. You know him?'

'Oh, Gavin,' Ray said amiably. 'Yeah, well I used to know him. He was a nice bloke and that other Aussie mate of his – Mick, was it? That's right. Probably the best photographer of the day, Gavin was. Toss up between him and Pennie Smith anyway. How is he these days?'

Well, there was certainly no bitterness in Ray's voice about the so-called enemy of old. He seemed genuinely interested in what my Antipodean chum was up to. Perhaps Gavin had been a bit jealous of him. He wasn't the type who liked being out-suaved and Ray was certainly one suave dude.

We got to Pizza Express and ordered some garlic bread, pizzas and Peroni beers. It was so empty at that time of night that we practically had the place to ourselves. 'Good call,' I said, looking around.

'Yeah, I always come here on the rare occasions I go to gigs these days. So,' he clearly still saw himself in the interviewer mode, 'have you met the rest of the band?'

Over the garlic bread I told him about my meetings with Steve, Lynton and Kevin. He laughed a lot at my description of Steve's tour of Portobello and sympathised with the Lynton interview.

'Well, he always was the quietest one, right from the start,' he said. 'The hardest one to get to know, definitely. I don't think he ever did give too much away.'

'So do you mind if I do a taped interview with you?' I finally asked, as the waiter delivered our pizzas.

'Yeah, OK,' he said, looking a bit wary. 'You know, it's kind of strange it being the other way around.'

I don't know if Ray had had an impressively anti-drugs grandfather as well, but his recall of the punk days seemed as sharp as Steve's. Perhaps a time that was so brilliant would always be crystal clear in your memory. He could really explain what it was like to be there, and why Blood Truth had been such a vital band.

I told him how taken I had been with the interview Stevens had given me.

'Ah, the testing-me-out interview,' he said. 'I got off lightly, I think. Vince was a pretty scary bloke, you know. He had a few fights with journalists he didn't like. I mean, so did Captain Sensible and Jean Jacques Burnel – even Marc Almond once chased a guy round a room with a bullwhip. But there was something about Vince that was more genuinely disturbing than any of them. That's why he was such a good frontman, but I don't think he was at all a nice person.'

'Really? Most of the people I've met so far seem to be almost in love with him.'

'Yeah.' Ray chewed his food thoughtfully. 'There are certain types of bloke who do tend to affect other blokes that way. I suppose he'd be the sort who'd get all the others to go over the top in World War One or something. The rest of the band, they were all lovely blokes, and they did all follow him over the top, in a way.'

'What do you think happened to him?'

Ray put his knife and fork down. 'What I honestly think is that he picked a fight with someone even bigger and nastier than he was. I think that was probably always the way it was gonna end with him.'

'Really?'

Ray caught my eye, looked away for a minute as if deciding something, then drew his peelers back level.

'It's weird thinking about all this stuff again. I've got a lot of good memories, but a lot of not-so-good ones too. Mainly around Mood Violet, to tell you the truth. See, I didn't know Blood Truth all that well, you know, I was never part of their family like Gavin was, I was just a journalist they got on with, so things were always friendly. But Mood Violet was a bit different.'

I hadn't expected this. But it was good. There was so much I didn't know about them. Maybe I was about to hear another berserker Leith story. Maybe Ray had once looked at Sylvana funny or something.

I was acutely aware of the hovering waiter, circling like a buzzard. I didn't want to get rushed out of there, so I ordered another couple of beers to distract him from our almost-finished plates.

'Yeah,' Ray continued when he had gone. 'See, the thing is, my ex-girlfriend discovered them. I was kind of involved in getting their career off the ground and helping her set up a label. Only...' He looked really uncomfortable. 'Would you mind turning that off a minute?'

Here we go again, I thought, instantly deflating. He's going to do a Kevin Holme on me now.

'Sorry,' he said, as if reading my mind. 'I'm not trying to be some rock star prima donna. It's just that this is personal stuff and, you know, I've got a wife and three kids and a quiet life these days. But my ex-girlfriend, Donna Woods, she dumped me twenty-three years ago, yet she still has the habit of coming back into my life when I don't want her to. Which is why I have to consider whether to help you or not.'

Ray tapped his fingers against the side of the table. His eyes looked strained. 'Because Donna is bad news, seriously,' he said, looking me straight in the eye. 'But if you want to get the real truth of the story, then you've really gotta speak to her. And then, if you do, there's no saying whether you'll be able to get rid of her again afterwards. Those goths in the Dev?' He gave a wry chuckle but he didn't look amused. 'They ain't got nothing on her.' I followed his troubled gaze, out into the Camden night.

I had thought Blood Truth were the Wild Bunch in this story. But having met Leith, and with Ray now saying this, it started to sound like the ethereal bollocks pedlars were the real Pandora's Box.

'Well, of course I'd like to speak to her if she's important to the plot…' I began.

'I tell you what,' Ray said. 'Let me speak to Allie. You know, the guitarist from the band. You should probably speak to him as well, but I'd like to get his opinion on this first.'

It was shades of Kevin yet again, but I had the feeling that Ray would keep his word. Why would he bother to meet me and then tell me all this otherwise?

'I'll call you back in the next couple of days, I promise,' he said. 'In the meantime, I suppose there's only one question we need to ask – do we really want to raise the dead?'

22

Party Fears Two

December 1980

Four months of sneaking around. Four months of late night assignations, snatched moments when schedules collided, illicit passions heightening the delirium of each encounter. Every time they parted, Donna felt as if he had taken another little part of her with him, another small chip off her heart, her brain, her self-control.

She could keep things normal on the surface while he wasn't around, she could go about her business in the same self-contained manner as she always had done, giving nothing away to anyone. That first mad night had been a lesson to her. She had fucked up that night good and proper. She made sure that it never happened again.

But this passion, this love, this fire he had lit inside her – it would not let her rest in peace. When she was alone, she felt afraid and angry. Angry that he always went back to that drippy Rachel he had dragged down from Doncaster, who clung to him like a limp wallflower. Angry that it had to be that way to keep the deception in place. The deception that would always be necessary, because the fear was stronger. The fear of the other person that Vince went to meet in the middle of the night. Of Tone – and what he would do to her if he ever found out.

Tone had been right, they were the same. They were both actors who loved duplicity. They were both haunted and shaped by what their fathers had done. They were both very different from the people they lived and worked amongst. And now they were both in love with the same man.

When Vince left her bed, as he always did, never once staying till the morning, Donna would listen to him drive away and cry so hard she didn't know how it could ever stop. She couldn't see a way out of this entanglement, yet to end it was unthinkable. She was trapped in lust. Trapped by her own flesh. This was what being a junkie was like.

Mood Violet and Blood Truth had both ended their tours in December with final shows in London. Mood Violet's was first. They'd sold out the Rainbow, the venue that had brought them all together in the first place, as if they had come full circle from wide-eyed spectators to owning the joint. Donna had been on the road with the band for most of their dates, diligently keeping an eye on Sylvana and Robin while her heart ached to be elsewhere. Things did seem to have calmed down between them. Perhaps it was the presence of Helen on the tour bus. That old camaraderie had reasserted itself to a certain extent and everyone seemed a lot more at ease. Everyone except Donna.

She'd known Blood Truth would be back in town the same night as the Rainbow. She'd had their dates imprinted on her mind; like a psycho stalker she kept track on every movement Vince made. But she hadn't expected Tone to call and ask her for a guest list. That had been a shock to her system and straight off she had wondered if somehow he had found out, that he was coming for her that night and she'd end up in the foundations of some new road or bridge before morning. He hadn't come to a Mood Violet gig for about two years.

But Tone was just being magnanimous. He'd had a good year, she'd had a good year, their bands were on one night after the other, let's live it up a bit and celebrate, was his gist.

She'd asked him if he was bringing anyone with him. She wanted him to say yes almost as much as she wanted him to say no. She hadn't seen Vince for three weeks by then. She was clawing the walls with pent-up desire.

'Put me down plus two,' he'd said. 'I'll see who else wants to come.'

It was so vague as to drive her wild. But in the end he'd turned up with Popeye Doyle and the scary-looking black man and she didn't know whether to laugh or cry. She'd ended up laughing mainly. Popeye – or Steve as he was really called – wasn't the sort of person you could stay miserable around for long. He was loud, rowdy and outrageously funny and he clearly fancied Donna from the moment he clapped eyes on her, which was all to the good. She flirted back almost as much, revenge on Vince who was no doubt back home tending to his weed, seeing as he wasn't with Tone. The black man, Lynton, was actually really sweet, shy and soft-spoken. They all watched the gig together from the side of the stage, the exact spot Donna had stood with Ray all those years ago. But Donna didn't even give him a second thought.

It was incredible how popular Mood Violet had become. The gig was a sell-out, and the crowd was ecstatic; pressed together they formed a kind of human sea, rolling in waves of black, green and purple round the rim of the stage. Hands reached out towards Sylvana, hands with scarves tied around the wrists or heavy with rows of silver bangles. The diaphanous layered dresses Helen had created in sea greens and purples to accentuate her Pre-Raphaelite otherworldliness were imitated over and over by the girls in the crowd, with the hennaed, crimped locks and the fringe that came down over the eyes. But it was the black-clad boys who made their affections known the loudest, who rucked around the front of the stage in ritual circles, throwing their arms up in the air at dramatic moments in the songs, piling up on top of each other's shoulders to get a better look.

The object of their affection sung with her eyes closed, swaying gently, reaching her own arms upwards at times, at others just holding on to the scarf-draped mic stand as if it were the prow of a ship, riding across this turbulent sea. At the siren's side, Allie moved backwards and forwards as he danced, raising his eyes every now and again to wink and smile at the crowd, coiling himself up in his leads sometimes when he became too enthusiastic. Behind them, Robin stood immobile behind banks of synths and amps. He looked like a mad professor loose in his lab but was more like an infernal conductor, controlling the invisible orchestra trapped inside his black machines.

'Would you give her one, Lynt?' Donna heard Steve say behind her.

Lynton laughed hard but didn't reply.

'No, come on,' Steve persisted. 'I want to know. Would you? Looks like everyone else here would, but I just don't gerrit.'

'She is very beautiful,' said Lynton diplomatically. 'And Stevie, please. Ask not whom you would give one to, but instead ask yourself – who would actually let you?'

Certainly no one else shared Steve's sentiments. The crowd didn't want to let her go. As the band came back to play their third encore, a rapturously received 'Splintered', a beaming Tone pulled Donna into a bear hug.

'You must be so pleased, Sis, look at 'em go,' he said. 'Look what you've done, eh?'

She tried to smile back at him, but the warmth and pride in his voice made her want to choke. Tone had treated her better than anyone else ever had. And she was busy betraying him.

'Oh, don't get all emotional, girl, it ain't like you.' He misconstrued her wonky mouth and blurry eyes. 'You're allowed to enjoy these things, you know. You worked hard enough for it.'

'If it wasn't for you...' she began but Tone waved his hands dismissively, reaching for the champagne bottle he had perched on an amp beside them.

'Shut up and have another drink,' he said.

After the gig, she took them into the dressing room, where there was a real atmosphere of euphoria. Even Robin had lost his surly expression and acted genuinely impressed when introduced to Tone, who was fervently complimentary about his musical ability. Tone had long been interested in pushing the boundaries with computers, so before long they were lost in a conversation about Rolands and Fairlights that would have been frankly incomprehensible to the rest of the room.

The two guitarists, Steve and Allie, bonded almost immediately. There always was an unspoken kinship between those that played the same instrument, and although they were both pushing their style in very different directions, these two were peas out of the same pod: big, amiable Celts, the respective older brothers of their bands.

Sylvana was staying close to Helen, but as Donna worked the room, she noticed Lynton drifting over to their corner. She wondered if she should offer a proper introduction – Robin looked happily involved in his conversation with Tone – but then decided to let nature take its own course. If he was going to throw one of his jealous strops she didn't want to be accused of facilitating it.

The usual liggers were all present and correct, Donna noticed. That Aussie photographer from the *NME*, busy ingratiating himself to one and all, laughing too loudly at other people's jokes. Donna had noticed the way he made friends and influenced people before and he was at it again tonight. He had a casual handshake that if you looked closely, seemed to be a way of slipping something to whoever he was talking to. She noticed him doing it with Lynton, as he barrelled over to interrupt the bassist's conversation with Sylvana.

Then again, maybe that was for the good tonight. For it wasn't to be a night of tantrums and tensions. Everyone was happy for once. It was true what Tone said, Donna reflected as she stood by the doorway, watching the carnival scene unfold in front of her, she had made all this happen. She did have something to really be proud of.

For the first time in four months, she forgot about Vince Smith and started enjoying herself. By about one o'clock, the management were regretfully but firmly trying to show the band and the twenty or so souls left in their dressing room the way outside.

Tone put an arm round Donna's shoulder as he made his way to leave. 'Come to the gig tomorrow, let me return the compliment,' he said. 'Or if you can't make it, invite everyone to my house on New Year's Eve. I'm gonna have a proper party this year. I've got a feeling 1981 is gonna be a good one.'

'Thanks, Tone,' Donna smiled up at him, fighting back the urge to suddenly confess to him exactly how she had been repaying his kindness in recent months. 'I don't know if this lot will be fit tomorrow, but we'll definitely come on New Year's Eve,' she said. She knew he wouldn't take no for an answer on that one, and it would be a damn sight easier to avoid Vince in a house full of people than at one of his own gigs.

'That's my girl,' Tone turned round and addressed his new friends. 'You hear that guys? Come to my party on New Year's Eve, Donna knows where. You're all very welcome.' Then he turned to leave, his two charges and the Aussie guy loitering behind.

'Cheers, Donna,' big Steve squeezed her hand almost painfully and regarded her with what he took to be an alluring expression but was actually the epitome of a cartoon letch. 'Thanks for yer hospitality, love. I'll be sure to show you some of mine whenever you like.'

'Come on, you dirty bastard,' Lynton pushed his friend out of her way. 'I apologise for him,' he said, taking Donna's hand in a graceful handshake. 'He's from Hull. He knows no better.'

Steve belched loudly. 'Gerrover, Lynt. She knows a real man when she sees one.'

'A cave man more like it.' Lynton raised his eyebrows in mock exasperation, then smiled. 'Anyway, I hope to see you at Tone's do. I'll protect you from his evil ways.'

If only, thought Donna, it was him I needed protecting from.

Sylvana felt a glimmer of hope for the first time in months.

Having Helen on the tour bus had made everything so different. It wasn't like they had gone back to how they were in the early days, it couldn't be – now they were driven around in a massive coach with bunk beds, a team of roadies and a tour manager, so there were no routes to plan, no freezing 4am sleeps in lay-bys with a fine layer of dew on your sleeping bag, no laughing and singing along to the radio. *The Partridge Family* was no more. Now they were fairly cosseted.

But the chemistry had altered. With Helen there, Robin didn't watch Sylvana's every move like a hawk, flashing her that look if she so much as dared to answer one of the roadies' questions or spent five minutes talking to a fan after the show, she knew what would happen. Those looks and that promise had gradually sealed her reputation as a glacial, stuck-up bitch throughout the music industry over the past year. Most of the time, people knew better than to even bother approaching her.

But with Helen aboard, he would leave her alone to talk with her old friend. At first this would only be for a matter of minutes, but gradually, as the tour went on and his guard was lowered, he ignored what they were up to for hours at a time. Ostensibly – and if anyone came within range of overhearing – they were talking about dress design, interiors and other permitted womanly subjects. But really, during those precious hours, Helen had gradually wheedled the truth out of her.

Sylvana had been keeping it close so long, it felt like she had been tied up inside a Victorian corset, her denial forming the rigid lines of whalebone that kept her together. When she began to loosen her ties, she thought she might suddenly collapse into a puddle of jelly and never get up again.

The hardest thing to admit was that she had fallen for the oldest trick in the book, had become for want of a better cliché a 'battered wife'. And the way that he did it was all so textbook too. The tears of remorse, the promises that it would never happen again, but at the same time, the gradual cutting her off from all her friends and family. Not that he had much to do on the family front. Her parents had all but disowned her for staying in London anyhow. It was only Ola that kept her going, putting money in her account each month to 'give you something to get by on', and Uncle Manny who sorted out her visa and let her continue living at Queen's Gate Gardens. Although if he had known the truth about Robin, who still slept in Helen's old room whenever he was about, she was sure that arrangement would soon come to an abrupt end.

Sylvana told Helen how she wished she had acted on her instincts and cut and run the first time it had happened but how, with a tour to do and an album to promote, she felt she couldn't let everyone else down. And at first, Robin had stuck to his promise that he'd never hurt her again, being kindness itself for the rest of that tour. Then gradually, as the months went by and the band got bigger and bigger, his dark side had reasserted itself, his rages triggered by the most stupid of things.

Things like fans throwing her black roses onstage, as they had taken to doing, in an act of gothic homage. Like the fan mail Donna passed on but she never got to read because he ripped it all to pieces in front of her, foaming at the mouth and calling her as many different variations on the word 'whore' as he could think of. Or like the guy from the *Melody Maker* who had really understood her lyrics and whom she had spent hours talking to, rapt with enthusiasm that she'd found a kindred spirit. The guy who was thirty years old and married – not that that counted for anything in Robin's book. That was the last time she'd been allowed to talk to the press without him glowering by her side, and gradually, she had been phased out of the process altogether. The last vestiges of any love she'd had for him had crumbled away at this point, and only the fear of not knowing what she could possibly do next had kept her there, under his thumb.

She didn't – she couldn't quite bring herself to – tell Helen exactly what it was that he had been doing to her, though. Robin was quite careful not to leave any marks where people would see them. His artistry with cigarette butts and bits of broken bottle were hidden on her body, underneath those layers of diaphanous chiffon Helen designed. Sylvana's shame at revealing them was too deep. It was her own fault she had ended up like this. Those scars, and the hideous pain that had caused them, was her reminder of her own folly.

All she could tell her best friend was that, in all truthfulness, she would rather die than stay with Robin.

Helen, in return, had acted like a cross between an agony aunt and a secret agent. Because she had to go back to London between some of the dates, she had been able to take Sylvana's door key, go back to Queen's Gate Gardens and take all her friend's most precious things to a place of safety. Her passport, her bankbook, her box of Ola's jewellery and other, sentimental artifacts had all gone into the bank vault where Helen kept her business stuff. She didn't suppose her own home would be safe enough if and when Robin found out.

Sylvana also gave her money to buy a suitcase and pack it full of everything she would need to make a quick getaway. These things made Sylvana feel stronger and after they had been done, between them they figured out a strategy of what to do next.

Her best plan, Helen reckoned, was to go to where Robin couldn't follow her – New Jersey – and lay low for a while. It was obvious, Helen said, that Ola would be able to bring her parents round and she and Allie would take care of getting Robin out of her uncle's place when the time came. Sylvana knew that if she confessed all to Ola, Manny himself would probably take care of that eventuality, but that was still something she was too afraid to do. Helen didn't push it either. She just got her to concentrate on one thing and one thing only – getting safely away.

The final thing that Helen had done for her that morning was to go and buy her a plane ticket. The flight left Heathrow at 4pm on January 1. They intended to go somewhere the night before, as is traditional on New Year's Eve, and get Robin so arseholed they could safely leave him passed out somewhere. Then they'd spirit Sylvana away before he came round and could do anything about it. Drastic maybe, but Sylvana knew that if she didn't do it now, with Helen's help, she'd possibly never have the courage to do it ever again.

Helen hadn't even told Allie. She had let Sylvana down once and couldn't afford to take any chances that their plot could get foiled. She intended that her husband would be as drunk as Robin. He would know nothing and therefore have nothing to answer for.

Up until that moment, they hadn't been quite sure what they would actually do on New Year's Eve. But now, Donna's friend had just given them the perfect cover. As they made their way out of the Rainbow, back to the tour bus for the final time, Robin was full of his new friend Tony Stevens and what a genius he appeared to be. He couldn't wait to go to his house, he kept saying, and see his personal synth collection.

Sylvana hadn't seen him so animated, so happy, for years.

At the back of the venue, in the cul-de-sac where the bus was parked, Sylvana stopped and looked up at the dirty London sky. God please, she prayed silently, under the streetlights that blocked out the stars, let me escape from this man. Please God,

I'll never ask you for anything ever again. But save me. Save me from Robin.

'Aren't you ready yet?' Steve bellowed up the stairs. 'We're gonna be late for all that free booze!'

There was no vocal response from the master bedroom of the squat, just the squeaking of floorboards and the sound of 'American Trilogy' being notched up another few thousand decibels.

'I dunno,' he turned to Lynton. 'Shall we just leave him to it?'

Lynton raised his eyebrows. Like Steve, he was suited and booted and eager to get to Tony's party. 'Where's Kevin got to?' he asked.

'Fuck knows.' Steve shook his head. 'Maybe she's doin' his laundry an' all.'

He nodded his head towards the kitchen door, through which the form of Rachel could be seen, dutifully ironing her boyfriend's trousers for the eightieth time, her black-rimmed eyes staring blankly into space. She'd dolled herself up hours ago in anticipation of this rare night out, but her party frock and make-up showed definite signs of wilting now she had spent the best part of the evening running errands in the kitchen, getting through half a bottle of vodka as she did so.

'Kevin!' Steve yelled. 'We're gonna hit the road, you coming or what?'

A figure appeared at the top of the stairs. Kevin was still in his underpants.

'I'll catch you up,' he said. 'I've got to make a phone call and I'm not ready yet.'

'So we see,' Steve noted. 'You saving your best pair for the ladies, Kev?'

'Something like that. Look, don't worry about me, I can find my way well enough. You lot get off and I'll see you later.'

'All right,' Steve shrugged. 'Ta ra then, Rachel,' he peered round the kitchen door.

Rachel looked up blankly. Steve was beginning to suspect it was more than booze that she was on these days. She looked as if she could barely focus on his face, let alone open her mouth to speak. All she could do was move that iron back and forth, back and forth.

'Careful, love,' he said gently. 'You won't have much left if you carry on doing that.' But she didn't seem to hear him.

Steve shook his head and turned back into the hallway. 'Right, let's go,' he said. The moon was high and the air was crisp with frost as they walked down Ladbroke Grove.

'Oooh, heck,' said Steve. 'I hope that Donna one's gonna be there. I'd shag the arse off that, I would.'

'You'd be fucking lucky, mate,' Lynton said, 'I reckon she sets her sights a little bit higher than you.'

'Oh, you do, do you? You reckon she'd rather have the black Leslie Phillips then, am I right?'

'I say!' Lynton mimicked said charmer.

'Well, you can't fool me with yer fancy talk. It's that Yank one you're after, eh, Lynt?' Steve goaded, bursting into a ridiculous impression of Sylvana's singing voice. 'Ooohhh eeehhh ah've lost my braaaaaa, I doooon't knooow where my knickers are…'

'Shut up,' Lynton said, trying to stifle his giggles. 'Look, here comes the bus.'

'Oh, aye,' said Steve. 'And I notice you don't deny it.'

They jumped on the 15, still laughing and bickering.

It was twenty past eleven.

'Not long now,' Helen whispered down Sylvana's ear as she passed her another glass of orange juice.

Sylvana smiled back at her friend, trying not to show the fear she felt inside. Trying not to betray the fact that now they were so close to completing their plan, she no longer knew if she could go through with it. The thought of what Robin would do if he caught her halfway through trying to leave, the guilt at what would happen to Allie and Donna if she didn't come back, the trauma of having to explain it all to her parents…It spun around and around in her head, like the beeping, squealing music blasting out of Tony Stevens's jukebox.

The house was packed to the rafters with revellers, and though they seemed to have managed to lose Robin and Allie for now, Sylvana's eyes kept darting to the kitchen door every five seconds. Maybe she could have relaxed into it a bit better if she'd had more than the one glass of champagne that Tony had handed her when they arrived. But Helen had made sure they stuck dutifully to the soft drinks ever since.

'The time for celebration's when you're safely on the other side of the Atlantic Ocean,' she kept reminding her. Sylvana was beginning to wish she hadn't told Helen now. Her nerve was failing her. Visions of her mother's face, looking like she'd just sucked on a lemon, saying: 'What did I tell you, Ruben, the child isn't capable of standing on her own two feet for a moment,' kept swimming into her mind. The vision was made still more harsh and surreal by the dayglo yellow the music was provoking. Dayglo yellow and shocking pink. The colour scheme in this house might well have been a manly monochrome but the music its owner liked was a migraine-inducing assault.

Sylvana wished they could escape back to the roof garden they'd been shown earlier, where palms and ferns made a gentle, almost mystical atmosphere. But Helen had been adamant that they stayed here, where there were too many people around them for Robin to dare make a scene.

For the last hour, he and Allie had been lost in the *Boy's Own* wonderworld that was the basement, messing about with some guys from a German electronic band in Tony's own mini-recording studio. Sylvana neither knew nor cared whether they were down there fiddling about on the banks of synths, going through Tony's British Library-sized record collection or playing on the full-sized snooker table.

All she knew was, while he was doing any of those things, he wouldn't be getting pissed enough for their plan to work. She had a horrible feeling that before the night was out, he was going to suss out what they were up to. Suss them out and make her pay.

For the past half an hour, she and Helen had been making polite conversation with that Lynton guy who had come backstage at the Rainbow. He seemed a really nice, well-mannered man, but Sylvana just couldn't hold the thread of the conversation.

'Oh.' She saw Helen frown. 'There's Allie.'

Sylvana followed her gaze, her heartbeat quickening. Allie was waving from the doorway. Thankfully, he seemed to be alone. She saw him mouth the words, 'Come here a minute, hen,' to Helen.

'Shit,' Helen looked dubiously at Sylvana, then Lynton, then back to him. It was obvious she didn't want to leave her there, talking to another man.

'Go and see what he wants,' Sylvana said, more sharply than she had intended.

'OK,' Helen bit her bottom lip. 'Great timing, Allie,' she muttered to herself, then tried to fix a bright smile to her face.

'I won't be a minute, I promise,' she said to both of them, and hurriedly made her way to her husband.

Lynton followed all this with a bemused expression on his face. 'Is everything OK?' he asked.

'Yes,' said Sylvana, wanting to scream the opposite. 'But I tell you what. Do you think you could slip a little something into this for me?' She proffered the glass full of orange. 'Brandy or vodka or something. I'm getting a little bored of this goody-two-shoes routine.'

'For your voice, yeah?' Lynton assumed. 'Well, I won't tell. I'll be back before you know it.'

For a second, standing on her own, Sylvana felt a measure of relief. Now that she didn't feel pressure from all quarters, perhaps she could work out a way of getting out of this situation without hurting Helen. Or Robin. Or Donna. Or…

'You look lost,' said a voice.

Sylvana looked up abruptly. There was a tall, handsome man standing right in front of her, with a shock of thick black hair and the most beautiful, violet eyes. For a second, she assumed he must be talking to someone else and turned her head around.

'No, I mean you.'

When she looked back, he was smiling. It was the kindest smile she had ever seen.

It was a quarter to twelve and Donna was raging inside. Tonight had been hell so far. Pure, exquisite torture.

It wasn't enough that she was going to have to spend the biggest party night of the year watching the man she loved with his drippy girlfriend while having to smile through it all like she was oblivious. Now, thanks to good old Tone, she was going to have to share that experience with her bloody band looking on. She was going to have to pretend that she was pleased to be out with them, when she was sick of the fucking sight of them. She was going to have to pretend to be worried if nasty Robin gave poor little Sylvana a dirty look during the course of the evening, have a fucking conference with Social Worker Helen about it and no doubt see the New Year in holding the silly cow's hand in a taxi.

She actually considered pretending to be ill to get out of it. But in the end, she found herself hammering her bank balance in Vivienne Westwood, picking out the most audacious outfit in there, a black-and-white rubber polka-dot dress with a waist cinched in to only eighteen inches and a hobble skirt. This, when teamed with her eight-inch patent stilettos and vertiginous hairdo – created by Louis, finished off with a white rose behind her right ear – made her look just like Cruella de Ville.

'Let him keep it in his fucking trousers when he sees this,' she had fumed to her reflection in her boudoir mirror. 'Let him want to fuck that drippy bitch instead.'

But, nearly three hours into the party, she still hadn't been able to put this theory to the test.

Despite the fact she had been at Tone's side for almost the entire time they were there, and it seemed that everyone else in the entire music business had come up to pay homage to him, there was no sign whatsoever of Vince.

Her heart had given a brief flutter when she saw Steve and Lynton coming towards them, heard them tell Tone that their singer was 'on his way'. But that ripple of excitement had turned into a millstone of despair as she had then found herself having to endure the incessant, coarse advances of that fucking Steve for the next two hours. Even Tone and Lynton had seemed to drift away with embarrassment and she'd actually found herself being glad of a rescue from the dreary old bag that commissioned her to write for *Time Out*, who fawned all over her new outfit for the next half an hour.

Well, the silly cow wouldn't think it was quite so fucking *a-mayyy-zing* if she'd tried to use the lavs while wearing the fucking thing. That was perhaps the greatest indignity of the entire evening so far – if not, her entire life. Donna couldn't roll the fucking thing back down over her arse; the rubber had got so hot it had stuck together like glue. The toilet she'd gone into was totally devoid of talcum powder, so in her increasingly frenzied attempts to prize it back down she had managed to get two of her false nails stuck to her backside and put another one right through the fabric. Donna had almost had a panic attack right there and then and screamed the house down. She didn't know where she had got the reserve of strength to make herself go back to the beginning, slowly and methodically to take off all her nails, throw them in the bin, roll the rubber down gently, bit by bit and then hide the hole she had made around her upper thigh by using her eyeliner to paint over her flesh.

She only knew that it was finally done, and she was taking deep breaths while staring in the mirror, when she noticed that the clock behind her was telling her there were only fifteen more minutes 'til midnight.

Donna tottered out of the door. She was on the first floor landing, where Tone's Scarlett O'Hara staircase looked out over his hallway and the champagne fountain he'd had installed for the evening. Naturally, this is where all the champion liggers were circulating. She leaned against the railings to take the weight off her feet, presuming that Tone would soon appear to lead them all into the NewYear's countdown.

Her eyes roamed the room, but for a minute she didn't quite take in what she was seeing. There were so many people down there it took a while to digest the scene properly, to work out their individual faces. But her eye was caught by the motion of someone moving through the crowd, away from the kitchen, towards the front door. Not one person, actually, but two. Someone really tall with his arm around someone much smaller, almost like he was shielding them.

Someone really tall with jet black hair.

Someone much smaller with blood-red locks.

Vince walking towards the door.

Sylvana in his arms.

Lynton had thought his luck had changed when he was finally left alone with Sylvana. But then, he also thought it would only take a minute to cross to the other side of the room and get her a brandy. However, the room was full of people and they all seemed to want to talk to him. First it was Paul, their music publisher from Exile, roaring drunk and full of tall stories that he wanted to share. After he had extricated himself from that one and finally made it to the table with the spirits on it, there were a couple of girls in a similar state of inebriation who tried to chat him up. By the time he had got away from their bindweed embraces, filled the glass and turned round to walk back, he could no longer see the girl he actually wanted to be with still standing by the door.

Instead he saw her friend Helen, looking around the room in a state of panic. He hurried his way back over.

'Oh there you are!' Helen almost shrieked. 'Is she with you?'

'No.' Lynton was dumbfounded. 'She was here a minute ago. I just went to get another drink and…'

'But if she's not with you, then where is she?'

'Maybe she just went to the toilet?' he suggested.

But the woman was totally panicked. 'Oh God, I knew I shouldn't have let her out of my sight.' She glanced at her watch. 'Are you sure she was here a minute ago? Only it's taken me ages to get back here and now it's nearly midnight…'

'Well,' Lynton noticed the time – it had taken him half an hour to get the drink, but he didn't want to worry Helen any more – 'maybe ten minutes ago. It takes so long to get anywhere in this house. But I'm sure she won't have gone far…'

As the words left his mouth, he could hear someone ringing a bell.

'Order! Order!' a voice shouted from the hall.

Someone else shut off the jukebox.

'Ten…' people began to shout, 'nine…eight…seven…'

Then round the corner a banshee came. Wild-eyed and black-haired, she launched herself at Helen, grabbing hold of the lapels of her jacket, screaming into her face: 'Do you realise what that little tart has done? Do you know what's she's up to?'

Lynton tried to move in to intervene.

'Six…five…four…'

'Get off me, Donna, what the hell are you doing?' Helen was falling backwards.

'Three…two…one…'

Lynton felt the fist intended for Helen connect with his lower jaw.

'Happy New Year!'

Part Three

23

Where the Shadows Smile

May 2002

Less than a fortnight after my meeting with Ray, I was on a train headed for St Albans and a meeting with Mood Violet's former guitarist Aliester McTavish.

It was the first Saturday in May, the Bank Holiday weekend, and it had dawned so hot and sunny I'd cracked out my finest Hawiian shirt for the occasion. With my cream slacks and Ray Bans, I felt like Al Pacino, a wise guy travelling incognito through the rolling fields of Hertfordshire. I was going to find out some old secrets, settle some old scores. For the first time since Louise left, I was actually feeling good.

The sudden heatwave wasn't the only reason for this either. It was the line of detection that had brought me here, something I'd managed to figure out for myself without Gavin's help. I had been right about Ray Spencer; he was no Kevin Holme. We'd had a couple more jars after our meal that night, across the road in the Dublin Castle, where we joined the old Irishmen gathered around the tables near the long copper-topped bar, the Ghosts of Camden Past as they so nearly were these days.

Ray must have decided I was worth trusting, as he told me a bit more about his involvement with Mood Violet and this woman, Donna Woods. She sounded like a kind of cross between Paula Yates and Janet Street-Porter and had been big news for about five minutes in the early eighties.

When the band had ended, he said, it had taken all friendships with it. Aleister had been the only one to come out of it unscathed, Ray reckoned, though the process had burned him to the extent that he never played in a band again. He was a music teacher these days.

Yet perhaps, after all this time, it seemed he might like to set a few records straight. Or even get some kind of acknowledgement for pioneering a type of music that all the kids were so happily ripping off these days.

I'd spoken to Aleister, or Allie as he told me to call him, a couple of days previously on the phone. Thankfully, he sounded nothing like Robin Leith. I knew that they came from the same small town on the outskirts of Edinburgh, but there was no harshness or implicit threat in his tone at all, instead he had a genial rumble. He said he would pick me up from the train station and drive me over to where he lived with his wife and kids on a smallholding just out of town. He even had the train timetable with him so we could work out which one I would take.

But he did sound one note of dissent. 'You'll just be coming on your own though, mind, not with your photographer pal?'

It was more of a statement than a question, although he did sound apologetic even as he said it. 'It's just that my wife...well, she doesnae like him much.'

Actually, I had intended to go it alone. I didn't think it was appropriate for someone who routinely referred to the band's singer as a fucking bitch to come up and have tea and cakes with the guitarist anyway, so I wasn't surprised to hear he wouldn't be welcome. Mood Violet were my own separate investigation, one that I doubted Gavin would be interested in anyway. Besides, he was off on one of his jaunts for the *Sunday Times* that weekend.

St Albans station was small and full of teenage girls tottering around in baby pink T-shirts with sparkly logos and jeans cut low enough for you to see their nylon g-strings disappearing up an inch of well-fed arse cleavage. No doubt they were all dolled up for a day 'up West' or whatever the local parlance was, all of them furiously texting, jabbering and chewing their nails as they went. A few youthful Jeremies, trying to disguise themselves as 50 Cent in hoods and jeans with waistbands around the knees, loitered by the payphone, thinking they looked hard.

So it wasn't difficult to spot the one middle-aged man in the place. Allie McTavish was broad and tall, but he hadn't run to flab the way Steve Mullin had. His crinkly black hair might have been frosted over with grey, but his tanned, weather-beaten face and strong shoulders suggested he'd been enjoying the outdoors life for the past twenty years, although there were still some traces of his former identity in his T-shirt with the big black Fine Power Tools logo, cut-off combats and Converse sneakers.

Allie was holding his car keys in one hand and a bag of shopping in the other. He raised the less encumbered limb when he saw me.

'Hiya, Eddie.' His voice was as friendly as his face. 'You found us OK then?'

'Yeah, this a great service,' I said. 'Much better than the tube.'

'Aye,' he nodded, leading the way out to the car park. 'We don't miss any of that shite out here. Beautiful day, eh?'

Allie had one of those sleek four-by-four jeeps, also in black, which he unlocked with the remote control on his keys, stashing his groceries in the back before opening the passenger door for me.

'Nice,' I said, appraising the vehicle.

'It helps with the kids I teach, you know,' he said and winked. 'They think I'm Dr Dre drivin' this. Helps with my own kids an' all. But unlike the housewives of Chelsea we actually do need an off-road vehicle where we are. As you'll see.' He spun us niftily out of the car park and out of the tiny city.

'You wouldn't think,' he said, as we stopped at a crossroads, 'that this was once the busiest road in Britain.'

'No, you wouldn't.' I took in the smart shops and comfortable-looking pubs, the well-heeled old market town ambience.

'Aye. This used to be Watling Street, the main road to London.' Allie accelerated away, down the hill. 'It's still the same road as the Romans built, really. This ends up being Edgware Road.'

'How long have you lived here?'

'Just over twenty years.'

We drove on winding lanes past rows of beautiful old white houses with thatched roofs and leaded windows. I had no idea this place was so genuinely ancient and well preserved. It made Guildford look positively nouveau riche.

'Looks like a great place to live,' I said, thinking, Mother missed a trick here.

'Aye, we took a chance but I wouldnae change a thing. My wife, Helen, she had a really successful fashion business, that was what gave us the money to do it. Mind you, if we were in the same position now, we'd probably have to move back to Scotland to get what we've got here.'

We'd left the city and were travelling down green, leafy roads, the verges white with the froth of cow parsley, mirages forming in the bumps on the tarmac ahead, shimmering in the midday sun. It gave me a sudden pang for the Surrey Downs and childhood days spent wandering with Dad through the woods while Mother cast aspersions at the WI fête. It was the only time the old boy had ever come alive, pointing out the various species of trees and flowers, birds and creatures to me.

My dad was a lot older than all my friends' parents. He had actually fought in the Second World War and whatever he had seen there, he still couldn't bring himself to talk about it. The

Downs were his solace, I think, that perfect piece of England that had never changed and represented everything he held dear. The only story he ever told me about that time in his life was the day that he was demobbed and was so happy to be free that he'd walked all the way back from the outskirts of London, over twenty miles, through the night. As the dawn came up he had reached the ridge of the Downs that overlooked Guildford, and as he stopped to drink in the splendour of that dawning day, in a clearing he had seen a group of weasels, dancing round in a circle.

'It was the most incredible thing,' his voice was full of wonder and his eyes took on a faraway gleam when he recounted the tale. But I could never understand what had so fascinated him. It was as if he had seen Blake's angels nesting in a tree, not a bunch of frolicking rodents. But then, I had never been one for bucolic bliss; I had escaped to the city as fast as I possibly could. Now, watching the expression of pride on Allie's face as he turned his jeep down a rutted side road, all but hidden by the tall hedgerows from the B-road we'd just been travelling down, I got the sense he would have recognised the old man's feelings.

And it made me feel sad, wondering if I would ever know what it was like to be a father.

'This was all my wife's idea really,' Allie was saying, as we bumped our way towards a white house with a red roof, surrounded by fields. 'See, her parents had a place like this, it's kind of how she grew up, she was always a country girl at heart. When she gave up the fashion business she wanted to start something else that was creative in a different way. We couldnae manage a lot of land, so we specialised in organic fruit, veg and poultry. I reckon only Helen and Prince Charles had the same idea back then. And it was bloody hard work, the first ten years, right enough. But it's all paid off now…'

We rumbled past the house to the end of a drive, where an old barn had been converted into a garage. Beyond was an orchard full of fruit trees, where little brown and black hens wandered around, pecking at the grass.

I don't think I would have made the same trade as Allie had. But he was certainly the healthiest looking ex-punk I had ever met.

'It's great,' I enthused. 'So do you work the land as well as your teaching job?'

'I dunnae have to now.' Allie led me towards the back door of his house. 'We're making enough money for Helen to hire a manager and she and the kids do the rest. I did miss my music...' He stopped for a moment, looked down at the ground and then back up, towards the horizon. 'So it was quite nice to get into teaching it. You know. Pass on a few old tricks to a new generation.'

We had reached the back door by now and after the brightness of the sun, it seemed impossibly dark and gloomy in there.

'Helen?' called Allie.

I heard a distant voice calling back, and after a couple of minutes, a woman appeared. She was almost as tall as he was, and strong-looking too, with long ginger hair tied back in a ponytail, an unmade-up face with wire rim specs perched on a little nose, and kind hazel eyes, flecked with green.

'Hello there,' she extended an arm that had round, hard, bicep muscles and gripped me in a handshake as firm as a man's.

'Go on out and have some lunch,' she said. 'It's all ready. I'll be with you in a minute.'

They'd made a patio area in the sun-trap outside the back of the house, surrounded by trellises twined around with grapes, passion fruit and honeysuckle that filled the air with a heady aroma. There were sturdy wooden chairs around a table and a canopy for shade, a tinkling fountain rising out of a little round pond. It almost felt like we were in the Mediterranean.

Such a bright, homely place for such a dark story to unfurl.

Once we had got settled with Helen's mounds of bread, cheese, chutneys, hams, scones and cupcakes, she came from the kitchen to join us. The small talk began to falter after we'd eaten as much as we could and it didn't seem like she was going to drift off and leave us to talk about old times. In fact, as soon as I broached the subject, Helen took hold of Allie's hand and they exchanged meaningful glances.

'Before we start,' he said uncomfortably. 'I have to level with you, Eddie. When Ray called us up, I wasnae really sure about digging up the past. We've had our fifteen minutes and there's no way either of us wants to go back to that life…'

'But I persuaded him to,' Helen cut in. 'Because of Sylvana.'

She fixed me with a steely gaze, although her voice remained amiable.

'Ray said that it was Gavin Granger who got you interested in this, so I suppose you have been talking to all his friends about her?'

I nodded.

'In which case, I bet nobody's had a good word to say, have they?'

'Er, not many of them, no.'

Helen grimaced and shook her head. 'They're all such bloody lying bastards.'

The venom with which she spat those words out was quite alarming.

'Sylvana never did anything to anyone, it was everyone who did everything to her. Do you know, I thought about her when Princess Diana went into that wall in Paris. I thought, are you happy now, you bastards? Got what you wanted now she's dead? It's the same misogyny that's at the core of the music business. If you're beautiful and perceived to have come from a privileged background, men want to destroy you. That's all they could say about Sylvie, that she was a spoilt Jewish princess. Never mind her talent, never mind the fact her parents actually treated her like shit, never mind that she was as fragile as glass. No, the fact she was so naturally gifted just made them want to stick the boot in still harder. Then it becomes Vince Smith was a genius and she ruined him.'

I expected to see smoke coming out of her ears at any minute, or for a black cloud to suddenly sail over the sun and send a lightning bolt down to fry my sorry male arse. Helen was fucking scary.

'What bollocks!' she went on. 'Sylvana sold thousands of records, hundreds of people came to see her gigs. Blood Truth barely dented the bottom of the indie charts. If anyone ruined anyone else's career, it was him, not her.'

Allie put a hand on his wife's back, muttered: 'Are you sure about this, hen?'

'Yes, I bloody well am,' she snapped. 'Get the tape recorder out, Eddie. If this is going on the permanent record, I want you to know the truth. You don't have to say anything, Allie. But I do. She was my friend.'

Meekly, I complied.

'Right,' she said, as soon as I had switched it on. 'This is what you need to know…'

It ended up being Allie who went back and forth from the kitchen, taking in the plates, bringing fresh drinks and disappearing to answer the phone when it rang. Helen had a lot to let out. Long shadows were cast across the lawn and the sun was turning everything that mellow gold of early evening by the time she was finished.

Thankfully, she hadn't poisoned any of those scones. I slowly realised that the vitriol of her initial outburst wasn't actually meant personally. Although good luck to Gavin, Tony or Steve if they ever crossed her path again.

According to Helen, Sylvana had been the innocent victim of a series of abusers. The picture she painted was so vastly different from everything else I'd been told that I couldn't work out why people had hated her so much. Especially Tony Stevens. He'd made out she was nothing but a gold-digging groupie, when it seemed obvious she was nothing of the sort.

'It was almost as if she had the words "kick here" painted on her forehead in some kind of invisible ink that only predators could read. Robin was the worst,' Helen said, 'which is why Allie hates to talk about it. They were childhood friends and Allie had always protected him – like all bullies, he was bullied himself first, of course. I understand that Robin had a terrible childhood. His father was a wife-beater and probably worse and the boys left Scotland thanks to him. Robin's father had put him in hospital. He broke his jaw. But the terrible thing was, it was to do with him stalking a girl and his behaviour towards women got worse, not better. I suppose, what he saw his dad do, he ended up doing. Only much more sneakily, nastily. I've read a lot about domestic violence since then and he followed all the classic patterns. But he never let anything show. She never had black eyes or anything.'

I got the cold chills then, thinking of what he might have done to Louise. I thought about telling Helen about my meeting with the bastard, but I didn't want to stop her flow.

'And the thing that still gives me sleepless nights,' she went on, 'was that he was doing it to her for years, for nearly the whole time they were together. But she never told me…' Her voice faltered and she stared for a moment into the distance, the corner of her mouth wobbling. 'She never told me until right near the end, the last tour they ever went on. And I tried, I really tried to get her out of it as soon as I knew. But it all went horribly wrong…'

Helen took off her glasses and picked up a napkin to dab her eyes. 'Sorry,' she said. 'It doesn't matter how many times I go through this in my head, I still feel that I failed her.'

As if by telepathy, Allie came back outside then, sat back down beside her with his big, muscled arm around her shoulder. 'Where are you up to?' he asked.

'New Year's Eve,' she replied.

'Yeah,' said Allie sadly. 'All the skeletons came tumbling outae the cupboard that night, eh?' He looked at me. 'I didnae know it then, but Helen and Sylvana had cooked up this plan to get her out of the country on New Year's Day, 1981. But we got invited to this big posh party at Tony Stevens's house on New Year's Eve and everything that could have gone wrong did go wrong.'

I felt an excited prickling, like hairs standing up on the back of my neck. I just knew Allie was about to make some vital connections, and despite his obvious discomfort and Helen's distress, I couldn't wait to hear it.

I remembered what Tony Stevens had told me back in January: 'Other people will probably tell you, continue to proliferate that tall story about them falling in love with each other over the sausage rolls at my Christmas party...'

Yeah, right, I thought. Let's have it.

'We'd not really met Stevens before,' Allie continued. 'But Donna, our manager, knew him really well and she'd brought him to our gig at the Rainbow a few nights before, with a couple of guys from Blood Truth, Lynton and Steve. It was the biggest gig we'd ever done and it had sold out an' all. I was on top of the world that night. See, I don't know if Helen told you, but that was the place that we met.'

Helen smiled lovingly at him as she put her glasses back on.

'Anyhow, we's all in high spirits, getting stuck into the rider and that, and at the end of the after-show party, he just invited us all. We thought, great, we'd nae proper plans of our own. So we all rolled up at his great big house in Little Venice, couldnae believe our eyes. The fuckin' guy was loaded all right, it was like a house of dreams with his own private recordin' studio in the basement. So naturally, us men end up down there, with some German electrobop guys, Ludwig and Leo, I think they were called, messing about with all these top of the range synths and sequencers. After a couplae hours of this, I thought, shite, where's my wife, she might be fed up of us ignoring her. So I went looking for her…'

Helen gave a mirthless laugh. 'Meanwhile, I was on Sylvie patrol. Our plan was to get Robin as drunk as possible so we could get to the airport in the morning while he slept it all off. She was so scared of him that I'd had to go to her flat while they were on tour, get her passport and everything and buy her a suitcase full of clothes and stuff to take away with her. She was terrified that if Robin saw a single thing out of place when they got back, he'd realise what she was doing. She was terrified that night too. I think as the hours went by, she was getting more and more afraid, either of actually going through with it, or getting caught out in the process. So I was watching her like a hawk, trying to make sure she didn't get pissed. Not that she was much of a boozer, but when she was unhappy, she tended to drink herself into a stupor, and I really think she was in that frame of mind that night. Silly girl was scared of hurting Robin's feelings, scared of hurting my feelings, scared of doing anything to get herself out of the situation.'

'So, unware of any of this, I come up and drag Helen off to the basement to show her all this amazin' stuff we'd been doing with these Germans,' said Allie.

'And I spent half an hour trying to get back upstairs again,' Helen said. 'I mean, I had left her talking to that Lynton guy from Blood Truth, we both liked him, so I thought she was safe enough. You know, so long as Robin didn't see them together. But I just had this awful feeling that if I left her, I would never see her again. And then, when I finally got back to the kitchen, there was Lynton standing there with two drinks in his hands and she'd disappeared. I started to panic then and he was trying to calm me down, saying she'd probably just gone to the loo or something else entirely logical but I just knew she'd gone, I just knew it. And then they started counting down to midnight, you know, the whole rest of the house partying away.' She shuddered. 'Then the next thing I knew, bloody Donna came running round the corner screaming blue murder at me and trying to beat me up. Only she missed and sent poor old Lynton flying across the room.'

'Blimey.' I tried to picture the scene. Obviously Ray hadn't been exaggerating about his ex. 'What was wrong with her?'

Allie and Helen exchanged glances.

'Well, what we didn't know was Donna had been having this secret affair with Vince Smith for months. And she saw Sylvie leaving the party with him about five minutes before I'd got back to the kitchen. Whatever it was that had been going on between them, the sight of him and Sylvie together sent her totally round the bend. Of course, Sylvie would have been completely oblivious and I don't even know if she ever found out about it, I'm sure he didn't tell her. No one knew until then. But Donna had always hated Sylvie anyway. The very first moment we met her she tipped a pint of beer over Sylvie's head to try and start a fight, but I stepped in and she didn't have the guts to take me on.'

I wasn't surprised about that. Helen looked like she could punch out an ox.

'Then, as soon as she found out that Sylvie was an heiress, she was bloody all over her, pretending to be her best friend. I tried to get rid of her for nearly two years, I knew she was bad news; all she ever wanted to do was social climb her way to the top. But as soon as she started seeing Ray Spencer and found a way of using him to get a record company all set up, there was nothing I could do. We were stuck with her. But she'd always kept her distance with me; she knew I didn't trust her as far as I could throw her. Until that night.'

'Aye,' Allie nodded. 'But it gets worse. That whole scene kicked off in Stevens's kitchen. It took three guys to get her off Helen and poor old Lynton was knocked unconscious. So old Stevens runs in and finds this whole bloody scene ruining his la-di-da party and he hits the roof too.'

'My God.' Helen shook her head. 'He got her in an armlock and pulled her out of there, still kicking and screaming. I don't know if he locked her in a padded cell or threw her back in the street or what, but he got rid of her somehow. Of course, everyone who is anyone was there, looking at all this chaos, taking it down. Must have embarrassed the hell out of him. Meanwhile, someone called an ambulance for Lynton, and there were a lot of people in that house that probably assumed the police would be coming too, so half the people there just scarpered. It was almost funny the way they swarmed out of there. So much for Happy New Year.'

'Me and Robin missed all of this, of course, we was still dicking around in the basement with the Germans. First we knew was some guy appearing in the doorway saying the filth were on their way and if we had any gear we'd better get rid of it fast. So we go upstairs to find Helen putting an ice-pack on Lynton's head, Stevens all red in the face and fuming and Sylvana completely disappeared. Which, of course, sent Robin off the deep end.'

'We calmed him down enough to get him back to their flat,' said Helen, 'and of course, she wasn't there. I had her passport and everything back at my house, so I went home, hoping she'd turn up there, while those two spent the whole night driving round, trying to find her. It's a miracle you didn't get arrested for drunk driving.' She took Allie's fingers in her own.

'Aye.' He nodded. 'Or driving under the influence of a fucking maniac. I'd seen Robin's moods before, but Jesus Christ, I'd never seen anything like he was that night. I probably shouldae just handed him in at Broadmoor there and then.'

'Sylvie was right though, he did suspect something,' Helen said. 'Didn't he keep saying to you, "I knew it! I knew it!"?'

'Aye, he did. And then he started threatening Helen. Things between us two went downhill pretty quick after that.'

'But you must have seen her again, otherwise how did she get to Paris with Vince?' I asked.

'After a week, that poor Lynton turned up to my stall in Ken Market,' said Helen. 'He told me that Sylvie was with Vince in some hotel somewhere, that she was safe and happy and that they planned to elope to France. She didn't want anyone to know, because by then Donna had told Robin what she'd seen, and he was going round threatening death to them both. And, of course, if she was too scared to face her parents about Robin, she didn't want them to know that she was about to run off with another bloke; they would have put a stop to that right there and then. But she wanted me to know that she would always be thankful to me for trying to help her and for being her best friend...'

Helen choked again then and had to spend a few minutes wiping away more tears.

'So, eventually, after a lot of sneaking around, I met up with Lynton at a fabric shop in Berwick Street and handed him the suitcase and all her things. We knew Robin had gone mad and was following us all around in case we'd lead him to her, so it was the only thing I could think of. I always went to that shop for my fabric, and I always came back with bolts of stuff in a suitcase.'

'God, how horrible,' I said. I decided then not to tell them about Robin threatening me. They'd been through enough of his debased behaviour for them to have to worry that even now he might be spying on them with field glasses from a nearby tree.

Eerily, Allie appeared to be reading my mind.

'You better hope he doesnae find out about you writing this book, eh?' he said.

'Do you know where he is now?' I asked, a tad hastily.

'No, thank Christ. Like I said, we cut our losses with London and moved out here as soon as we possibly could. We didn't realise, but Helen was four weeks pregnant with Luke at the time we went to that party. If old Lynton hadn't got in the way of Donna, things couldae ended up immeasurably worse. We didnae tell anyone in the music business what we were doing, no one knew but our families but we couldnae have our first child growing up with all that madness around us.'

'God, so it was all over, just like that?' I said, remembering Louise and her suitcase.

'More or less.' Helen had recovered her composure. 'I never did see poor Sylvie again. The last I heard from her was the week before she died. She called me from Paris totally distraught because her grandma had died. I think that was why she did what she did. I think that just pushed her over the edge. 'Cos from everything we saw and heard about Vince Smith after she died, I think her knight in shining armour was a very dark prince indeed. She just went out of the frying pan into the fire. I suppose the grimmest irony was that Donna had spent all those years chasing after Sylvie's cash, and lover boy just waltzed off with the lot. Not that it ended up doing him any good. I like to think he came to a very unpleasant end. I like to think of him in a cold, dark, unmarked grave…'

'And that,' Allie, 'is where the story ends.'

I took the hint and switched the tape recorder off. 'Well,' I said. 'Thank you very much for talking to me, both of you. It can't have been easy and I really appreciate it.'

'Nae bother.' Allie got to his feet. 'Shall I run you back to the station now?'

'Thank you, that would be great.'

Helen stood up and offered me another of her bone-crushing handshakes. 'Just remember,' she said, 'to tell it like it was. Tell the truth about her for once. That's the least she deserves.'

Conversation was muted as we drove back over that tranquil, leafy landscape, gilded by the slowly sinking sun. Now I really understood why they loved it so much here. It was a sanctuary, a place to bury the past and bring up a better, cleaner future.

'So,' Allie finally said, as we approached the outskirts of St Albans. 'Are you going to talk to Donna then?'

'I don't know,' I said honestly, not relishing tangling with a female equivalent of Robin. 'Part of me thinks I should. I mean, today has been great, I'm really thankful to you and Helen 'cos I wouldn't have got to the truth any other way. So I kind of feel that for the sake of the book I should meet her. On the other hand, Ray said that if I did, I might end up not being able to get rid of her.'

'Well,' Allie frowned. 'If you want my advice, I'd stay the hell away. Her and Robin are the last two people you want knowing where you live.'

'Was she really that bad? If she looked after your band for all those years…'

'Whatever madness got uncorked that night,' Allie said solemnly, 'it never got put back into the bottle. Donna was all right up until that point. Helen never liked her, true enough, but I never saw the harm in her, she always did the most for our career that she possibly could. But after that night, forget about it – she showed her claws, she was as mad as Robin. And her whole world crumbled without Mood Violet. She lost her main band and without that, the rest of her business went up the Swanee pretty quickly. She ended up with nothing after being the virtual Queen Bee of that scene for so long. If you were to meet her now, I'd say you'd meet the most viciously bitter woman alive.'

By now we had reached the train station car park. 'Well,' said Allie. 'Whatever you decide, good luck to you, man. You'll no doubt need it.'

He raised a comical eyebrow, but I think he was deadly serious.

'Thank you,' I said, unlocking my seatbelt. 'And tell Helen, I won't let her down.'

'Aye. Well. Safe home, Eddie.'

It was still a beautiful, warm evening, but I felt a little shiver as the genial Scotsman drove away. I felt that my supposedly inspirational story of a band who never got their due was starting to get hijacked by dark forces of insanity and obsession. All was not as it had seemed in the shiny new world of post-punk. Should I delve into it, head first, do a real exposé on what the music business did to people? Or should I just stick with what I had, take the safe route away from any other ghouls I might dig up from their long sleep?

'Youz goes proddin' around amongst the deed like this an' don' be surprised a what springs up outta the coffin,' mad Robin Leith had warned me. Could this Donna be even worse than him? And what was I – a man or a mouse?

'Safe home, Eddie.'

Safe home…

24

The Flowers of Romance

January 1981

'I am lost,' she told him. 'I shouldn't be here and I don't know how to get out of it now.'

The words just fell out of her mouth and for a moment she was shocked she had uttered them to a complete stranger. Although there was something familiar about this man. She had the strangest feeling she had met him before and that it was perfectly logical she should talk to him this way. Either that or she had made him up in a dream. Whatever it was, she felt that she already knew him.

'Well, that's no good then, is it?' he said. He had a deep voice, with some of the Northern inflection she had caught in Lynton's. As he spoke, she put two and two together. She had seen him before, or at least his picture. On the pages of *Sounds*, *NME* and *Melody Maker*.

'Are you the singer in Blood Truth?' she asked.

'Vincent Smith, at your service.' He stuck out a hand and she took it. It was cool and strong. 'And I know who you are. You're Sylvana.'

His eyes were an incredible colour. Fringed with long, dark lashes, they seemed to dip from deep blue to violet as he turned his head in the light. Her favourite colours; the colours of twilight; the colours she had named her band for. The hideous spectral din emanating from the jukebox seemed to dim in his presence.

'Oh.' Sylvana had no idea he might have been reading the same papers as she did or would even be interested if he had. 'Yeah, that's right.'

'So were you not invited then?' he said. 'Did you sneak your way in to take a look at the pop stars?'

The way he said it, she couldn't help but laugh. Nothing could have been further from the truth.

'That's right,' she said, playing along. 'And I was so disappointed in them, that now I want to leave. Although I did like the bass player from your band. He's somewhere over there, if you want to find him.'

Sylvana reluctantly dragged her eyes away and cast them around the room. Lynton seemed to have been absorbed into the throng of bodies around the tables of food and drink; she couldn't see him at all, although her new companion was that much taller he probably had a better view.

'That's all right,' Vince followed her gaze, caught sight of Lynton ensnared in conversation with Paul King, and smiled. He'd heard enough of their publisher's travellers tales to know the bassist wouldn't be back here in a hurry. 'I see enough of him as it is. I'd rather find out why you don't want to be here.'

Those words brought her back to earth with a bump. Robin, after all, was in this house somewhere, only metres away from where they stood. Helen would probably be back any minute as well, to keep her under house arrest until she could ship her back to bloody Glo who would probably ground her in New Jersey for the rest of her life. No, that was so unfair to Helen, she was trying her best to help, but what use would going back home really be? Whichever way it went, she would be trapped somewhere against her will.

Sylvana felt a wave of panic rising within her. What was she doing, talking to this guy as if there was a chance of her being able to date him, or leave with him, or do anything normal whatsoever with him? What was she doing entertaining such thoughts when she was about to be forced into the most monumental decision of her life?

'Oh God.' She tried to say something more, but the tears welled up in her eyes, tears of exasperation, fear and rage, tears of the perennially put-upon who had buried her real feelings too deep too long.

'Hey,' Vince put a gentle finger on her cheek and caught the hot drop in the end of it. 'I thought you were supposed to be some kind of ice maiden. But you're not, are you? Are things really that bad?'

His eyes were so concerned, his voice so soft, she wanted to break down right there and then. She nodded, not daring to say anything more.

'Well, I know what you mean.' His eyes did one more scan around the room. 'I can't see anything but a load of arseholes and hangers-on in this room, stuffing themselves with Anthony's free booze like pigs round a trough. No doubt the rest of the house is the same.'

He paused. 'Do you want to go somewhere else?'

Sylvana looked up at him sharply. There was no trace of mockery in his eyes; rather, he was inclining his head towards the door, one eyebrow raised in suggestion.

He couldn't have said more magical words.

She could do it, couldn't she? She could just walk out of here right here and now while Robin and Helen were looking the other way, go someplace else, someplace they wouldn't know about. Then she wouldn't have to catch that plane tomorrow. She wouldn't have to go home with Robin and suffer another night of his insane rage. She could get away and work out what to do from a safe distance.

With the help of this beautiful stranger.

'Yeah,' she whispered and at last her heart felt free. Yeah, that's what she was gonna do.

'Right,' Vince enveloped her in his right arm. 'Come with me.'

The journey from the kitchen to the front door felt like the most perilous voyage she'd ever been on. There were so many people to wade through she was sure that at any moment she'd feel a hand on her collar and get hauled out of Vince's arms. But he held onto her tight and pushed his way through, ignoring a couple of people who called out his name. Sylvana's heart was hammering as he opened the front door. She had made it. She had actually made it.

It was as if he knew what was going on inside her mind. They stood on top of the front steps for a moment as Vince looked left and right up Blomfield Road, seeing if the coast was clear. Then he whispered in her ear: 'Let's scarper!' and they ran down the steps, out of the gate and up the road, not stopping until they had reached the end of it and stood panting on the bridge over the canal.

'I think we did it,' Vince said, looking back down the road to make sure no one had followed. Sylvana followed his gaze, then her eyes dropped to the scene below. Away from the pressure and the noise and the hellish forced conviviality of that house, the night was a different world. On each side of the canal were moored a line of barges, painted up like gypsy caravans, a whole separate community living under the noses of the big mansions that lined the street. Some of them were having their own New Year's celebrations and they had decked out their craft with fairy lights to add to their magical presence, so that they looked like little floating grottoes that cast dancing reflections across the surface of the water. People stood on deck drinking and the blur of their laughter and conversation spilled out into the night air, along with a decidedly different tune to what had been playing at Tony's – the shiny pop of ABBA's 'Super Trouper'. Something about the purity of those girls' voices gave Sylvana hope.

Vince smiled at her. 'Come on,' he said, grabbing hold of her hand. 'We're not safe yet.'

He led her across the bridge and down the other side, past a pub on the corner where more revellers were singing along boisterously to 'Start' by The Jam, and down a little side road that came out to a sudden roar of traffic by the side of the Westway.

They stood on the corner by the traffic lights, blinking in the sudden shift from pretty Little Venice to the heart of the concrete basin. Above their heads, the vast arch of the flyover blocked off the view to Paddington beyond. It was the point where West London was cut in half.

'It's pretty easy to get a cab from here,' said Vince. 'We can go anywhere you like. So where do you fancy?'

Sylvana's heart danced. She was leaving her old life behind; she had a right to celebrate that as much as all these other people were celebrating the start of 1981. Not only the right, but also the means. Although both of them had agreed that Helen should keep hold of her passport for safety, Sylvana had decided to keep her chequebook and bank card on her, and still had them, in the black velvet bag she carried, its bootlace straps wrapped around her wrist.

There was plenty of money in that bank account. It was time for a revolution.

'Do you think they still have a room at the Ritz?' she asked him.

His mouth dropped open. 'The Ritz?'

'Or Claridges. Or the Hilton. Anywhere with a bit of class, anywhere those music business scumbags don't hang out. Don't worry; I can pay for it. So long as you've got some money for a cab, I can take care of the rest.'

A broad grin spread across Vince's face.

'You really weren't joking about being disappointed with Anthony's party, were you?' he said.

'No,' she said. 'I've had enough of that whole scene. As from now,' she felt a rush of liberation as strong as the feelings of despair she'd had at the party, 'I quit my band. Mood Violet is over and I'm hereby emancipated. You want to celebrate that with me?'

Vince looked both astonished and delighted. 'Well,' he said, catching sight of a yellow light gliding towards them and sticking his arm out as he did so, 'like I said, I'm at your service.'

'Good,' Sylvana smiled as the cab pulled over. 'Then let's get lost.'

The cabbie decided their venue for them. The centre of London was closed off to traffic; they'd have to get out and walk through the celebrating hordes if they wanted to try their luck at Claridges or the Ritz. But he could get them to the Hilton on the other side of Hyde Park.

The cabbie had his radio on and somewhere between Paddington and Park Lane, they heard the countdown to midnight begin. Sylvana and Vince stared at each other, smiling like naughty children who'd given their parents the slip. Then, as the announcer yelled '*Happy Noooooo Year!*' like some Butlin's bingo caller and the banging of fireworks filled the air, suddenly they were kissing. The longest, tenderest kiss Sylvana had ever known. The diametric opposite to Robin with his urgent tongue-grinding and clumsy, needy caresses. Kissing Vince was like kissing an angel, tender and beautiful and erotic, like swimming in a turquoise sea in a pink and golden sunset.

When she opened her eyes he was staring back at her with what looked like awe.

'Park Lane Hilton,' said the cabbie.

Wherever this new confidence that bloomed within her had come from, it completely energised Sylvana. Things she would never have dreamed she could do before suddenly became the merest trifles – almost, she realised, as if she had somehow tapped into her mother's persuasive powers and knew how to get exactly what she wanted.

Like getting a room in the Hilton. The lies tripped off her tongue like honey as soon as the snooty concierge gave her a doubtful look and asked in a patronising tone: 'Isn't this an odd time to be checking in to a hotel room, madam?'

He probably did have a point. There was a party going on in full swing around them, lines of the aged well-to-do finally letting their hair down and doing the conga round the hallowed Hilton halls.

'My husband and I just got back from New York. Our flight was delayed and our luggage is following us on, so we've had more than enough hassle for one evening,' she told him, laying her accent on thick and deliberately emulating Glo's haughty demeanour. 'We were told that you had the most accommodating service in London. But if that's not the case, then we can certainly take our business elsewhere.'

She had put her chequebook down on the desk where he could check out the fact it was with Coutts, the bank whose cheques were instantly honoured, the bank the Royal Family did their business with.

'Safer than the Bank of England, my gel,' as her grandma had told her.

The clerk looked her up and down and started to blush. She guessed that a woman dressed as she was, in a velvet imitation Paul Poirot cape and a bouffant of bright red hair, should not have been the sort of woman he'd expected to have an account at the Queen's bank.

'Certainly we can accommodate you, madam,' he said. 'I was merely pointing out that this is an unusual hour and an unusual day. Now, let me see...' As he consulted his bookings, Sylvana cast a backwards glance at Vince, who was trying to hide behind a potted palm in the middle of the foyer until the reservation had been made. Neither of them had been sure if his thick-soled Robot creepers and black drape suit and pink shirt with bootlace tie were strictly what constituted the correct dress code.

Now he was surrounded by partying pensioners with party hats at skewed angles on their heads, blowing party trumpets in his face. One old dear even tried to goose him as she danced drunkenly past. He regarded them with an expression of total disbelief.

'Ah, here we are, madam.' The concierge was all politeness now. They had a room, on the 25th floor, so they could see out across the whole of London. Sylvana decided to take it for a week. Even if Vince wasn't staying, she needed to be somewhere safe; somewhere Robin would never think to look. Twenty-five storeys up over Park Lane ought to do the trick.

She tried not to laugh the whole way up the elevator with the stony-faced bellboy who obviously did not think them appropriately dressed. She delighted in palming him a quid from her purse with a sarcastic smile and watching him go red as he pocketed it.

Then finally, with the whole of Hyde Park spread out before them, illuminated by strings of fairy lights glimmering for as far as the eye could see, they were alone.

'Well,' said Vince. 'Now that we're here, what were we running from?'

'Everything,' Sylvana said. 'My whole life. It's all been one great big goddamn mess and now I've got to straighten it out. Thank you for getting me out of that place. You don't know how much you've done.'

'You're a mystery, aren't you?' Vince raised his fingers and softly ran them down the side of her face. He stared deep into her eyes as if trying to divine her thoughts. 'Here was I thinking you were some massively successful singer, happily married…'

She shuddered as he said those words and cut his sentence off.

'No, I'm not married, thank God. I was never quite as stupid as everyone thought. I was never a total pushover.' Her words sounded harsh to her ears and she stopped, wondering what he was thinking. 'I'm sorry,' she said quietly, 'you probably think I'm crazy, don't you? Running off from that party and bringing you here when I've only just met you.'

'No, I don't think you're crazy at all,' he shook his head. 'I've been in this business long enough. I've found out for myself what you think it's gonna be is not how it turns out. And as you could probably tell, I didn't particularly relish seeing in the New Year with all those creatures either.'

Confidence revived, Sylvana looked up at him with a smile.

'Well, let's order some champagne from room service and celebrate the fact that we didn't.'

They lay side by side on the huge double bed, suspended above the glittering city, drinking the ice-cold champagne and telling each other all about their lives. Occasionally their fingers entwined, or he wound a strand of her hair around his finger. But Vince was supremely delicate with her, as if he were afraid he might break her if he came on too strong.

She told him about her childhood in the gilded prison in New Jersey and was surprised to hear that his own background had similar echoes. For a start, they were both beneficiaries of the rag trade. Vince said he came from Wensleydale, a huntin,' shootin' and fishin' part of North Yorkshire and had grown up in a mansion built by his textile-magnate grandfather. A big, rambling stone house up on the moors that was never properly heated and always overflowing with dogs, children and a succession of exasperated nannies. It sounded a lot happier than the childhood she had known, but Vince said that the good times had come to an abrupt halt when he was sent off to public school at the age of nine.

'Bloody sadistic places they are,' he told her. 'You had to spend your whole time fending off advances on your arse. I'm not joking. And I was a little wimp when I first went there, a right little cry-baby who got beaten soundly every night before bedtime and blubbed for his mummy on his pillow. Luckily I had a growth spurt when I was thirteen and grew about a foot overnight. Once my weight had caught up with that, people gave me less of a hard time.'

School holidays compounded his isolation from his brothers and sisters. While they were off riding to hounds, he'd be up in his room, reading Beatnik literature and listening to the radio, getting more and more introverted and suspicious that he must have been a changeling baby. He'd been hooked on Elvis since he was a little boy and liked to imagine he would grow up to be a singer like The King – until he heard The Sex Pistols. That was when he'd decided to go to art college, to try and meet some people to form a band with. He'd always been good at art, as well as music and English so he got into his nearest college easily. His dad hit the roof. Like Glo and Ruben, Smith senior already had a career mapped out for Vince, and when his son rebelled, he disowned him.

'No son of mine behaves like a bloody puff.' Vince imitated his father's final speech to him. 'Mixing with limp-wristed, Marxist degenerates at a bloody art college when you've a good, solid future ahead of you. You go there and you'll never come back. You'll not be any son of mine any more.'

Like Sylvana, Vince hadn't been back home for a very long time.

He told her how he met Steve and Lynton at a Sex Pistols gig in Doncaster, how Steve had tried to hide him in the van on the way home but he had woken up and thought he was having a vision of Elvis which was really a pendant hanging over the rear-view mirror.

Sylvana laughed and said she had met her own band at a

Damned gig about a year later. Then she started telling him what had happened with Robin. 'I thought he was so amazing to begin with,' she sighed. 'You see…'

She paused, wondering whether it was wise to continue. But they had shared so much already, and after all, tonight had been all about throwing caution to the winds. 'I don't know if you can understand this,' she said. 'But when I hear certain words and all music, I can actually see colours.'

She stared hard at Vince.

'Wow,' he said, looking genuinely interested. 'What do you mean? A wash of colour over everything, or like coloured shapes dancing around in the air?'

'It depends what the sound is. If it's harsh, like the music in that house tonight was, it's like big blocks of colour in abstract shapes, really bright and quite brutal. But the music we made was more like swirls and patterns, like a whirlpool of the colours of sky at twilight. The most beautiful colours, I think. That was why the band was called Mood Violet. That was the colour I mainly saw when Robin and Allie first played me their tapes.'

Vince's own twilight eyes were round with amazement. 'Wow,' he said again. 'How amazing to see the world through your eyes. God, I wish I could do that.'

'It's not always amazing. Sometimes it's hideous. My mother thought I was crazy, that I was making it up to get attention, so she sent me to all these shrinks to try and straighten me out. I hate to say this, but Robin was the first person who seemed to understand what I was saying. He told me he could see colours too, and his music proved that to me. It was so easy to write lyrics and sing to it, it just seemed to flow out of me. But I was so wrong about him. Like everything else,' she dropped her eyes to study the bubbles in her champagne glass, 'that was just one of his lies. He delighted in telling me so, the last time he was angry.'

'Oh, little Sylvana,' Vince put his own glass down, took hers and put it on the bedside table. Then he wrapped her in his arms, dropped delicate kisses on her forehead, her eyelids, her face.

'Do you want to see what else he did to me?' she finally had the courage to say. 'Do you want to see how fucked up my life has become and why I need to get away from it?'

'Only if you want to show me,' whispered Vince.

She rolled out of his arms, sat on the side of the bed for a moment, gazing out at the sparkling, revelling city below. If Vincent Smith was all that he seemed to be, then he would have to pass this test.

She stood up and unbuttoned her dress, her back still to him. Stepped out of it and draped it across a chair. Then she turned to face him, still wearing her bra and knickers. With those still on, he could see it well enough, and if he was going to turn and run in disgust at the sight of it, she didn't want to be left here naked and alone.

She watched the horror bloom on his face as he took in the rings around the top of her breasts, a bouquet of burns made by cigarette ends. At the purple arcs carved above the line of her knickers, abstracts made with broken glass that curved down still further where he couldn't yet see.

'Oh, my God,' he finally said, sitting up and swinging his legs over the side of the bed, looking up at her face at last. 'My poor darling. He did that to you? That ugly bastard did that to you?'

Sylvana nodded.

'Come here to me,' Vince stood up and strode towards her, picked her up like a child in his arms and carried her back to the bed.

'No one's ever going to hurt you again, I promise.' He stared deep into her eyes. 'I'm not going to let them. Christ, no wonder you needed to get away.'

His fingers traced around the patterns of her scars, and as he dropped his eyes she saw a single teardrop on his thick black lashes.

'Does it still hurt?' he asked.

'Not physically. And the rest of it, I try to blank from my mind.'

'Jesus. If I ever see him again, he's a dead man.'

'I'm never going to see him again. I don't know how yet, but I'm getting as far away from him as possible,' Sylvana said. 'Whatever it takes.'

Sylvana suddenly felt completely wiped out. The fact that Vince hadn't rejected her, the fact that she felt safe in his arms, meant that her struggle was over. Now the events of the night were catching up in a sudden, soporific wave.

'Gosh,' she said. 'I'm sorry, I feel really sleepy all of a sudden.'

'I'm not surprised,' said Vince. 'When you go through something traumatic and come out the other side, that's the natural reaction. Your body shuts down to let you repair yourself. You go ahead and sleep; I'll be guarding you. No ginger Jock wanker's coming anywhere near you ever again.'

'Vincent Smith,' she said, her eyelids heavy, her vision swimming in a purple haze. 'You really are an angel.'

When she woke up, he was still staring at her, with an expression of such love and tenderness she wondered if she was still dreaming. The events of the previous night fast-forwarded through her mind.

'God, it's really true,' she said. 'I am here with you.'

Vince stroked her hair. 'Sylvana, I've been thinking. All night I've been thinking,' he said, and his voice was gruff with the lack of sleep. 'I've never met anyone like you before. You're pure genius.'

'No, I'm not,' she said quickly. 'I'm an idiot. I—'

'Shhhhh,' Vince put a finger up to her lips. 'Yes, you are, Sylvana. Now I've met you, I don't ever want to be apart from you.'

She didn't say any more. She just started to kiss him and he kissed her back and it was what it should be like; no timidity, no revulsion, no suppression, just love, deep love, like she'd never known before, like part of her had known all along this would happen and now she'd finally found him.

Hours later, exhausted and giddy, collapsed on their backs with their fingers entwined, Vince said. 'Can I finish my sentence now?'

She laughed. 'What sentence.'

'Well,' Vince rolled over onto his front, took hold of both of her hands and looked her straight in the eye. 'As I was saying, before you so rudely interrupted me with all these terrible physical demands, I was thinking all night long about what to do about this situation we find ourselves in. Deciding that having met you, my life would be wholly incomplete if I wasn't sharing the rest of it with you. Wondering whether you would do me the honour of being my wife?'

She laughed, for a moment still thinking he was mocking her.

'I'm serious,' he said. 'I've never been more serious about anything in my life. Marry me, Sylvana, and I'll take you away from this dreadful place and all the rest of the shit that's been following you around. I'd never joke about something like this.'

'But what…What about the rest of your life?'

'The rest of my life can sort itself out. I just want to be with you.'

'You're really not joking, are you?'

'Woman,' he said, thickly putting on his Yorkshire accent, 'will you marry us or what?'

She started laughing again, delighted. 'Yeah, all right then. Yes, yes I will.' And she carried on laughing.

25

Crush the Petals on the Floor

May 2002

I couldn't decide what to do about Donna. For the rest of the Bank Holiday weekend I tried to weigh up Allie's warning about her innate personality defects against what there possibly could be to gain from meeting her. All the time, the unwelcome spectre of Robin Leith kept popping back into my mind, rasping his dire warnings against waking the dead. It all went round and round in my head while I tried to keep myself gainfully employed transcribing the tapes and avoiding Mother's calls.

I was overdue for a visit and I normally caved in to pressure around Bank Holidays, but I still hadn't found the courage to tell her that me and Louise were kaput. I knew what would happen if I did. She would wonder how on earth I was going to manage to keep the flat on with my sporadic earnings. She would muse that I might be better off giving it up; start spinning the web to try and snare me in my own shortcomings and drag me back to Guildford. To assuage my sorrows with burned oven pizzas and gravy that you could cut with a knife.

I couldn't be doing with that. Of all the things I was afraid of, that was by far the worst. I wished I could have sloped off with Christophe for a few days of alcoholic rumination, but he had gone to some rock'n'roll weekender with his new bird, in bloody Great Yarmouth of all places, so he was no good to me. I pictured him wearing a Kiss Me Quick hat in force nine gales and pissing rain, wandering up and down a tatty seafront full of SAGA holidaymakers and one-eyed yokel children. That kind of made me feel better. But not for very long. I was starting to get cabin fever and I couldn't concentrate on work, couldn't settle in front of the TV, couldn't find any solace in any kind of music at all.

In the end, I thought, fuck it. It was seven o'clock, Sunday night and everyone else was lapping up the rays and enjoying the long weekend in the company of a significant other. I couldn't stay put in my stuffy mausoleum with dead singers and fucked up rock'n'roll casualties from another era for company. I may as well go out for a wander, drop into the few pubs worth going to, see if anyone I knew was about and up for a few beers. You know, try and at least act as if I had a life.

Just as I had decided this, the phone rang. 'Oh, piss off, Mother,' I said aloud, but something kept me lingering by the doorway while the answerphone clicked on. I suppose, in my most futile fantasies, I was hoping it might still be Louise, admitting she'd made a mistake and wanting to come home. Seeing Helen and Allie's cosy set-up had upset me more than I wanted to acknowledge.

But the voice that came out of the machine was a most unexpected one. 'Hello, Eddie, it's Kevin Holme here. I'm sorry it's been such a long time. I said a couple of days, didn't I? And that was a couple of months ago. Anyway, I—'

I ran back over to the phone and swooped it up. 'Kevin,' I said. For a moment there was just the squeal of the answerphone protesting as I clicked if off and I had a hideous feeling I had just gone and cut the connection.

But then I heard: 'Eddie?' His little voice sounded dubious.

'Kevin, hi,' I said, trying to sound as cheerful as possible. 'How are you?'

'Oh, I'm fine. I didn't know if you were still going to be there. I lost your number for a while and I only just found it. Would you believe, it was still in the pocket of the jacket I was wearing that day I met you. Like I say, I'm sorry it's taken so long, but things have been a bit hectic since I saw you, d'you know what I mean? I got asked to go on a tour of Japan and there was a few other things I had to see to that took me longer than I thought...'

He carried on in this slow, plodding manner for another few minutes, while I started to wonder if it would all come to any point soon.

'No need to apologise,' I tried to chivvy him along. 'Are you back for a while then, now?'

'Oh yes, you know, I still live here, like. It's just not often that I go away for so long these days. They're quite crazy, those Japs, you know. Don't seem to matter to them how long in the tooth or past your sell-by date you are. It's still all punk rock to them. Somethin' else, they are, really.' He gave a little chuckle and I tried not to start grinding my teeth.

'Are you still writing the book then?' he finally enquired.

'Yes, yes, I am. I've met Steve now, and Lynton. It's going pretty well...'

'Oh, that's nice. How were they? Doing all right for themselves, still, are they?'

'As far as I could see.'

'Oh, that's good. I don't see much of them any more, as you know, but I still like to hear that they're doing OK.'

I had a sudden fear that I was actually caught up in the middle of one of Alan Bennett's thought processes and I'd never come out again. Had Kevin only managed to find my phone number again when I was in the worst of all possible moods, just to taunt me with his fey Northern banalities? Was he doing this on purpose to punish me?

'So, anyway, I've been giving it some thought, this interview you wanted to do…'

'Oh, have you? Really?' Subconsciously I put my hand on my hip and started nodding.

'That's right,' he said and sighed. 'Do you remember, I told you about Rachel?'

I tried to. 'Vince's old girlfriend?' I dredged up from memory.

'That's right. Well, I've talked it over with her and I've decided that I will do another interview with you.'

'Well, that's very good of you. And her. Thanks, thanks a lot.' I really tried not to sound sarcastic but I think he caught a hint of it.

'All right then,' his voice gruffened a shade and speeded up. 'Have you got any spare time then, this week? Only I could meet you Thursday, if that would suit. Same place as last time?'

'Thursday…' I pretended I was consulting some diary or other. In reality, all my pages were blank for the foreseeable. 'Yeah, that would be fine, Kevin. What time shall we say?'

'Let's make it midday, shall we? Just come and ask the barman, like you did before. Oh and Eddie…'

'Yes?'

'Would you mind coming on your own again? Not with Gavin, like?'

This was becoming a popular refrain. 'Of course not, Kevin, I'll be there at noon, this Thursday, upstairs at the Red Lion, was it?'

'That's right,' he sounded doubtful again, even as he said it. 'I'll see you then. All right, Eddie. Ta ta.'

'See you then, Kevin, bye.' I put the phone down wondering how boring that was going to be. I was fairly sure that now I had Steve's interview, I had the best of Blood Truth. I didn't think Kevin was going to have much of worth to add to it.

As I looked up again, my eyes lighted on a couple across the road, strolling along, hand in hand. He had dark hair, oiled back into a quiff and a Hawaiian shirt. She had a sleek black bob with a fringe cut over her eyebrows.

They probably didn't look anything like us really, but it seemed to me I was watching a timeslip of me and Louise coming up here for the first time, nearly eleven years ago. When we were young and in love.

I stared at them until they had disappeared. The will to step outside in the sunshine and go looking for a drinking companion slowly drained out of my body. Instead, like an automaton, I went as far as the shop downstairs, bought a bottle of Jack and came back up to my festering pit alone. Drew the blinds, put *Scarface* on the DVD and let Al Pacino really articulate what was going on inside me.

By the time Thursday had rolled around, the bright weather had rolled away, replaced by the usual grey skies and dirty, recidivist rain. Or maybe that was just the climate in Stoke Newington perpetually. Even the one bus that went up there didn't seem to relish its task. You had to leave early if you needed to rely on the 73. It's not that old cliché that you wait half an hour then three will come at once; more like you wait an hour and seven all pull up in a clanking crocodile, snarling up the traffic the length of Essex Road so that you feel you have reached purgatory on the top of a Routemaster.

The Red Lion was its usual cheerful self too. The congregation was a bit thinner on the ground than on my last visit. Some old biker with a grey goatee steadily emptying his pockets into the fruit machine, a thickset, middle-aged bloke with a black mop top who looked like a lost Ramone leaning against the bar in tight black jeans and a sleeveless T-shirt that revealed far too much of a paunchy torso.

The hideous cacophony of Guns 'N' Roses 'Welcome to the Jungle' blared from the jukebox. The air was stale and deathly, the sweetish stench of unclean carpet mixed with the spent smoke of a thousand dog ends, eau de rock'n'roll funeral parlour.

Speaking of which, the goth barman was still there, trying to stay awake while listening to Stokey Ramone's war stories, which were delivered in the monotone of the permanently pissed and drug damaged. I was surprised to see his eyes light up when he saw me, but I suppose even I was preferable to Our Great Night at The Marquee with Chelsea in 1979.

'Hey, you was right, mate!' he hailed me enthusiastically.

Really, I thought, that would be the first time.

'About Blood Truth. I got Kivin to burn me off a CD of their stuff. Who woulda thought it, eh? It's fuckin' choice!'

This information didn't go down too well with Stokey Ramone.

'Blood Truth,' he creased his formidable brow, 'I remember them. Bunch of Northern arseholes.'

'Nah,' the barman shook his head. 'They were genius. Do you want a pint, mate?'

'Yeah, make it a Four X,' I said.

'Northern arseholes,' repeated Stokey, staring into his pint.

The barman waggled his pierced eyebrow at me to convey this was normal behaviour from the tosser and I rather enjoyed the fact that he now had something to wind him up about.

'Nah, it's on the house,' he said when I reached for my wallet. 'He's upstairs waiting. You know the way.'

Kevin was perched on the same barstool, with his mineral water and paper, exactly as I'd left him the time before.

'Oh, hello, Eddie,' he said as I came in.

'Hi, Kevin, good to see you. I hear you have a new fan.'

We shook hands and I sat down opposite him.

'Oh, you mean Richard downstairs?' Kevin smiled. 'That's right, I have. He'll be the first one in the queue to buy your book, he will.'

He waited until I had settled myself, my tape recorder and my pint down comfortably. Then his face became serious.

'Now, Eddie, you know what I said to you last time, about how I feel about Vince? Right, well, what I'm about to tell you will probably explain. It's not an easy thing to go through, d'you know what I mean? But as I've said, Rachel thought that you should know this, just in case you do manage to find him alive somewhere. Have you got any further with that, by the way?'

I shook my head.

'Good, well I hope you don't,' he said. 'No offence, mind. Not to you, any road.'

He picked up his glass of water and took a delicate sip.

'Are you recording?' he asked. 'Right. Well, you wanted to know why Vince put me in hospital, didn't you? It was because I knew his guilty secret. Steve and Lynton never did and they probably still don't to this day. They had their own problems at the time, like enough.'

He sighed. His eyes dropped to his paper beside him, and his left foot bounced unconsciously up and down. This was obviously pretty hard for him and I suddenly felt guilty for dismissing him as a boring inconsequential. Just like everyone else had always done.

'It were New Year's Eve, 1980, the last year we lived in that squat I was telling you about,' he said, his eyes still fixed on the newsprint. 'We was all invited to a party at Tony Stevens's house – big, posh gaff he had, up in Little Venice.'

For a minute I thought I was having a flashback all of my own. This was the same night Helen had been talking about.

'I was running a bit late from the others 'cos it's me mam's birthday, New Year's Eve, and I'd got to go out to make a phone call to her. It sounds daft now, I know, but we were that skint that I'd been going through all my drawers, coats and trousers and all the nooks and crannies in me room to try and find enough two pence pieces to last a couple of minutes. You probably can't imagine that, having grown up in a world of mobile phones. But in them days a phone were a luxury and we certainly didn't have one in that house.

'So, any road, because of all this, Steve and Lynton were ready to go long before I were. I was still upstairs in me underpants when they called us to go. So I just told them I'd catch them up; it worked out better for me that way, meant I could stop off at the phone box first on the way to the bus stop.

'So they went off and I was just getting myself dressed. I knew Vince was still in the house, he'd been playing his bloody Elvis all time at top volume, I were getting right sick of hearing it. Then suddenly,' he raised his eyes up to look at me again, 'it gets switched off and I hear him clattering down the stairs.

'Well, that's them off then, I'm thinking. But then I hear something else. Vince shouting. I couldn't make out what he were saying, he were too far away. But this shouting's followed by a load of crashing about. I got a bit frightened then. Wondered if someone had broken in or summat. So there I was, trying to get my jeans on and my boots all laced up when I hear the front door slam and someone running away up road.

'By now, I'm brickin' it. I'm sure it's burglars and that Vince has interrupted them and had some kind of fight. So I creep out onto landing as quietly as I can, trying not to stand on a creaky floorboard or owt, in case they're still down there. But it's all gone totally quiet. So now I'm thinking, what if them burglars have just got off up road and left Vince lying in a pool of blood? And I start walking downstairs, dreading what I'm gonna find down there.'

Kevin dropped his eyes again and shook his head. Took his glasses off and rubbed the lenses with the tails of his shirt. His left foot was still bouncing, as if he was tapping out some soundtrack to the horror that was unfurling in his memory. I daren't say a word in case he stopped.

'At bottom of stairs,' he said, putting his glasses back on, 'to your right, there's the kitchen. Well, the door's open and the light's on – but it opened outwards, d'you know what I mean, so I can't see in there. So I just stand there for a minute, trying my best not to shit meself. I can feel hairs standing up on the back of my neck, just like they say you do.

'Then I hear this like low, moaning sound and I'm thinking, oh Christ, they have, they've brained him. So then I goes running into kitchen. And there were someone lying in a heap on the floor all right. Only I can see right off it's not Vince.'

He raised his eyes and they were wells of pain. 'It were Rachel. Poor, bloody Rachel.'

'Shit,' I said. 'What happened?'

'It were awful, Eddie. Just fucking awful.' He shook his head, took his glasses off again and rubbed his eyes.

'What had happened was that Vince was basically tired of Rachel. He'd been ignoring her for months and she were slowly turning into this zombie that we saw but never heard. She were pumped full of drugs by then, of course, which we'd all been trying not to notice. But she must have really wanted to go to that party, she'd got all dressed up and she'd been ironing his shirt for him in kitchen for hours, waiting for him to come and take her to the ball. Only he didn't want to take her, did he? He wanted to sow his wild oats, like usual. So they'd had an argument in the kitchen. He'd lost his temper and…Well, I don't exactly know what he'd done. What it looked like were he'd just picked up the whole bloody ironing board and thrown it at her. With bloody iron still sitting on the end of it, still plugged into wall. Then he'd just run off and left her there.

'I think the board had probably hit her and knocked her out, you know, the metal edge on front of it or summat. Either that or she'd fallen when he'd thrown it and hit herself on sideboard. She'd fallen over any rate, and the ironing board was lying on floor beside her. But it were worse than that, Eddie. Much worse. Bloody iron had fallen on top of her. It had come off the side of her head. It were there, burning a hole in carpet. But it had already burned another hole. On the side of her face.'

'Jesus!' My mouth dropped open.

'Yeah. I rang the hospital as quick as I could, like. But she started coming round before the ambulance got there, she was just whimpering with pain, her whole body was shaking like a leaf, I've never seen anything like it. And I didn't really know what to do for the best, I honestly didn't. I thought she were gonna die. All I could do was hold her hand and tell her help were on its way. But I just felt helpless, really helpless. And it seemed like they were never gonna get to us. It seemed to go on for ever, until the ambulance men came and properly sedated her. And, God, Eddie, the smell of it will never leave me. The smell of burning flesh.'

'Shit,' I said, trying to picture the scene. 'What did you tell them when they got there? Didn't they want to call the police?'

Kevin's eyes dropped back down to the floor. 'I had to make up a lie, Eddie. I had to tell them I thought it were an accident.'

'Why?'

''Cos I were trying to protect her, of course,' he shouted. 'Sorry,' he stopped himself short. 'You don't get it, do you? I couldn't tell them anything else 'cos I knew she'd been tekking heroin. And I knew there'd be some in the house. And the last thing that I wanted was for her to wake up, with half her face burned off, to find she were under arrest. Funnily enough,' he shrugged, 'the doctor told me later that it were probably a mercy she were so off her face. It had numbed her, apparently. Stopped her feeling the pain so much when she came around. Some mercy, eh?'

'Oh God,' I said. 'I'm so sorry, Kevin. No wonder you didn't want to go into it.'

'No,' he agreed. 'But if you want to know the truth, that's what Vince was capable of.'

There was a pause while we both necked what was left of our drinks and I lit a cigarette.

'So what happened next?' I finally asked. 'How come the others didn't know anything about it?'

'Well,' said Kevin. 'I spent the whole night up the hospital with her, St Mary's in Paddington. Horrible place, that. When she finally came round and was allowed to speak to me, she begged me not to tell anyone.'

'What? Why?'

'I never did understand her reasoning. I think…I dunno. I think she were probably ashamed. Ashamed she'd let herself get into such a position. You know, Rachel came from a really good family. She were a really bright person. She were studying at St Martin's while we were in that squat. That's what her parents thought she were doing, mekking a career for herself in art world.'

He gave a harsh, humourless laugh.

'And they were about to come down and find out different. Imagine what they must have thought.'

This time, the *déjà vu* was deafening. This was almost exactly what Helen had said about Sylvana. There was a pattern here. Rich, awkward, artistic women coming to a horrible end when they met Vince Smith. This book I was writing was changing every time I did a new interview. It was on a horrible downer, a dream mutating into violence and ruined lives. Was there ever a music biz story that didn't end up this way?

'And anyway,' Kevin went on, 'when I finally get back to the house, there's a whole other world of drama going on. Some bloody Scotsman and a mad woman called Donna trying to kick bloody door in 'cos Vince has copped off and disappeared with some bird called Sylvana. On the same bloody night he did that to Rachel.'

'That's unbelievable,' I said.

'Not if you don't have a conscience.'

There was another, awkward silence.

'Do you want another drink?' I offered. I knew I bloody needed one.

'Yeah. Thanks, Eddie. I'll have another mineral water.'

'You sure you don't want anything stronger?'

He looked at me like I was stupid.

'Do you really wonder why I don't?'

This time it was me who had to look away. 'No, I'm sorry, Kevin. No, I don't.'

I went back downstairs, my head in a spin.

Stokey Ramone was asleep with his head on the bar. Kiwi Richard was polishing glasses, nodding his head along to 'Sweet Home Alabama.'

'Same again?' he asked brightly when he saw me.

'Yeah,' I said, trying to raise a smile.

He wouldn't let me pay for this round either, so I promised him a free copy of the book when it ever came out. His response was enthusiastic enough to wake the sleeping Brudder.

'Bastards,' he said, and slid off his stool, staggering bandy-legged towards the Gents.

This time, when I came through the door and looked at Kevin sitting all on his own, staring sadly at his paper, I didn't see him as the unregarded little drummer. Instead, I realised what he really was. The biggest man in Blood Truth.

'So,' I said tentatively. 'I take it Vince didn't realise the magnitude of what he did that night? Until you put him straight.'

'That's right,' Kevin nodded. 'Oh, I sat on it long enough, like. About two months I kept that information to myself, 'cos that were what she wanted, like. But in the end…Everything unravelled so fast after that night. Everything just went wrong. I suppose I didn't really tell you the truth last time, about that Sylvana. 'Cos I did hate her too. I hated her as much as Steve did, but for completely different reasons. I hated her 'cos that bastard just swanned off with her, after he did that to Rachel, just swanned off without a care in the world. I doubt he would have even come back if we didn't have that tour booked in the States. And that were nightmare enough, I tell you. For a start, he brought her with him. I had to sit there on that bus, night after night, while they were simpering over each other in the corner, thinking about that hole in Rachel's face. Sit there while Lynton turned into a junkie and Steve turned into an alcoholic. While we got bottled off by rednecks and had the KKK threaten to kill us in Alabama. But it was him I hated most. And I let that hatred grow inside me, until finally we were alone.

'So, yeah. After we staggered back from the States, we had to mek that album. Tony Stevens somehow managed to banish Sylvana off premises – well, for a week, anyway. And it were all going so well. Steve smashed his guitar to pieces and stormed off in a mood. Lynton just disappeared into the night, as he so often did in them days. And then it were just me and him.

'So that's when I told him what he'd done. I described what it looked like in graphic detail, how I'd felt when I was waiting for the ambulance. And how her parents had had to put her in a sanatorium to get her off the heroin habit he'd given her, hide her away in a place where no one they knew could see what had happened to her. How he had basically, totally ruined her life.

'And he listened to this all with this scornful expression on his face, like I were a raving madman mekking this all up. Then he said, "You know what your problem is, Kevin? You're too soft you are."'

'You're fucking joking.'

'I'm not, Eddie. That's when I lost it. God, it must have looked funny. Like a Yorkshire terrier trying to pick a fight with a Doberman or summat. And the rest, as they say, is history.'

'Jesus Christ.' I was at a loss as to what to say now.

'Not really the story you were looking for, is it?'

Well, that put it in a nutshell. 'No. No it isn't.' I took a long swig of my beer. 'So what is Rachel doing now?'

'Not a lot. She's still in and out of sanatorium all the time. She has her good days, when she goes back to her parents' house, walks out on moors, draws a little bit. Then it all gets too much for her and they have to tek her away again. It's not a life, not really. So you see now why I had to protect her. If you really want to do her a kindness, you'd not publish any of this. You'd just tek it on board and think about whether you really do want to find him again.'

Those words followed me out of Stoke Newington, through the grey miasma of the long road home. Followed me back up to the flat and hung in the air around me.

It was horrible, and it seemed to be getting worse.

The trouble was, the more horrible it became, the more I wanted to write it. The mystery was gaining a new momentum, and where I had been dispirited a few days ago, now I was seized by the conviction that what I was discovering was increasing in importance. I knew what I had to do next.

I had to go after Donna.

26

The Art of Falling Apart

January 1981

As Tony lifted the glass to his lips, Steve noticed that his hands were shaking. Eleven o'clock in the morning and he's got the DTs, he thought. Reminds me of my Da.

He'd never seen his boss look so rough before. Hollow cheeked, blurry-eyed, not just unshaven but with a plaster over his top lip where his unsteady hands had obviously done battle with a razor. Steve wondered if he'd asked him down to this pub because he daren't show his face at work looking such a fright.

Vince had been gone for a week now. And what a week that had been.

'So you've finally heard from him then?' Tony drained his whisky down in one, lit a cigarette with his fumbling fingers.

'Aye,' Steve winced. Of all people, he'd expected Tony to be the strong one. But the chaos that had erupted when the clock struck twelve on New Year's Eve seemed to have turned everyone he knew into a walking disaster.

As far as Steve could make out, it had all gone wrong at the point during the party when he'd had to leave Donna to go off for a slash. Up until then, he had been thoroughly enjoying himself, tucking into Tony's hospitality, pretty sure he'd be getting his oats before the evening was out.

He'd had a wander on his way back, looked around the place a bit. Old habits die hard, and Steve's fingers still gave a little prickle as he opened bedroom doors and cast his eyes over antique furniture and fine porcelain. Stevens's brass had gone a lot further than any other record company boss he'd known. Far beyond old Don, that was for sure. And to think he'd once considered Dawson the musical Don Corleone.

All this, he was sure, was not merely the result of a few successful records. This was how Steve imagined the landed gentry lived.

His perusal came to an abrupt end when he opened one door and found a mass of writhing bodies on the bed, some of whom, he gradually worked out, were the members of a suddenly famous punk-turned-pop band. They appeared to be enjoying both heterosexual and homosexual favours all at the same time, though it was quite hard to tell what was female from what was male. Steve had never seen so many naked bodies contorted into so many ludicrous positions all in one place, never heard such moaning and groaning.

'Can any one join in?' he finally asked, as no one seemed to be paying him any mind.

The eyes of the most famous member of the ensemble immediately snapped open. He looked a picture, he really did, framed between the young girl bucking away on the end of his cock and the pair of dangling, hairy bollocks suspended over his forehead.

'Who left the fucking door unlocked?' the pop star screeched and a few seconds of highly amusing squealing and scrabbling later, Steve found a Victorian chamber pot hurtling towards his head. He only just dodged it in time, hearing it smash to pieces on the closing door.

Downstairs, people had started to count down the New Year. Steve followed the source of the sound, realising he'd lost his drink somewhere on the way.

Donna was not where he'd left her, but neither was anyone else. They'd all congregated around the staircase and the hall, leaving unattended bottles and glasses all over. Steve took one look at the throng and decided to minesweep for a while rather than fight his way through. He found a half-full bottle of Bollinger and an empty glass and sauntered in the opposite direction, looking for the master bedroom. He wanted to see how Tony Baloney really lived.

Up on the top floor, another gaggle were clustered around the steps leading up to the roof, where the sound of shrieking laughter indicated yet more inhibitions being lost. Steve walked past, strolled the length of the landing and back, casually turning door handles as he did, ready to say he was looking for the khazi if anyone asked him. But the door to every room up here was locked.

Ah well, Steve thought, at least he's not stupid.

He stopped by the sash window on the landing to put down his drink and roll up a fag. That done, he pushed up the bottom of the window and leaned out onto the sill, staring over Tony's back garden. It was even more like *The Godfather* out there. White fairy lights had been strung up in the pine trees, illuminating a gravel patio full of Roman statues, all nudes and nymphs, arranged tastefully around clipped privet hedges. Oh aye, thought Steve, bet he comes out here for his orgies in the summer time and all.

No sooner had that image had flashed through his mind than a sight appeared below him that made the roll-up drop from between his lips.

The door was flung open, casting an orange light onto the scene. Tumbling out came Tony, wrestling a wildly flailing Donna.

He put her in a headlock while he slammed the door behind

them, then tried to drag her up the path away from the house while she pulled backwards, her heels thrashing on the gravel.

'Get off me, you fucking queer!' she shrieked, pummelling him with her fists.

Tony managed to drag her around the back of one of his topiaries, so that no one looking from the back door could see them. Then he grabbed hold of a huge handful of her hair, pulling her head back and forcing her down on her knees. 'You've really gone and done it now,' he said, his voice quiet but ominous with menace. 'All I done for you, girl, and this is how it ends up?'

Donna panted and writhed in his grasp, her eyes flashing with defiance even as her teeth gritted with pain.

'Fucking homo queer,' she yelped.

'Why, thank you, darling,' Tony's face twisted into a snarl, 'I'll see you live to regret that remark.' Then he started pulling her again, away under the branches of a tree, away from Steve's sight.

Steve started legging it downstairs, pushing his way through the throng. As he reached the main stairway, he could see people hurrying into their coats, hear snatches of conversation about a fight and the cops coming.

But all he could think about was Donna being dragged across that garden. Just the way his Da used to drag him off for a hiding. He skidded into the kitchen, ready to punch Tony Stevens through the nearest wall.

And saw Lynton trying to get up off the floor, a vaguely familiar woman with short, spiky hair helping him, pressing an ice pack to his forehead.

'What the fuck?'

'It was Donna,' said the woman. 'She just went mad. She came down here screaming her head off and punched him clean out.'

Steve's gob fell open.

'Ambulance on its way,' someone shouted behind him.

Lynton was shaking his hands, wobbling around on unsteady legs.

'I don't need no ambulance, man,' he groaned.

'Oh, fucking hell.' Steve just managed to catch him as he pitched forward out of the woman's arms. 'Lerrus get clear, can you?' he shouted at the gawping moon faces pressed around him. 'Lemme get him somewhere he can lie down.'

'I'll take his legs,' the woman said. She was the only person in the room who seemed capable of rational thought. Together they got him into one of the lounges, hoisted him onto a sofa, scattering pissed liggers like confetti as they went.

After that, the woman disappeared and ambulance men appeared in her place. They flashed a pen torch into Lynton's eyes, put a neck brace round him and lifted him onto a stretcher.

'It's probably only concussion,' one of them said to Steve. 'But let's get him out of here, eh?'

There was a lot of screaming going on in the hallway as Steve followed them out, a mêlée of bodies hustling for the exit. For a second he caught sight of the woman who had helped him, red-faced and animated in argument; then of Tony's face in the kitchen doorway, white as a ghost as his party dissolved around him.

The back of an ambulance seemed like a quiet place of sanity after that.

They took Lynton to hospital because he'd hit his head as he'd fallen on the floor and they needed to be sure he hadn't fractured his skull. It was dawn before they discharged him, with a huge headache and a lump on his jaw the size of a duck's egg. Steve called them a mini-cab from the numbers pinned up around the payphone in reception. He'd been drinking the vilest coffee he'd ever tasted from the vending machine for three hours by then. As they staggered into the freezing cold beginning of 1981, Steve felt like the most sober man alive.

Lynton crashed out as soon as they got home, but Steve couldn't rest. There was something wrong with the house too. No one was in it. There was a strange, nasty smell lingering on the air.

It suddenly occurred to him that he hadn't seen Vince at the party. Nor Rachel. Nor Kevin. And there was no sign of any of them here either. Every room was deserted. In the kitchen, there was a huge burn in the carpet, the source of the noxious odour.

He remembered Rachel moving the iron back and forth, back and forth, and a horrible feeling of impending doom settled in Steve's stomach. But the ironing board had been packed away, the iron itself standing cold on the sideboard.

He was sitting on the stairs, still trying to puzzle out what the fuck had gone on, when Kevin came through the front door at midday.

'What the fuck…?' Steve began.

Behind his wire-rimmed specs, Kevin was hollow-eyed with exhaustion.

'Don't ask,' he said, and went to walk past him up the stairs.

'Kevin?' Steve caught his arm.

Kevin shook his head. He looked like he'd been crying. 'I'll tell you later, Stevie. I can't think straight any more. I'm going to bed.'

Steve dropped his arm and put his head in his hands. He must have dozed off for a while, perched on the stairs like that, but then Steve always had the ability to set like concrete when he went to sleep. The next thing he knew was Kevin tapping him on the elbow with a mug of steaming tea, saying: 'Thought you might like this.'

'Ow!' Steve came back to consciousness with a nasty crick in his neck, wondering for a moment where on earth he actually was.

'What? Oh, er, thanks, Kevin.' The aroma of the brew woke his stomach before his brain was fully engaged. 'Fucking hell, I'm starving!'

'I were just about to put cooker on,' said Kevin. 'We've not got much in, mind. Will a fry-up do you?'

'Sounds fucking great.' Steve stood up and stretched, feeling his elbows and knees crack as he did so. He followed Kevin into the kitchen.

'What time is it?' he asked. It was dark again outside, but that was no indication at this time of the year.

'Four o'clock,' said Kevin, lighting the gas ring. 'I tried to have bit of kip, but I couldn't really settle. Thought maybe a full stomach might help. It must be nearly twenty-four hours since I last had owt.'

'So,' Steve attempted to connect events in his head, fuzzy though it was. 'What happened to you last night then, Kevin? Did you not manage to make it up to Party of the Year?'

Kevin carefully laid out four rashers of bacon in the middle of the pan, watched them start to sizzle.

'No,' he said. 'There was a bit of a to-do in here when you left.'

'What do you mean?'

'Well.' Now he was slicing the two remaining button mushrooms they had in the fridge as finely as he could manage. 'Vince and Rachel had a bit of a falling out. An argument, you might say, about going to that party. He went off on his own and left her here…'

'Oh,' Steve nodded, 'I gerrit. So you had to mop up the tears.'

'Something like that.'

'Bad luck, son. Where is she now, like?'

'Well,' Kevin carefully flipped the rashers over, scattered his mushrooms into the pan. 'That's just it. She's not here any more. She's left him.'

'Right,' Steve said and yawned. 'Well, I suppose that's no great surprise, is it? I wouldn't have put up with him half as long as she did. Suppose it's always at this time of year everything comes to a head. Gone home to her mam then, has she?'

'That's right,' nodded Kevin, carefully cracking an egg into a cereal bowl, tipping it in the pan, then doing a second one the same way.

'Oh.' Steve noted his technique. 'That's a good idea, Kevin. You don't break the yolks that way, do yer?'

'No,' said Kevin as he pulled open the door of the cupboard above his head, stood there for a moment with his back to Steve, examining what was in there. His voice sounded a little wobbly for a moment when he said: 'Oh, great, there's still some beans in here. Do you want some, Stevie?'

'Oh aye, and chuck us a bit of fried bread in there if there is any.' His stomach was rumbling by now at the smell of the bacon. 'Thanks, Kevin.'

'That's all right,' Kevin's voice was back to normal. He pushed the rashers and the mushrooms to one side, laid down two slices of bread in the middle of the pan to soak up the fat. 'So did you see Vince at this party then?'

'No,' remembered Steve with some surprise. 'No, I didn't. D'you know what, I don't think he even got there. Maybes he'd been invited somewhere else; somewhere he didn't want us to find out about. I was gonna say somewhere more posh, but believe me, Kevin, I don't think there is anywhere more posh than Tony Bloody Stevens's gaff. Apart from Buck House, mebbe. No, it has to be another woman, doesn't it? Christ. I don't know what they all see in him.'

'Me neither,' Kevin nodded, flipping the bread over and then taking a tin-opener to the beans. 'Nearly done now, Stevie. Do you want to put kettle on, mek us another brew to go with it?'

'Aye,' Steve pushed himself off the corner of the doorframe where he'd been leaning, walked over to the sink. Looked down as he was filling the kettle and noticed the burn in the carpet again.

'Aye,' he said, motioning at it with his head, 'were that part of argument an' all?'

Kevin nodded.

Steve whistled. 'All's I can say is, good job it weren't round Tony Baloney's. There would have been fucking hell to pay.' He plugged the full kettle back into the wall, turned it on at the switch.

Kevin took a couple of plates from the rack by the sink. 'I'll just put these under grill for a moment, heat them up,' he said.

'Your mam did train you well, didn't she?' Steve laughed.

'Aye,' Kevin shrugged concession. 'I suppose she did. Oooh heck, Stevie, I completely forgot – where's Lynton got to? I've not made him any.'

Steve raised his eyebrows. 'Now there is another story.'

'Oh yeah?' Kevin had taken everything out of the frying pan and arranged it on their plates. There was a loud gushing sizzle as he tipped the beans into the hot pan.

'Poor old Lynton got his head brayed in last night. By a lass.'

'You what?' Kevin spun round with a look of amazement on his face.

'Oh aye.' Steve poured boiling water into the teapot. 'Some lass went a bit mental and lamped him one. I don't actually know why. I had to end up tekkin' poor sod to hospital, we were in there most of night. Some party, eh?'

'Oh God,' said Kevin, turning pale. 'What hospital were that, Stevie?'

Steve put the teapot down on the table. 'Fucked if I know. I just called us a taxi when they let him out. I didn't really tek much in, tell you truth. And after all that, he just wanted to sleep it off. He's probably so full of sedative he'll be out for rest of day.'

'Right,' said Kevin in a tiny voice, turning the gas off under the beans and piling them onto the plates.

'By 'ell, look at that,' Stevie stared ravenously at the plate.

'Tomato sauce?' asked Kevin, going back to the cupboard.

'Fucking brilliant.'

For a moment, there was silence as they got stuck in, Kevin pouring the tea, Steve banging out as much ketchup as he could over the top of his steaming feast.

'Fucking hell,' Steve picked up his knife and fork with relish. 'How much am I looking forward to this?'

Kevin never got a chance to answer that. The next minute

there was an almighty crash as a brick came flying through the window, smashing its way into the sink and sending shards of glass across the room.

'What the—?' Steve leapt to his feet, outraged. A hammering started at the front door. Along with the freezing cold blast of air from the ruined window came the noise of angry shouting.

'Right, you, Smith! Ya sneaky English cunt! Your tea is oot!'

Kevin flew under the table, curled himself up into a little ball.

Steve made for the front door, flung it open and stared into the mad eyes of the rat-faced keyboard player from Mood Violet. For a second both of them regarded each other with some shock, the other not being who they had expected to see.

Then Robin started up again. 'Where is he? Where is your lover boy? You hidin' him in there or what?' He tried to look past Steve into the house. 'Hoy, Smith! I've come fer you. And wha's mine...'

'What the fuck are you talking about?' Steve spluttered. 'You've just put a bastard brick through my kitchen window!'

'Get oot ma way,' Robin tried to push past him, but Steve's frame filled the door.

'You're not listening to me!' Steve roared and grabbed hold of the lapels of the Scotsman's coat, pushed him away from the front door and up against the outside wall. It took all of his might to do it. Robin may have been a foot shorter and three stone lighter but he was possessed with the superhuman strength of the insane.

'What the fuck are you doing here?' Steve demanded, pushing his fists further into the bony shoulders, forcing Robin up against the brickwork, pinioning him there so he couldn't move his arms.

Robin's eyeball's bulged. 'Get off! Get off!' he screamed, writhing in Steve's grip like a sack of ferrets, twisting his head from left to right, trying to find the space to headbutt his opponent. Up close his pitted face and saucer eyes were the picture of dementia. He looked disgusting.

'Are you gonna tell me or what?' Steve bellowed.

'Vincent Smith!' Robin said and spat a huge wad of green right into Steve's face. 'He's got mah girrul!'

'Ugh, you cunt!' Steve brought his knee up sharply, as hard as he could, into Robin's groin. The shriek that emitted was enough to wake the dead, but at that end of Ladbroke Grove, no one cared to put their heads out of the window to see what was going on.

Steve let him drop, writhing to the ground, got in another kick to his kidneys.

'Whass happening, man?' Lynton was suddenly beside him on the doorstep, his forehead creased, holding onto the side of his face. Panting, Steve opened his mouth to answer.

'Oh no,' Lynton said first. 'Not that fucking bitch from Hell...'

Steve wheeled round. Rocking and swaying on the pavement across the road, her arms drawn tightly around her chest, was Donna. Or perhaps more accurately, the remains of Donna.

She appeared to be wearing nothing but a satin nightdress with a mohair jumper over the top, hardly enough to keep out the bitter cold. Her legs were bare and scratched to fuck and she wobbled on the concrete in a pair of stilettos. But the most shocking thing about her was her hair. The beautiful black mane she'd been so proud of now looked like the wings of a half-plucked cockerel. Huge clumps of it had been pulled out from the side and the crown of her head.

She looked at them staring at her and started to laugh – a high-pitched, hysterical noise, hideous to behold.

'Oh, Jesus Christ and Mother of God.' Steve's mind spun back to what he had seen going on in Tony Stevens's garden.

'Get back inside,' he told Lynton. 'Keep the door fucking locked until I come back in.'

Lynton backed off slowly, his eyes round with horror. He slammed the door shut.

Robin was still rolling on the ground making gurgling noises. Steve kicked him one more time for luck then ran across the road.

Donna stopped laughing as he approached. She cocked her head to one side and looked at him as if she was trying to place him.

'What the fuck's happening, Donna?' Steve said, not knowing whether to reach out for her or not. She looked totally destroyed but he had already seen what she'd done to Lynton. 'What are you doing here?'

'We've come for Vince,' she said, in the voice of a child. 'Vince and Sylvana. They are here, aren't they?'

'What are you talking about? What's that mad cunt doing throwing bricks through my window?'

Donna put her hand over her mouth and snorted. 'Oooh. That was a bit naughty, wasn't it? But Vince deserved it, you see. He's done a very bad thing to both of us.'

She smiled a smile that was as deranged as the face of the Scotsman, her eyes unfocussed, pupils like black holes. Dried, congealed blood stuck to the tufts of hair on the side of her head. Only one night ago, Steve had been trying to get her into bed. Now it looked like she was more fit for Bedlam. What the bloody hell had Stevens done to her?

Instinctively, he reached to touch her. 'Get off!' she shot away from his grasp. She wobbled around for another few seconds, then kicked off her shoes and started running back down Ladbroke Grove. 'I don't know you!' she shrieked as she ran. 'Get away from me!'

'Donna!' Steve's mind was now totally in turmoil. 'Come back! I'm not gonna hurt you! Let me help you, please...' He started to run after her, but he was so done in from the exertions of subduing Robin on top of the night before that he only managed a couple of yards before he fell back, exhausted.

He couldn't bring her inside, what was he thinking of? Lynton would do his pieces.

He put his hands on his knees and tried to get his breath

back, tried to clear his head. Glanced back over the road. Robin had managed to get to his feet and was shuffling away in the other direction, listing like a drunkard, catching hold of lampposts to steady his journey. Still Steve had no idea what was going on. Perhaps he was having a nightmare. Perhaps he'd wake up soon.

A police siren cut through such fanciful thoughts. The blue light flashed past him, the headlights momentarily illuminating Donna, who was still running, running over the railway bridge, running like she was fleeing the hounds of Hell. Fuck knows where she was going to. But a run-in with the boys in blue was the last thing Steve needed now. He turned and went back to the house.

'Well?' Tony demanded. 'Where is he?'

The desperation in the other man's eyes made Steve feel sick to his stomach. No, Stevens was far from being a strong man. He was a weak, bullying ponce. Steve had seen the truth of him all right. So he decided to string his answer out.

'One of his druggie mates dropped by the house. I was out at time so I couldn't tell you who, but he gave Lynton a number to call. Lucky Lynton was in, really. Kevin's been hiding under the bed since the mad Jock smashed our window; he won't open the door to no one. And I think he's got a point, don't you? I don't really think it's safe for us to stay in that house much longer. 'Cos it comes to something when you can't call police to come and take away the lunatic that's threatening to kill you on your own doorstep 'cos if you do, you're gonna get evicted. And I've boarded up that window for now, but it sort of draws attention to us, don't you think? That and the non-stop circus outside.'

Tony nodded hastily as Steve spoke, crushing his cigarette out in the ashtray and immediately lighting another.

'Yeah, yeah,' he said impatiently. 'I'll sort out somewhere else for you soon as I can. By the end of next week, I promise.'

'I'm sure you have your contacts,' Steve said.

'Yeah.' Tony's voice turned slightly menacing. 'As you have yours, Stephen. Now tell me what's happened to Vince.'

The two men eyeballed each other for a tense moment, cigarette smoke hanging on the air between them.

'I don't like being called Stephen,' said Steve. 'It reminds me of my Da. Come to think of it, so do you.'

A muscle jerked underneath Tony's left eyeball. Rage blazed in his eyes. But he managed to keep his voice level when he eventually spoke. 'I apologise, Steve.' He extinguished his current cigarette more slowly and deliberately than the last one. 'Now please, just tell me. Where is Vince?'

'Paris,' said Steve, leaning back in his seat to regard the effect this bombshell would have. 'The Flying Scotsman was right. He has run off with that lass from Mood Violet. He needed someone to go and get her passport for her…so they could elope.'

Tony's eyes closed and he leaned forwards, putting his head in his hands. It seemed to Steve that he shrunk before his eyes, his shoulders sagging and his chest caving in.

'You fucking queer.' Donna's words echoed through Steve's brain. Now it was all starting to fall into place.

When Tony finally looked up, his eyes were sad and old.

'Here's the number.' Steve laid the crumpled piece of paper he'd been carrying in the pocket of his jacket down on the table between them. 'It's the Hilton. You might be able to catch him before he goes. You never know; he might invite you to the wedding. Make you his best man or summat.'

'Thanks,' said Tony dully, pocketing it without looking at it.

'Right,' said Steve, getting to his feet. 'I'll leave you to sort out our accommodation problem then, shall I? In the meantime, none of us fancy hanging round here any more, so we'll be back in Hull. You might want to send someone to fetch Vince's stuff for him, if he still wants any of it. But you don't have to worry about Rachel, if you even were. She's moved out already.'

Tony looked up at Steve and nodded. It was hard to tell whether he'd even heard what had just been said.

'Ta ra then,' Steve headed for the door. When he left, Tony was still sitting there, staring into space.

27

Watching The Detectives

May 2002

'Hello, Eddie.' Tony Stevens's voice purred down the line. 'I've got a bit of news for you. I've finally found our Monsieur Pascal. He's alive and well and living in Deauville.'

This was a surprise. I pressed the button on the remote control, turning down the sound that had been blaring out from the stereo. Since I'd got up that morning, I'd been back in 1981, listening to *Butcher's Brew* with fresh ears after Kevin's revelations. I was intent on deciphering the lyrics, now that I understood they weren't as abstract as they seemed.

'Wow,' I said, impressed.

'I had a chat with him just now and he still seems very *compos mentis*,' Stevens continued. 'He remembers all about the case, I hardly had to jog his memory at all. And he kindly said I could pass his number on to you, and that he'd be happy for you to talk to him. He might have retired ten years ago, but there's plenty of life in the old dog yet.'

'That's fantastic,' I could hardly believe my luck. 'Thanks, Tony.'

'Not a problem.' He sounded fairly pleased with himself too. 'Let me know how it turns out. Even if he can't add anything more to what I've already sent you, at least it gives you a bit of colour.'

'Damn right it does,' I said. 'I was thinking of going over to France to see the place for myself, but if his memory's that good he can probably set the scene a lot better. That's just great.'

I jotted down the number Stevens gave me. After what had happened with Louise my vain notion of going to Paris had gone right out of the window. I had no mind to be mocked by the city of lovers now. But this was just what I needed.

The old detective was as sprightly on the phone as Stevens had implied. He still had all his files, he said, in an accent that hadn't strayed far from its Gallic roots, despite the amount of time he'd spent in England. He said that now he was connected to the Internet, it was easier to search for any fresh news on old cases. That if I wanted him to, he'd start digging around a bit, see if anything came up. He still had some old police friends left from back then. Still a few of the old codgers left. He sounded genuinely delighted to have been asked to help out.

We exchanged email addresses so he could send any relevant information my way, then we could talk over the details on the phone.

'I cannot promise you anything, Monsieur,' he said. 'This trail was tricky enough when it was still warm. But I will do my best for you. What say you give me a week and then I can have it all straight in my own mind at least? And you never know, maybe someone can pop out of the woodwork to help us.'

I was almost jumping up and down when I finally put the phone down and got on to Gavin straight away. I'd done enough sneaking around behind his back for the time being, I thought, and anyway, this lead had come from his contact.

Gavin sounded mildly amused at the thought of a geriatric

gendarme coming to our aid. He suggested we got together to discuss the questions we could put to him.

'Have you come across anything else new yourself?' he asked me.

Lucky I was on the phone. If this had been a face-to-face conversation I might not have been able to meet his eye. 'Hmmm,' I dithered, searching for something I might throw him that wouldn't involve my extra-curricular activities with Ray Spencer. Then I remembered. The magazine Christophe had given me. 'Well, there is something I need to show you,' I said. 'A magazine article with a picture of Vince in it. It doesn't say much, but there is one interesting thing – there's a girl with him in the photograph. A girl with blonde hair. Now if I remember rightly,' I reeled my mind back, 'Pascal's report mentioned a mystery blonde. Maybe this is her.'

'Right,' Gavin sounded surprised. 'You'd better bring her over then, mate. See if we can ID her.'

'Right you are,' I said.

'Oh, and one more thing,' Gavin cut in before I put the phone down. 'Would you mind letting me see Pascal's report myself? It might help.'

He sounded a little rankled.

'Sorry, I didn't realise you hadn't,' I said. 'I'll bring it right over.'

I started to get a bit nervous on the way over. Wondered if, by some jungle drum or other, Gavin had found out that I'd been seeing another journalist behind his back. I hadn't heard him sound so curt before. But I managed to head that thought off before it went too wild. He'd probably just been rankled that Tony had sent me the report and not copied him in on it. He didn't like to be left out. So Christ knows how he would feel when I did have to fess up about Ray, but we'd cross that bridge when we came to it.

My worries evaporated as soon as I got to Elgin Crescent, dispersed by the smell of freshly-brewed coffee in Gavin's sunny kitchen and the way he rubbed his hands together as I unloaded my bag on the table.

'Right, mate,' he said, disposition now as fair as the weather. 'Shall we take these outside and read 'em?'

Looked like Gavin was taking the task seriously. In an uncharacteristically scholarly fashion I'd never seen him adopt before, he donned a pair of reading glasses to scan the closely typed pages, whistling between his teeth as he came to the most intriguing bits.

'Reckons he was hooked up with gangsters, hey?' he said, as he reached the part about Marco 'the Arab'.

'The French coppers didn't sound too helpful, though, did they?' I asked.

'Nah,' Gavin shook his head. 'I guess for them it was just another case of wiping the scum off the streets and who cares so long as they're outta here.'

He rubbed his chin thoughtfully. I waited until he'd finished his slow trawl through the document, underlining certain sentences and suggesting a few questions, before showing him the magazine. 'Here you go,' I said. 'What do you make of her?'

Gavin stared hard at it, then jerked his head back. He pushed the magazine out in front of him, as if he could see it better from a distance, then pulled it back in to under his nose and lifted up his glasses to squint at it.

'Jeez,' he said, 'that chick looks familiar.'

'Really?' I leaned over to see if there was something there I'd missed. But she didn't look familiar to me.

'You mean she's not some Parisian streetwalker?'

Gavin frowned. 'I don't think so, mate, but I suppose she could be. It's just something about the expression on her face reminds me of someone…'

Then he shook his head. 'Nah, it couldn't be. The hair's totally wrong for a start.'

'Who do you think it was?'

Gavin picked up his coffee cup and took a thoughtful swig. 'This chick called Donna Woods. You come across her yet?'

I frowned myself, tried not to give anything away. 'She was Mood Violet's manager, wasn't she? I must admit, I'm not quite up to speed on their set-up yet,' I lied. 'Although I suppose I should be by now.'

'She ran their record label.' Gavin nodded. 'Vada, yeah, you heard of it?'

I nodded.

'Right. But by the time this picture was taken...' he scrutinised the notes Christophe's girlfriend had translated '...that would have been November 1981. She was in the loony bin by then.'

'The loony bin?' I echoed.

'Ah, in case you hadn't got that far, Donna was another one of Sylvana's casualties,' Gavin said, peering at me over the top of his specs. 'I guess she had to deal with the fall-out from her side of things – the madness of Robin Leith for one thing, losing her livelihood for another. Only she didn't deal with it. She went berko. Had to be sectioned for her own protection.'

'Really?' I could feel my palms starting to sweat. I glanced away from his gaze, around the raised rockery and the hollyhocks that were nodding on the gentle breeze, bumblebees humming amongst them, going about their work. Tried to push the madness and darkness away.

'Yeah,' Gavin said. 'Funny the things you forget. I hadn't given her a second thought in all of this, but I suppose she was just as fucked up by it as everybody else.'

I looked back at him and he was staring hard at the photo.

'So that couldn't be her then?' I asked, trying not to fidget in my seat.

'Well, like I said, it does look like her,' Gavin strained his eyes over it one more time. 'But, nah,' he shook his head and put the magazine back on the wrought-iron garden table. 'I don't see how it could have been. I mean, even if she was out of hospital by then, what would she have been doing there anyway?'

'I haven't a clue.' I shrugged nonchalantly, but inside bells and whistles were going off in my brain.

So Gavin didn't know about her secret affair with Vince either. And if it was her…If it was her, I had to meet her. That decided it, right there and then.

Good as his word, Pascal got back to me a week later. He'd emailed me some correspondence he'd had with an old police mucker of his, which I printed out pronto before calling him up to go over it.

'*Alors*,' he said, 'Now, we get down to business. Now you have everything I have about your Vincent Smith. You are familiar with the report I compiled for Monsieur Stevens, yes?'

'Yes,' I said, pressing play on my tape recorder. I'd taken the precaution of using a phone bug for this, just in case I couldn't take down the notes fast enough. 'You don't mind if I record this, do you?'

'Not at all.'

'It didn't seem like the French police were much help to you?'

'*Non*,' he said, 'but of course, they had their reasons. Monsieur Smith had got himself too much of a reputation. After the death of his wife, he'd fallen in with a bad crowd. Drug dealers, pimps, prostitutes. Not serious criminals, you understand, but the petty lowlife that clog up Pigalle, the vermin you are always having to clean up after. Some of them are Algerian and Moroccan and, I am afraid to say, there was and still is a lot of racism in France about these people. The police do not care if they disappear, it is merely one problem off their patch. Do you know anyone besides Monsieur Stevens who knew Monsieur Smith well, Eddie?'

'Yes,' I said, 'Gavin Granger, the photographer I'm doing the book with. He was a pretty close friend of Vince's.'

'Did he give you any idea why his friend would have wanted to do such things? Why he didn't come back to England when his career and those who loved him were all there?'

'Only one reason,' I said. 'Heroin.'

'Ah,' Pascal replied. 'I see. This is a problem I found at the time. All of Monsieur Smith's acquaintances were what we would call unreliable witnesses. Junkies will tell you anything if they think they will get rewarded for it. They will make up tall stories to throw you off the scent, like the girl who told me that they called him The Vampire. I think she thought I was a reporter and would give her some money for saying this. Of course, I had to offer a little bit around here and there to get anyone to say anything. But I think Monsieur Smith flashed his money around too much with these people. They seemed very put out that he was no longer around to subsidise them.'

'Oh,' I said, 'that reminds me. Did you ever find out who the mystery blonde was?'

'*Non*. It was only from these unreliable locals, after the fact, that I hear about this woman. All I know is, she wasn't one of the usual crowd. She wasn't a known prostitute. But you see, the girls that go through these places, they do not last for long. I doubt we would be able to trace her now.'

Right, I thought smugly, that makes me a better detective than you are. 'So,' I pressed on, 'what about these documents you've sent me?'

'Well, as you know,' the old man said, 'my best theory about Smith was that he deliberately vanished. So what I ask myself is, where would he go?

'This Marco, the pimp or whatever he really was, the guy he was hanging out with. It is said he smuggles drugs up through Marseilles, so the first thing that occurs to me is that Monsieur Smith would go in this direction. South. To Marseilles itself, or beyond, perhaps to Casablanca or Tangiers. These are the sort of places he would seem attracted to – they are lawless and mysterious and full of the drugs he likes. They also have a mythic resonance, and I think your Monsieur Smith, he is a romantic, he likes these things.'

'You're dead right,' I said, surprised. I hadn't expected him to think in such a writerly fashion, but maybe I shouldn't have been surprised. The French are a literary lot, after all.

'So I ask around a bit amongst the friends I still have and this time, I ask not just about Smith, but about this Marco too, just in case they stayed in cahoots. If you take a look at the first document…'

I trained my eyes on my print-out.

'And I found something that could be quite interesting. I think that this Marco is actually one Mert Ibci.' I looked at the strangely spelt name on the paper. 'Not an Arab at all, but a Turk, so you see how useful these racial generalisations can be. Anyhow, I managed to ascertain that this man was arrested in February 1982, in Marseilles, for possession of hashish with intent to supply. He wasn't charged in the end, but he turns up again here three more times for petty drugs offences and pimping before he vanishes off the radar in the spring of 1983. What is of particular interest is that on his file there are a list of known associates and one of them is an Englishman who calls himself…Donald Dawson. Does this name have any relevance to you?'

The hairs on the back of my neck prickled. 'Yes,' I said. 'Yes, it does. That was the name of Vince's first manager.'

I scanned down the document. There it was in black and white. Shit, Gavin was going to love this. 'From what I know,' I said, 'Vince didn't part with Dawson on very good terms.'

'*D'accord*,' Joseph said. 'Then I think we could have the two of them here. The trouble is, this only gets us a couple of years down the line. All we can do now is follow Mert Ibci and he only turns up again one more time, so far. Go to the next document I sent you.'

I rustled my pages, straining to keep up with him.

'This time, five years later, in Seville, Spain. Here he is charged with living off immoral earnings and sentenced to three years in prison. After this, *pfhutt!* Nothing. Not yet, anyway. But as I say, I will keep in touch with my contacts. It is hard with a transient petty criminal like this Ibci, because I have only sources left in continental Europe. If he has gone to Africa, like we suspect, I doubt I will find a thing. And of course, there is nothing to say that Monsieur Smith kept in with him, even as far as Seville. But you are sure,' he emphasised, 'that this Dawson character is most probably our man?'

'It's got to be,' I said. 'It sounds just like the sort of joke he'd make.'

I remembered Ray's article: Don Dawson's the King of Nothing Now.

'Wow.' My head was swimming. 'That's just…amazing.'

'The game is afoot, my friend.'

'Wow,' I repeated, trying to process it all.

'You have any other questions?' the detective asked.

'Let me see,' I quickly scanned down the notes I'd prepared with Gavin. He seemed to have answered everything we'd thought of. But still his line about Vince absconding to Casablanca intrigued me.

'You seem to have had quite a good sense of Vince's motivations. Did you form an opinion on his character?'

Pascal chewed on this for a moment. 'This man's character was the most difficult thing for me,' he said. 'Normally, people follow a pattern, whether they are a good man or a psychopath. But Smith does not seem to do this. I hear many different things about him from many different people; none of them gave me the complete picture. I know that he is a very artistic man and I know that he likes to align himself with outsiders and outlaws; this is a myth that many creative people find attractive. I know that he loved his wife, and this made many people around him very angry. I think that her death could have made him more erratic, but I still don't understand why he would want to live the life of a petty criminal when it is clear he has a very good mind. I think he is very much a romantic, and that can be a very dangerous thing. We French know all about that, of course.'

'Do you think that's why he stayed in France, then? That he felt more at home there?'

'It could be. He certainly chose the most infamous quarter to make his home.'

'But apparently, he was quite religious too,' I said. 'Or so Tony Stevens told me. That's why I found it interesting that he lived in the part of Paris where the red light district is overlooked by that beautiful church, saints and sinners together, if you like.'

'The Sacré Coeur, you mean? Ah. Well, this church is not what it seems to be either. Do you know the story of the Sacré Coeur?'

Obviously not.

'The basilica of the Sacré Coeur was built in expiation for the massacre of the Communards,' he said.

'Er?' I began and he laughed, then explained.

'There was an uprising in Paris, in 1871, against the Third Republic, during the Franco-Prussian war. The French leaders had signed a treaty with the Germans, which was high treason for the people of Paris. The Communards were working-class people, supposedly republicans, but actually anarchists who were already sick of what the Republic had become and wanted the people to run the city themselves. So they try and take the city over. The French army was ordered to put them down with extreme violence.

'Now the butte of Montmartre, the hill on which the church now stands, it used to be a chalk mine. It is the highest place in the city and it seemed the easiest to defend. Hundreds of the Communards hid there. So what did the army do? *Phfft!* They dynamite the exits of the mines, burying the whole lot of them alive. That beautiful white basilica that you see there now, it is built on top of a hill of blood, a mass grave of our own, and yet built to atone not for this sin, but for the sins of the Communards. You see, the Sacré Coeur itself is an emblem of the royalists and right-wingers; it is telling the people to stay in their place, even after we have had this so-called revolution. So for me, the saints and sinners are not side-by-side in Montmartre. It is a place for sinners only.'

'I see,' I said. Or at least, I thought was beginning to.

28

Shot by Both Sides

January 1981

'I feel horrible doing this,' said Kevin, opening the wardrobe door.

The day before they left the squat, Rachel's parents had arranged to send a van to collect her belongings. Kevin, Steve and Lynton dawdled nervously in the room she'd shared with Vince, gingerly attempting to separate their former flatmates' belongings, cringing with anticipation at what they were likely to discover.

They'd packed up her college things first. Her paints, charcoals, pastels and pencils were kept in a workman's toolbox. There were sketchbooks and scrapbooks, reference books and a big portfolio of finished work. Most of her canvasses had been hung on the walls, but Lynton found another pile of them on top of the wardrobe, wrapped in an oilcloth and tied together with string.

He lifted them down and put them on the bed.

'Should I check what this is?' he said.

'Suppose so,' said Steve, glancing round at Kevin, who nodded apprehensively.

They were three studies of Vince in thick oils, looking over his left shoulder, a stark white face against a sludge-grey background, the multiple tattoos running down his arm rendered in black and blood red. The girl in the Martini glass with *Man's Ruin* written underneath had long since been joined by an array of daggers, disembodied eyeballs, tumbling dice and forked flames.

The first one was a straight portrait and that was unnerving enough: Vince in a foul mood, his eyes dark with menace, looking like he was about to coil out of the canvas and stick a knife in you. The second one, she'd abstracted his features Cubist style, so that Vince became a series of curves and angles, a geometry of black, white and red. The third was a homage to Edvard Munch's most famous painting: Vince's face as a skull-like mask, mouth hanging open in a silent scream, eyes completely black. She'd turned the tattoos into a sacred heart that flamed across his shoulder.

They stared at them agog.

'God,' said Lynton finally. 'These are scary, man. Shit.'

Steve cocked his head to one side, regarding the third one.

'I think she's captured the real Vince here,' he said. 'D'you think she was designing our next album cover or what?'

'Put them away,' whispered Kevin. 'I don't want to look at them.'

Lynton and Steve exchanged glances. Since that night with the Scotsman, Kevin had withdrawn into himself so much it was like living with a ghost. Today, coming back from his morning trips to the newsagent and the phone box, was the first time they'd had a proper conversation out of him since then and that was only about packing up Rachel's things.

Which was why Steve had decided they'd be better off back home for a while.

Lynton rapidly reassembled the pictures in their wrappings. 'I'll start taking this downstairs, shall I?' he offered.

'Aye,' nodded Steve. 'I'll do this,' he nodded towards the dressing table, where it was obvious who the make-up and jewellery belonged to.

'She didn't tek much with her, did she?' he mused, packing bottles into his cardboard box.

Kevin stood by the open wardrobe. 'It don't seem right to touch her personal things,' he said.

Steve came over and put an arm around his friend's shoulder. 'It's all right, Kevin, you don't have to do it if you don't want to. You go and pack up your own things. I'll see to this.'

Kevin was shaking. Steve realised he was trying not to cry. 'It's all right,' he repeated, although he doubted that it was. 'We're getting out of this shitehole tomorrow. Tony's going to find us a proper place to stay, it won't be anything like this, I promise you. Or else,' he muttered more to himself than to Kevin, 'his precious Vince won't have a career any more, will he?'

Kevin gave a huge sob and slipped out from underneath him. 'S-sorry Steve,' he tried to say. 'I just can't...' and with that, he ran out of the room, into his own, slamming the door behind him.

'Jesus wept.' Steve shook his head. 'Vincent Smith, you treacherous bastard, what the fuck have you done to us?' He went angrily back to the dressing table and continued packing as fast as he could. He found Rachel's works in the second drawer down, wrapped up inside a velvet box.

The ferry churned its way across the choppy grey sea, a trail of seagulls squawking in its wake. The wind was high and raw, flinging stinging drops of rain against Sylvana's face as she stood on the prow of the ferry, wrapped in a floor-length black coat, her red hair billowing out behind her.

Vincent had preferred to stay inside in the bar with his Paris guidebook, but Sylvana had wanted to be out in this. She wanted to feel her escape, every motion of the waves, while she savoured how life had suddenly turned itself around.

Vincent had been such an angel since the moment they met. Every day they'd stayed in that hotel he had been busy arranging things; getting her passport and her suitcase back from Helen, working out how they could get married by special licence and sorting out somewhere for them to stay in France. He thought that Paris was the most romantic place on earth, so that was where they should go. She didn't ask how he had done it all. She assumed that Tony, with his big house and all his money and contacts, would have had something to do with it. People with that much money seldom had problems with officials.

She didn't question whether it was the right thing to do, nor pause to reflect on the mistakes of the past. All she felt was the urge to travel forward, away from those dark days as quickly as she could, to blot Robin and everyone associated with him out of her mind. The love she now felt for Vincent was so overwhelming it took precedence over all other considerations. It even drowned out the tiny voice in her mind that reminded her that at least she ought to tell Helen what she was up to, after all Helen had done and tried to do for her.

Helen would understand, she told herself, shaking the guilt out of her mind. Of course she would. Once she knew the true Vincent she'd be so happy for her. Vincent was a genius. The way that he spoke, he could make sense of everything, could straighten out the jumble in her mind better than any of Glo's shrinks ever could. It came down to love and creativity, he said, two sides to the same coin, qualities that she had in spades, even if she didn't realise it. He could help her reach her true potential. This was just the start.

She knew it wasn't exactly the Cunard Line, Sealink ferries from Dover to Calais, but Sylvana wanted to feel the way Ola had when she had set sail to New York all those years ago, heading for a new life with her new husband by her side. Not that she'd had the courage to call her grandma yet either. But she was sure Ola would be pleased for her when she eventually did. So despite the wind, despite the spiteful rain and the roiling, chundering landscape of leaden sea and sky that stretched out before her, she was enjoying the wild ride across the Channel.

The ride to freedom.

When they finally hit the A63 back towards Hull, Steve gave up on the radio. If he had to hear 'Imagine' or 'Starting Over' one more time he'd be tempted to throw bloody thing out of the window. So what, John Lennon was dead. He'd never meant owt to Steve.

Their ride back up north had been without conversation, the dull countryside of Hertfordshire and Northamptonshire, Lincolnshire and Nottinghamshire passing in a grey blur of low cloud. Now the humped mounds of slag heaps, the black arcs of pit heads, the rows of cooling towers and endless pylons demarked the boundary between the agricultural south and the industrialised north. It gave Steve a shiver, thinking what fate could have dealt him. To end up in one of those places, down a pit or in a factory, on the docks like Grandad Cooper, slaving his guts out for the money to get pissed on a Friday night and forget about it all.

Inside, the fear that Vince's disappearance would send him back there, snatch defeat from the jaws of victory. That the world of tour buses and recording studios, riotous fans and fawning journalists would fade away into the fog like the road behind him; that in the end, that was all that was really fit for the likes of him.

'You got any tapes?' he asked Lynton, slumped in the seat beside him, staring out of the window at the flat, monotonous land. 'I can't listen to this shit any more.'

Lynton nodded languorously and reached down to pick up the army surplus bag at his feet. There was a clicking of plastic as he foraged amongst the tapes. 'Here,' he said finally, selecting one and sticking it into the machine.

A mournful, brooding trumpet note coiled up through the air like cigarette smoke, blending in perfectly with the bleakness of their surroundings.

'What's this?' asked Steve.

'*Kind of Blue*,' Lynton said, leaning back in his seat and closing his eyes.

'Oh.' Steve realised, as he took the turning back into Hessle, Lynton was finally playing him Miles. 'Yeah. That makes sense.'

They took the train from Calais to Gare du Nord, watched the sun go down in a molten pink sky and saw Paris appear out of the darkness in a fairy tale of lights.

'Wow,' Sylvana breathed. 'It's so beautiful.'

Although she was less sure of that when they left the grand environs of the station and turned out onto the main road. The buildings here slouched alongside the pavement in dark huddles, eyeing them through baleful yellow slits of windows, as if loitering with intent. There was that strange atmosphere of menace that always lingers outside major termini, along with the opportunist hawkers, fly-by-night cab drivers, pickpockets and streetwalkers.

People jabbered at them in harsh voices as they passed: dirty, broken-looking people with pinpoint eyes, bad teeth and folds of wrinkled skin. Even with Vince so tall and purposeful beside her, Sylvana wondered whether it would have been wiser to go straight to the cab rank.

Worse still, this road seemed to lead to an even more dangerous place. To a world of peep shows and sex shops, lit up in gaudy neon, where lank young men in leather jackets barked out leering words that even without her schoolgirl French she fully understood. A street where drunk men lurched suddenly out of dark doorways and staggered across their paths, where tired-looking women gazed out of windows with glassy eyes.

Sylvana was tired now, her feet were aching and the cold was biting into her. Even though Vince was carrying her suitcase, with his own army kit bag slung casually over his shoulder as if it weighed nothing, the thought that they so obviously looked like tourists in a place like this, in a place like Times Square for Chrissakes, started to terrify her.

Where were they going? Why was he taking her here? This wasn't part of her romantic plans.

As if he could read her mind, Vince squeezed her hand reassuringly, said: 'Not much further now.'

Sylvana's stomach dropped. Had he booked them into some flea pit above a strip joint?

But almost as soon as the words left his mouth, they seemed to come out of the den of prostitutes and thieves. Their path rose upwards and into streets of elegant white houses with little bars and cafés tucked underneath them; the atmosphere of sickness and menace disappeared like a puff of smoke, leaving behind the enticing, magical Paris she had expected to see.

From one of the cafés, the sound of a saxophone lingered on the air, along with the reassuring blur of conversation. They came into a square and up above of them, bathed in floodlights, was the most beautiful white church she had ever seen, crowning the top of the hill.

Vince stopped. 'The Sacré Coeur,' he said, staring up at it and then back down at her, his eyes alight with excitement. 'The Sacred Heart. What could be more romantic than that, eh?'

Relief and fatigue washed over her. 'Oh, Vince,' she said. 'I was worried back there. I thought you were taking us the wrong way…'

He put his arm around her shoulders, squeezed her close. 'I'm sorry,' he said. 'I didn't realise it would be quite such a colourful journey. That was the famous Pigalle – it's only like Soho, really. I don't think they bother you if you're not an obvious mark, but I didn't mean to frighten you.'

'Don't worry,' she said, trying to banish the faint anxiety that still fluttered in the corner of her mind at his easygoing approach to their personal safety. This place they had ended up in was perfect, after all, and it wasn't his fault what they had to walk through to get there. How could she doubt him?

'I'm just a bit tired and cold, I guess. Is our hotel very far?'

Vince smiled, and swept his arm to the left. 'No,' he said, pointing to the handsome white building on the corner, his eyes dancing in the streetlights, the curve of a smile on his lips. 'It's right here.'

There were two witnesses at Vince and Sylvana's wedding: Tony Stevens and a tall Australian called Gavin Granger, who took some commemorative snaps for them as they got in the Cadillac Tony had hired. They'd arrived the night before and up until that moment, Sylvana had just about forgotten that walk through Pigalle and how it had made her feel.

They had had the most incredible week until then. They had walked all around the city each day, drinking in all its sights, from the Louvre to Notre Dame to the Musée Gustave Moreau. They drank cocktails in L'Hotel where Oscar Wilde uttered his famous last line about the wallpaper and combed the flea markets to buy outfits for their big day. Vincent chose a vintage tuxedo and a blood-red shirt; Sylvana found an antique velvet dress in exactly the same colour, with a beautiful white lace collar. Miraculously, it fitted her like a glove. The old lady she bought it from said in her faltering English that many people had tried it before but none were petite enough to wear it; but it looked like it had been waiting for Sylvana to come for it all along.

At night they had walked along the Seine, finding Left Bank cafés to pretend to be Existentialists in, or, nearer to their hotel, little jazz bars in Montmartre that looked like they hadn't changed since the 1930s. Vince knew so much about the history of the place. He knew where Picasso had lived, where Zola had written his masterpieces, from which he could quote, where André Breton had begun his joke on the art world. He was so inspiring that already they had written lyrics to about ten songs together.

But he was so spiritual too. Every morning Vince went up to the Sacré Coeur to light a candle. Sylvana had never known very much about the Roman Catholic faith before, but Vincent told her that every candle lit was a prayer of love, and he was getting all the angels on their side so that, although they were getting married in a register office, God would still be happy.

'*Mazel tov*!' she said to that.

But when they got back to the hotel to find the two men waiting for them, she felt inexplicably awkward. These were two of Vincent's best friends, but they seemed very cool towards her, very aloof. She had one drink with them to attempt some form of conversation, but when they continually ignored her, talked over her head to each other and Vincent, she decided that there was one wedding rule she was going to keep.

'I think I should leave you guys to it,' she announced, when Vincent suggested another round. 'Isn't it tradition for you to have a stag night anyway?'

Vincent looked puzzled. 'You sure, darling?'

He looked so beautiful with his hair falling forwards slightly over his eyes that her heart ached to have to leave his side. But it was enough for her that tomorrow they would be man and wife. Let these rude bastards have him for a few hours, they were never gonna get what she was.

'Course I am, honey.' She looked around at the other two; saw the expressions of relief writ large on their features. 'You all enjoy yourselves. I want to take a long bath so I can look my best for you tomorrow.'

And she leaned over and gave him a long, lingering kiss, enjoying the curdled expressions of the other two when she opened her eyes again. She supposed she was going to have to get used to this kind of jealous behaviour. It obviously came with the territory of a man like Vincent.

In fact, she had enjoyed spending a long evening pampering herself and going to bed early. Thoughful Vincent hadn't even woken her up when he got back in, whatever time that was. No, there was nothing that anyone could do to take away her joy on her big day.

Not the low whispers and sarcastic expressions of her witnesses before the ceremony. Not the fact that Vincent was so nervous that he dropped the ring as he went to put it on her finger and had to scrabble around on the floor for a minute to retrieve it. Not even that afterwards they all had to go and have dinner together, paid for by Tony, before he and his surly sidekick got their plane home. That Tony's last words were a pointed reminder about the album Vince had to come home to make, how he'd be seeing him *very soon*.

Because now she was officially Mrs Vincent Smith. Or to use his full family name, which he didn't like to but she found secretly thrilling, Mrs Vincent D'Arch Smith. Nothing else mattered.

And Vincent seemed to have a new gleam in his eye the moment they were alone. He took her hand and ushered her back upstairs to their room, singing 'Love Me Tender' in his best Elvis baritone as they went.

Four hours and two bottles of champagne later, she felt just about spent, satiated on love and drowsy with drink. She was just about asleep, when she felt him nudge her arm gently.

'Darling,' he whispered. 'Don't go to sleep yet. I've got something very special for us to try.'

'What's that?' Sylvana fluttered her eyelids open.

'I don't know if you've ever done this before, but I promise you this is going to make you feel better than you've ever felt before. Better than you ever thought possible.'

'Mmmm.' Sylvana shut her eyes, trying to imagine what that could be. She thought they had just about gone through everything that made her feel that way.

But when he didn't make a move towards her, she opened her eyes again and saw Vincent sitting on the end of the bed, fashioning some kind of joint from one of his cigarettes and a packet of white powder.

She blinked, sat up and tried to work out what he was doing.

'This,' he said, turning back to her and firing the fat cigarette up with his Zippo, 'is going to make you see even more colours than usual.'

He inhaled and an extremely beatific smile spread across his face. 'Beautiful,' he murmured, passing it over to her. 'You try.'

'What is it?' Sylvana looked at the joint as if he was holding out a poisonous snake.

'It's powdered dreams, honey. No need to be afraid.'

Is it opium, she thought? Or some fancy French thing she'd never heard of? Sylvana was woozy with drink already; she'd never been able to handle it well. And drugs were another country. She had never taken more than a quick draw on a reefer, had always declined the wraps of speed that used to go around on the Mood Violet tour van to stop Allie from falling asleep at the wheel. She knew drugs were part of the industry, but she'd always been afraid of them. Not that she'd ever ventured to the Lower East Side or anything, but she knew New York had been a city awash with heroin zombies when she'd left, a dark, lawless place.

But she took it anyway. If he thought she would like it, then at least she would give it a try. Still warm with love, she put it to her lips and inhaled.

The tobacco burned the back of her throat, making her cough, but she didn't feel any other sensation. Not then, anyway. Without saying anything, she passed it back to her new husband, who took it from her like he was receiving some holy sacrament. With every puff, his body relaxed, sprawled out across the lovely French bed, his expression became more and more dreamy.

The second time she took a puff, it was as if all the strength had suddenly drained out of her arms. Her vision went a cloudy yellow and she felt a surge of overwhelming nausea.

'Oh, my God,' she said, staggering to her feet, shoving the offending cigarette back into Vincent's hand.

'What's wrong, darling?' he said, with the same, silly smile plastered all over his face.

She couldn't stop to tell him. She only just blundered across the room in time to get to the toilet and heave the contents of Tony's wedding dinner down the porcelain. Her body spasmed as she did, as if someone was kicking her hard in the stomach. She tasted the steak frites and fish soup all over again as it poured out of her like a foul fountain, cold sweat breaking out on her forehead, her arms full of pins and needles.

Then Vince was behind her, stroking her back, holding back her hair from her face.

'I'm sorry, darling,' he whispered. 'It happens like this sometimes, the first time. But you'll be OK.'

For one second, Sylvana's mind spiralled back to that bedroom in Leicester, Robin screaming obscenities into her face. Then she blanked it out. No. This couldn't be happening to her again. Another huge spasm pushed a brown, partially digested stew out of her mouth and into the toilet bowl, flecked the side of her mouth that she'd painted with such care only hours before.

'There, there,' Vincent flushed the loo, pulled off some toilet paper and gently dabbed around her mouth. 'Here, my baby.' He ran a flannel under the cold tap, put it over her forehead.

She retched again and again until finally, only an acrid line of saliva came out. She'd got rid of everything, but still her stomach lurched against her, trying to force out the poison that was now inside her blood. Stars danced in front of her eyes.

This was not how it was supposed to be. But so began Sylvana's married life.

29

Miss the Girl

May 2002

Gavin's reaction to my interview with Pascal was not exactly what I'd expected. I'd rushed straight over to show him the print-outs and discuss what the detective had said, thinking he'd be wired by the revelations – the thought that we might actually be on Vincent's trail at last.

Instead, he listened to me blurting it all out in silence, then got up and started to walk up and down the room. The revelations had clearly shocked him. He kept shaking his head saying: 'Donald Dawson, eh?' or 'Seville? *Tchuch*!' stroking his chin and staring out of the window into his garden. My print-outs flapped in his hand. Ocassionally he stopped circling the room like a caged tiger and stared at them, only to shake his head and resume his troubled pacing once more.

I wondered what kind of internal conversation he was having with himself, because it was deep enough to block me out entirely, almost as if I had ceased to exist.

'Well,' I eventually said to him. 'Do you think the old boy's onto something, then?'

'Hmmm?' Gavin came round slowly, as if he had been dreaming with his eyes open. 'Shit, sorry, mate. I was miles away. What did you say?'

'Are you feeling OK?' I asked him.

He shook his head. 'Not really, mate. I feel a bit weird, to tell you the truth.'

He walked over to the fridge and pulled himself out a beer. Cracked it open and took a gulp.

'Shit,' he said. 'Sorry, mate, d'you want one too?'

'Ah, OK,' I said and he passed one over.

'Did it upset you, hearing all that stuff about Vince?'

Gavin sat down opposite me, screwing his face up into a frown. 'I don't know if upset is the right word. Unnerved is maybe better.' He shook his head again. 'Or unsettled, perhaps. I guess what it is, is, I'd kinda got used to the idea that Vince was dead and I accepted it. Now, after all these years, this old guy has got me thinking that maybe it's not true.'

He looked up at me, spreading his fingers as he spoke. 'Maybe he isn't dead. Maybe he has been hanging around in Tangiers or Casablanca for all this time, playing at being a gangster with his little Turkish mate. This Pascal's got him pegged pretty good, considering he never met the guy.'

'That's his job, I suppose,' I said, lighting a Marlboro and imagining Vince in a smoky bar, with a big ceiling fan whirling over his head, listening to the pianist playing one of his songs. A jazz version of 'The King of Nothing' – that would be something.

'So now I'm thinking, what if we actually find him?' Gavin's eyes were pained. 'I mean…I dunno. It's a big what if, but…'

'It would be pretty amazing,' I hedged. I didn't want to upset him by saying how great it would be for the book.

'Yeah,' he winced. 'Amazing, but also…pretty painful, I guess, in a lot of ways.'

'Mmmm,' I nodded, trying to look at it from his point of view. 'There's a lot of questions you'd want him to answer...'

'And what if he never wanted to be found? I mean, if he is alive, he's done his best to appear dead this past twenty years. He obviously never wanted to come back. Shit, I dunno. What if we find him and it's the last thing he wants? I mean,' Gavin put his head in his hands and rubbed his forehead, 'from what the guy was saying, Christ knows what kinda shit he's got himself into over the years.'

He tortured himself like this for about another hour and I probably wasn't too much help. Although I did my best to assure him that if Vince had stayed lost for this long, he'd probably stay lost for ever, I was already thinking the opposite. Hoping the opposite. But I didn't want to appear mercenary.

'I mean,' I said, 'they never found that Richie Manic, did they?' It was the best argument I could think of.

'No,' Gavin agreed, 'but that's because he jumped off the Severn Bridge.'

Quite possibly, that was true. But I soldiered on. 'Well,' I said, 'do you fancy a drink? Maybe a stroll down the 'Bello would do you good, get some fresh air?'

Gavin hesitated. 'Nah,' he finally said. 'No offence, Eddie, but I feel like I need a bit of time on me own right now. I need to let this all sink in.'

I let him get on with it. I was on fire. I knew what I had to do next.

Back home, I put the picture of Vincent and the mystery woman on my desk, next to the picture of Donna from *Time Out*. I couldn't see much of a similarity, but that was probably because I'd never met the woman in the flesh. Lucky, then, that I knew a man who had.

I scanned the picture from the French mag, turned it into a Jpeg.

By then it was ten o'clock. I couldn't phone Ray at this time of night, so I sent it in an email to his work, hoping he'd open it and get back to me in the morning.

He did. 'Where did you get that picture?' was the first thing he said.

I told him. 'Gavin's first reaction was to think it was Donna,' I said, 'but then he seemed to doubt himself. You probably know what she looks like a lot better than he does, do you make it for her?'

'Yes,' he said. 'I do. I never saw her with her hair done like that, but it's the expression on her face. The classic Donna sulk. Blimey,' he paused and I imagined him scrutinising the image on his computer the way Gavin had done the magazine page. 'Yeah. I'd say ninety-five to ninety-nine per cent for sure, that is her. But as to what she was doing there, I couldn't begin to tell you. This was *after* Sylvana was dead, yeah?'

'Yeah, and a month before he disappeared off the face of the earth.'

'Fucking hell, Eddie,' Ray's voice dropped to almost a whisper. 'Fucking hell. You really could have a story here.'

'That's what I was thinking.'

'You're gonna have to talk to her now. Or should I say, I am.'

'What do you mean?'

Ray sighed. 'If she finds out what you're really up to, she'll be after money and that is when she turns into the monster you don't want to meet and will never be able to get rid of. Let me think. What magazines do you write for, Eddie?'

I reeled off a list. He stopped me at the most likely one, a music, film, and books monthly.

'*Cut-Ups*, yeah. You got a good contact there?'

'Sort of,' I said, 'though it's been a while.'

'Why don't you try to pitch them a story, so as you've got it as legitimate cover and you make some money out of it at the same time? 'Cos she might just check up on you. I know: say you want to write about the Lost Faces of Punk, the people behind the scenes that have been forgotten, and you think she's an interesting character. Even if they say no, it's better to tell her something along these lines. Because her vanity will get the better of her if she thinks she's finally going to get some recognition and she'll be a lot more gracious.'

We thrashed around a few more names we could possibly add to this feature and then he had to go, his boss was breathing down his ear. I was starting to feel lucky, really lucky. So I called the guy I knew on *Cut-Ups* and sure enough, he seemed to think it was an original enough idea to give a spin. He said he wouldn't commission it officially until I had made sure I could contact all the people I wanted to and that they would speak. But if I could do that, I could have two thousand words, no problem.

It really couldn't have worked out better. Now I had my cover, and, if nothing ever came of it, Donna could check up on me all she liked and there'd still be a valid excuse for the feature not running – no one else would talk.

Almost delirious with excitement, I banged out an email to Ray, saying that I had got the story rolling. He replied that he would be in touch as soon as he could. When the phone rang shortly afterwards, I lifted it up with glee, ready to congratulate him on his quick work.

'Edward!' It was like a sudden ice bath. Her tone was strident, with a fearful undercurrent of outrage. At once, I knew the game was up.

'Oh hello, Mother,' I said.

'I've just seen Louise's mother in Waitrose,' she said. 'She informed me that the two of you have split up. That Louise is no longer living with you and hasn't been for *almost a month*.' The last three words emphasised in a wobbling soprano.

'Well, er…'

'I've had a terrible shock, Edward. I had to tell her I had no idea about any of this. Why haven't you told us?'

'Well, it's not been easy for me either,' I tried to protest. 'I didn't think it would work out like this. I thought we were just having a trial separation...'

'A trial separation?' said Mother. 'You were never even married in the first place, Edward. What on earth are you talking about? According to Mrs Wilkins, that's precisely why Louise left you. She didn't think she had a future with a man who wouldn't commit himself to her.'

'But I did ask her...' I began, screwing up my eyes and praying for the gift of articulate speech. It was impossible. Hell hath no fury like a mother scorned.

'Oh, and when was that? While she was packing her bags to leave?'

'Oh bloody hell...' slipped out of my mouth before I could stop it.

'Don't you dare use that language with me! I'm your mother! I know you, Edward, probably better than you know yourself. And I understand perfectly why that poor girl felt she didn't have any other choice. Now then. I want you to stop skulking round in London and come up here and explain yourself. Your father and I will expect to see you on Friday evening, for the weekend. We won't be kept in the dark any longer!'

'But I...'

'No buts!' The volume of this last statement was faintly terrifying. 'It's months since you've shown your face. Are you really too terrified to tell your own mother when something this important happens to you? What do you think I'm going to do to you, eat you? For heaven's sake...'

Then she did a most uncharacteristic thing. 'Speak to your father,' she said. 'Maybe he can talk some sense into you.'

I think Dad was as startled by this assumption as I was. 'Hello, Eddie,' he said, sounding as always, slightly shell shocked. 'Er, your mother's not very happy I'm afraid. I think it would be for the best if you'd come and see us this weekend, if that's not too inconvenient. We don't want her upset, do we? I mean, any more than she is already. All right, old bean?'

After a whole weekend of that, I understood how Gavin had felt at having his world suddenly turned upside down. As I had suspected, Mother saw my split with Louise as the ideal opportunity to drag me back to 'the nest', where she could make sure I was eating properly, writing my future bestseller to deadline and meeting a good selection of horse-faced, thirty-something spinsters whose mothers also frequented the Con Club.

Nothing could have been more terrifying than waking up that Saturday morning, staring at my ancient Thomas the Tank Engine wallpaper while the morning sun crept underneath the navy curtains and Mother crashed about in the kitchen directly below, twittering 'For the Wings of a Dove' as she started murdering breakfast.

Nothing could be worse than returning to that.

But strangely, throughout the ordeal of that weekend, I found I had an unexpected ally – Dad. He came into his own on Saturday night, after a day in which Mother had exhausted herself on the subjects of my emotional state, her embarrassment at having to apologise to Mrs Wilkins for Louise's emotional state and perhaps more pertinently, my finances.

He had tried some mild interjections throughout the day. Along the lines of: 'Well perhaps that's up to Eddie, dear, it's his life after all,' and, more provocatively, 'A man's finances are his own affair, dear, and he is nearly thirty'. She had almost reached for the smelling salts by that stage, and soon after, clasping her handkerchief to her cheek, announced she was going to bed.

As soon as the coast was clear, he began rummaging around in his writing desk and came out with a bottle of single malt. 'False bottom in there,' he explained. 'Old army trick. She doesn't suspect a thing. Let's keep it that way, eh?'

He put his finger to his nose as he said it. It made me see him in a completely different light and, over a couple of glasses of the contraband, we had the closest to a heart-to-heart discussion we'd ever known.

'Shame about Louise, she was a lovely girl,' was all he had to say on the matter. 'But I expect you had your reasons and you've no need to explain yourself to me. It's just that your mother, well, she has a hard time coming to terms with the world we live in today. She's had a sheltered life, in many ways. She's never really moved with the times. She expected you to be married with children by now, but as I've tried to tell her many times, you can't plan another fellow's life for him, even if he is your son.'

He raised up his glass then, squinting at the pale liquid inside. 'Good bottle this,' he said.

'Yes,' I agreed, because I was suddenly rather impressed with him despite the fact I would rather have had Bourbon. Dad was revealing his hidden depths. I wondered how many other silent rebellions he had staged over the years.

'Thanks for understanding, Dad. It really wasn't easy for me...'

'Afraid to tell her, I know,' he nodded. 'Silly thing is, of course, she's more afraid than you are, she just doesn't know how else to react. Always jumps boots first, does Mildred.' He nodded to himself and I nodded along with him.

'Dad,' I said, 'remember that walk you used to take me on, over the Downs?'

'Aha,' he said, eyes brightening. 'Where I saw the weasels, you mean? My favourite part of England, that will for ever be.'

'Well, is there a pub near there or something, where I could take you both for Sunday lunch tomorrow? Then maybe we could go for a walk afterwards.'

I had never seen him look so delighted. 'Do you know, I believe there is. Coach and Horses, I think it's called, but I can soon look that up in my *AA Guide*. We went out there once before, with a couple of your mother's friends. Good Sunday roast they did too, if memory serves. That would be just the ticket, Eddie.' He nodded emphatically. 'Good thinking, old chum.'

There was nothing wrong with Dad's memory at all. The food in the Coach and Horses was a blessed relief, especially considering the alternative. Mother still hadn't quite calmed down, still had to make loud remarks about the pinkness of my lamb and how could it be safe to eat, although she did deem her own well-roasted beef perfectly satisfactory.

I had to do the driving so I couldn't partake in anything contraband there, but I noticed that Dad kept mother's glass of red topped all the way through the meal. As a consequence, she had mellowed enough by the end of it to consent to a short walk and even admit that this had been rather a good idea.

Poor old Dad couldn't move very far or very fast any more, but he was still as enthusiastic as I remembered from my boyhood, once let loose in his own Jerusalem.

'Look, Eddie, willow warbler,' he pointed out. 'And is that… yes! I thought so. Pied wagtail. Pretty little fellow, what? Look at his tail going.'

Thankfully, it was a beautiful afternoon and the Downs basking in the summer sun, lush with oak and ash, were a symphony in gold and green. All of us, I think, forgot our woes for the time we were out there, just listened instead to the languorous breeze rippling through the leaves, the twittering of the birds all around us and Dad's occasional Bill Oddie commentary.

When it was finally time for me to leave, the tears in Mother's eyes were not ones of rage.

On the doorstep she took my hand and leaned over to give me a kiss. She smelt of powder and Tweed. Her hand was thin and frail and her kiss as light as tissue paper. 'You'll be all right, won't you, Edward?' she almost whispered. 'Just don't be a stranger any more.'

'Of course not,' I said, finding tears in my own eyes. I looked over at Dad, who smiled and stretched out his hand.

'Chin up, Eddie. And thanks for a marvellous afternoon.'

I felt a strange kind of melancholy as I rode the train home, staring out of the window at the fields of ripening wheat turning mellow gold as the sun dipped downwards and spread its final, brilliant burnished glow across the land. I didn't know who I felt the saddest for – Mother for her disillusion, Dad for his stoic acceptance, myself for losing Louise. All of us, I supposed, for our lives turning out so differently from what we had expected.

I no longer felt like the resentful child who had woken up in his old bed on Saturday morning, though. I felt that I had learned something valuable after all, this weekend. Perhaps, for the first time, I actually felt like an adult.

Someone had left a newspaper lying on the seat beside me, a *Camden New Journal* at that. They must have been making their escape in the opposite direction to me.

The headline was a welcome home all right: *Camden Now Officially UK Murder Capital.* I picked it up, sighing, wondering what fresh horrors awaited. The first sentence pointed out that the 'Murder Mile' began at Camden Town tube, right where I was headed next.

But before I could take in the gory details, my mobile buzzed in my pocket.

It was Ray and he had promising news. Absent-mindedly, I stuffed the newspaper into my bag and forgot all about it.

30

No Fun

February 1981

Lynton put down the battered paperback book on the table in front of him and rubbed his eyes. Outside, Route 78 seemed to stretch forever into the Georgia night. Inside the steel juggernaut that was transporting them from Atlanta to Birmingham, Alabama, the atmosphere was close: sticky with humidity and festering bad vibes. Lynton had a dread feeling that things would be coming to a head soon, that Birmingham would be the place to make it happen.

For the past two weeks, everything had been getting steadily worse. This tour had started under a black cloud; the three of them returning from extended exile in Hull full of apprehension. Vince had turned up for their London rehearsals with a moon-eyed Sylvana clamped to his arm and it soon became apparent that she wasn't going to move very much further.

Lynton had cringed at the sight of her. He couldn't believe that he had entertained ideas about her himself, that he had actually gone to that party on New Year's Eve even thinking that he might get lucky. It seemed like it had happened to another person, another lifetime ago. Now she was the last person anyone wanted around.

Even Kevin had been uncommonly hostile towards her. Lynton had expected Steve to blank her; he'd made no secret of what he thought about it all, he was seething with resentment for their sudden state of disarray. But Lynton had never seen Kevin cut another person dead like that before, ever. Kevin, who would sign a hundred autographs after a gig, who would uncomplainingly talk to the most moronic admirer long after everyone else had left and then selflessly clear up everyone else's mess, seemed to have become the worm that turned.

When Sylvana shyly offered him her hand he'd looked straight through her and walked past, so she was left standing there, red in the face. She stayed out of the rehearsal rooms after that, but Vince wouldn't take a hint. Or maybe he saw it as a declaration of war. He was determined that as far as the American tour went, she was going with them. A constant reminder of events everyone else would have far rather forgotten.

When Vince left the studios at night, he went back to the posh hotel she was keeping him in. The rest of them either kipped down on mattresses on the floor, or made do with any sofas that were on offer at friends' houses. Usually that meant Lynton and Kevin reprised their original roles of sleeping guard over the equipment while Steve went off to get bladdered – only in much unhappier circumstances than in their original tour van.

They still didn't have anywhere proper to live, despite Tony's incessant promises that they would be sorted soon. His words and his demeanour rang hollower to them by the day. As if they had already tacitly admitted that things were nearing an end, none of them had brought much back from Hull after New Year. Apart from their equipment, they were surviving on the bare essentials.

Rehearsals had not gone well. They'd all walked around each other like cats with their hackles up, waiting to see who'd make the first move. It was hard enough to go back to the stuff they knew off by heart, let alone revisit the new material they had been working on just before Christmas. The chief mind game was spinning out between Vince and Steve. Both of them kept deliberately fucking things up whenever a song was starting to reach coherence, each of them testing the other out to see how far this piss-takery would go. No one exploded, but the screw was tightened every day, and every night Steve started drinking earlier. The clock was ticking on a walking timebomb.

As they flew out over the Atlantic, a journey that should have been so full of hope and excitement, the three of them sat separate from the lovebirds, under their mutual black cloud. Lynton still could hardly bear to look at Sylvana; nor could he entirely discredit the nagging feeling that somehow he had brought all of this upon them in the first place, by opening his mouth about finding her attractive within Vince's earshot. Hadn't he learned a long time since that anything you admitted you wanted Vince would do his utmost to get for himself? Was it too ridiculous to think that he'd only married this woman to piss Lynton off? Had he been imagining the way Vince had slyly winked at him when he'd said: 'You've met my wife before, haven't you?'

It gave him a headache thinking about it, and that was another thing. Lynton seemed to have had a headache ever since they arrived in America and the stultifying atmosphere on the bus right now wasn't doing anything to help it. It was the same headache as the one he'd come round with after Donna KO'd him; a dull, throbbing tattoo down the left side of his temple and inside his eye socket. He knew the brain scans he'd had at the hospital had all come back clear, but Lynton was also secretly worried that he'd been done some permanent damage that night, something that the doctors couldn't see. Because this headache was unlike anything he'd experienced before.

On top of all that, America didn't seem to be taking kindly to Blood Truth. The best night so far had been the first one in New

York, where they'd managed to sell out the legendary CBGBs – something that had lifted their spirits no end. Until they actually got there and realised that CBGBs was about the same size as the Hull Adelphi and hardly much more salubrious than that little pub. Still, all the city's punks seemed to have turned out for them and, with the charged atmosphere that already existed between the four of them acting like a lightning conductor, their set had been blistering.

Old songs mangled into new shapes, while the most recent ones suddenly took on the new, urgent life they had refused to find in rehearsals. The magic of their being together took over from their individual discomfort and the crowd felt its charge, rode on it. Up on that tiny stage with the condensation flooding down the graffitied walls in danger of electrocuting the lot of them, Lynton had felt truly alive again. Afterwards, he had stood open-mouthed in amazement as not one but two Ramones came up to offer their congratulations.

He and Steve had ended up at some wild party on the Lower East Side that night, being offered every form of vice that the Big Bad Apple had to offer. In the high of the moment, they had managed to convince themselves that maybe everything would be all right.

They'd been allowed one day to rest and recover after that gig, then they'd been gathered together by the young guy Tony had sent with them to be their tour manager, an executive posing as a positive punk who spelt his name 'Nik' and attempted to dress the way the band did. Only he made such fundamental errors as wearing their T-shirts to their gigs, under the pinstriped suit jacket and skinny jeans he thought made him look the part, with a fluorescent pink skinny tie knotted round his neck and worse still, matching fluorescent pink plastic winklepickers. Nik was full of the genuine enthusiasm of one who had no idea of what he was letting himself in for.

They were slightly more heartened to make the acquaintance of their driver for the next month, Earl, and his gigantic articulated rig. They'd never seen a lorry so big or so gleaming as this mobile Silver Bullet, as Steve immediately christened it; it certainly put the British standard tour coach to shame. Inside it had bunks at the back and a lounge in the front, with its own fridge and a Hi Fi that looked like it had been designed by NASA. With a roadie from New York, a young Italian American who looked like Travis Bickle and rejoiced in the name of Mouse, in the middle of a hailstorm, they started their journey across the badlands.

The novelty of the coach's luxuries began to fade when they slowly realised that, for the next month, they'd be spending about fifteen hours a day confined in it, with only a couple of overnight motel stays on the way. Just as the novelties of the truck stops with their bizarre novelty shopping items – replica route signs; glow-in-the-dark Jesus pendants; *Real Truckers*' tapes; fundamentalist preacher stickers; and the hornet-coloured tablets called Stingers that were like legalised speed for roadhogs – began to pale next to the sour looks and muttered comments of the folk inside them.

Outside New York, to the rest of America, they were a travelling freak show.

The further south they went, the more Lynton had the unnerving sensation they were moving back in time, into a world of swamp and cotton and white clapboard churches that had forever been hostile to a man with black skin. A world his jazz heroes had told him all about was now prickling at the core of him, almost as if his own blood was singing him a warning. Maybe it was; maybe his ancestors had toiled in servitude in similar lands, fashioning the music that kept their souls alive even as they broke their backs labouring. He wouldn't ever know. But he *felt*. And it seemed his instincts were quickening. Earl, who himself looked like a bowlegged cowboy with a drooping moustache and a black Stetson parked firmly on the back of his head, seemed to stay closer by his side when they got out to stretch their legs and eat. He didn't say anything, but Lynton just knew he was watching his back.

He stared at the back of Earl's head now, at the neck thick with muscle and the long black ponytail that snaked out of the Stetson and ran halfway down his back. At the jaw that stoically chewed tobacco in time to the Hank Williams tape he listened to as he drove. Lynton had never particularly liked country music before, but Hank's lonesome keening had lodged itself permanently in his brain, as haunted and lost as the landscape they travelled through. It mingled there with Billie Holliday's lament of strange fruit, hanging from the trees. He realised he was drinking almost as much as Steve now, although it didn't seem to afford him the respite that was coming in loud snores from behind him.

Washington DC was the last place where Lynton had felt safe. That had been a mainly student gig with a fairly polite audience, all with white faces, he noted. Their playing had not quite been touched by the quicksilver magic of New York that night, but it was still enjoyable enough for them to forget their differences for the duration.

But since then…

Baltimore, the venue half empty. Norfolk, Virginia mainly hostile stares and indifference, just a handful of the local weirdos making a show of themselves in front of the stage. Steve disappearing with a couple of girls afterwards, a nervous, two-hour wait for him to get back on the bus, Nik pacing and wondering if he hadn't been mugged down some dark alley, infecting the rest of them with his fretful agitation. Steve eventually turning up arseholed, singing 'The Irish Rover', something that freaked him out when Lynton tried to joke about it the next day, because Steve couldn't remember any of it and worse than that, it was his Da's favourite song.

Tonight's gig, left four hours ago in Atlanta, had been heavier going still. Two good old boys had parked themselves right in front of Lynton, giving him knowing winks and then making gestures as if they were jerking a rope around their necks. At one time, Vince would have picked up on this, would have been down off the stage sorting them out in a second. But Vince didn't seem like he was entirely on the same stage as the rest of them. Vince was glassy-eyed and mumbling his words, tearing off his shirt and then falling over. The first beer cans had started coming their way at that point, gathering momentum as Vince staggered back to his feet and flapped his arms, shouting vague, incoherent threats. Steve had saved the day by catching a full one as it flew in an arc towards his head, then, without missing a beat, bowling it straight back over-arm to his attacker. That had raised a cheer, bought them a bit more time. Steve had seized it, deftly segueing the hideous non-version of 'The Crooked Mile' they'd been demolishing into the viperous opening chords of 'Grumble' and then, as if this ancient routine had awoken Vince from his narcotic haze, they had pulled it all back from the brink.

It was only during those fraught few minutes between disaster and redemption, when Steve searched out Lynton's eyes for support, that he had finally noticed the Dukes of Hazzard down there. In an instant, he had come over to Lynton's side of the stage to grind his Les Paul at them from his sweaty leather crotch, with his top lip curled and an expression of pure psychosis in his eyes. Pulling expressions of disgust, they'd moved away, but Lynton could still feel his heart hammering all the way out of the venue. In the car park, Earl was lounging by the bus, idly swinging a metal baseball bat. *As if he had known.*

Lynton couldn't stop his eyes from darting around the darkened lot, couldn't stop his hands from shaking until he was safely back on the bus and they were on the highway out of town.

Then it had gone into what was becoming their routine. Vince and Sylvana went immediately into the bunks at the back of the bus. Nik counted the money, doled out the PDs, put everything else in his little safe box and then retired with it clutched to his chest. Sometimes he'd try and stay up drinking with the rest of them, or sit up front and bother Earl, but not tonight. Lynton, Steve and Kevin sat around in the front with Mouse, who, as usual, was spilling over with enthusiasm to recount his Tall Tales of CBGBs.

They all liked Mouse, they really did. He seemed not to mind working his arse off for fuck-all money so long as he got to hang out with the bands he thought were cool. He was funny too, with his quickfire delivery and his pained attempts to keep his hair perfect against all the odds of his chosen profession. But none of them wanted to know about it that night. All Mouse could have heard was the continual cracking of cans being opened and Zippos clanging open and shut. In the end he'd gone up the front to sit with Earl, leaving them to their introspective misery.

Kevin was the only one who wasn't numbing himself with drink or some kind of drug, legal or otherwise. Kevin still read the local papers and fanzines he picked up wherever they went to try to get a better idea of this strange new country they were in. Kevin still got his camera out and faithfully recorded each venue and truckstop and sight of interest along the way. He still had a notebook in which he diligently wrote down notes on each gig and ideas for new songs. Lynton guessed that, unlike the rest of them, Kevin was doing this to try his best to hold on to some sanity and normality, the way he had always done.

Keep your head down, Kevin, and with luck the fists will fly above your head. He had gone to his bunk about two hours ago with the earplugs they'd been given on the plane.

Lynton and Steve had carried on ploughing their way through tonight's slab of Budweiser. 'Fucking weak, pissy, Yankee crap,' was Steve's opinion on that. 'What I wouldn't give for a decent pint of Tetley's. I tell you what, Lynt, I'd rather be back in Hull.'

Then he'd done his trick of falling asleep with the crushed can still inside his fist. He'd fallen over sideways since, into a foetal position, his Homburg hat tipped over his eyes.

Lynton wished so hard that he could sleep. He'd thought that reading might help him nod off. But maybe it had just been the wrong choice of book, Flannery O'Connor's *Wise Blood*.

The sign flashed past in the Silver Bullet's huge headlamps as Earl steered them into the next state.

The Heart of Dixie. Sweet Home Alabama.

Load in was at 4pm at Cropper's Lounge, a long, low building made out of clapboard with a big neon sign over the door, on the Southside of Birmingham. This was supposed to be the liberal side of town, where a cabal of artists and writers had set up shop in the early seventies. The youthful rebellion had slowly spread out from their revolutionary bookshops, coffee shops and bars to fashion the area into the live venue hub of the city. So Kevin informed them, as Earl drove them in from the motel on the outskirts of the city where they had been allowed to crash out for most of the day.

Lynton vaguely took in what he was saying, staring out of the window at the high ridge of the Appalachian mountains, which rose up like great, jagged giant's teeth, green and grey under the scudding clouds. They were so much bigger than any mountains he'd ever seen before that they almost looked as if they had been painted onto the sky.

He hadn't managed to sleep until they'd disembarked the Silver Bullet at four in the morning. Then, when he'd finally got a surprisingly enormous double bed in front of him, he'd crashed straight out. Luckily, Lynton got to share with Kevin on this tour; Steve was bunking in with Mouse, so he didn't have any of the usual snoring and farting to put up with. His slumbers had seemed blissful at the time, but now he felt woozy, the way you did when you'd slept through the middle of the day, and he'd woken up with the same headache, a dull fuzz in the side of his head.

Kevin had some headache pills; they came in a little plastic dispenser here like Tic-Tacs back at home and were just about as effective. Maybe what he needed was some food; they were due to get some once they turned up at the venue.

Marty Cropper, the guy who owned the bar, was obviously one of the old hippies from Kevin's guidebook. A tall, rangy man with long frizzy hair tied back into a ponytail, and a matching handlebar moustache and sideburns that had probably been bright red once, but were now softened out with an abundance of grey. He and Earl greeted each other with slaps on the back as if they were friends from way back. They certainly had the same aura about them, like two outlaw bikers who had come to heel a bit in their middle age, but not that much.

Inside Cropper's Lounge was a horseshoe bar with a seating area to the left, red leather booths around the outside, smaller, round pine tables in the middle and the obligatory pool table. Narrow and skinny from the front, it went back a long way, with a big dance floor and a wide stage beyond it, decorated with steers' horns and red velvet drapes. Psychedelic posters covered almost every wall, but there were a few more modern ones: the *London Calling* cover and *Never Mind the Bollocks*.

Lynton started to relax a bit as he looked around; this wasn't the hillbilly hellhole he had been expecting. Genial Marty ushered them into the booths, brought them pitchers of cold beer, iced water, corn chips and salsa and the menus. The freak show divided into its usual components: Vince and Sylvana sat with Nik, the rest of them took over a corner. The only difference to usual was that Earl joined them this time, when he normally ate alone.

The food came fast and the plates were piled high. Once he had half a warm, spicy burrito inside him, Lynton found he was actually enjoying himself.

'Hey Earl, you know this guy?' asked Mouse, after Marty had deposited another jug of beer and iced water and taken away the empties.

Earl, sucking the meat off a spare rib with his moustache drooping over the side, nodded his head. 'Uh-huh. We were in the Marines together.'

'No way!' said Mouse. 'That's some coincidence.'

'Not really.' Earl put the gnawed bone down and reached for a toothpick. 'We buddied up in Korea, rode together for a while after we got back. His interests have always been the same as mine, 'n' this job takes me out this way often enough.' He nodded towards Nik, sitting across the room listening avidly to whatever Sylvana was saying as he picked daintily through a salad. 'I always try and make sure if I take a band out, they play a night in this place. Marty's good people. You don't get a lot like him out these ways.'

'Where exactly you from, Earl?' Mouse continued his interview.

'Bacon County, Georgia.'

'You're shitting me?' Mouse laughed.

Earl grimaced stoically, as if he was used to this response. 'Bacon County, Georgia. You look it up on the map, dumb rodent.'

'What's it like there?' asked Steve.

'Shit,' said Earl, simply. 'Hard land, hard people. I signed up for Korea, they didn't have to come and git me. That'd tell you just about all you needed to know.'

Steve nodded admiringly. 'Right. Mebbe they should twin it with Hull, where we come from.'

'You folks all come from Shit too?' Earl let a small smile curl around his top lip. 'Well, apart from Mouse here, 'cos we all know he come from Fairyland. It ain't so bad though, is it? Think about it. If we all didn't come from Shit in the first place, we wouldn't have had nothin' to get away from.'

His words stirred something in Lynton's brain. 'That sounds like a line from that book I was reading.'

'Flannery O'Connor, yes, sir, it is,' Earl winked at him. 'I saw you reading that. That's a great piece of art, that book.'

'Get to fuck!' exploded Mouse. 'Earl's an artist and we didn't know it.'

Earl's sardonic grimace returned and he cuffed the roadie round his shaved head like a large bear might reprimand his cub. The laughter went on as Mouse rolled about in his seat, squeaking expletives and pretending to be mortally injured. Earl got to his feet, shaking his head. 'Now if you gentlemen will excuse me, I'm headed back to my bunk. I'll see y'all later.' He doffed his Stetson and turned to go, then had another thought and turned back to look at Lynton.

'You folks take my advice and make the most of ol' Marty's hospitality here tonight. There ain't nothing else worth seeing round here, you don't mind me saying.'

As he said it, that tiny worm of fear started to uncoil again in Lynton's stomach and the smile froze on his face as he watched Earl walk away.

No one else had read any other meaning into those words. They all carried on laughing and joking. He tried to push it out of his mind, reassuring himself that nothing bad could happen to him here, not in a liberal hippy place owned by an ex-Marine who could probably dismantle a redneck with his bare hands.

But that worm, it wouldn't go away. It wriggled all through soundcheck, so he had to concentrate hard on what would normally come naturally, so that he was all fingers and thumbs over the easiest of parts. It twisted and turned as they met the support band, a local three-piece called Three-Legged Dog. It wouldn't let him take in what they were playing when it was their turn to warm up, except that the singer had one of those harsh old Appalachian voices he would have expected to hear from a grizzled old man who played a banjo, not a regular-looking guy with short hair who was about twenty.

Give me a beer, the worm seemed to say to him, give me a beer and I might go away. All right, he thought. I'll make the most of ol' Marty's hospitality.

Marty's backstage spread was the best they'd ever had. More Mexican food, a bottle of tequilla and decent-looking beer called Dos Equis. Lynton started getting stuck into those, and felt an immediate relief as the first one went down. Then Vince picked up the tequilla, holding it up to the light and studying the yellow liquid. 'I've heard this is good,' he said. 'Anyone want to give it a try?'

'You wanna be careful on that,' Sylvana warned him. 'That stuff can turn you funny.'

Vince looked at her with the most disdainful expression any of them had ever seen him use on his new bride. 'Sweetheart,' he said, 'isn't it time you were powdering your nose or something?'

Lynton saw the shock and hurt bloom in her eyes. Then she meekly caved in. 'Sure, honey,' she whispered. 'I didn't mean to cramp your style.' She sat back down in the furthest corner of the room. Nik jumped up and went over to her side, started gabbling away to try and hide the embarrassment of the moment.

Vince didn't even bother to look her way. Instead, he fixed his gaze on Lynton. 'Lynton,' he said, his eyes glittering. The bleary mess who'd so nearly ruined everything the night before seemed to have vanished. In its place, spruce Vince looked razor-sharp in the Smith & Wesson T-shirt he'd picked up in a truckstop, black Sta-prest trousers and his big brothel creepers. 'You game?'

Lynton shrugged. Vince unscrewed the bottle, poured out a shot and handed it over. Then he poured one for himself and raised up his glass. 'Cheers!' he said.

Lynton sensed a challenge in Vince's eyes. The worm squirmed to rise to it. 'Cheers!' he returned. They clinked glasses and then poured the liquor down their throats.

'Wow,' Lynton licked his lips. 'That's really good.'

It was as well. The tequilla seemed to anaesthetise the worm and filled him up instead with a pleasing glow. 'Give us another one, Vince.'

After they'd downed another two, Steve grabbed the bottle out of Vince's hands.

'Give us it here, you great puff,' he said, and raised the whole thing to his lips. A second later he was coughing and spluttering. 'Fucking hell!' he said. 'That's fucking dynamite.'

The bottle had gone before the support band got onstage. Their enthusiasm for its contents seemed to wipe away all the animosity between them, and they found themselves laughing together for the first time in months. It was like Sylvana and all the rest of the baggage faded to the back of the room, out of sight, out of mind. When they heard Three-Legged Dog starting their set, Steve nodded towards the door.

'Let's go and check them out,' he said. 'They seemed like good lads.'

Out the front, the place was packed. To Lynton's relief, it all seemed to be students, hippies and a smattering of punks. They stood in front of the stage and cheered on the Dog, who played a harsh, angular type of stripped-down blues, made all the more compelling by the vocals. The tequilla making him light-headed, Lynton found his mind conjuring up all sorts of visions to that keening, hard-lived-in voice. It reminded him of Earl's Hank Williams tapes and the shapes of the mountains that surrounded this city, a voice directly descended from the Scottish crofters who'd been displaced here, bringing nothing but their songs and stories with them.

'*High and lonesome, dead and gone,*' he caught above the sound of the singer's guitar. That voice resounded with all of those qualities. Told it like it must have been a hundred years ago.

Vince, however, didn't seem quite so taken with the music as with what they'd just been drinking.

'I'm gonna find that Marty,' he declared. 'I'm gonna get us another bottle of tequilla.' And he plunged off through the crowd towards the bar.

Vince didn't return until the band had finished and Steve and Lynton had gone back into the dressing room to offer their congratulations. Lynton was really drunk now, but it was in a good way, the worm had gone and with it, the sense of disorientation. Now he felt like he could strap on his bass and play note perfect, that he'd left all his fears behind in the bottom of that yellow bottle. He'd been wrong about tonight, it was going to be the best gig of the tour, the one that brought them all back together.

Then Vince came through the door.

'Did you not find Marty, then?' Steve clocked his empty hands.

'I've just seen something I shouldn't have seen,' said Vince.

'You what?' Steve frowned. 'You been doing drugs or summat?'

'No,' Vince screwed up his brow. 'I wish I had.'

'Then what's up with yer?'

At that moment, Marty's head came round the door. 'Five minutes, folks, if you'd be so kind,' he said.

'Look…' Vince started, looked at Lynton and then stopped. 'Look, it's nothing. My lovely wife was right. That stuff really does fuck with your head. Come on, let's do it.'

'Is everything OK?' asked Kevin, wandering up with his hands taped and his drumsticks at the ready.

Lynton looked at Vince's face. He wasn't bullshitting. Something had happened to him out there. But he couldn't think about that, or that worm would come back. He had to keep it together and play this gig.

'Yeah, yeah,' Vince waved him off.

'All right then.' Kevin looked at Lynton. 'Our usual?'

Lynton nodded, felt the sweat break out on the back of his neck. His bass was waiting for him on the left hand of the stage. He just had to walk out there and get it.

His legs felt wobbly as he picked his way across the stage, but the bass felt safe in his hands. He wouldn't look, he would just do it. *Safe. Easy*. The first notes, deep and heavy, plucked their way out of his fingers and his body started to sway with them, let them take him. He heard Kevin come in behind him, brushing across the top of his drums.

Yeah, you hillbillies, he thought, you've heard your music, now you can hear mine.

Kevin's drumbeats built up, slow and mesmerising, the two of them locked in their own voodoo. All he had to do was keep looking down, not out at the audience. From his right, Steve's guitar slashed across their rhythm and he heard a cheer go up from the crowd. Keep looking down, Lynton, keep it together.

Then Vince was right beside him, closer than he should be, his elbow pressed against his shoulder, raising his mic up. *'I am the king of this wasteland!'* he howled. *'I am the king of nothing!'* Then he was down on his haunches, leaning forward right into the crowd.

Lynton couldn't help it. He saw the motion out of the corner of his eye. It was like some strange, slow-motion action replay of their first ever gig, the time when Gary Dunton came steaming through the crowd with his moronic mates in tow. Only this time, what was headed their way looked a whole lot bigger and more horrible than those schoolyard tyrants.

He saw a big, sweaty moon face and piggy little eyes that were black holes of hatred boring into Vince. He saw the red mouth opening and the words that formed on its lips: *'Nigger lover.'*

His stomach did a double flip and he involuntarily stepped backwards, looked sideways, saw Steve with his head tipped back, lost in the moment; saw Sylvana behind him at the side of the stage, staring at Vince as if her heart was breaking; then saw the bottle of beer fly through the air and go smashing right into the singer's face.

Vince fell backwards, his hands splaying out sideways, his eyes rolling back in his head. Sylvana started screaming.

Everything seemed to happen in slow motion after that. Like two sharks scenting blood, Marty and Earl finned through the crowd towards the pudgy-faced assailant, who was whooping with delight at his direct hit. A couple of Marty's ex-biker bouncers came up behind him and he soon wasn't smiling any more as he was hoisted out of there bellowing, the crowd parting to let the procession through.

Steve was down on his knees beside Vince, who had got up onto his elbows and was staring around in disbelief. The bottle that had hit him had been full, so it hadn't broken against his skin but bounced off onto the stage and smashed, showering the singer in glass and foam. Nik appeared to be holding back a hysterical-looking Sylvana at the side of the stage, while Mouse and Steve hauled Vince to his feet. He swayed there for a moment and the crowd whooped in approval.

Either he looked worse than he felt or the cheers had brought him back with a bang. He raised his hands up in his preacher's pose, acknowledging his audience's support, then turned towards Steve and whispered something in his ear. Grinning from ear to ear, the guitarist stepped forwards towards his own mic and said: 'Thank you, everyone. We'd like to remind you all, these boots kill fascists.'

Another huge cheer and Steve started playing the first chords of 'Dead Loss', the song they had written in 1977, about Dunton and his friends.

Lynton shook his head, trying to clear the image of the redneck from his brain, trying to remember how the song went as Kevin picked up the beat behind him. It was hardly likely anyone in the audience knew this song at all, but they were so behind the band now that they virtually erupted.

Steve keeps deliberately going back in time, Lynton realised. He thinks it will make things better.

But it didn't work for Lynton. As much as he could see everyone else getting off on it, the rest of the gig seemed like a dream. It was almost as if he was standing outside himself, while the musician part of him played on as if on autocue. But he couldn't feel anything.

All he could see was that pudgy white face of hatred. And those words: *Nigger lover. Nigger lover.* He couldn't feel anything for the music any more – even as Vince threw himself into the welcoming arms of the crowd and was borne aloft like their new messiah, lying on top of outstretched hands, watching his own band as he sang. Even as the crowd begged three encores out of the band, passing up beers they had bought themselves to urge them on.

Even when it was over, and Marty was laying on more beers backstage, apologising for the bottle-chucker, explaining that he tried to run a clean place without any of that scum getting in, but he hadn't known the guy's face or he never would have got past the door.

Earl had enjoyed taking the man down and throwing him out. He was delighted that the band had responded the way they did, particularly Steve, who he kept clinking bottles with and declaring: 'Like I said, it's good to come from Shit.'

It had all been quite a laugh for Steve and Vince. Even Kevin was knocking back the Dr Pepper with a grin. They had triumphed over adversity and now they were all slapping each other on the back and congratulating each other. They were all right.

All white.

But not Lynton. There was a hollowness inside him that separated him from all the others. They couldn't begin to understand the way he felt. But there was one thing he still desperately needed to know.

'What was it you saw?' he asked Vince, two nights later, as they rolled through another night towards Memphis, Tennessee.

Vince raised his eyebrows. 'When I went up to the bar,' he

said, 'that fat guy was standing there staring at me. I asked him what his problem was and he just smiled. There was a little pool of spilt beer just beside him on the bar, and he put his finger in it and drew the letters KKK. Then he wiped it away and smiled at me again. I thought he was just trying to fuck with my head…'

'But now he's gone and fucked with mine.' Lynton put his head in his hands.

'Vince,' he said, hearing the words spilling out of his mouth without even meaning to say them. 'I don't know how I'm going to get through the rest of this tour.'

Vince put a gentle hand on his shoulder. 'I know a way,' he said.

31

Teenage Nightingales to Wax

June 2002

I stood at the bottom of the Trellick Tower, looking for the right buzzer. Funny how Gavin had thought Donna had disappeared off the face of the earth, when she had been just around the corner from him all along. And in West London's most newly-fashionable address too.

I'd always thought the Trellick was a bit of a monstrosity myself, apparently Ian Fleming had too – naming one of his most famous villains after its architect, Erno Goldfinger. But the Trustafari had been paying up to a third of a million quid for some of the flats up here, ever since the council had let them be tarted-up and flogged off with a nice concierge service installed to boot. Despite the fact that the building was still circled by little hooligans on stolen bicycles trying to sell you: 'Rocks, hasish, coke', and a housing estate that rattled and boomed to the sound of about ten different pirate radio stations. Apparently the views were just amazing. Well, I'd soon find out.

As per Ray's instructions, I'd come alone, at three o'clock on a Tuesday afternoon. The concierge was giving me sideways glances, even though I'd shown him some ID, a bit tetchy about his gated community in the sky. But finally, I found the right bell.

Donna's voice on the intercom sounded as I had imagined: flat and sardonic. 'Thirteenth floor, love,' she rasped. 'And that ain't a joke. You have to get out of the lift on the twelfth and walk along the balcony, take the first set of stairs going up on your right.' I wondered, as I whooshed up the lift, if her face would look as hard as she sounded.

It was a fairly complicated set-up, the Trellick. The lifts only went to every third floor, so you had to walk the rest. I could imagine how scary the long, grim corridors would have been in the days when the GLC owned the building and heroin addicts supposedly laid in wait to mug you in the side rooms Goldfinger had envisioned being used as macramé workshops. They were all locked up now. There was no one about as I made my way to Donna's door.

There was a rattling of locks and chains as she opened up. It sounded like she could remember those bad old days only too well but I was on edge myself, wondering what kind of fright her appearance would give me. Finally, the door opened a crack and she stood there, leaning against the frame, staring at me with eyes so dark they looked like they were all pupil.

Ray had told me she was half-Spanish; her mother's folks had been evacuated here like many others during the war, when Tommy needed the Rock of Gibraltar to shield Europe. It had given her that black hair and strong, handsome face. Now there didn't seem to be much left of either.

Her hair was clipped short, probably only a number three or four all over. It was iron-grey, flecked with white in big patches around the sides and on the top. Her face had that strange, bloated and drained look that many eighties casualties seemed to have been left with, as if all their cheekbones had collapsed into saggy half moons and all the nutrients had been sucked out of their skin. Though to her credit, unlike Boy George and

Steve Strange, Donna hadn't tried to plaster over her crumbling architecture with a cement mixer full of foundation and black eyeliner. In fact, she didn't seem to be wearing any make-up at all, which, combined with her buzzcut, gave her the look of an aged Greenham Common protester. She certainly didn't look like the madwoman of legend, but neither did she look much like her former self.

The only thing left of beauty were those huge, black, Spanish eyes. Which were travelling up and down me with a most insouciant glint in them. 'Hmmm,' she said, raising one eyebrow and a slight smile. 'Anyone ever tell you, you look like Dave Vanian?'

I felt myself blushing. 'No, I, er, can't say they have,' I blurted. 'Do I?'

'Yes,' she said, looking pleased, drawing back the door properly. She was shorter than I'd expected; her body a well-rounded figure of eight shrouded in black like a proper ex-goth Spanish Mama. A voluminous long black T-shirt on the top half, ankle-length skirt on the bottom and an incongruous pair of pink fluffy slippers sticking out at the bottom. Yet again, though, there were faint traces of the old Donna in the thick, twisted silver torque around her neck and long, dangling earrings.

'So you're Eddie, are you?' she said, offering a hand that was perfectly manicured, albeit with black nail varnish, and adorned with a heavy silver ring on each finger, silver and turquoise bangles rattling on her wrist. 'You'd better come in then.'

Her hallway was dark after the brightness of outside, painted purple, with nothing but a coat-stand and a telephone table in it. Donna's slippers made a gentle slapping noise as she walked ahead of me, her ample rear swinging from left to right. 'This way, love,' she said, opening the door ahead of us.

Expecting an altogether more goth interior, I stood on the threshold in shock. Donna's front room was amazing. A vast panorama of London stretched out in front of me, as far as the eye could see, and all at once I understood the Trustafarian lust for the place. Not just the view, but old Goldfinger's brutalist glass, steel and blond wood interior, which looked like it had hardly been changed, only added to by Donna's own shockingly suave pieces. A huge red leather sofa on chrome legs that faced out towards the window, with two smaller ones at each side. A black Japanese lacquer table between them, with one of those long, black and white glass sixties ashtrays that looked like shapes made by the inside of a lava lamp poised at an angle on top. A miniature palm tree in a round black pot by the door that led out onto her balcony. Every surface shining and pristine.

'Wow!' I said involuntarily.

'Yeah,' said Donna. 'It ain't bad, is it? It was a bit of a shock to me the first time too.'

'Did you buy this place then?' I couldn't stop myself from asking.

'Nah,' Donna shook her head. 'Believe it or not, I inherited it. The only decent thing my old man ever done for me was pop off right when they turned this place around.' She smiled grimly. 'S'ironic, really. You couldn't get me near the place for donkey's. The Tower of Terror they used to call it, and they weren't joking, it was like *Dawn of the Dead* round here.' She nodded to herself. 'Anyway, Eddie, can I get you a drink? Tea, coffee, orange juice? Or you can have something stronger if you like. I don't indulge myself any more, but I always keep some in for them what do.'

Well, I was still a bit nervous of her, so I started on coffee, but I couldn't help thinking that Donna didn't seem to be mad at all. Granted, she looked like she'd lived a life and a half, but all the apprehensions I'd had about her living in a smelly flat full of cats and crystal balls vanished in the afternoon sun that poured through her window. She did quiz me about how I knew Ray, but we'd already sorted that one out in advance. We'd met at a record company party and I, being an old music paper junkie, had recognised his name and come over all the adoring fan. Flattered, he'd kept in touch ever since.

'You should be interviewing Ray for this feature and all,' she said, with surprising loyalty. 'He was by far the best punk journalist. He was the one who went to all the gigs, the one the bands all wanted to give their demo tapes to. But he's the only one that hasn't gone on to make a living from pedalling the same old phony punk war stories over and over again. Shame, ain't it? I'd far rather look at him on those bloody nostalgia programmes than poncey Paul Morley droning on and on or even worse, that wanker Garry Bushell.'

She was surprisingly funny too. I really found myself warming to her, imagining how Ray must have fallen for her, this mouthy punk Eliza Doolittle. Strangely, as the afternoon progressed and she kept up her steady flow of amusing anecdotes, I even started to realise what the physical attraction was too. Her face got better, the more you looked at it, the more animated and alive it became as she told her stories – which were studded with outrageously libellous insults and blackmail stories on just about everyone from the punk scene you could think of.

And, as much as I tried to keep such thoughts from my head, you could tell what she must have once been like – a bit naughty, a bit *dirty*, a wink and a promise on those arched eyebrows like she could do you like you'd never been done before.

But after we'd spent three hours reliving all the highs of her youth, I knew that we were heading towards the inevitable low, the unhappy ending, at speed. When we'd got to the point when she realised Sylvana was getting beaten up by Robin on a regular basis, her demeanour changed, the light slowly drained out of her face, and she played with her rings and ruffled her spiky head continually.

'Bad times,' she said, staring off into space. I thought I was going to lose her then, but she made an effort, pulled herself back from it.

'Look,' she said, 'do you want another drink?' She obviously needed to do something with her hands. 'Another coffee? Or do you want a beer or something? Sun's over the yard arm now, Eddie.'

Why not, I thought, I could do with a bit of Dutch courage myself now. She seemed a lot happier when I accepted her offer, brought a cold bottle of Grolsch back from her fridge and watched me pour it into a glass with an expression of near contentment.

'I only keep the good stuff in, Eddie. I've always tried to live that way,' she said and then sighed. 'I suppose you know how it all went for me, did Ray tell you?'

'You don't have to talk about it if you don't want to,' I said, giving her my most sympathetic eyes, while desperately hoping she'd still spill.

She ruffled her hair again, tucked her legs up underneath her and hugged her knees. 'There ain't a lot to say, really. My band split up, my business went to the wall, I ended up in a psychiatric unit for six months and then in and out of them places for the next five years. No one wanted to know me then, I can assure you. Ray's the only person from them years what did anything for me in the bad times.' She couldn't stop the bitterness from giving her voice an edge as she said this. She blinked hard, turning her head to look out of the window for a moment, before turning back to me.

'And as you can see, the medication they put me on ain't done wonders for my looks over the years. It keeps you calm but it bloats you out at the same time – so, you get your mind back, but not your body, not your face. I think it horrifies people to see that, you know. Too much of a reminder of their own mortality, I s'pose. I was beautiful once, Eddie. You probably wouldn't credit it to look at me now…'

'Don't say that,' I said, and actually I meant it. 'You've done one helluva lot better than some of the people I've met—' I stopped myself then, just before the words came tumbling out that would have thrown mine and Ray's carefully constructed plan into jeopardy '—doing this feature,' I finished.

'Yeah well,' Donna shrugged, 'I expect most of them got that way doing illegal drugs. I'm the only one who was forced to take legal ones. Ironic, ain't it?'

'Considering how much you did achieve, though,' I said, trying to wing the conversation round from anything else that might slip me up, 'weren't you ever tempted to go back in to management, or PR or something?'

She gave me a look as if I was the one on medication.

'Management? PR? I was a punk, Eddie, for fack's sake. Not some big business flunky. It did use to mean something, then... But by the time I was finally well enough to face the world again, it weren't a place I understood no more. You think about it – and you can shove this in your piece, it'll give you some perspective – it only took ten years from Johnny Rotten singing 'God Save The Queen' to them load of rock star ponces doing facking Live Aid. I mean,' she rolled her eyes, 'Bob *facking* Geldof. Do you know what I mean? From the shittest Johnny-come-lately punk band there ever was to the Jesus of the Jet Set. What a player. What a rotter. What a facking *cahnt*.'

The way she said it made me laugh so hard I had tears in my eyes. Donna liked this. I could tell by the way she twirled a few more insults in Geldof's direction, delivering them like an out-take from *Derek & Clive Ad Nauseam*.

'More tea, vicar?' she asked, picking up my empty bottle.

As she sashayed back off to her fridge, I found I could hardly keep my eyes off her arse. Pull yourself together, Eddie! I told myself. This woman looks like an old, shaved lesbian. You can't possibly fancy her. Think of England! I managed to think of another question by the time she returned. 'But haven't you noticed how fashionable early eighties music is nowadays? Every time I turn on Jools Holland he's got some new bunch of pale-faced twats with Mohicans sounding like a cross between Gang of Four, The Cure and The Bunnymen. Weren't you ever tempted to re-release the Mood Violet back catalogue on CD? Surely you could make a fortune off of that nowadays.'

Donna sat back on the sofa with a huge sigh, rubbing her forehead. 'Yeah,' she said. 'You would think so, wouldn't you? But it ain't that easy. That band were facking cursed, Eddie. They curse me to this day.'

It was like a sudden stormcloud had descended into the middle of that sunny evening. Donna shook her head, stood up and walked over to the window.

I was bewildered. 'What do you mean?' I said, following her.

She stood with her back to me, gazing down on West London, her fingers twisting over her silver rings. 'Thing is,' she said without turning round. 'I don't actually own the rights to Mood Violet's back catalogue. I had a secret business partner, you see. He fronted me the money and in return, he got to earn a certain percentage back from their records, whereas I just got a cut off the tour and the swag.'

She turned around and her black eyes were strained, fearful. 'I shouldn't be telling you this, Eddie. Even Ray don't know nuffink about it. Talking about old times has loosened my tongue and that ain't good.' She shivered despite the heat, wrapped her arms around herself.

'Look,' I said, 'I'll turn off the tape recorder. I doubt it's even caught any of this conversation from here, but you can rest assured, I won't put anything into this feature you don't want. You've been very kind to give me so much of your time today as it is. If you want me to go now, I fully understand.'

'Nah, nah, it's not that. Please, don't take offence, Eddie. Sit down and finish your beer. Only, if you don't mind,' she nodded towards my dictaphone, 'keep that thing off for now.'

She came and sat back down again, but she was still agitated. I could have called it a day then and left with a bit of character for the book that it would have been the poorer without. But I didn't want to stop there. I wanted to know why she was in that photograph with Vince and I had a feeling we might be teetering on the verge of it. Something else too. I had started to care about what had happened to Donna. Despite what everyone had said about her, I had started to like her.

'I shouldn't do this,' she said. 'But could I ponce one of your fags?'

'Of course.' I passed the packet over and she took one out, lit it hurriedly and inhaled as if her life depended on it. Then she started coughing, ended up laughing.

'Facking hell,' she said. 'You're bringing out all of my dark side, Eddie.' She looked me up and down slyly. 'It's 'cos you look too much like Dave Vanian. I used to fancy him something rotten.'

Whatever it takes, I thought, although I had to admit, I was still getting a bit of an embarrassing stir myself. 'Did you ever make his acquaintance?' I asked, raising one eyebrow in the Roger Moore fashion that Louise had once amused me with.

She laughed a bit more, then shook her head, stubbing the half-smoked fag out in the ashtray so hard it snapped in half. 'Nah,' she said. 'More's the pity, he was a proper gent by all accounts, was Vanian. Nah. Muggins here ended up with the booby prize to end 'em all. Not that I thought so at the time, of course. I thought I'd snagged the facking Prince of Darkness, I did. Thought he was a facking prince an' all. Trouble was, so did everyone else.'

I did my best to look puzzled.

'As you probably know from your punk studies,' she said, 'Mood Violet fucked up because my singer, dear little Sylvana, ran off with big bad Vincent Smith.'

I nodded, trying to keep the excitement from shining through into my eyes.

'Yeah? Well, what you don't know was that at the time that happened, for my sins, I was facking the wanker myself. What a facking carve-up that was.' She shook her head, then looked me straight in the eye and said: 'If you want a real facking story,

Eddie, you should write something about him. You could write a whole book about his exploits.'

The next second seemed to take a million years. I could feel a lump rising in my throat and a slight loosening at the other end of my abdomen while those black eyes held mine in a steady, unblinking gaze.

Shit, she can't know, I told myself furiously. How could she know? Keep that smile on your face Eddie, prove to her you're a stand-up guy.

Then she shook her head and laughed. 'Nah, scratch that. It wouldn't be a very smart idea to go sniffing down that alley.'

'Oh,' I tried to regain my composure, 'why is that then?'

'Because,' Donna leaned back in her seat, 'everyone who's ever got near him is either mad, lost or dead and in some people's cases probably all three. Like Robin. I mean, as I said to you before, I don't even know where he ended up and I suppose I was lucky in comparison – at least I had proper *psychiatric care*,' she pronounced the last two words with deep sarcasm. 'But he had that effect on people, did Vince. He really was in a league of his own.'

'So how come you fell for him?' I ventured.

'It's took me a long time to work that out,' she said, playing with one of her rings. 'But what I finally realised was, Vince was the ultimate addiction. 'Cos I didn't have any before I met him – I was careful not to. But he worked out what my weakness was without me even knowing that I had one. Then, over a period of months, he exploited it, until I was totally dependent on it. When he knew I was, he took it away. With most people, it was drugs. That was what he worked on his band, his hangers-on, silly little Sylvana. But with me, Eddie, with me it was love.'

She looked so vulnerable when she said it, so little and alone, I felt a real stab of pity for her.

'I would have followed that wanker to the ends of the earth,' she went on, 'despite the fact he'd ruined my whole life for me, as casual as you like. The first time they let me out of that funny farm, I was probably more mad than when I went in. See all these white patches here?' She pointed to the sides of her head. 'That's from pulling all my hair out when he ran off with Sylvana. I had to learn to curb that sort of behaviour or they never would have let me see daylight again. So the first thing I learned was be sneaky. I needed to be an' all, I'd made so many enemies by then. But I found out where he was. With Sylvana gone, I stupidly thought I could get him to come back to me. You'd have thought I'd have learned my lesson by then, wouldn't you? But nah. I had to go to Paris incognito in a stupid blonde wig and make a right fool of myself all over again. He done a bunk after that, did his disappearing act what you've probably heard about. But Vince was too much of an arsehole to leave it like that with me.' She shook her head. 'I'm sorry, Eddie, I'm ranting, nasty habit of mine I will admit up to. D'you want another beer?'

By then I would have agreed to anything. Anything to keep her on this story. Anything to get her to the end of it. I tried to stop my left foot from bouncing up and down as she went back to the fridge. Looked at the nuclear sunset instead. The Trustafari were right, you got a fucking amazing view from the Trellick. All of West London disappearing in a molten haze of orange and red. Skies like you wouldn't believe.

'What were we supposed to be talking about?' she asked as she came back.

'I'm not sure myself,' I laughed. 'Blimey, Donna. It's like an acid trip, that sunset.' I knew I was talking shit, but I thought if I did, she might get bored and go back to the story.

'I wouldn't know,' she said, 'I've never done one.'

'Neither have I,' I admitted, 'but that's how I'd imagine it to be.'

And I wasn't imagining her sitting down a bit closer to me.

'Ah, that wanker Vince. Nah, you don't wanna know about him.' She shook her head and I knocked back half the beer virtually in one, forgetting even to pour it in the glass. My head was starting to swim. Donna looked at me with that glint in her eye again, like she'd had at the front door.

'Do you know how I cured myself, Eddie?' she asked. I shook my head, wiped my lips with my cuff. 'There was only two things I was ever good at, you know, and I realised I'd have to use at least one of them to survive on me own. First one was hairdressing. Well, why would I bother to do that, I was bored to tears with it as a teenager. Silly cows coming in with their little pictures of Farrah Fawcett-Majors or Debbie Harry, thinking you could do their face for 'em while you were at it. Then getting all upset afterwards when they still looked ugly. Fack that for a game of soldiers. I just do me own hair now, clip it all off like a man. I can't kid myself I'll ever be beautiful again, and after all, a fat lot of good it did me in the first place.'

Her eyes were fierce now and my knees were turning to jelly. Her left breast was perilously close to the side of my face and the room was far too hot.

'So what do you do?' I uttered weakly.

'I put on a wig,' she said, 'strap myself into a corset and beat the living shit out of silly little men.'

That should have been enough to see me out of the door and out of that tower like a streak of greased weasel shit. But as the words left Donna's mouth, I found myself with an enormous hard-on. The next thing I knew, her hand was on top of it, and she was leaning over me saying, 'Thing is, Eddie, I kind of miss having a normal fuck. Especially with a man what looks like Dave Vanian.'

And all those months of loneliness, all those nights of crying over Louise, all those stories of Vince and Sylvana and Steve and Donna and Helen and Allie, they all swirled round in my head like a rush of mad voodoo and all I wanted was her mouth over mine and my cock inside her and her huge tits right in my face and her huge arse right on top of me, grinding me into her red leather sofa while the sun set in a blaze behind us, all of West London aflame, coming into the lava flow of that sky and her thighs.

And then I must have passed out because the next thing I knew the room was dark and I was lying on the sofa with my flies open and a horrible cold mess congealing on my belly. Donna was sitting next to me, calmly smoking one of my cigarettes.

'You all right now, love?' she said as she saw me open my eyes. 'The bathroom's back through the hallway, on the left. I think you probably need to clean up a bit.'

My head was hammering like I'd downed a vat of beer, not just three, or was it four bottles? I tried to piece together what terrible spell she must have cast over me for it to end up like this as I staggered to my feet and made tenuous steps towards her bathroom. All I could think was, thank God she didn't turn the light on, as I really, really didn't want to see what I had just done.

Her bathroom was as stark as the front room. Everything chrome, everything spotless. In her mirror, my face looked a hundred years old. I tried not to heave as I patted down the mess on my shirt with some toilet paper, shoved everything back where it properly belonged. I splashed more cold water on my face, tried to bring myself back to my senses, knowing only now that the main thing was to get out of here.

Donna had put a low wattage lamp on when I finally picked my way back to the front room. It cast her in a better light than I had expected.

'I've called you a cab,' she said kindly. 'My usual firm, they won't be long and they won't charge you much either.'

I felt a wave of nausea as she said the word 'charge', but I fought it down, I really didn't want to piss her off now. Though on the contrary, Donna was looking pretty pleased with herself.

'I remembered what we were supposed to be talking about,' she said, as I gingerly sat back down, noting that my dicataphone was still where I had left it and my bag didn't appear to have been disturbed.

'Oh?' I said, doing my best to smile.

'You wanted to know about Vince, didn't you?' she said. 'I was telling you how he wouldn't let it finish with me, weren't I?'

I just nodded. I had no idea now where she would go next.

'Yeah,' she said. 'After he did his big disappearing act, he kept sending me postcards. Just so as he could keep me under his thumb, just so I could never keep my head straight. First it was from Marseilles. Then it was Tangiers. Travelled around a bit, I can tell you, but he always wanted me to know how well he was doing for himself, how happy he was that I wasn't with him.'

She was smiling a strange, glassy smile. I wondered if her medication was starting to wear off, but perhaps she really was just grateful for a clumsy fuck with someone who reminded her of her youthful crush.

'Seville was the next place,' she went on. 'He thought he had it good there for a while. But then it all went quiet for a few years so I thought he must have got nicked or something, 'bout facking time an' all. But that weren't it. Nah. He found a better place. A place where no one knew him from Adam; a place where he could run things without the law bothering him or nuffink. A place,' she snapped her fingers and her bangles jangled at her wrist, 'where they do all their living by night. Do you want to know where that place is, Eddie? All them people think he's been dead all this time, but he ain't. If only they knew.'

She gave a hollow laugh. I would have thought that she was mad, that she had just been playing with me all afternoon and evening if it wasn't for the fact that, thanks to Joe Pascal, I knew she wasn't lying. Then she looked at me sadly. 'He's in Lisbon, Eddie. That's what you wanted to know.'

The buzzer rang loudly, cutting through the sound of my jaw dropping.

'And that'll be your cab.' She stood up. 'You got all your stuff?'

'Er, yes, yes, thank you.' I stuffed my tape recorder back into my bag, made a quick rummage through my pockets as she walked ahead of me towards the front door. Everything was exactly where it should have been.

She picked up the intercom. 'He'll be down in a second,' she said into it, then turned to me. 'Where to?' she asked.

'Camden,' I said, my mind reeling too much to even think to make up an alternative.

'Camden,' she told the cabbie, then replaced the receiver.

'Well, I hope you got everything you came for.' Donna opened the front door and stood aside to let me pass.

There wasn't an answer to that, so I didn't give one. Instead, I offered her my hand. 'Thanks, Donna,' I said as she took it.

'Eddie,' she said as I stepped into the hallway.

I looked back into her black Spanish eyes.

'Safe home,' she said and closed the door.

I don't remember the journey home, or stumbling into my bed. The next thing I knew was the phone was ringing, my head was splitting and the clock by my bed said the time was half-past ten. For a moment I couldn't think where I was or what I was doing. But then, as the answerphone clicked on, I was given an all too clear reminder.

'Eddie,' came Ray's voice. 'I'm just checking to see if you're all right. Blimey, mate, I don't know what you did to please Donna, but she thinks you're the best thing since sliced bread. I've just had her on the phone singing your praises. You're lucky you're not twenty years older, mate, or I'd be seriously worried about your chances. Anyway, give us a ring when you get the chance. Ta-ra.'

Donna. Jesus. I clasped my hand to my aching head as it all flooded back to me. I fucked Donna.

I felt sordid and sick inside. How had she beguiled me that way? Had I wanted to get into this story so badly that I literally had to go where Vince had been? Had I been chasing the *Time Out* vamp with the chopsticks in her hair or had her fried remains been trying to resurrect her own youth via some infernal sex magick when we did what we did? Either way, it was an unholy communion.

And yet…I dimly realised from what Ray had just said that she hadn't told him about it. And more than that.

She had told me where Vince was.

That thought propelled me out of bed. Yesterday's clothes were all over the floor in a mess. I dumped them in the already overflowing laundry basket and made straight for the shower. Ten minutes of alternate hot and cold blasts of that and I'd cleared my head and rid my body of any faint, lingering aromas of last night's performance. Now wasn't the time to dwell on that. Now was the time to work out how to tell Gavin I'd come about this information.

I thought, as I put the kettle on and poured Crunchy Nut cornflakes into a bowl, I'd have to be a bit careful about what I said to him. I didn't want him to know I'd seen Donna. Perhaps Monsieur Pascal could be of assistance.

I poured cold milk over the cereal, moved over to the Mac, powered it up and stood there in my dressing gown, rapidly filling my face and working out what to say. Pascal was old school. Blokes of his generation could generally be relied upon to be discreet.

As soon as I was up and online, I had it. I wrote:

Dear Joseph, I've had a bit of a tip-off about Vince Smith. Now, the person who told me did so in strict confidence and I'm not altogether sure if they're not just a random nutter, but they seemed to know enough to convince me this is worth a try. For instance, they knew about Marseilles and Seville and confirmed he had been in Tangiers, as you suspected. Only could we please keep the information between ourselves, and if anything comes of it, tell the others it came from one of your comrades? It's just to protect my source, as all good journalists must.

I sent that little beauty off, wondering what else I could tell Gavin if Pascal didn't have any snouts in Lisbon. In the meantime, I called Ray, assured him that everything had gone well and proceeded to laugh off the source of Donna's enthusiasm for my good self through gritted teeth. 'She kept saying I looked like Dave Vanian,' I told him.

'That'll be it!' he said. 'Course. I'm not too on the ball, am I? I hadn't noticed it myself, but I suppose there is a bit of a resemblance. Well, enough for her fevered brain anyway. She always was obsessed with Vanian.'

'Well, she was very complimentary about you,' I told him, trying to change the subject. 'She said you were the best punk journalist of them all and I should be writing about you.'

'Yeah, well,' Ray brushed the compliment off. 'We'll see. She's being nice for now, but we'd better hope she hasn't developed too much of a crush on you, *Dave*...'

'Yeah, yeah.' It was just as well he couldn't see me squirming in my chair.

By the time he'd rung off, Pascal was flashing in my inbox:

```
Let me assure you any information you give me will be treated in the strictest confidence. I understand perfectly that you need to protect your source and compliment you on finding one so quickly. You must be quite a detective yourself!
```

Well I was beginning to think so. I replied:

```
Thanks Joseph I didn't doubt your discretion. My source—
```

I liked that word, made me sound like a professional, not someone who went round shagging mentally ill, middle-aged dominatrices

```
—said that they had heard from him recently and that he was living
```

```
in Lisbon. If you know of anyone there, maybe they could take a
look around. I have no idea if he's still using the Dawson alias,
but from what I can gather he's still involved in some kind of
drugs thing.
```

Pascal thought he might have a friend of a friend in Lisbon. By the time I had finished the morning's correspondence with him, last night's hangover had all but disappeared in the rush of anticipation. So what if I had done something slightly unsavoury to get the information I needed, I told myself. I'd still got it. And by Christ, if we found Vince, then this book would be heading for the top of the bestseller lists. They could make a documentary out of it, or a film. Even, maybe, I'd win some prizes for it, like I'd dreamed way back in cold November on Gavin's couch.

I supposed I could start work on Donna's tapes, get it out of the way as fast as possible, keep moving on while I waited to see what Joseph could find. At least I knew I'd stopped recording well before all that stuff had happened that I didn't want to think about. And in the run up to that, it had been mostly gossip, if I remembered rightly. The things I had really needed to know I didn't need a tape recorder for.

I rummaged around in my bag and found the dictaphone, and with it that *Camden New Journal* from the train back from Guildford. Hmmm, I thought, this could be interesting, I was more in the mood for that kind of shit now. Eddie Bracknell, Ace Detective, in his secret hideout overlooking the Murder Capital of Britain. That would be a few moments distraction before I got down to Donna's dirty laundry.

I got myself another coffee and a packet of digestives and sat down to read it. There had indeed been a hefty upswing in the murders around these parts, hardly surprising when you took a look outside at some of the citizens of the parish. Some of the crimes were pretty gruesome. Bodies in carrier bags shoved into wheelie bins. Bodies in suitcases thrown into Regent's Canal. A lot of stabbings, gang warfare the police reckoned, to control the drugs racket, but some of them just stupid après-pub bust-ups or crack addict muggings gone wrong. Even a couple of drive-by shootings, proper South Central Los Angeles behaviour.

They'd written a list of everyone who'd been murdered between Camden, Chalk Farm and Kentish town in the past six months. My eyes trailed down the list. And my blood turned to ice.

January 12: A man's body found under a bridge over the Canal between Oval Road and Regent's Park. Slumped against the wall, he had been dead for at least twenty-four hours when a concerned passer-by realised he was not simply sleeping or inebriated. The pathologist subsequently found heavy trauma to the back of the skull, made by a blow with a hammer or similar blunt instrument. An emaciated homeless itinerant and heavy drug user, the man was identified through his dental records as Robin Gordon Leith.

'I took care of that thing for you,' I heard Christophe say, loud as a bell in my head. Christophe, sitting by the fire in the Lord Stanley, surrounded by smoke, looking supremely contented, like he'd just had himself a fine meal. Christophe of whom I'd heard so little from recently. Christophe who was so sure my problems with Leith were over.

Because he knew for sure. 'He won't be bothering you again, believe me.'

Eddie Bracknell, Ace Detective, shagger of middle-aged dominatrices and keeper of the secrets of the dead, presides in his secret hideout in the Murder Capital of Britain, himself an accessory to murder.

32

Wait For the Blackout

May 1981

Steve sat backstage at the Lyceum Ballroom, staring through rather than looking at the copy of *Sounds* in his hands. That record that had nearly killed them to make, that Lynton had so cryptically titled 'Butcher's Brew', was number 25 in the actual charts. Tonight's gig had sold out within a day of the tickets going on sale. It seemed the Great British Public had missed Blood Truth while they'd been away, couldn't wait to have them back.

Tony had been equally moved. He'd got them all separate flats, with fixed low rents, from some mate of his who had a few coming up in Ladbroke Grove all of a sudden. Couldn't have them working and sleeping in the studio now, could he? How thoughtful. Steve now had a flat of his own with plenty of space, no need to share, no need to worry about the pigs or the neighbours. Welcome home, lads.

But Steve didn't feel welcome, or popular, or vindicated. He felt bereft.

He'd lost Lynton in America, back in the Deep South somewhere. He had a suspicion it was en route to Memphis, which would have made it just perfect for Vince. The birthplace of the King and Lynton's heroin addiction. For the first time since they'd met, Lynton had shut Steve out. The trio that had been united on their way out to the States were now splintered. Steve had spent the last two weeks on the Silver Bullet almost exclusively talking to Mouse and Earl, trying to figure out what had happened, what he'd done wrong. Kevin had just kept his head in a book, ignoring everything else between one venue and the next. Steve couldn't blame him for that. Swotty Kevin Holme always kept his head down.

But Steve had been hurt, hurt to the core. Every time he tried to start a conversation, Lynton brushed him off and turned his back on him. Every time Steve sat down next to him, Lynton went to the back of the bus, to Vince and his silly American bitch. Their last dates had been horrible, messy disasters. He hadn't even bothered to play the right songs, had deliberately gone off into a world of his own just to fuck the rest of them off. Blood Truth were just sport for the audiences who bothered to turn up, target practice for lobbing beer cans. Steve didn't blame them either.

The only good thing that had come out of the whole, horrible mess was meeting Earl. Earl had seen what was going on, hadn't passed comment, but had invited Steve to ride shotgun with him most nights, told him his life story as they rolled across the States. When they'd parted, in the vacuous enormity of LAX airport, the big man had pressed a number into Steve's hand. 'You ever wanna try and get somethin' else goin' on out here,' he'd told him, 'you give me a call. You're good people, Steve.'

Steve still had a faint hope that things might get better back in London but they didn't. Despite the new flats, despite the fact Tony had managed to get rid of Sylvana for almost an entire week. Most of the songs on this album had been collaborations between Vince, Lynton and their mutual friend, with dimbo Sylvana nodding off in the corner. Steve had been shut out yet again. He'd smashed four guitars in a week. Kevin, meanwhile, had got his head kicked in. Steve didn't know why. He just knew, when he saw the poor, battered face in the hospital next day that he wanted to put Vince in the next bed. But Vince, with that sixth sense he had that always told him in which direction trouble was coming, had already fucked off back to Paris.

Steve had got so drunk that week he'd been woken up in the gutter outside his flat by a street cleaner; got carried out of a party he had no memory of even attending, apparently crying his eyes out; and had even found himself on the roof of the Scala cinema, after an all-night Stanley Kubrick programme, staring down into Pentonville Road as if he'd just come out of a dream, only two steps away from oblivion.

He'd pulled himself together after that, he'd had to. Good old Tony Baloney had booked them a tour, and he needed all the money he could get. The one thing he'd managed to hang on to was Earl's phone number. Once they'd done this last night in London, he was going to be out of there, on a plane to San Francisco where Earl had assured him there were plenty of bands who needed a guitarist of his calibre. Kevin was going to split as well. He'd always had plenty of offers to join other bands, and now he was going to take up one, with a band from North London who had met while following Blood Truth around. Maybe they would treat him with some respect. Poor bugger had earned that at least. Steve and Kevin's grim secret was their only weapon against the indifference of the rest of them. The only way they could keep what was left of their pride intact.

Not that this tour had been a shambles, oh no – the opposite in fact. Steve looked upon it like the end of *The Wild Bunch*, going out in a blaze of glory, burning everything down so that no one could follow them. This band had been his whole life; he could give it nothing less. He had played each night like his life depended on it, even the new songs, the songs he hated, he had made incandescent with his simmering rage, raising the game of the rest of them while he did it. Kevin had been behind him all the way, a fucking little powerhouse; they were channeling each other's energy now, giving the punters something to remember for the rest of their lives. They could give them nothing less either. Afterwards, Steve had sated himself not with drink but with which ever beautiful lass was throwing herself his way that night, and they were getting more beautiful, seemingly by the day. Steve was bloody thankful to all of them. Tried to give them something to remember him by and all.

And now...Now the hours were ticking down on his teenage dream.

He thought of Johnny Rotten, how America had fucked it for the Pistols too, then pushed the thought away; too many memories were coming hot on its heels.

He folded up the music paper, put it down on the bench beside him unread, Johnny's words in his head. *Ever had the feeling you've been cheated?*

Sylvana sat on the bed in the apartment in Montmartre. She had never felt so lost or alone.

Vincent had insisted she had to stay here while he did this one last tour, to protect her against Steve and what he was likely to do when he announced he was leaving the band. So that as soon as he was back they could be together for always, without anyone's interference. Those songs they had written together, in Paris and on the tour of the States, would form the basis of their first album. They would be the post-punk Nancy and Lee, he said. Getting a deal would be easy.

Sylvana didn't know if she even liked Nancy and Lee. She didn't know very much any more, if truth be told. Life had started to blur around the edges shortly after her wedding night, shortly after he had given her that first taste of the dream stuff.

She hadn't been sick again after that first time. She had instead found that state of bliss and perfect happiness Vincent told her would come to her, that feeling that no one else would ever be able to hurt her again. God, it had been the best sensation she'd ever felt; all her fears and doubts had melted away as she realised Vincent was right yet again. Before they'd had to go on that goddamn tour, they'd spent weeks in bed, just writing songs and poems together, wrapped in the golden arms of their dreams. The rest of the world had just faded into the background, almost ceased to exist at all.

America had been a shock to her system. She couldn't believe the hostility of Vincent's band. Steve had nothing but sarcasm for her, wouldn't even look her in the eye. Little Kevin, who looked so harmless, radiated silent hatred in her direction. Even that Lynton who'd been so nice to her before had totally blanked her for the first two weeks. Thank God Vincent had managed to bring him around, the last two weeks had been kinda OK, although there were always some hairy days when Vincent couldn't seem to magic any of the stuff they needed out of the air like he usually could.

Sylvana had not been prepared for withdrawal. The shivers, the cold shakes, the constant itching. At first it hadn't been so bad, just like a cold with added layers of anxiety, but it had brought out other qualities too, in both of them. Vincent had turned on her a few times during that tour. It was nothing like the way Robin had treated her, that mad, relentless rage. No, with Vincent it was the opposite. He became cold, sarcastic, as if she was nothing but a pathetic child he had no interest in looking after. The first time had been that bikers' joint in Alabama. The way he'd spoken to her, in front of everyone, Sylvana had felt like her world was about to fall apart. Then when that redneck had thrown a bottle in his face, after that, he'd been back to normal again, attentive, loving. Maybe it had scared him, she thought. But she'd seen it again, several times since then. One moment he'd be all over her, the next…well, he wouldn't be there.

She'd tried to stay in Paris while they recorded the album, really she had. Vince had left her with enough stuff to keep her going, had given her a number to call if she ran out or got scared, of a guy called Marco who he said would sort her out. But Sylvana was too scared to ring the number. She was scared of using her schoolgirl French for anything other than the barest essentials. She had spent one week sitting in on her own, timidly venturing across the road to the boulangerie when she got really hungry, picking up bottles of water in the little shop on the corner, fumbling with the strange francs she wasn't used to using. But without Vincent, she didn't have the nerve to go out exploring the fairy-tale city at night. She just sat in her darkened room, staring out at that big white church he loved so much, remembering the candles he had lit for their love, only a few short months ago. In the end, she could stand it no longer. She got a taxi to the airport, bought the first flight she could back to London.

She prayed the cheque wouldn't bounce. She hadn't dared to look at her bank balance for weeks now. There had seemed to be a bottomless amount in January. But that was nearly six months ago and she'd been paying for nearly everything since then. Sylvana had a dreadful feeling she was spending faster than Ola was putting in, that it would all run out, and then what would she do?

She would have to phone home. And how would she begin to explain her plight?

At least Vince was pleased to see her when she turned up at the studios, even if no one else was. And this time, that Tony had sorted him out with a flat so she didn't have to fork out for any more hotel bills. Sylvana couldn't believe how relieved she felt to be back in London, to be able to speak to another person in English again. Which was bad, she knew because Vincent wanted them to live in Paris. She vowed she'd spend the time in the flat, with her French phrasebook, making herself confident about using the language. She thought she might even call Helen; she'd longed for her friend's company while she was in France, but now that she was back in London, she wondered if Helen would be angry with her for the way she did a flit and never contacted her. She couldn't seem to bring herself to pick up the phone. She didn't want to go out either, there were far too many people she dreaded bumping into, most of all Robin and Donna.

So in the end, Sylvana ended up spending most of her time at the studio. Luckily, it seemed that Vincent and Lynton were doing most of the album themselves; they'd already written a bunch of songs on the tour bus in America, so Steve and Kevin were hardly ever there. Steve seemed to hate her even more now, so much so that when she first came into the room where they were recording, he took one look at her, smashed his guitar against the wall and walked out. He was staring at her the entire time he did it, as if he was attempting to convey to her that he would much rather be picking her up by the neck and dashing her head on the floor. If he was trying to frighten her, it certainly worked, at least until the next time she'd had a hit.

Kevin had had some kind of accident towards the end of their session, Sylvana didn't know what. A car crash or something on his way home, bad enough to put him in hospital. She didn't get to find out the details as shortly after that, they went back to Paris and found themselves this little apartment, which seemed so chic and homely when Vincent was here sharing it with her. She especially loved the bathroom with its marble washstand and the bath with little legs. The French were so much more stylish than the English. If only she could speak their language as easily as she'd fallen in love with their capital city.

Thank God, she'd had enough left in her account to put down the deposit and pay the first month's rent. But she couldn't understand why there hadn't been any more put in it. If Ola didn't come through soon, she reckoned she could only pay the next month and then that would be it. Maybe Glo had something to do with it. Maybe she'd found out, and this was her way of shutting her down, getting her to come back home.

And that just couldn't happen. She prayed that Vincent would be coming back home with some money this time.

Because, even though he was her husband now, Sylvana was too scared to tell Vince how perilous their finances had become, or to inquire about the health of his own bank balance. She knew his father had cut him off, he'd told her that right at the beginning; and his income from his records was way below what she'd managed to make from Mood Violet. She suspected he was too embarrassed to tell her; men never liked having less money than women did, it was emasculating for them. They were the hunter-gatherers after all.

She had been alone with this problem for a week now. She could chase it away with a smoke every couple of hours, but it would only come back again. Vincent had started to inject the stuff while they were in London; he said you got a much better high off it that way. But Sylvana couldn't bring herself to do it. That would be nasty. That would be like being a proper addict.

She hated being alone here, she was so really, really alone. Vincent could seemingly go out and make friends everywhere they went, but Sylvana had never had that kind of self-confidence. Deep down inside, she was still Dumpy and Dopey.

And something even worse had happened that day. When she'd woken up this morning, the colours had gone. When she started to hum a tune, the colours didn't dance in the air the way they had always done, directing her thoughts and her lyrics. For the first time, she'd seen the world as everyone else presumably saw it and she was terrified. The magic had gone. She'd sat here for hours, rocking backwards and forwards on her bed, trying desperately to will them back, humming and singing her way through her entire back catalogue. But nothing. She knew what it must be. It must be the heroin. There now, she'd finally admitted it to herself. It wasn't magic dreaming powder. It was heroin. And it had gone and robbed her of the one thing that made her special. It had taken her dreams away.

Tears streaked her face. She had to speak to Ola, she just had to. Ola would find a way of explaining it all to Glo; Ola would know exactly what to say and do, she always had done.

Gathering all her courage up in a knot inside her, Sylvana reached for the phone. Her hands were shaking as she dialled the familiar digits. Please God, let Ola answer the phone, she thought, please. I'll never touch that dirty stuff again if you just let it be her and not my mother.

'Hello?' Glo's voice on the other end of the line dashed her one, fragile hope.

'M-mother?' Sylvana began.

'Oh, dear God in Heaven, is that my little girl?'

'M-mother, I'm so sorry…'

'Are you all right, Sylvana, where are you? Where have you been? Why haven't you called us for all this time? We've been going spare with worry for you, darling, please tell me you're all right.'

Sylvana started to cry. Of all the reactions she'd expected from her mother, this tone of anguish and concern and yes, even love, was the last thing she'd thought she'd hear.

'Oh darling, darling,' Glo said, and then called out, 'Ruben, honey, pick up the other line. It's our little girl.'

'Mother, I didn't realise,' Sylvana tried to find the right words to say. 'I didn't mean to hurt you and Dad like this. I just got into a bit of a situation…'

'Sylvana, darling, where are you?' her father now joined in.

'I'm in Paris,' she said. 'I'm all right, I'm fine, I just had to leave my band and have a little time on my own…' She couldn't bring Vincent into this yet. She'd have to tell them that later.

'What happened, what went wrong?' asked Glo. 'Why did you have to go to Paris of all places? You could have come back home.'

'I don't know,' Sylvana started sobbing again.

'*Shhhh* now, no one's angry with you,' Ruben said gently. 'Just so long as you're OK, that's all we care about, isn't it, Gloria?'

'Oh, Daddy,' Sylvana choked the words out. 'Is Grandma there?'

There was a long silence from New Jersey. For a moment, Sylvana thought she had lost the connection. Then she heard her father sigh and say, 'Oh, honey. I don't know how to tell you.'

'What?' Fear gripped her heart like ice-cold fingers. 'What is it, Daddy?'

'Your grandmother,' said Glo, 'has passed away.'

33

Watchmen

June 2002

Everything happened in a mad rush after that.

Reading that paper sent me into a tailspin, the biggest panic attack of my life.

By the time I'd seen Robin Leith's death notice, the *Camden New Journal* had been out for a week. If anyone in the music press had seen it, if anyone was left who still realised who the dead itinerant once was, it would be all over the place by now. So I googled it immediately, scanned down the list of entries with my heart hammering so loud in my ribs I swear I could hear it reverberating down my ears.

Only the same old Goth websites that had brought him up in the first place were linked to Leith's name and Mood Violet. Only the same old stories I'd been reading back in November; nothing new. Nothing on the *NME* online; nothing in any of the papers. I was sweating so hard by the end of my search I had to go and have another shower, try and calm myself down. Tried to think. Robin had died six months ago. Presumably any attempts at a police investigation had petered out by now. Presumably his rancid remains had long been turned to ash in some industrial incinerator. He hadn't had much of a family life, had he? Didn't seem to have had any friends left at the end either. No one to claim his body.

Like Donna said: mad, lost and dead. Nobody cared.

In all that time, I'd been talking to the few people who had remembered him and none of them had heard about his death. For a second I had a mental idea to do a massive ring round of all of them, just to say hello, see if any of them dropped it into the conversation. I stopped myself even as my hand hovered over the dial, realising that I would probably sound like a gibbering idiot, realising further that if any of them had read the same paper as me then surely they would have rung me first.

Tried to reassure myself again: no one's missed him yet, no one ever will. More importantly: no one knew I'd been to see him except Louise, who wanted nothing more to do with me, and Christophe, who wouldn't be telling any tales either.

That was what finally calmed me down. No one had anything to connect me to the dead man. Thank Christ, I hadn't mentioned meeting him to anyone. All I had to do was stay as far away from Christophe as I could and if I did bump into him, try my best to act as if I'd never picked up that paper, for if I hadn't, I'd still be none the wiser. I only wished I'd left it on that seat, unwanted and unread.

I looked around the room, taking stock of everything in it. Louise had been right all along; we should never have stayed here. Now I had the means in front of me to get out, I had to take it. I had to just forget about all this and get on with finishing the book, with finding Vince Smith. Then I could get the hell out of Camden, once and for all.

It might have been an uneasy week but it seemed, for once, that fate was on my side. No one called to ask if I'd heard about Robin. Nothing appeared in any papers. PC Plod didn't turn up on my doorstep and ask me to accompany him down the station. Everything stayed quiet on the Murder Mile, or at least, my part of it. To keep myself busy, I forced myself through the transcript of Donna, wove her colourful stories through the narrative I already had, got everything in order that I possibly could and just prayed that Pascal would come through.

After seven days, I got another email.

My contact in Lisbon has come up with something positive. He has been trawling around the Barrio Alto to see what he could find. This is the perfect place for our Monsieur Smith, a place of many musicians and a lot of decadence; it almost sounds like the Paris of my youth. There are a lot of underground members' clubs, and enough people who owe my friend a favour. Anyhow, he has found that a man matching the description of Monsieur Smith, a tall, middle-aged Englishman who always wears a suit and carries a cane, is a regular of one of these clubs in particular. He likes the Fado singing of one man who performs here on Friday nights and often turns up to see him, usually in the company of persons of a certain reputation. The Englishman is something of an enigma; apparently he has been coming here for many years, yet no one is sure of his business. It is assumed he is some kind of dissolute lord, a man of independent wealth anyway, as he has good manners and always tips heavily. If you like, and you want to take a chance on it, I can tell you the places to visit. And, as you wish, you may tell your friends I have found him with the help of my contact and nothing else. Call me if you want to discuss it further.

With my heart in my mouth I dialled the number. Pascal was almost purring as he went over his findings, threw in a few more details about his friend Luís Carbone who had done the sleuthing. A retired detective who had spent most of his life on the Portuguese equivalent of clubs and vice, he still knew the right places to search and people to ask even if he had been off the force for nearly twenty years. The only thing Pascal was doubtful about was that if this was Vince, he had no criminal record in Lisbon and had never been linked to any nefarious activity – though it seemed that he kept the company of plenty who had and did.

'Did your friend check out the Don Dawson alias?' I asked him.

'*Oui*,' said Pascal, 'came back negative also. Maybe he has gone straight after all this time. Maybe he has made his fortune and is enjoying his retirement, is possible, *n'est-ce pas*?'

'Perfectly,' I agreed.

'Anyway,' he continued, 'Lisbon is not so far away, you can get a cheap flight, spend a weekend there on holiday, even if you don't find him or it isn't him, it won't be a wasted journey. After all, this was once one of the greatest cities on earth. Even Lord Byron thought so.'

Too right, I thought, a cheap holiday away from this dump is precisely what I do need. I gushed my most grateful thanks down the phone, took a deep breath and called Gavin.

I really wasn't sure how he would react. He had been so sombre when we left each other the last time that delight was not the first emotion I anticipated from him. I wasn't wrong either.

'Jesus,' was the first thing he said. 'You're not making this up, are you, Eddie?'

'Honestly, I'm not. Check your inbox, I've forwarded the email to you.'

Actually, this wasn't quite true. I'd sent an amended version of his first email to Gavin, omitting the last two sentences and making out that this was the result of one of his own trails.

'Fuck,' was all he said to that. 'Let me take a look. I'll call you back.'

Ten minutes later he did. 'Shit, can you believe that old guy?' was what he said. 'Sorry if I was a bit short with you earlier. Like I said to you before, I'm having trouble taking this all in. D'you want to come over? I'm gonna give Tony a call, see what he thinks. I think we might all need a cold one to wash this down with.'

He was still on the phone to Stevens when I arrived on his doorstep.

'Tony's in New York,' he said as he cut the connection and ushered me in. 'He's got some industry seminar thing over there at the moment, which I didn't realise, managed to wake the poor bastard up at six in the morning. As you can imagine, he's pretty shocked about it too. But he thinks we should go out there.'

'So you both reckon it's him then?'

Gavin went straight to the fridge, removed two cans of Red Stripe and placed one firmly in my hand. He cracked his own open, took a long swig and then wiped his mouth, leaning back and shaking his head.

'To be honest with you, mate, I don't know how it can be possible. Vince Smith, back from the dead.' He took another swig. 'But Tony believes it all right. He's probably booking us flights out there right now.'

I pulled the ring on my own can. I hadn't had a drink since that night at Donna's, hadn't wanted the taste of it anywhere near me. Strangely enough, I hadn't missed it either. After the performance in the Trellick Tower and the shock of the *Camden New Journal*, I'd been more afraid of where it might lead me if I did let myself go.

I took a delicate sip and said: 'Do you want to go, though? Or do you think it's all some wild goose chase cooked up by a senile old man?'

Gavin laughed and shook his head. 'Mate, I truly honestly don't know what I think. But I guess we've come this far, we might as well go for it. After all, what have we got to lose? If it isn't him, we get to spend the weekend in one of the coolest cities in Europe. And if it is, well…' He raised his can. 'Well, I guess I get to ask the mongrel where the bloody hell he's been.'

'I'll drink to that,' I said, raising my own can, feeling my appetite coming back.

'Right then,' said Gavin. 'Let's get online and grab some cheap flights.'

By the end of the afternoon, we had it all worked out. We'd leave next Thursday, call Joseph's mate on the Friday and see this club for ourselves. We'd hang around another couple of days, come back on the Monday morning. That way we could get the cheapest last minute deal and have enough time, if it was Vince, to try and talk to him. We found a Best Western Hotel that was only thirty quid a night and Gavin put it all on his credit card, his enthusiasm now palpable.

'I can't believe we're doing this,' he kept saying. 'Get me another cold one, tell me I'm not dreaming.'

He didn't want to think of any game plan in advance, though. 'Too much of a headfuck,' he considered. 'Let's just take it as it comes. We'll work it out if and when we come to it.'

Satisfied he had achieved everything we needed, he rang for some pizzas and more beers and it ended up just like it always had, us putting on the old videos, staying up until it started to get light again and me falling asleep on his sofa. Which, as it happened, was the best rest I'd had in a long time.

I stayed for a late breakfast, took a stroll with Gavin around Portobello before leaving. It was a glorious day, the beginning of June and the whole place was humming. The beautiful people stretching their long tanned legs across the pavement next to the Ground Floor Bar; the sounds of dub reggae pumping out from the Rasta emporium on the next corner down; the traders calling out their end-of-the-day specials; slices of watermelon pressed to the mouths of a hundred hot, happy faces.

'D'you know what?' I said to Gavin. 'I'm gonna start looking for a flat round here.'

'Yeah?' he said. 'Well, good luck, mate. We're gonna need to sell a lot of copies. But, I guess, it is still possible to find a cupboard under someone's stairs for less than a million bucks.'

'You never know,' I said.

'You got that right.'

It was still a perfect evening when I got out at Camden and even the detritus by the tube and the bus queue by Sainsbury's couldn't bring my spirits back down. I wove my way through the lot of them, humming to myself, picturing a little mews pad somewhere round the back of Portobello. Then, just as I was walking past that pub on the corner opposite Camden Road BR, the one that had been closed for a year after the opening night's murder and had suddenly opened its doors again as Fink, I heard a voice right up close behind me.

''Allo, 'allo.'

I spun round into Christophe's smiling face.

'Long time no see, Eddie.'

He was looking dapper. Tanned almost walnut, looking like he didn't have a care in the world, blue Hawaiian shirt, grey StaPrest trousers and deck shoes.

'Where you been, mate?'

My mouth opened, shut and then opened again. 'Er, you know, just working on the book.'

'Oh yeah?' he said, exhaling smoke from his casually held Rothmans. 'How's that going then?'

'Yeah, yeah, it's good, you know.' I could feel my grin tightening into a rictus. Christophe must have noticed it too; he gave a little frown and another laugh. 'You all right, mate? You look like you're about to shit yourself.'

A horribly high-pitched bray came out of my mouth. 'Had a bit of a late one last night,' followed it, sounding equally insincere. 'I just need to crash out, you know.'

'Oh,' said Christophe, not looking at all convinced. 'That's all right then. Thought for one moment that wanker might have popped up out of the woodwork, started bothering you again.'

'What?' I said, feeling faint.

'You know, that wanker from the Dev. The one you were so worried about. He ain't come back again, has he?'

I tried to take it all in. I couldn't believe what he was actually saying – mocking me right here in the street, in broad daylight. Nor the expression of complete sincerity he was feigning to go with it.

'Are you taking the piss?' I asked.

'No,' he said, and suddenly looked angry. 'Are you? What's the matter, Eddie? Have you been hanging out with your new rock star mates too long to remember who your real friends are?' He flicked his cigarette past my left earhole, so close I could feel its heat.

I put up my hands, terrified, knowing now what he was capable of. 'No, no, Christophe, I didn't mean that,' I gibbered. 'I really appreciate what you did for me that day, it was way beyond the call of duty. I'll owe you for ever…'

He frowned when I said this, so I laid it on even thicker: 'And I'm sorry I haven't been in touch recently, I've just been all over the place with this book, and then my mum found out about Louise, and you know what she's like…'

'Yeah, yeah, all right, don't get your knickers in a twist,' he said, looking embarrassed now and raising his eyebrows. 'It would just be nice to see you now and again, that's all I'm saying. You don't need to give me all that shit about owing you one, just come out some time and buy me a beer, meet the bird after all this time.'

''Course I will.' I was so relieved now I thought my legs would give way. 'Look, I've got to go away the end of this week, but I'll be back on Monday and we'll get together then, I promise.'

'I'll hold you to it,' he said, pointing his fingers towards my nose in the shape of a gun. 'Sometimes I wonder about you,' he joked, back to the *Goodfellas*. 'You may fold under questioning.'

Then he raised his hand, turned the gun into a wave and sauntered away, back down Camden Road.

Never had I been more glad to get on an aeroplane in my life. Landing in Lisbon was one of the most amazing descents I'd ever seen. The verdant green, steeply terraced hills gave me the impression we were in South America rather than Portugal, and at any moment I expected to see an Inca temple rising up out of them. It looked completely different to the Med resorts and Spain that I was used to. Lord Byron had indeed described this region as 'this glorious Eden'; I had looked up Joseph's reference to him on the Net. Lord Byron and the King of Nothing both came here to lose themselves.

The air that hit as the plane doors opened was hotter still than England, like standing in front of an open oven door. I loved this kind of weather and so did Gavin. He said it reminded him of home.

All the way from the airport to the hotel the city unfurled its treasures – parks full of palm trees, beautiful white mansions, wide boulevards. I couldn't wait to get out in it, and no sooner had we checked in and freshened up than we were walking back out, ambling up through the little parks and twisting roads that led us up to the clifftops, where enormous piles of pink, yellow and white mansions sat in an aura of quiet, crumbling magnificence.

To our left, the city spread out like an amazing funfair, spires and turrets and castellations rising up and down the steep curves of the hills. To our right, the enormous red suspension bridge arched across the bay, just like the Golden Gate. Another thing they said about Lisbon, it was like a European San Francisco, right down to having been partially destroyed by an earthquake two hundred years ago. But this place was older, more mysterious. It was early evening and the light was perfect, a pink tinge to the sky giving everything a dreamlike quality as if the whole vista had been fashioned by an Impressionist painter at the height of his powers.

'Forget Portobello Road,' I said to Gavin. 'I think I want to live here.'

'It's a beauty all right,' he agreed, his pale blue eyes roving over the horizon. I wondered what was going through his mind, whether he was excited, apprehensive, or even afraid of what we would find amongst this enchanted cityscape. I felt that a thousand secrets were whispering on the breeze, beckoning us to follow their siren call.

We weren't following a map, just drifting. The place had looked small enough from my copy of the *Rough Guide* and Gavin was one of those people who could always find his way back home. We took a leftwards curve around the little promenade we found ourselves on and came to the most incredible pub either of us had ever seen.

Pavilhão Chinês Bar was a big old building, once apparently a department store, now housing the most mind-boggling collection of collections in every available space of its lavish interior. We stood on its threshold with our eyes out on stalks as an array of tin toys, model railways, Toby jugs and steins jostled for attention amid political posters and the immense mahogany bar with a carved Bacchus hanging over it, summoning us to partake forthwith.

'Ah,' said Gavin, 'looks like we've made a bit of a find here.'

He ordered us caiphirinhas from the surly-looking barman and they tasted like heaven to our parched throats. We wandered through rooms where glassy-eyed stuffed animals looked down at us and customers sat on rococo chairs under enormous cuckoo clocks.

Eventually we found ourselves a corner patrolled by tin soldiers and sat, still craning our necks around the room.

'I know we've only been here five minutes,' I said. 'But I can see why someone like Vince would want to stay lost in a place like this.'

Gavin nodded, his eyes still taking in every surface. 'Yeah,' he said. 'I've got a feeling, Eddie, that this is the place. I reckon we're gonna find him.'

I could feel it too.

We ordered more drinks, stayed at the bar this time, so we could eyeball another corner of this house of fun. As more and more people filled the bar, it all started to get a bit much and I started to feel light-headed. So we decided to go and find some food, to explore the city more.

It had started to get dark, an enormous moon was hanging low in the sky and our path took us round until we were standing high on a hilltop, looking down a steep drop to the city below. It looked even more enticing all lit up, a vertiginous web of sparkling lights enticing us on to more adventure, and a little funicular railway trundling its way up the slope towards us.

'That looks like fun,' said Gavin. 'Let's see where that goes.'

The wooden funicular was disgorging women with their shopping, old men with their backs bent, cigarettes dangling from the corners of their mouths, and tourists with shining eyes. The driver looked just like Tom Waits and as soon as I saw him, the *Raindogs* LP started playing in my head; it made the perfect soundtrack. We rode down the practically vertical railway, down to a big square of enormous Art Deco buildings that was teeming with life. We followed the crowds into a side street where we found a shopfront no bigger than a doorway.

A *ginginha* bar. According to the *Rough Guide*, this was a legendary cherry brandy that could cause hallucinations and was lethally addictive. The scene certainly bore the latter quality out. The dour-faced proprietor banged out shots to a waiting queue that resembled a cross between the inmates of a dole office and a bookies.

'Jesus,' whispered Gavin 'they look like junkies.'

I nodded, looking at the landlord, keeping up a slave driver's rhythm as he dished out his wares. 'Shall we try some?'

'Might as well,' he shrugged. 'I doubt you can get hooked on your first go, eh?'

It tasted less like meths than I'd suspected, just potently alcoholic cherries.

'Maybe it's like absinthe,' I said as we put down our glasses. 'You need to do loads before you start seeing things.'

'Could be,' said Gavin, 'but I reckon I've seen enough round here. Let's try and find the Barrio Alto, that's where the fun's supposed to be. This feels a bit too much like the badlands.'

He was right. The streets around the *ginginha* bar had a darker, more dangerous feel. Not only were they lined with the cherry brandy addicts forming huddles around similar establishments, but guys cruised up to you whispering that old Camden mantra about hashish and other sundries, while curled up in doorways were tattered rags of homeless that put the inmates of Arlington House to shame. African, a lot of them looked, with Third World diseases to show for it. I saw one man with what looked like a bunch of over-ripe grapes protruding from the side of his face. His arm stretched out listlessly in front of him; even begging was too hard-going for him now and no one wanted to look into the hell that was etched into his features for more than a second. Maybe this city was more like London than I'd realised: Byron's Eden was only one funicular ride up from this squalid Purgatory of lost souls. It crystallised Vince's purpose here still more clearly in my mind, though I didn't share this thought with Gavin.

We retraced our steps until we were back in the square, where a hotdog seller told us that the Barrio Alto was back the way we'd come, up the funicular and turn left, then right. Tom Waits would deliver us from evil once more. I whistled 'Jockey Full of Bourbon' all the way back up, trying to blank the grape-faced man out of my mind.

Here was the place indeed. Another warren of streets lined

with bars, most of them decorated with the blue painted tiles that were unique to this city. We found a café called Hell's Kitchen and, amused by the name, went in to find a trendy, funky, low-lit joint. A tank of Chinese dragon fish idly circled behind the bar, backed by a row of vintage soda siphons that the proprietors of Lounge back on Portobello would have killed for. We ordered steak, chips and beers and sat down, chuckling at Lisbon's ability to out-cool the coolest parts of London. Strangely, neither of us mentioned Vince again. It was almost as if we would break the spell if we did and then never find him. Or at least, that's how it felt to me.

By eleven o'clock, the Barrio Alto was heaving. 'A place,' I heard Donna's voice in my head, 'that does all its living by night.'

I was starting to feel a mellow blurring round the edges, a nice kind of drunkenness that I put down not just to the alcohol but to the power of the city itself as we wandered out again. With his keen nose for a hip spot, Gavin stopped suddenly in a little doorway with a modest sign that I would surely have missed. Bar Ártis, it said. There was an ancient brass bell and a spyhole in the door.

Gavin waggled his eyebrows. 'Look at this, Eddie, this must be one of those members' bars that Luís fella was on about. Let's give it a try, eh? They can only say no, after all.'

'Yeah,' I nodded, 'why not?'

Gavin pressed the bell with his long index finger.

A couple of seconds and the hatch moved back across the spyhole.

'Gavin Granger from Sydney, Australia,' said Gavin, 'and Eddie Bracknell from London. *Flâneurs* of the night.'

I had no idea what that meant but it seemed to do the trick. The hatch closed and the door opened. We went down a narrow staircase lined with thirties posters to the sound of Charles Mingus's 'Theme For Lester Young' and the ambient buzz of conversation on the air. Down below was the perfect beatnik cellar: wood-panelled walls, old leather armchairs, those tables in the shape of artists palettes that were so fundamental to the fifties, and a corner bar overhung with pictures of Mingus, Miles, Ornette and Bird. Groups of black-haired people bent over the seats in intense conversation, smoking furiously over their drinks.

'My God,' I said to Gavin, 'you've done it again.'

'Yep,' he cracked a wide grin and wove his way towards the bar.

Then everything seemed to go into slow motion.

As we neared the bar, I noticed a man sitting with his back towards us. He was extremely long and lean – too long, it seemed, for the bar stool he was sitting astride, which was rocking backwards as he leant on the counter top. He had on a white suit, elegantly cut, and long, pointed, shiny black shoes protruded from the bottom of his trousers. My eyes travelled up his lanky form to a thick head of iron-grey hair, slicked back with pomade.

I knew, even before he turned around.

I knew, just as Gavin got a foot behind him and his head slowly swivelled, as if he also knew, also sensed a presence there he hadn't felt in a long time.

The curve of the cheekbones, the whiteness of his skin, the black eyebrows and piercing, dark blue eyes, set in an expression of puzzlement as they clocked the features of the man moving directly towards him.

'Gavin,' said Vince.

'Vince!' cried Gavin.

34

Requiem

June 1981

It was colder now. So much colder and darker.

The colours completely gone. Sylvana bereft in her room full of ash, full of grey. The last of the junk coursed its way through her system as she fell back on to the covers, the tangled, sticky sheets so clammy with the coldness, the bone-chilling coldness. All she could see now were visions in white, like ghosts chasing around her head, whirling wraiths of indeterminate form, ectoplasm coiling around her.

She knew now she was never going back to New Jersey.

The tickets Glo had wired her the money for were still beside her bed. Along with the note she was supposed to leave for her parents, which would make their pain less now that she could no longer understand her own.

Now that she could no longer understand anything.

Her bags were still packed by the side of the doorway, where darker shapes moved in more tangible form. But she couldn't reach them, not now. She would never reach them. She tried to move her arm, her left arm, the one nearest to the door, but that was the arm that the needle had gone into and it felt weighed down with lead now.

Her eyes rolled in their sockets.

The dark form by the door moved closer. It almost appeared human. There was something she had to remember and it flashed for a second before disappearing again.

The wraiths circled her head, beckoning her into their world. It was cold, so very cold, and grey as ashes.

It came to her at last that that brightness, those colours, they were only supposed to last for a while. She had blazed them, though, she had blazed them through her own mind and into others; she surely would not now be forgotten, not now she was dying so far from home?

For a moment, the ectoplasm reminded her of the waving hands of the people who had once stood in front of the stage, gazing up at her with adoring eyes, the shapes of their hands as they reached out to touch her, as if she knew the secrets of their minds, as if she, of all people, could offer them succour.

Then they parted and rushed away, the dark shape now taking all the space in her vision.

Cold, so very cold.

Then a warmth on her cheek, the brush of lips, the murmur of a voice. The voice of an angel. 'Sleep tight, my love,' it said.

Her eyes rolled into the back of her head.

There was nothing more.

35

Rise

June 2002

A slow smile played over his lips. His skin was still like alabaster, scarcely a line on it. Well, they say that heroin preserves you well. Maybe he had a portrait in his attic; or maybe it was the hair on his head that was his picture of Dorian Grey.

'I wondered how long it would take you,' he said. His voice had the perfectly modulated tones of the urbane, artistic Englishman. He didn't look surprised at all, just slightly amused. I looked down and noticed that in his right hand he held a black cane with a silver top, just like Joseph's friend had said he would.

'Well,' said Gavin, recovering his composure quicker than I'd expected. 'I didn't want to rush things, mate. I wanted to take a look round the place myself first.'

This was high sarcasm even for Gavin. I couldn't believe he'd come out with it. After all, tomorrow we were expecting to maybe find him, with the help of our guide. Not here. Not now. Not so easily.

But Vince Smith chuckled, enjoying the bon mot. Maybe it

was Gavin's dry, Aussie savoir-faire that had impressed him in the first place. Maybe he expected no less.

Then he turned his head and looked at me.

Everybody had said it was his eyes that did it and I was no exception. In the dim light of the little cellar bar I couldn't make out the famous violet colour, but I could see how deep and still they were, like pools.

'And you are, sir?' he said.

'E-Eddie,' I stammered, 'Eddie Bracknell.'

He moved the cane over his legs, from his right hand to his left. 'I take it you know who I am, then, Eddie.'

I nodded, dumbstruck. Started to wonder if I was hallucinating, if that cherry brandy's mystical powers were just kicking in. Or if I had actually gone to bed hours ago in an alcoholic stupor and was merely dreaming all this.

He nodded and turned back to the bar, said something in Portuguese that I couldn't follow. A couple of seconds later, he was passing over bottles of beer. 'It's a local brew,' he said to me. 'I think you'll like it.'

Then he turned back to Gavin. 'You approve then,' he said, 'of my manor?'

Gavin shifted slowly from one foot to the other, a tiny sign of unease. 'It suits you,' he said.

Vince smiled and his face became amazingly illuminated, like a thousand flashbulbs were going off around him. I remembered a line I had read about Joan Crawford once, that she always brought a full rig into a room with her. The brightness of real stars.

'I thought you would,' he said. 'Although they don't have the live music here on a Thursday, you'll have to wait for tomorrow night for that.'

He looked back at me. 'There's a guy here, a local guy called Paulo Borges, as in the popes of infamy,' he said. 'Looks a lot like Roy Orbison, sounds like him too. You ever heard Fado singing, Eddie?'

'No,' I said, feeling incredibly stupid and small.

'You'd love it,' he said, his eyes slowly wandering up and down my Hawaiian shirt and Chinos. 'You look like a guy who knows his Dean Martin. You know those old Neapolitan love songs he used to do, in Italian, when he really used to sing like he meant it? Well, they're a bit like that, full of loneliness and yearning. The Portuguese have a word for it that doesn't exist in any other language, they call it *saudade*; nostalgia for a time that never really existed. I have a feeling you know all about that, Eddie.'

His deep blue eyes bored into me as if he could read every thought I had ever had. I had a strange feeling then, like the ground was falling away from under me. I grabbed hold of the bar, felt Gavin's arm come underneath my left shoulder.

'Steady, mate, are you all right?' he said.

'Y-yeah, just felt a bit light-headed.' I shook my head. This was all too surreal.

'It's a bit hot and close in here,' he said, over my head to Vince. 'Maybe we should get some air.'

He sounded a bit menacing, as if he realised Vince had been playing with me and didn't like it.

Vince raised his bottle and took a swig. 'As you like,' he said. He put the empty back down on the bar and slid gracefully off his stool, turning to bid the barman goodnight in slurred language that sounded like a drunken Sean Connery.

We followed him back up the steps and out into the Barrio, which was now so chocka as to resemble Soho on a Saturday night. It was lucky he was wearing that white suit or we would probably have lost him in the maze of winding streets so thronged with people now, the bars that had been shut earlier now pumping out loud music, bleeping electronica that sounded abrasive to my ears. Luckily, Gavin kept his hand on my shoulder, steering me through it all. I had one of those odd, comforting, pissed thoughts that he and Vince were the tallest people here, so of course they could follow each other. The Portuguese seemed pretty small, mainly.

After a while I realised that we were on that promenade bit again, over the harbour.

'Do you feel all right now, mate?' asked Gavin.

Vince was standing under a palm tree, some way ahead, gazing out to sea. He looked like the perfect colonial gentleman in his white suit and cane and I wondered if he did that deliberately to provoke a reaction. But why would he, if he was trying to keep a low profile?

'I should stop drinking,' I told Gavin, 'I can't seem to handle it any more. But I wasn't expecting any of this to happen.'

Gavin shook his head. 'I think situations like these are better done drunk,' he said. 'I don't know what I could have said if I was sober.'

'Fair point.'

We drew level with Vince. He was smiling softly as he stared across the bay, the lights dancing on the water as a big cruise liner slowly pulled out of its dock, sounding a mournful horn like it was sad to be leaving. Was he glad to have been found at last? Had this all been some kind of game? Would he soon be regretfully leaving Lisbon too?

'I suppose you'd like to see my hideout,' he said, turning to face us, the smile still creasing the corners of his mouth.

'One of these stately piles along here, is it?' Gavin asked, gesticulating to the clifftop houses we'd been admiring earlier.

'He really is like Sherlock Holmes, isn't he?' Vince looked at me delightedly. 'I mean, I'm sorry, Eddie, I'm sure it could so easily be the other way around. Only you look a lot more like Dr Watson.'

'And I wondered why I missed you,' said Gavin.

Vince's house was actually set back from the clifftop, a slightly crumbling-looking villa surrounded by rambling wisteria and a tangle of palm trees, as if it was deliberately shutting itself off from the world around it. It certainly looked like the perfect hideout.

There were steps up to the front door where two stone lions, cracked with age, sat one on each side of his doorway.

'Not bad,' said Gavin. 'Looks like you could do with a few servants or something though, eh, mate? Keep the place in order a bit?'

He was doing his best to joke, but he sounded strained, nervous. Like I was feeling. I wondered if we should make some excuses and ask to meet up with Vince tomorrow. But then, of course, by tomorrow he would probably have vanished all over again. Fate had brought us here now. We had to see it through.

Vince opened the door and snapped on a light. There was a long corridor with a marble floor and panelled walls, illuminated by a dusty chandelier. The place smelled old and dusty, like no one had been living in it for years. Vince put his cane down in an elephant's foot stand, in which there was also an umbrella. I noticed that the silver top was fashioned into the shape of a skull.

'This way,' he said, snapping on another light and leading us into his lounge.

Unlike the musty corridor, this really did look lived in. It was a big room, with great, high ceilings and bay windows framed with long, red velvet drapes. At first sight, everything in the room seemed red, or red and gold to be more precise. From the dark crimson wallpaper flecked with gold fleur-de-lis, to the velvet chaise longue, chipped rococo chairs and the huge gilt-framed mirror hanging over the fireplace that reflected the whole scene back. Standing right in front of that was a three-foot-high plaster Madonna.

There was another chandelier hanging from the ceiling, an actual leopardskin rug on the floor. A huge stone gargoyle was propped up next to the fireplace and, by the window, one of those massive round candle holders like they have in churches that look almost like medieval torture devices. Next to that was a grand piano.

An odd assortment of canvases adorned the walls. Some of them were old pictures, scenes of Lisbon, probably, that he must have collected while he was here. But the one that dominated was an oil painting of a woman with long, flowing hair and huge sad eyes, painted in shades of violet.

Vince saw me look at it.

'You know who that is,' he said. 'That's my wife.' He spread his arms wide and bowed towards it. 'To whom I owe it all.'

Me and Gavin traded sideways glances. It was like we had entered the room of a mad old aristocrat in a Hammer horror movie. Christ knows what he was expecting but I still thought I would wake up any minute in my room in the Best Western, blaming it all on the cherries.

'Drink, anyone?' Vince had moved to the far corner of the room now, where there was an old fifties bar. It was a perfect specimen. Red, gold and cream, decorated with martini glasses and cocktail shakers. From behind it, our host pulled a green bottle and three glasses.

'The Green Lady,' he said. 'Lisbon's most infamous export. Have you tried any yet?'

Absinthe. I had been trying to avoid that stuff ever since James and Jocasta had started going mad for it about three years ago, when it had finally been made legal in Britain, if only without the wormwood that was the whole point of it in the first place.

Vince picked up one of those vintage soda siphons and examined its contents, then blew a little into a glass. 'Ah, good,' he said to himself. 'It still works.' He looked up at us.

'Sit down, sit down,' he urged, 'make yourselves at home. After all, you've done an excellent task so far, you deserve rewarding.'

I looked at Gavin.

'Play along with him,' he whispered. 'I think he's completely out of it.'

I sat down gingerly on one of the old chairs. Vince was arranging things on a tray. Once he seemed satisfied he had everything he came over with it, pulling a little table round in front of us and then drawing up a chair of his own.

'What I really love about this stuff,' he informed us, 'is the whole ritual that goes with it. What you do is this: first, pour some absinthe into each glass,' he meted out the pale green liquid between three antique-looking glasses, with thick, square bases. 'Then, you take this special instrument.' He raised up an old, battered silver spoon so that we could see the slots in the middle of it and the scorch marks underneath it. 'Put a lump of sugar on it.' He demonstrated, picking up a lump with a pair of tongs out of a little round bowl. 'Then melt the sugar into the absinthe.' He extracted a Zippo from his top pocket, put the flame to the spoon. 'Actually, a candlestick works better, but still, you get the idea. Then, when all that's done, you add water to taste.'

He squirted each glass with his soda syphon. '*Et voilà!* See the Green Lady dance.'

He proffered a glass to Gavin and me. I realised Gavin was right, Vince did seem totally out of it. His pupils were enormous. It made me feel better about being in this strange house with him, because a loaded man surely wasn't a dangerous man, even if he was being more than a tad eccentric, showing us this bizarre ritual that was so much like cooking up.

I took the glass from him. It was big and heavy and had been beautifully cut. The green liquid shone beguilingly within it. I took a sip. It tasted like vile, sweetened Pernod. Another reason I had never bought into the absinthe fad back home. I had never liked that aniseed taste.

'Good, yes?' said Vince, tipping his own back.

'Fucking vile, mate,' said Gavin for me. 'Don't you keep any cold ones around here?'

'You always were a philistine,' said Vince mildly. 'Will a bottle of port do you? Another thing they do rather better around here.'

After more rummaging behind his bar, he came back with a dusty bottle and three more, smaller, more delicate glasses.

'I hope you won't have the indecency to complain about this,' he said.

It looked a whole lot better, deep, ruby red. It was really too sweet for my palette, but even so, immensely preferable to what had gone before. Once Gavin and I had made approving noises, Vince sat back in his seat, looking satisfied.

There was a long, not-at-all-comfortable silence.

I stole a glance over at Gavin. He was staring at Vince with an expression halfway between hurt and admiration. Vince himself was staring at his glass of absinthe, holding it up to the light as if he could see the green patterns of the Lady dancing around the room.

Well, fucking hell, Eddie, I thought to myself. I think you've got yourself a dynamite ending. In the court of the Mad King of Nothing…

Then Vince leaned forward suddenly, sharply. 'So now we're all comfortable,' he said, looking straight at me, 'I wonder where you think this story ends.'

'I beg your pardon?' I started, in a voice not unlike Mother's.

Vince grinned. It reminded me of that grin Christophe was wearing in the pub that day. Satisfied. Satanic.

'I mean, I know why you're here,' he said. 'Or should I say,' he flicked a glance over to Gavin, 'why you think you're here.'

His eyes sparkled like the drops on the chandelier. I felt that faint feeling again, like my blood was slowly draining out of me.

'You've been writing a book about me, haven't you? With the help of Gavin here, of course, my oldest, most faithful fan. He convinced you that because I had disappeared so long ago that by now I was probably dead. Only you are a journalist, aren't you, Eddie? You're not prepared to take anyone's word when there's always another possibility. That's good,' he said, his eyebrows raising. 'That's what a journalist should do. After all, you don't want to come out with any old shitty cut-and-paste job, do you? I should think not. I deserve better than that.

'So you did a bit of digging, talked to a few people. Started to think otherwise. That it was possible to find me. *Et voilà!* Here you are. Well done, Eddie. Tell me, who was it who finally tipped you the wink?'

'It was Pascal,' said Gavin gruffly. 'That old detective from Paris. Would you believe, he's still alive? Tony found him again.' He shook his head. 'Tony never gives up the faith.'

'Ah,' said Vince, leaning back into his chair again. 'Is that right, Eddie? The old Frenchman who couldn't find me in his own city actually managed to find me here. Most impressive.'

I tried to swallow. As surely as he seemed to have been reading my mind all evening, I knew that Vince knew there was more to it than that. He knew who had told me. It was only Gavin who didn't and I sure as hell didn't want to fall out with Gavin now. 'Yeah,' I said feebly. 'That's right.'

'So,' said Vince, 'what do you think happens now? Do you get the comeback interview with me, bring me back to a world that had chosen to forget me, rehabilitate me like Rick Rubin did with Johnny Cash? Because my kind of music is very popular again, isn't it?'

He examined my slack-jawed face, my bewildered, nodding head with an expression of intense satisfaction. 'I can read the Internet just as well as you can, Eddie,' he said, as if explaining it to a child. 'I can see all the potential you can. I could become an icon, couldn't I? A greater star than I ever was in my youth. And I dare say poor old Steve and Lynton would be so overwhelmed to see me that they'd be back in the band like a flash. Although,' he grimaced and waved his right hand dismissively, 'I doubt Kevin would be so keen. Though, he could easily be replaced, couldn't he? I gather Rat Scabies is still doing the rounds...'

I looked over at Gavin. He appeared frozen in his seat, his knuckles white around his glass of port.

'Yes, it would be marvellous, wouldn't it? I would be a star, you would have a bestseller, and good old Anthony could make another million quid off his back catalogue. Everyone's a winner, right?'

He smiled that full-beamed smile at me again, raised his glass to me and drank the green liquid down in one.

'Only,' and his face fell theatrically. 'There's just one problem about all of that.'

'Oh?' I said.

'Oh,' he nodded grimly and stood up. 'She,' he said, pointing to the portrait of Sylvana, 'she wouldn't like it.'

Oh dear, I thought, he is out of his head. Not to mention, totally mad. We should get out of here.

'Look,' I said, standing up. 'If that's the case, then forget about it. We never found you, we never came here. The book ends with you disappearing into the Paris night and nobody's any the wiser. Me and Gavin will meet up with our contact tomorrow, you won't be where he thinks you are, it will all peter out. But we will have written a tribute to you anyway. To Blood Truth, the greatest band that never was. After all, you said we deserved some reward for finding you. Right, Gavin?'

Gavin looked up at me. His eyes were bloodshot. He must have had too much of that port on top of everything else.

'He's quite poetic, isn't he?' said Vince. 'I can see why you make a good writer. But please, sit down, Eddie, let me finish. After all, you can't come all this way without finding out the end of the story.'

I sat back down slowly, aware of little stars dancing in the corner of my eyes. Gavin had his head in his hands now. Maybe I'd end up carrying him home after all this. If my own legs would still carry me.

'Now, Eddie,' Vince stood under the portrait of his wife. 'How do you think it was that I came by all this wealth?'

'Drugs,' I said. 'That's what Pascal reckoned. You and that

Marco, or Mert, or whatever his name really was. International drugs dealers,' I said it as if I was having one of my *Goodfellas* conversations, but even as the words left my mouth I realised the potency of them. 'Well, of course, I can understand why you wouldn't want any of that coming out,' I backtracked furiously. 'But you know, Gavin would never betray you about that and neither would I. None of that would be mentioned. None of that at all.'

'Oh, Eddie,' groaned Gavin. 'You doofus.'

But Vince waved his hand, as if dismissing the subject.

'Of course I know that, Eddie. And romantic though your ideas certainly are, I'm afraid the answer is much simpler. It's been staring you in the face all along.' I followed his gaze up to the portrait of Sylvana. 'You did your research on her, I hope,' he said.

'I thought I had,' I said.

'Sylvana,' said Vince slowly, 'was an heiress. A proper heiress. She wasn't just a little pixie princess, making up pop songs for a living. When her grandmother died, which she did when I was on my last tour of Britain, my lovely wife came into a multimillion dollar fortune. And when God, in his infinite mercy, came for her so quickly after that, I, as her distraught next of kin, automatically inherited that fortune from her.'

I frowned, still not getting it. 'But she killed herself,' I said. 'That wasn't your fault. You really loved her, everyone said so.'

'Ah,' Vince shook his head sadly. 'Not everyone, Eddie. For one, her parents doubted my good intentions. They couldn't prove anything, of course, but they seemed to believe I had led her into bad ways, despite the very real pain I was feeling for her loss.'

I stared at him. His mouth started twitching, twitching up into a grin. Then he started laughing, a horrible, shrill cacophony, a sound that matched the mad light dancing in his eyes.

'Jesus Christ,' I wheeled round to where Gavin was now standing behind me. 'Gavin, let's go.'

But Gavin just stood there, shaking his head.

'Don't ask him for help!' hooted Vince. 'He was the one who helped me clear up all the mess in the first place!'

'Gavin?' I said urgently, grabbing hold of his lapels. 'Come on, let's get out of here. He's completely mad, can't you see? I know he was your friend once, but Jesus, Gavin, look with your own eyes!'

He wouldn't look. He just kept staring at the floor.

'Do you want to take confession now, Gavin?' said Vince. 'Let the poor boy in on our little joke and rest your weary conscience?'

Gavin slowly raised his head. Tears were running down his cheeks. 'Eddie,' he said softly. 'I should never have shown you that video. I'm sorry, mate.'

'What are you saying?' I was aghast. Realisation was dawning like a penny, slowly spinning on its axis, getting ready to drop.

'I tried to stop things going this far, really I did. I dunno, I guess I never really believed you'd actually think you could write a book. I had you pegged as a lazy lush who just liked talking shit a lot; I thought you'd soon lose interest when it all became too much like hard work. But no, you surprised me; you were really into it. Things were moving, weren't they, Eddie? So I thought again, tried to nip it in the bud another way. I sent Robin after you, to see if he would put you off,' he said. 'I didn't count on you having that mate of yours.'

'What?' The penny was spinning faster now, louder, like the rushing sound in my ears.

'You sent Robin after me? You?'

He nodded. 'I wasn't on a press trip that time, mate. Who else do you think could have told him?'

'I don't know, I...'

'And who else could have given him your number?'

I felt the hot tears spring behind my own eyeballs now. 'And you – you saw Christophe whacking Robin?'

'I saw your mate giving him a good kicking down by the canal.' Gavin's voice was flat now. 'That was a bad move. Robin would have only come back for more after that and then he'd have blown the gaff, told you it was me who sent him. You can't trust the mad. I should have known that from the start. But I fucked up, so I had to put it straight.'

'What do you mean?'

'Eddie, why are you always so slow?' he said it almost fondly. 'Acutally, it was pretty easy once your mate had finished with him. Piece of rubble over the head, *pfft*! Put him out of his misery. But it wasn't the end of you. You kept going, didn't you, kept making connections faster than I could. Then Jesus Christ,' his voice raised an octave, 'Bloody Stevens found that stupid old French bastard and the two of you were well away. It was hard for me, Eddie.' He looked at me with ravaged, searching eyes.

When they come for you, I remembered from my favourite film, *they come for you with a smile. The people who have cared about you your whole life.*

'Do you know what it's like to keep a secret for twenty years? To hide it from everyone? To go through it all again when we saw Lynton and Steve, not to mention Tony, the poor, deluded, bloody bastard. Can you imagine what it did to me, keeping up the appearance that I was going along with it all? Keeping up the smiles and the jokes, making out like I thought the same as they all did. Secrets are like a stone in your pocket, Eddie. The longer you keep them, the more they weigh and they go on getting heavier and heavier until you can't bear to carry them around any more.' He put his head in his hands.

'Do you understand now?' said Vince, by my side now. 'Good old Gavin. My most faithful fan. I rewarded him well, of course. That flat in Elgin Crescent must be worth a packet by now. And of course, his tenancy agreement means that if there's ever any cleaning up to be done again, he takes care of it.'

'But,' I said, 'but why are you telling me all this now?'

Vince gave a regretful smile. 'Because this is how the story ends. Your reward was to hear it. No one else ever has.'

'But—' I saw my whole life flash before me and in it, I saw Gavin typing emails to Joseph Pascal '—but you can't do anything to me. People will come after me. He told Pascal we were coming here to find you. He knows where you are. If I go missing, he'll be straight on your case.'

'I'm sorry, Eddie,' said Gavin. 'Those emails you saw me typing, well, I never sent any of them. Just like I was never on the phone to Tony Stevens. You'll notice how, by amazing coincidence, we bumped into Vince before we could hook up with Joseph's friend? Well, it wasn't amazing coincidence at all. Nobody knows you came here, do they?' he said, wearily. 'You told me yourself you didn't bother to tell your parents, in case they were worried about where the money was coming from, right? Louise has left you, there's nobody waiting for you in Camden. So as far as anyone knows, that's still where you are. In fact, we both are. And in a couple of days, I'll start ringing you up and won't be able to find you. Your flat will have been broken into, your computer will have been stolen, there won't be anything left to say you've ever been here. And sadly, nothing left of your book either.'

'He's really good at this,' Vince said, nodding. 'He's a tragic genius, you know. He even got Sylvana to write her own suicide note.'

'How?' I said. I should have felt scared by then, really scared. But instead I felt surreal, like I was watching some mad piece of theatre, not really partaking in it at all.

'Didn't he tell you that he trained as a chemist in Australia? Photographs aren't the only things he likes developing, you know. He's very clever. I bet you've never seen him looking sick, have you?'

I shook my head, thinking back to all the hangovers I'd had that had never affected him. I just thought he'd had a better metabolism than me.

'As for Sylvana,' Vince continued, 'he just fed her the right chemical combination, slipped it into her drink, made her feel like she was dreaming. Probably how you're feeling right now.'

He was right. That whooshing light-headedness, it was coming back stronger now.

'You never did like to get your round in, did you, Eddie?' said Gavin sadly.

'I think I need to sit down,' I said.

'Yes,' nodded Vince. 'It's better that way. Now Eddie, please, don't feel bad. Nothing's going to hurt you any more. You're going to be safe and warm and protected. Here, I'll play you some of that Fado. You'll see what I mean about it.'

He must have slipped the needle into my arm shortly after that, because I did feel a nice, safe, warm feeling flooding up through my veins. The room took on a magical kind of glow, like swirls of colour were dancing around me. Under the chandelier I could see Vince and Gavin and it looked as if they were dancing too, in each other's arms, to that old-fashioned Fado that I could hear vaguely in the corner of my mind.

The colours, I noticed, seemed to be coming from that portrait on the wall, the one of Sylvana. Only they weren't just violet any more, they were all the different colours of the rainbow. It looked like she was moving with them, stepping out of the frame. Her hair was like red seaweed floating in the water and her eyes were as green as emeralds. She opened out her arms to me and I felt myself float towards her, into the colours, into the light.

Epilogue

TIME OUT, July 3, 2003

It has been a year now since *Time Out* contributor Eddie Bracknell went missing from his flat in Camden Town under mysterious circumstances. Eddie, who was a month short of his 30th birthday when he was declared a missing person, had been a valued contributor to this as well as many other London-based titles, writing with authority on music, film and popular culture. He continues to be sorely missed by all those who knew him.

At the time of his disappearance, Eddie had been going through a split with his long-term partner and was believed to have been suffering from depression, although he had never indicated to his friends or family that he had any suicidal inclinations. Whether he had left his flat with a passport or any credit cards could not be properly ascertained, as the place was found to have been ransacked when his anxious parents called round two weeks after he had last been in touch with them. His computer was taken and important personal documents could also have been stolen. No money was ever withdrawn from his account. His file remains officially open.

If you believe you have seen Eddie, or know of his whereabouts, please ring the Missing Person's Helpline on…

Donna put the magazine down on her coffee table and shook her head sadly. Poor Eddie, she thought. I bet I know what happened to him. I could have told him not to go following that Vince Smith around.

She sighed, fought the urge for a cigarette and picked up the magazine again. Studied the picture of Eddie's face, his big brown eyes looking mournfully out of the frame as if he knew all along that something bad was going to happen to him.

Kevin had told her all about this Blood Truth book months before he'd turned up on her doorstep. Kevin was the only one out of the old firm she still saw. They had met again, years later, at one of the clinics she'd been sent to, where some ropy old guitarist friend of his was getting counselling for methadone addiction. They'd bonded over the dog-eared copies of *Tatler*, laughed at how all waiting rooms stocked the poshest titles, just to rub it in how low you'd sunk. Stayed in touch ever since.

So it had pissed her off to begin with, all that old bollocks about an article for *Cut Ups* Eddie and Ray had fed her, as if she couldn't be trusted with the truth. Still, she supposed, she couldn't blame Ray for that; she had led him a pretty merry dance in the past. And as for Eddie, she couldn't bring herself to be nasty to him either, not when he looked so much like Dave and especially not when he'd treated her so nicely.

Her last postcard from Vince had come almost exactly a year ago; that was when she realised she wouldn't be seeing the journalist again. Pity, that. *But hold steady, Eddie, help is at hand. You won't be forgotten around here.*

She flicked onwards through the magazine until she came to the music section. The picture on the opening page put a smile back on her face.

Tony Stevens of Exile shakes hands with his new signings, The Illuminated

read the caption. Underneath it went into the usual froth about how the band had attracted a massive following through their website and the free CDs they burned themselves and gave out at gigs, how they were the way forward with their edgy, modernistic take on post-punk and all that waffle. Better still was the guff about Stevens, pioneer of the original class of '77 and how he was so excited to be part of something so brave, so youthful and so full of energy all over again. It made her laugh, it really did.

But not as much as the picture.

There they were, all standing on Shepherd's Bush Green, in front of his office; she could just about see the exact spot from up here. Four skinny young men in black jeans, white shirts and black hair. One in particular stood out from the rest; he was taller and much better-looking, if she did say so herself. He didn't need to dye his hair like the others did, his was all natural. Had the eyes to match, the Spanish eyes.

Tone was looking at him with an expression she recognised well.

She wondered when he would realise there was something very familiar about his new signings and the spirit of '77, something very close to home.

They had taken her baby away from her when he was born. That had been the worse time of her life. She had struggled over to Paris to try and tell Vince about him, hoping desperately that if he would only recognise the child as his own they might give him back to her. But of course, he hadn't. He'd just laughed in her face.

Donna had resigned herself to having lost her baby for good along with everything else. She didn't even allow herself the fantasy that some day, he'd come looking for her.

But he had. As soon as he was eighteen. He told her he always knew there was something missing in his life, that it had come as no surprise when his foster parents had told him.

Marcus, they had called him. It suited him. He was beautiful, more beautiful than she could have ever dared hope for. All of Vince's height and slender limbs, but none of his arrogance. With her hair and eyes and olive skin. Something else from Vince they had soon found out about, after they had reacquainted themselves and she had gradually told him about his real parents and what they had once done. His musical talent.

No wonder they were the hottest new band in Britain. And the most intelligent too. Donna hoped she had helped Marcus to avoid the pitfalls of being beholden to any cunt in the music business and this Internet lark had certainly helped. Direct produce from the studio to your desktop, no fat, suited wankers in between. It had meant that, as soon as they had gate-crashed the charts – such as they were these days, you only needed to shift about fifty CDs to get in there now – the record companies had come slavering after them.

But Marcus had chosen wisely. He hadn't gone for the biggest cheque. He had gone for the record company that had the most history. History that he could relate to. History that he could use to build on, to assure himself a glowing future.

And there he was now, holding the hand of destiny, captured in a flash for all eternity by Tone's faithful photographer, Gavin Granger.

All of them none the wiser.

For now, at least. All that was to come, and would come, in its own delicious time. She would enjoy each minute of what was to come next, let it unfurl as slowly as it liked.

After all, Donna had waited a long time for this, almost a lifetime. But now she could see it at last.

A gift from the past. A future.